Adrian McKinty was born and grew up in Carrickfergus, Northern Ireland. He studied law at Warwick and politics and philosophy at Oxford before emigrating to New York in 1993. In 2008, he emigrated again, this time to Melbourne, Australia with his wife and kids. Adrian's first crime novel, *Dead I Well May Be*, was shortlisted for the Ian Fleming Steel Dagger Award and was picked as the best debut crime novel by the American Library Association. The first of the books in the Sean Duffy series, *The Cold Cold Ground*, won the 2013 Spinetingler Award; the second, *I Hear the Sirens in the Street*, was shortlisted for the Ned Kelly Award and longlisted for the Theakston's Old Peculier Crime Novel of the Year Award. The third, *In the Morning I'll Be Gone*, won the 2014 Ned Kelly Award. The fourth, *Gun Street Girl*, was shortlisted for the 2015 Ned Kelly Award.

"Adrian McKinty's Sean Duffy thrillers set in 1980s Belfast come thick and fast, but the quality remains constant . . . The tension between McKinty's competing love of tight, formal puzzles and loose, riffing dialogue is what makes the Duffy novels such a joy . . . enormous fun"
John O'Connell, *Guardian*

"Someone who always delivers: Adrian McKinty . . . he's very good at taking the story in a direction you don't see coming"
Val McDermid

"One of the great crime series . . . brilliant" *Sun*

"McKinty is a gifted man with poetry coursing through his veins and thrilling writing dripping from his fingertips"
Sunday Independent

"McKinty has all the virtues: smart dialogue, sharp plotting, sense of place, well-rounded characters and a nice line in what might be called cynical lyricism" *Irish Times*

ADRIAN McKINTY

POLICE AT THE STATION AND THEY DON'T LOOK FRIENDLY

First published in Great Britain in 2017 by Serpent's Tail,
an imprint of Profile Books Ltd
3 Holford Yard
Bevin Way
London
WC1X 9HD
www.serpentstail.com

1 3 5 7 9 10 8 6 4 2

Designed and typeset by Crow Books

Printed and bound by CPI Group (UK) Ltd, Croydon, CR0 4YY

A CIP record for this book can
be obtained from the British Library

ISBN 978 1 78125 692 3
eISBN 978 1 78283 279 9

Police at the station and they don't look friendly,
Police at the station and they don't look friendly to me . . .
Tom Waits, "Cold Water", 1992

It only takes two facing mirrors to construct a labyrinth.
Jorge Luis Borges, *Seven Nights*, 1977

PROLOGUE: YOU CAN'T TRUST A SPECIAL LIKE THE OLD-TIME COPPERS

Blue dark, red dark, yellow dark.

Snow glinting in the hollows. The Great Bear and the Pole Star visible between zoetroping tree limbs.

The wood is an ancient one, a relic of the vast Holocene forest that once covered all of Ireland but which now has almost completely gone. Huge oaks half a millennium old; tangled, many-limbed hawthorns; red-barked horse chestnuts.

"I don't like it," the man behind the man with the gun says.

"Just put up with it, my feet are getting wet too," the man with the gun replies.

"It's not just that. It's these bloody trees. I can hardly see anything. I don't like it. It's spooky, so it is."

"Ach, ya great girl ya, pull yourself together."

But it is indeed spooky out here, in the hulking shadows of these venerable oaks, four hours after midnight, in the middle of nowhere, while Ireland sleeps, while Ireland dreams . . .

The little rise is a deceptively steep incline that takes my breath away and I can see that I am going to need my new inhaler if it keeps up. The inhaler, of course, is back in the glove compartment of the car because I haven't yet acquired the habit of taking it with me everywhere. Not that it will make any difference in a few minutes anyway. A bullet in the head will fix an incipient asthma attack every time.

"Hurry up there," the man with the gun growls and for emphasis pokes the ugly snub nose of the revolver hard into my back.

I say nothing and continue to trudge at the same pace through the nettle banks and ferns and over huge, lichen-covered yew roots.

We walk in silence for the next few minutes. Victim. Gunman. Gunman's assistants. It is a cliché. This exact scene has played out at least a thousand times since 1968 all over rural Ulster. I myself have been the responding officer on half a dozen bodies found face down in a sheugh, buried in a shallow grave or dumped in a slurry pit on the high bog. The victims always show ligature marks on the wrists where they have been cuffed or tied and the bullet is always a headshot behind the left or right ear usually from less than a metre away and almost always from above.

Trudge, trudge, trudge we go up the hill, following a narrow forest trail.

If I was so inclined I could believe in the inherent malevolence of this place: moonlight distorting the winter branches into scarecrows, the smell of rotting bog timber, and just beyond the path, in the leaf litter on the forest floor, those high-pitched unsettling sounds that must be the life-and-death skirmishes of small nocturnal animals. But the pathetic fallacy has never been my cup of tea and I'm no romantic either. Neither God, nor nature, nor St Michael the Archangel, the patron saint of policemen, is coming to save me. *I* have to save me. These men are going to kill me unless *I* can talk or fight my way out of it.

A fire-break in the forest.

Sky again.

Is the blue a little lighter in the east? Maybe it's later than I thought. The interrogation didn't seem to go on too long but you lose track of time when you're tied to a chair with a hood on your head. Could it be five in the morning? Five thirty? They've taken my watch so I can't know for sure but wasps and bluebottles are beginning to stir and if you listen you can hear the first hints of the morning chorus: blackbirds, robins, wood pigeon. Too early in the year for cuckoos, of course.

Who is going to teach Emma about the birds and their calls when they shoot me? Will Beth still drive out to Donegal so Emma can spend time with her grandparents? Probably not. Probably Beth will move to England after this.

Maybe that would be for the best anyway.

There's no future in this country.

The future belongs to the men behind me with the guns. They're welcome to it. Over these last fifteen years I've done my best to fight entropy and carve out a little local order in a sea of chaos. I have failed. And now I'm going to pay the price of that failure.

"Come on, Duffy, no slacking now," the man with the gun says.

We cross the fire-break and enter the wood again.

Just ahead of us on the trail a large old crow flaps from a hawthorn branch and alerts all the other crows that we are blundering towards them.

Caw, caw, caw!

Always liked crows. They're smart. As smart as the cleverest dog breeds. Crows can recall human faces for decades. They know the good humans and the bad humans. When these thugs forget what they've done to me this morning the crows will remember.

Comforting that. My father taught me the calls and the collective nouns of birds before I even knew my numbers. *Murder of crows, unkindness of ravens, kit of wood pigeon, quarrel of—*

"Don't dilly-dally, get a move on there, Duffy! I see what you're about! Keep bloody walking," the man with the gun says.

"It's the slope," I tell him and look back into his balaclava-covered face.

"Don't turn your head, keep walking," he says and pokes me

in the back with the revolver again. If my hands weren't cuffed I could use one of those pokes to disarm him the way that Jock army sergeant taught us in self-defence class back in 1980. When you feel the gun in your back you suddenly twist your whole body perpendicular to the gunman, presenting only air as your hands whip around and grab his weapon hand. After that it's up to you – break the wrist and grab the gun or kick him in the nuts and grab the gun. The Jock sergeant said that you've got about a 75 per cent chance of successfully disarming your opponent if you're fast enough. Lightning turn, speedy grab, no hesitation. We all knew that the sergeant had pulled those statistics right out of his arse but even if it was only one chance in ten it was better than being shot like a dog.

Moot point this morning, though. My hands are behind my back in police handcuffs. Even if I do spin round fast enough I can't grab the gun and if I suddenly make a break for it I am sure to fall over or get shot in the back.

No, my best chance will be if I can talk to them, try to persuade them; or if that doesn't work (and it almost certainly won't) then I'll have to try something when they uncuff me and give me the shovel to dig my own grave. I will certainly be going into a grave. If they just wanted to kill a copper, they would have shot me at the safe house and dumped my body on a B road and called the BBC. But not me, me they have been told to *disappear*. Hence this walk in the woods, hence the man behind the man with the gun carrying a shovel. The question is why? Why does Duffy have to disappear when killing a peeler would be a perfect morale boost for the cause at this time?

There can only be one reason why. Because if my body actually shows up it'll bring heat on Harry Selden and Harry Selden, despite his professions of innocence, does not want heat.

The gradient increases and I try to calm my breathing.

Easy does it now, Sean, easy does it.

I walk around a huge fallen oak lying there like a dead god.

The earth around the oak is soft and I slip on a big patch of lichen and nearly go down.

"Cut that out!" the man with the gun growls as if I've done it on purpose.

I right myself somehow and keep walking.

Don't dilly-dally, he said earlier.

You don't hear that expression much any more. He must be an older man. Older than he sounds. I might be able to talk to a man like that . . .

Out of nowhere a song comes back to me, played 4/4 time by my grandfather on the concertina:

My old man said "Foller the van, and don't dilly dally on the way".

Off went the van wiv me 'ome packed in it, I followed on wiv me old cock linnet.

But I dillied and dallied. Dallied and dillied,

Now you can't trust a special like the old-time coppers,

When you're lost and broke and on your uppers . . .

The concertina playing is note perfect but the singing . . . my grandfather, who was from a very well-to-do street in Foxrock, Dublin, can't do a Cockney accent to save his life.

Isn't that strange, though? The whole song, lurking there in my memory these twenty-five years.

Oh yes, concertinas look fiendishly complicated, Sean, but they're easy when you get the hang of them.

Really?

Sure. Have a go, let me show you how to—

"Jesus, will you hurry up, you peeler scum!" the man with the gun says. "You think you have nothing to lose? We don't have to make this quick, you know. We don't have to be easy on you."

"This is you going easy?"

"We've let you keep your bollocks, haven't we?"

"I'm going as fast as I can. You try walking through this lot with your hands cuffed behind your back. Maybe if you undid these handcuffs, which you've put on far too tight anyway."

"Shut up! No one told you to speak. Shut up and keep bloody moving."

"OK. OK."

Trudge, trudge, trudge up the hill.

The slope increases again and the forest is thinning out. At the edge of it I can see sheep fields and hills and perhaps to the north that dark smudge is the Atlantic Ocean. We are only a forty-five minute drive from Belfast, but we are in another world completely, far from planes and machines, far from the visible face of the war. Another Ireland, another age. And yes, the stars are definitely less clear now, the constellations fading into the eggshell sky. Dawn is coming, but dawn won't save me. I'll be dead before sun-up if they are even halfway competent, which I think they are.

"What is the matter with them?" the man with the gun mutters to himself. "Hurry up you two!" he yells to the others.

I've been told not to look back, but this confirms what I've suspected. Of the five men who lifted me, one is waiting back at the car, one is waiting at the bottom of the trail to be a look-out and the other three are going to do the deed itself.

"All right, no one told you to stop, keep going, Duffy!" the man with the gun says.

I shake my head. "I need to catch my breath. I'm asthmatic," I reply. "I'm having trouble breathing."

"There's nothing wrong with you!"

"I'm asthmatic. They diagnosed it at my physical."

"What physical?"

"My police physical. I thought it was just too much smoking but the doctor said I had developed asthma. I've got an inhaler."

"Rubbish!"

"It's true."

"Did you bring your inhaler?"

"Nope. It's back in the glove compartment of my car."

"What's going on? Are we going to top him here?" one of the two others asks, catching us up. The one complaining about the spooky trees. The one with the shovel.

"He claims he's got asthma. He says he can't breathe," the man with the gun says.

"Aye, cold morning like that will give it to you. Our Jack has asthma," this second man says. Younger than the man with the gun, he's wearing a denim jacket, tight bleached jeans and white sneakers. The shovel is an old model: heavy wooden handle, cast-iron blade, low centre of gravity . . .

"I don't believe in asthma. Asthma's a modern invention. Fresh air is all you need," the man with the gun says.

"Well, you can talk to our Jack's mum, she's been to the best doctors on the Waterside, so she has."

The third man reaches us. He's smaller than the others. He's wearing a brown balaclava and a flying jacket.

No, not *he*. It's a woman. She didn't speak during the car ride but if I'd been smarter I would have twigged that that smell in the back was her perfume. Thought it was the car's air freshener. She also is carrying a gun. An old .45. Look at that gun. US Army issue. 1930's model ACP. That's been in somebody's shoebox since the GIs were here in WW2. There wouldn't be any suffering with a weapon like that. Wouldn't even hear the shot. An instantaneous obliteration of consciousness. Wouldn't feel anything. Sentience into darkness just like that. And then, if Father McGuigan is correct, an imperceptible passage of time followed by the resurrection of the body at the End of Days . . .

"Is this it? Is this the spot?" she asks.

"No, we've a wee bit to go yet," the man with the revolver says.

"Can we just do it here, we're miles from everybody," shovel man wonders.

"We do it where we're told to do it," the leader insists. "It's not far now, anyway. Here, let me show you."

He unfolds a home-made map on thick, coarse paper. It's like no cartography I have ever seen, filled with esoteric symbols and pictograms and mysterious crisscrossing paths and lines. The guy's an eccentric who makes his own maps. In other circumstances entirely we'd probably get on like a house on fire.

"What is this? Some new thing from the Ordnance Survey?" the woman asks.

"No! God no. 'Ordnance Survey', she says."

"What is it?"

"Each one of us should make a surveyor's map of his lost fields and meadows. Our own map. With our own scale and legend," the man with the gun says.

"What do you mean 'our lost fields'?" the woman says irritably.

"He's quoting Gaston Bachelard," I say.

"Who asked you? Shut up!" the man with the gun snaps.

"Gaston who?" the man with the shovel wonders.

"Look him up. There's more to life than the pub, the bookies and the dole office, you know. Asthma my arse! There is no asthma. Have you noticed that none of us have fallen? Have you noticed how quickly our feet have become accustomed to the ground?" the man with the gun says.

"Not really," the woman replies.

"For the last half hour our eyes have been secreting rhodopsin. We're adapting to the dark. That's why you have to get outside, away from artificial illumination. Good for the eyes, good for the soul."

"Rhodopsin?" the woman asks.

"It's a protein receptor in the retina. It's the chemical that rods use to absorb photons and perceive light. The key to night vision."

"What on earth are you talking about, Tommy?" the woman says.

"No names!"

"Ach what does it matter if we use our names? Sure *he*'s going to be dead soon, anyway," the man with the shovel says.

"Doesn't matter if he's going to be dead or not. It's the protocol! No names. Did youse *ever* listen during the briefings? Bloody kids!" *Tommy* mutters and folds away his map in a huff.

"Is it much further?" the woman asks.

"Come on, let's get moving," Tommy shouts, pointing the gun at me again.

Trudge, trudge, trudge up the hill, but it must be said that I have learned much in this little interaction. The man with the gun is about forty-five or fifty. A school biology teacher? All that stuff about protein receptors . . . No, he probably read all that in *New Scientist* magazine and remembered it. Not biology. Doesn't seem like the type who was smart enough to get a pure science degree. Geography, maybe. Bit of a hippy, probably a lefty radical, and that was definitely a Derry accent. We almost certainly went to the same rallies in the early 70s. Definitely a Catholic too, which would mean he's probably a teacher at St Columb's, St Joseph's or St Malachy's. That's a lot to work with. And he's the leader, a couple of decades older than the other two. If I can turn him the rest will snap into line.

A big if.

"Rhodopsin my foot. I fell," shovel man says, passing the woman the water bottle. "Twice. And it's going to be worse going downhill. Mark my words. We'll all be going arse over tit. You'll see."

The woods are thinning out a bit now and in the far west I can see headlights on a road. Ten miles away, though and going in the other direction. No help from there.

A gust of clear, elemental wind blows down from the hilltop. I'm only wearing jeans and a T-shirt and my DMs. At least it's my lucky Che Guevara T-shirt, hand-printed and signed by Jim Fitzpatrick himself. If a dog walker or random hiker finds my body a few years hence and the T-shirt hasn't decayed maybe they'll be able to identify me from that.

"Careful on this bit!" Tommy says. "It's mucky as anything. There's a bog hole over there. Dead ewe in it. But once we're through that, we're there."

We wade through a slew of black tree roots and damp earth and finally arrive at a dell in the wood that must be the designated execution spot.

It's a good place to kill someone. The ring of trees will muffle the gun shots and the overhanging branches will protect the killers from potential spying eyes in helicopters and satellites.

"We're here," Tommy says, looking at his map again.

"There must have been a better way to come than this," shovel man says, exhausted. "Look at my trainers. These were brand new gutties! Nikes. They are soaked through to the socks."

"That's all you can say? Look at my gutties! Complain, complain, complain. Do you have no sense of decorum? This is a serious business. Do you realise we're taking a man's life this morning?" Tommy says.

"I realise it. But why we have to do it in the middle of nowhere halfway up a bloody mountain I have no idea."

"And here's me thinking you'd appreciate the gravity of the task, or even a wee bit of nature. Do you even know what these are?" Tommy asks, pointing at the branches overhead.

"Trees?"

"*Elm* trees! For all we know maybe the last elm trees in Ireland."

"Elm trees my arse."

"Aye, as if you know trees. You're from West Belfast," Tommy snarls.

"There are trees in Belfast. Trees all over the shop! You don't have to live in a forest to know what a bloody tree is. You know who lives in the woods? Escaped mental patients. Place is full of them. And cultists. Ever see *The Wicker Man*? And big cats. Panthers. *The Sunday World* has a photograph of—"

"Gentlemen, please," the woman says, reaching us. "Are we finally here, or what?"

"We're here," Tommy mutters.

"Well let's get this over with then," she says.

"Uncuff him and give him the spade," Tommy says.

Shovel man uncuffs me and leaves the shovel on the ground next to me. All three of them stand way back to give me room.

"You know what to do, Duffy," Tommy says.

"You're making a big mistake," I say to him, looking into his brown eyes behind the balaclava. "You don't realise what you're doing. You're being used. You're—"

Tommy points the revolver at my crotch.

"I'll shoot you in the bollocks if you say one more word. I'll make you dig with no nuts. Now, shut up and get to work."

I rub my wrists for a moment, pick up the shovel and start to dig. The ground is damp and soft and forgiving. It won't take me ten minutes to dig a shallow grave through this stuff.

Everyone is staying well out of shovel-swinging range. They may be new at this, but they're not stupid.

"I'll be glad when this is over," the woman whispers to the younger man. "I'm dying for a cup a tea."

"And I could do with a ciggie. Can't believe I left them back at the farm," he replies.

"Tea and cigarettes is all they can think about when we're taking a man's life," Tommy growls to himself.

"It's easy for you, you don't smoke. I . . ."

I turn down the volume so they're nothing more than background noise.

I think of Beth and Emma as I dig through a surprising line of chalk in all this peat. *Chalk.*

Emma's smile, Beth's green eyes.

Emma's laugh.

Let that be the last thing in my consciousness. Not the babel of these misguided fools.

Shovel.

Earth.

Shovel.

Always knew that death was a strong possibility in my line of work, but it was absurd that that banal case of the dead drug dealer in Carrickfergus could have led to this. As standard a homicide as you're ever likely to see in Ulster. Ridiculous.

Earth.

Shovel.

Earth.

Shovel.

Gasping for . . .

Having trouble breathing again.

Gasping for—

Gasping for—

They think I'm faking it.

I have taxed their patience.

Someone pushes me and I go down.

Spreadeagled on my back in the black peat.

"Let's just top him now," a voice says from a thousand miles away.

"Yeah, all right."

Above me tree-tops, crows, sky.

And the yellow dark, the red dark, and the deep blue dark . . .

1: NO HAY BANDA

County Donegal is certainly not the wettest place on planet Earth; 130 inches of rain a year in Donegal may be a typical average high, but that's nothing compared to, say, Mawsynram in India, where over 400 inches of rain can fall in a calendar year. Crucially, however, that rain comes during the monsoon and the monsoon only lasts for about ten weeks. The rest of the year in Mawsynram is probably rather pleasant. One can imagine walking in the foothills of the Himalayas or perhaps taking a guided excursion to the tea plantations of Barduar. Donegal may not have the sheer amount of precipitation of Mawsynram but it makes up for this in the dogged persistence of its rain. Rain has been measured in some parts of Donegal on 300 days out of the year and if you add in the days of mist, mizzle and snow you could be looking at a fortnight in which some form of moisture does not fall to earth.

It is somewhat of a paradox then that until the arrival of cheap packet flights to Spain, Donegal was the preferred holiday destination for many people in Northern Ireland. All my childhood holidays were taken in Donegal at a succession of bleak caravan sites on windswept, cold, rainy beaches. Scores of parents wrapped in thick woollen jumpers and sou'westers could be seen up and down these beaches driving their small, shivering children into the Atlantic Ocean with the injunction that they could not come out until they had enjoyed themselves.

My memories of Donegal had never been particularly good ones and when my father took early retirement and my parents moved to a cottage near Glencolumbkille I was a reluctant visitor.

Things had changed, of course, with the birth of Emma. My folks demanded to see their granddaughter and Beth and I had driven out there for Christmas and now here we were again in the early spring. Glencolumbkille is in the Gaeltacht, with almost everyone in these parts speaking the quaint Donegal version of Irish. It is a little whitewashed place straight out of *The Quiet Man* with a spirit grocer, a post office, a pub, a chapel, a golf course, a small hotel, a beach and a cliff-path. A pleasant enough spot if you didn't mind rain or boredom or the hordes of embedded high-school students from Dublin practising their Irish on you. One of these kids stopped me when I was out getting the milk. "Excuse me, sir. *An gabh tu pios caca?*"

"No I would not like any cake, thank you."

He tried again, this time apparently asking for the way to the bandstand.

I explained in slow, patient Irish that there was neither a bandstand nor a band in Glencolumbkille.

He cocked his head to one side, puzzled.

"There is no bandstand. There is no band. *No hay banda, il n'est pas une orchestra.*"

"Oh, I see," he said in English. "No I was looking for the way to the beach hut, we're supposed to meet at the beach hut."

"It's just over there *on the beach*. And the word you're looking for is *bothán trá.*"

"Thanks very much, pops," he said and sauntered off.

"Pops, indeed," I muttered as I bought the milk and a local paper and I was still muttering as I walked back to the house where Mum and Beth were talking about books.

My mother, Mary, had taken immediately to Beth, despite her being a Protestant, monolingual, well off, younger and, worst of all, not a fan of Dolly Parton.

"Don't you even like 'Little Sparrow'?" she had asked on hearing about this calamity.

"I'm so sorry, Mrs Duffy, it's just not my cup of tea. But I'll listen again if you want me to," Beth had said conciliatingly.

This morning they were talking about Beth's master's thesis which she was trying to do on Philip K. Dick, something the stuffy English department at Queens were none too happy about. My mother's sympathies lay with Queens, as, secretly, did mine.

"But Mr Dick, apparently, is only just deceased. You can't tell if a writer's any good or not until they're dead a generation, at least," Mum was saying.

Beth looked at me for support but there was no way I was stepping into that minefield.

"Milk," I said, putting the carton on the kitchen table. "And I've brought Dad his paper," I added quickly, before nimbly exiting and leaving them to it.

My father also had taken to Beth and he discovered that he enjoyed the company of his daughter-in-law and granddaughter so much that while we were here he even, temporarily, lost all interest in his beloved golf and bird-watching. At night he would talk to us in low tones about Emma's prodigious achievements in ambulation, speech and the manipulation of wooden blocks.

"Talking at six months! And almost walking. You can see it. She wants to walk. Standing there, thinking about it. She said 'Grand-pa'! I heard her. That girl is a genius. I'm serious, Sean. You should start speaking to her in French and Irish. She'll be fluent by the time she's one. And you should have seen her make that Lego tower. Incredible . . ."

My parents' cottage faced the ocean and at the far end of the house there was a little soundproof library with a big double-glazed plate-glass window that looked west. Dad's record player was over twenty years old and his speakers were shite, but his collection was eclectic and pretty good. Since moving to Donegal he had discovered the works of the English composer Arnold Bax, who had spent much of the 1920s in Glencolumbkille.

I walked down to the library, found a comfy chair to look through the local newspaper and put on Bax's really quite charming "November Woods". Dad came in just after the strange, muted climax which was so reminiscent of the instrumental music of the early Michael Powell films.

"Hello, Sean, am I bothering you?"

"No, Da, not at all. Just listening to one of your records. Arnold Bax isn't bad, is he?"

"No, you're right there. He's wonderful. There's a lightness of touch but it's not insubstantial or frivolous. His heyday was the same time as that of Bix Beiderbecke. It's a pity they couldn't of played together. Bax and Bix. You know?"

"Yes, Dad," I said, stifling a groan.

He sat down in the easy chair next to me. He was sixty-five now, but with a full head of white hair and a ruddy sun-tanned face from all the birding and golfing, he looked healthy and good. He could have passed for an ageing French *flaneur* if he hadn't been dressed in brown slacks, brown sandals (with white socks) and a "Christmas" jumper with reindeers on it.

He handed me the *Irish Times* crossword and a thesaurus. I gave him the thesaurus back. "That's cheating," I said. "What clue is bothering you?"

"Nine down."

"Nine down: 'Melons once rotten will drop off branches.' It's *somnolence*, Dad. It's an anagram of *melons once*."

"Oh, I see. This is the world's worst thesaurus anyway. Not only is it terrible, it's terrible," he said and began to chuckle with such suppressed mirth that I thought he was going to do himself a mischief.

"Are you still on for tomorrow?" he asked. "I've been sensing that you don't want to do it, son."

My father's senses were completely correct. I didn't want to do it. Tomorrow we were driving to Lough Derg, about fifteen minutes inland from here, where we were going to get the boat over to Station Island for the St Patrick's Purgatory pilgrimage. You could do the pilgrimage twice a year: in the summer (which is when nearly everyone did it) or during Lent. The whole thing had got started 1,500 years earlier when, to encourage St Patrick with his mission among the Godless Irish, Jesus Christ had come down from heaven and shown St Patrick a cave on Station Island that led all the way down to Purgatory. Ever since then it had been an important place of pilgrimage for devout Catholics from all over Europe. My father had never been a devout Catholic but his interest in Lough Derg had been kindled by Seamus Heaney's new book-length poem "Station Island" about his own pilgrimage to Lough Derg. Heaney's poem and his slew of amiable interviews all over Irish TV and radio had made the place sound spiritually and philosophically fascinating and in a moment of weakness I had agreed to my father's request to accompany him; but now, of course, that we were on the eve of our journey I was not bloody keen at all. The idea of spending three days fasting and praying with my dad while walking barefoot around a damp, miserable island with a bunch of God-bothering weirdos didn't sound like my idea of fun.

"Oh, Sean, I'm glad you're still enthusiastic. It'll be good for all of us. Beth, Mary and Emma will get some quality time together and you and I will get closer. Maybe even closer to God, too."

"I thought you didn't believe in God. That's what you told Father Cleary."

"Well, Sean, when you get to my age, you think to yourself that there's more things in Heaven and Earth . . . you know?"

I didn't know if I believed in God either but I believed in St Michael the patron saint of policemen and I owed my thanks to

The Blessed Virgin, who, I reckoned, had helped change Beth's mind about the abortion in Liverpool nearly a year ago.

"Wouldn't you rather do the pilgrimage in the summer like normal people?" I asked.

"Nope. The Pope says that if you do a pilgrimage to one of the traditional sites during Lent it'll be particularly blessed, so it will."

"Hark onto Alfred Duffy quoting the Pope. Alfred Duffy who forced Dr McGuinness to teach us about Darwin. What's happened to you, Da? Did you get hit in the head with a golf ball or something?"

He grinned and leaned back in the chair, his watery blue eyes twinkling. "Oh, I just remembered what I wanted to ask you. You're on for the quiz tonight? We've never won yet, but with you on our team I think we have a good chance of beating the GAA."

"Will it be in English? If Beth wants to come?"

Dad smiled at the mention of Beth's name. "Ah, you got a good one there. You know it doesn't bother us that she's a, you know . . ."

"Red-head?"

"Protestant."

"Is she a Prod? I hadn't noticed. Well that explains everything."

"All you have to do now is marry her and your mother will be in clover."

"A wedding? Come on, Da. All our lot down one side of the church, them lot down the other?" I said, not mentioning the fact that Beth had told me never to even think about proposing to her. "And Beth's father isn't exactly a fan of mine," I added.

"What does he do again?"

"Builds houses."

"He works with his hands. I like that."

"Like Gwendolyn Fairfax I doubt very much if he's ever seen a spade. He got the firm from his father. All he seems to do is sit in his office and think up the street names for all his new developments."

"What does he name them?"

"Mostly after obscure members of the royal family. Some Bible stuff. I only met the man twice and if I hadn't been armed with my Glock I think he would have tried to beat me to death with one of his golf clubs."

"Ah, golfer is he? He can't be all bad. What's his handicap?"

"Handicap? Well, he's got an eighteenth-century mind-set, he's stinking rich and for recreation he golfs at Down Royal or sails about on his bloody great yacht. Is that handicap enough?"

"Yes, you've said she comes from money. Down Royal though. I'd love to play that course. You couldn't possibly ask if I—"

"No, I couldn't! I've told you, he's not my biggest fan."

"Maybe if you made what they used to call 'an honest woman' of his daughter he wouldn't be so hostile."

"Dad, trust me, a wedding is not in the cards."

"Well, I'm not going to try to force you. Every time I've tried to force you to do anything it hasn't worked. Backfired in me face, so it has. I still regret sending you off to that bird-watching camp on Tory Island. You cried and cried and I don't think you ever picked up a birding book again after that."

"Damn right. To this day I can't tell the difference between a woodcock and a bog snipe," I said and my father, who was easily pleased, erupted into gales of laughter (for, of course, as I'm sure you know, a woodcock and a bog snipe are the same thing).

Dinner that night was a high-spirited affair. One of Dad's neighbours had caught a massive sea bass and mum had cooked it in a white wine sauce with scallops and potatoes while Beth and I took Emma down the beach to throw stones at the breakers.

We sat in the dining room under the portraits of JFK and the Derby-winning horse Shergar (both assassinated in their prime) while a turf fire burned in the range and rain lashed the windows.

Beth, Emma and Mum stayed at home while Dad and I trudged to The Lost Fisherman for the village's big event of the week if you didn't count mass on Sunday (and fewer and fewer people did, with each fresh week bringing a fresh church scandal). Dad introduced me to all his golfing cronies and told them that with me on the team we were sure to crush those arrogant bastards from the GAA.

In the event the GAA performed poorly and by the final general knowledge round it was between the golf club and the bowling club for the prize pool of fifty quid. Marty O'Reilly said that there would be a tie-break question.

"This is the question and I want you to be very precise with your answer. No shouting out from any of the other teams. All right, here goes. What were the very first words spoken from the Apollo 11 astronauts on the surface of the moon? Everybody get that? Good. As usual, write your answers on the card and bring them up. I'll give you two minutes to think about it. Stop that! No whispering from any of the other teams!"

"The very first words from the moon?" Davy Smith said in a panic but I knew there was no need to worry because my dad was grinning to himself.

"Never fret, Alfred knows," I said.

"Do you know right enough, Alfred?" Big Paul McBride asked.

"Look over there at them bowling boys. They think they know the answer but they don't!" Dad said, almost rubbing his hands with glee.

"What's that supposed to mean, Da?"

"A lot of people think the first words spoken on the surface of the moon are 'That's one small step for man – that's one giant leap for mankind.' But it's not. It's not even 'That's one small step for *a* man', which Armstrong claims he says. That's what Armstrong said when he first stepped off the bottom rung of the ladder of the lunar lander, but him and Aldrin had been talking in there for an hour by then."

"What is it then?" Jeanie Coulhouln asked, on the edge of her seat.

"I'll tell you what else it's not, it's not 'Houston, the Eagle has landed', either. Everyone thinks it's that, but it's not that," Dad insisted.

"OK that's what it's not. What's the right answer?" Jeanie asked.

"Well," my father began, smiling at us beatifically like the Venerable Bede. "Not many people know this, but as the lunar lander, the Lem, as it was called, was touching down on the moon they had a little light to let them know when they'd actually touched down. It was the contact light and as soon as they touched down on the surface Buzz Aldrin had to tell Armstrong that the contact light was on so he could turn off the engines. So they touch down and the light comes on and Aldrin says 'Contact light', ergo the very first words spoken on the moon were 'Contact light'."

"Are you sure now, Alfred?" Big Paul said, poised with his pen. "This'll be the first time we've ever won outright."

"I'm sure," Dad insisted.

We wrote our answer on the card. The bowling club wrote down their answer and we both handed the cards up to Marty.

Marty grabbed the microphone and dramatically shook his pinched, aged face from side to side. "Ladies and gentlemen, you are not going to believe it! Both teams got the wrong answer! Both teams got it wrong so this week there's no clear winner and we're going to divide the pot. The bowlers wrote 'That's one small step for man' and the golf club lost their heads completely and wrote 'Contact light', but the right answer, is, of course: 'Houston, the Eagle has landed'!"

When we got home the rain had stopped, so Beth, Emma and Mum met us at the beach at the end of the lane.

"How did it go? Did youse win?" Mum asked.

"I don't think Dad wants to talk about it, there was a bit of a shouting match at the end there, let's just get inside and change the subject," I said quickly.

Dad, who was still red in the face, said nothing and marched down to the library, where we heard discordant and angry music that might well have been Bax and Bix.

The next morning I packed for the pilgrimage to Station Island with sleet and hail hammering the windows. It was the first week of March but we were still firmly in the grip of winter. I sat on the window ledge and caught my breath. For the last few weeks I'd been having trouble catching my breath in the mornings. If I wasn't worried about a diagnosis of cancer or emphysema I would have gone to the doctor before this. I'd cut way down on the smokes, maybe it was time to cut them out completely?

"How are you doing, Sean?" Beth asked and before I could answer added: "You shouldn't look so gloomy, I think this will be great for you and your Dad."

"You really want to know how I feel?"

"Is it going to be something positive?"

"I have nothing positive to say. Will you take two negatives?"

"No."

"Jesus, Beth, I really don't want to go on this bloody trip. I only agreed because I thought he'd forget all about it."

"Sean! Phone!" my mum shouted from the living room.

I walked down the hall and picked up the receiver. "Hello?"

"Sean, I'm really sorry to bother you on your holiday."

It was Detective Sergeant McCrabban. I'd recognised his dour, sibilant Ballymena intake of breath before he'd said a word.

"That's OK, Crabbie old son. It's always a pleasure to hear from you."

"How's your trip going?"

"It's all right, Crabbie. It's pouring, but, you know, that's to be anticipated in Donegal. Everything OK there?"

"Yeah, everything's fine."

"So to what do I owe the pleasure of this call?"

"Well, you told me to call you if anything interesting came up."

"And has something interesting come up?" I asked expectantly.

"There's been a murder."

"What sort of a murder?"

"Someone killed a drug dealer."

"Doesn't sound so interesting."

"No, but they killed him with an arrow. Shot him in the back with an arrow, so they did."

"Injuns?"

"Well . . ."

"Or that miscreant from Sherwood Forest who gives the local law enforcement agencies so much difficulty?"

"Here's the bit that I thought might get you intrigued. This is the second drug dealer that's been shot with an arrow in as many days."

"Two drug dealers. Both of them shot with arrows?"

"If you want to be technical about it – and I know you do – they were actually crossbow bolts."

"From the same crossbow?"

"We haven't removed the bolt from the second victim yet. We've only just discovered him."

"I see. And this first guy?"

"He lived."

"Well, that's good. I suppose. Where was he shot?"

"In the back like victim number two."

"Did he happen to see who shot him?"

"Maybe, but it's the usual thing. He's not telling us anything."

"Of course not."

"So do you want to come back for it? Or do you want me and Lawson to handle it? Up to you, Sean, but I thought I'd let you know. Our first murder in nearly a year, and a weird one at that . . ."

I lowered my voice. "Crabbie, just between us, you're a total lifesaver, mate. Have you heard of a thing called St Patrick's Purgatory?"

"No."

"No, why would ya, you big Proddy heretic."

I quickly explained the nature of the pilgrimage and what my dad wanted us to do.

"So you see, Crabbie, if I have to rush back to Carrickfergus to help solve this crossbow-wielding-vigilante-potential-serial-killer case I won't have to go to that bloody island and get verrucae, mildew and trench foot."

Crabbie, however, was not one to shirk off religious obligations lightly. "No," he said reflectively. "I think you should do that thing with your father. It sounds very holy, so it does."

"Crabbie, listen, I'm coming back. Saint Patrick and all the sinners in purgatory can wait."

"All right, I won't let anyone disturb the crime scene till you get there. When do you think that would be?"

"It's a one and a half hour drive back to Carrickfergus. If the baby wasn't in the car with me I'd be there in an hour, but as it is I'll have to leave the wife and kid off first and take it easy on the roads. Be there in an hour and a half. Maybe eighty eight minutes, OK? Anything else going on?"

"Did you hear about John Strong?"

"What about him?"

"He's moving on."

"To the choir invisible?"

"To Assistant Chief Constable."

"Same thing, really. Finally someone we almost like up at command level."

"Aye. And listen, what do you know about Bulgaria?"

"Uhm, decent defence and midfield, lacks imagination up front. Why?"

"I'll explain when you get here. 15 Mountbatten Terrace in Sunnylands Estate," Crabbie said.

"Sunnylands Estate – why am I not surprised? All right, take it easy, mate."

I hung up the phone and went into the kitchen with a downcast look on my face.

"What's the matter, Sean?"

"Mum, Dad, I'm really sorry but I have to go back to Carrickfergus. There's been a murder. Suspected serial killer. Maybe even a vigilante. It's action stations at Carrickfergus RUC. Top brass have been on the phone. The BBC. You know how it is."

"What does this all mean, Sean?" Dad asked.

"I've got to get back. It's all hands on deck. We'll have to do Saint Patrick's Purgatory another time."

I could see the look of relief flit across Dad's face. "Oh dear. Dear oh dear. I'm disappointed, son. I really wanted to go," he lied like a trooper.

"I know, Dad. I wanted to do it, too. We'll just have to go in the summer when the weather's better. Or next year."

"Yes! When the weather's better."

"A murder, Sean? You haven't had one of those for a while," Mum said.

"Nope. This is the first this year. Some drug dealer shot in the back with an arrow."

"Like Saint Sebastian," Mum said sadly.

"Saint Sebastian was shot in the front, love. Several times. You remember the painting by Botticelli," Dad prompted.

"So who am I thinking of that was shot in the back?"

"Jimmy Stewart in *Broken Arrow*? He was shot in the back. *He* survived but poor Debra Paget, his beautiful Apache wife, she died," Dad explained.

"Debra Paget," Mum said thoughtfully.

"She was shot by Will Geer who, of course, went on to play Grandpa Walton," Dad explained.

This was heading the way of all their conversations so I knew

I had to nip it in the bud. I pointed at my watch. "Really sorry about the pilgrimage, Dad. I was so looking forward to it. But someone has to keep the streets safe," I said but neither of them was really listening to me.

"Is Jimmy Stewart still alive?" Mum asked.

"He is too! And in fine fettle. He was on Gay Byrne just last year," Dad insisted.

"Debra Paget, I know that name," Mum said.

"Of course you know Debra Paget!" Dad insisted. "She was Elvis's girlfriend in *Love Me Tender* and she married Chiang Kai-shek's nephew. In real life that is, not in *Love Me Tender*."

"Oh yes, that's right. I remember, now," Mum said, satisfied.

I pointed at my watch again. "Listen, guys, it's been great, but duty calls."

We packed our bags, gave hugs all round and ran outside into the rain.

I looked underneath the BMW for bombs, secured Emma in her car seat and got Beth comfy in the front.

I got in the driver's side, turned the key in the ignition and we both grinned as the Beemer's throaty, fuel-injected six cylinder engine roared into life.

Eighty-eight minutes later I was at the crime scene.

2: JUST ANOTHER DEAD DRUG DEALER

A smallish crowd had gathered in front of 15 Mountbatten Terrace in Sunnylands Estate. No doubt the crowd would have been bigger if it hadn't been raining and this wasn't a Monday. Monday was one of the two signing-on days at the DHSS and more or less everyone in this particular street was either unemployed or on disability and therefore needed to sign on. This had not always been the case. When the Sunnylands Estate had been built in the early 1960s Carrickfergus had three major textile plants and the shipyards in nearby Belfast employed over twenty thousand people. Now the factories had all been closed, the shipyards were down to a rump of 300 men at Harland and Wolff and every scheme the government had tried to bring employment to Northern Ireland had failed miserably. Emigration or joining the police or civil service were your only legitimate options these days. But illegitimate options were to be had joining the paramilitaries and running protection rackets, or if you were a very brave soul you could try your hand at drug dealing.

Independent drug dealers were few and far between because the Protestant and Catholic paramilitaries liked to make an example of them from time to time to show the civilian population that they, not the police, were the ones who could be trusted to "keep the streets safe for the kids". Of course, everyone east of Boston, Massachusetts understood that this was hypocrisy. In a series of agreements worked out at the very highest levels in the mid 1980s the paramilitaries from all sides had effectively divided up Belfast between themselves for the dealing of hash, heroin and speed and the two newest (and most lucrative) drugs in Ireland: ecstasy and crack cocaine.

Such independent drug dealers that there were had to be very discreet or pay through the nose if they didn't want to get killed. Obviously this particular dead drug dealer hadn't been discreet or hadn't paid the local paramilitary chieftain his cut. I'd been thinking about the crossbow bolt in the car. Guns were to be had aplenty for the paramilitaries but a private citizen might have difficulty getting one, which made you think that maybe some kid has a heroin overdose and his dad goes out looking for justice. He can't get a firearm but you get could bows and crossbows at a sports goods shop . . . Something like that, perhaps?

I parked the BMW and got out of the vehicle. It was a grim little street and it must be truly hell around here in the summer when the only distractions to be had were hassling single women at the bus stop and building bonfires. Frank Sinatra's upbeat "Come Fly with Me" was playing from an open living-room window, but the crowd of about twenty people was sullen and malevolent. I could almost smell the stench of cheap ciggies, unwashed armpits, solvents, lighter fluid and Special Brew. They were mostly unemployed young men who had been drawn away from wanking over page three by a murder on their door-steps. I hated to leave my shiny new BMW 535i sport on a street like this, but what choice did I have?

Several wee muckers came over and began touching the paintwork.

"Get your hands off that," I said.

"Are you a policeman?" a very little girl asked.

"Yes!"

"Where's your gun, then?"

I patted my shoulder holster.

"What type of gun is it?"

"A Glock. A man called Chekov sold it to me. I figure I'll use it at some point." Pearls before swine but hey it's these little things that keep you going. I tried a different one on the girl: "Why don't blind people skydive?"

"Dunno, mister."

"Because it scares the crap out of their dogs."

No smiles at all. I was going to have to go slapstick with this lot and it was too early in the morning for Buster bloody Keaton.

"Is that your car, mister, or did you knock it?" a tall particularly sinister-looking child asked with an unsettling lisp.

"Why aren't you in school, sonny?"

"I got a note from the Royal. I get these terrible headaches. I only go to school when I want to go now," he explained.

"What's your name, son?"

"Stevie, Stevie Unwin," he said and I filed the name away for the future, when the thing in his brain that was giving him the headaches would drive him to the top of a tower with a rifle.

"Mind the car, Stevie, don't let anyone put their paws on it," I said, giving him the customary fiver and began walking towards the crowd. "Step aside there, step aside," I said. The crowd parted reluctantly and with hostility, people muttering highly original things like "bloody peelers" and "bloody cops".

Like Jules Maigret I arrived at the *scène du crime* thoroughly existentially jaded. But lucky old Jules never had a scene like this. The dead drug dealer was lying face down in his front yard, halfway up the garden path. He had orange hair and was wearing a sleeveless denim jacket that said "Slayer" on it in rivets. Under the denim jacket was a bright blue motorcycle jacket. To complete the ensemble he was wearing bleached white jeans and cowboy boots. The crossbow bolt was sticking out of his back, near his left shoulder.

I was surprised to find that the body had not been cordoned off and there was no evidence of forensic men or forensic activity. Indeed, the crowd were so close to the corpse that their cigarette ash was blowing onto the deceased, contaminating the crime scene.

My blood began to boil. In another police force you would have called this chaos. One didn't employ words like "chaos" or "fiasco" to the fine boys of Carrick CID, at least not in my presence, but if this wasn't chaos it could certainly do chaos's job until the real chaos came along in the shape of Ballyclare RUC or Larne RUC or those fuckheads from over the water.

"Everyone get back!" I said, physically pushing some of the onlookers away from the body. "Back there, onto the pavement and put those cigarettes out!"

Where were the forensic officers? And why weren't there uniformed officers on crowd control?

What the hell was happening?

Was this some kind of ambush? No, the spectators would be a lot more cautious if there was about to be a hit. A forensic officer tea break perhaps? That was more likely given their strange ways, but they'd never have buggered off leaving a bunch of eejits dropping cigarette ash over their corpse.

The crowd was nudging up again behind me. "Get back, I said. There's nothing to see here, he won't be doing any tricks, he's not friggin Lazarus."

I examined the victim while the crowd watched me expectantly and Sinatra sang "Chicago", which he did on the British but not the US version of this album. I could take or leave Sinatra, mostly leave, and the record was getting on my nerves. "And somebody turn that effing stereo off!" I yelled and almost immediately the record got yanked with a vinyl-scraping zzzzzipppp!

Now all was silence but for the wind among the crisp packets and shopping bags and the braying of a goat attached by a brick to a piece of rope in the overgrown yard of the house next door that was attempting to reach over said fence and eat the victim's shoelaces. It wasn't getting close but it too was slobbering all over the crime scene.

"And somebody move that goat!" I said.

"And who might you be when you're at home?" a woman asked with an East Belfast accent that sounded like broken glass under a DM boot.

I reached in my pocket for my warrant card but it was back with my bags at Coronation Road.

"Detective Inspector Duffy, Carrick CID," I said flashing my video club membership card in lieu of my police ID.

Suitably impressed, the crowd moved back a little.

I pointed at a likely lad whose Liverpool FC scarf was a sign of above-average intelligence.

"Sonny, do me a favour and move that goat away from the fence," I said.

"What'll I do with it?"

"See that shopping trolley over there filled with bricks? Tie it to that. Here's a quid for a good job," I said.

He grabbed the rope, went next door and tugged the goat away from the body.

"Right! What happened here? Where did the other police officers go?" I asked the crowd, but now everyone was staring at their shoes and saying nowt. The ever present/ever tedious Belfast rule: *whatever you say, say nothing* had come into effect.

"There were other police officers here this morning, where are they now?"

Silence.

The rain increased a fraction and a mist began rolling down the north road from the Antrim Hills. A man on all fours, perhaps with species dysphoria, was attempting to communicate with the goat.

Christ, this was depressing. It didn't help when an ice-cream van pulled up, parked itself at the end of the street and began playing a selection of television themes. Its haunting version of

EastEnders brought a few punters over.

This police/honest-citizen liaison was getting me nowhere. I lit a ciggie and went inside the house where I was met by a distracted and visibly upset Detective Constable Lawson coming down the stairs.

"Oh, sir, thank God you've got here at last!"

"What's going on Lawson? Why isn't my crime scene secured? Where's forensic?"

"I'm so sorry, sir, it's been a bit of a crazy morning. I was just on the phone, I was just trying to call them, I wasn't sure what number, I . . ."

"Call whom?"

"Forensic."

"Surely they were notified by dispatch?"

"Yes, sir. They've been and gone, sir."

"They left?"

"Yes, sir," Lawson said, his lip trembling and his bright blue-green eyes on the verge of tears.

"Are they finished?"

"No. They didn't even get started. Chief Inspector McCann said it was an unsafe work environment. He said it was union regulations."

"What union? What are they . . . Why isn't the victim even covered with a police blanket? He's getting rained on, ashed on and there's little kids staring at him."

"I'm so sorry, sir. I did ask for permission but Inspector Dalziel sort of dismissed my request."

"*Inspector* Dalziel?"

"He got promoted while you were away, sir."

"Let me get this straight. *Inspector* Dalziel arrived from the station and took over the crime scene?"

"Yes, sir."

"And wouldn't let you put a police blanket over the victim?"

"No."

"Why?"

"He said the goat would probably eat it and ruin police property. He may have been being sarcastic, sir, I wasn't sure . . ."

"Why didn't you control the goat, Lawson?"

"I mentioned that as well, sir. I said that the goat was slobbering over the fence, potentially contaminating the crime scene."

"And what did Dalziel say to that?"

"He said that that was forensics's problem. And then he said that the goat was on someone else's property and we'd need permission to enter the house next door to take the goat away from the fence."

"We're the Old Bill. We can do whatever the fuck we want, son!" I said, really angry now.

I noticed that my fists were clenched and my face must have been bright red. Kenny Dalziel had the same effect on everyone he worked with and the bastard was not going to give me a heart attack. I forced myself to take a couple of deep breaths and calm down.

"I'm sorry, sir," Lawson said, all trembly-voiced.

"It's not *your* fault, son. Where the fuck is Sergeant McCrabban? He's supposed to be in charge of—"

"That's what I mean by crazy. I thought you knew, sir. Oh gosh. I thought someone had told you!"

"Told me what?"

"Deauville's wife, sir – Deauville's the victim, sir – she stabbed Sergeant McCrabban when he tried to get her off the body so the forensic officers could do their work."

"Holy shit! Crabbie was stabbed! Why didn't you tell me that straightaway?"

"I thought you knew, sir."

"How would I know? I only just got here. What happened? How is he?"

"Uhm, I was just on the phone with him. Apparently he's fine, sir. No stitches, just a tetanus shot. She stabbed him with a fork.

He didn't want to go to the hospital in the first place but—"

"What happened?"

"Mrs Deauville was very upset. Sergeant McCrabban tried to move her away from the body and she stabbed him in the shoulder with a fork. She's a foreigner, I think. We had to report the stabbing, of course, and, uhm, Inspector Dalziel showed up. He ordered Mrs Deauville placed in custody and he ordered Sergeant McCrabban to report himself to the Royal Victoria Hospital as per the injury-at-work regulations."

"Christ! And then what?"

"And then the forensic team left, saying it was an unsafe work environment."

"And the forensic officer is this McCann fellow, eh? Don't know him. OK. Then what happened?"

"And then I tried to secure the crime scene . . . and the goat . . . and Inspector Dalziel . . ."

I bit my tongue. It wouldn't do to let young Lawson hear my full profanity-laden tirade against a superior officer. "And then Inspector Dalziel left with Mrs Deauville?" I asked.

"Yes, sir."

"Probably the first arrest he's made in years," I couldn't help but mutter.

"Unfortunately Inspector Dalziel took both constables off crowd control to restrain Mrs Deauville in the back of the Land Rover, so that just left me here, sir."

"Are forensic coming back, or what?"

Lawson flipped open his notebook. "Chief Inspector McCann said that with 'police officers being stabbed and with a hostile crowd in front of the house this was not a safe crime scene for his men to do their work', so they were withdrawing until the crime scene was secured."

"Withdrawing to the nearest pub I'll bet."

"I wouldn't know about that, sir."

"So Dalziel left just you to control the crowd, canvas witnesses and conduct an entire murder investigation?"

"Yes, sir. I'm sorry about all this, sir," he said, correctly inter-
preting the look of horror on my face. For this was a nearly
perfect fuck up – all we needed now was a newspaper reporter
or a random inspection by the Chief Constable.

"All right Lawson, we've got to move fast before the press or
a local councillor gets here. Go upstairs, get a clean bed sheet
if you can find one and cover up the victim's body. I've already
taken care of the goat. Once you've done that, get the crowd
back onto the pavement and if you are able please urge them to
go indoors."

"But how, sir?"

"Shoot someone in the kneecaps every five minutes until the
rest get the message?" I suggested.

"Sir."

"Just use your natural authority. I'll call the Royal, check in
on Crabbie, call forensic and get a new team down here pronto.
Now, go!"

Lawson found a clean sheet in a linen closet and I called the
Royal Victoria Hospital. They looked for Crabbie in Casualty
but he had already discharged himself and was on his way back
to Carrick, which was typical of him. Crabbie was one of the
good guys: solid, dour, competent, hardworking, uncomplaining
– a thousand men like him and you could do anything: feed the
world, build a bridge across the Bering Straits, terraform Mars.
There wasn't another like him in Carrick RUC and I'll bet at the
Royal he didn't even ask the nurses for high-dose opiates, which
is what I would have done. I hung up and called my old mate
Frank Payne from forensic and told him about the behaviour of
CI McCann, to which he was suitably outraged.

"Kids today, eh, Francis?"

"You can say that again."

"So you'll send a team down pronto?"

"Aye. I'll scratch your back and you scratch my back."

"If you mean I'll owe you a favour, yes. But I'm not going near that hairy back of yours, it's like Mirkwood in there."

"Just hold the fort there, Duffy, and I'll have a team down there in half an hour. Sunnylands Estate?"

"Yeah."

"Fucking nightmare there, is it?"

"Not as bad as some of the estates in these parts. To describe it as a UVF-ridden shithole filled with whores, druggies and scumbags would be ungenerous."

"Aye well, do me a favour and don't let the crime scene get contaminated, eh? I'm just back from an arson in Larne and them boys from Larne RUC were tramping size tens all over the shop."

"Typical. You know what they say, Frank? What's the difference between Larne and a yoghurt?"

"Dunno."

"You leave them both alone for sixty years and the yoghurt will grow a culture."

"Hilarious, Duffy, don't give up the day job."

I hung up with Frank and next I called my boss, Chief Inspector McArthur, explaining to him that we needed half a dozen constables for witness canvassing and crowd management. It was a relatively slow day at Carrick RUC, so he said that that shouldn't be a problem as long as it didn't involve over-time.

"I don't think over-time will be necessary, sir. I'd be surprised if anyone saw anything at all, sir. Not anything they'll admit to us. We should have the canvassing done in an hour or two."

"And how's Sergeant McCrabban? I heard he was attacked?"

"He's already discharged himself, sir."

"I hope he doesn't put a claim in."

"He won't, sir. This is John McCrabban we're talking about here."

Another police officer might have taken three months off

on disability or even sued the station for compensation, but Crabbie wouldn't do either of those things.

"I'm relieved to hear it."

"Sir, I'm also pretty sure Sergeant McCrabban won't be pressing charges so could you please have Mrs Deauville released from the cells and brought up to the CID Incident Room? Maybe have a WPC give her a cup of tea?"

"That's not going to be possible, Duffy."

"Why's that, sir?"

"Inspector Dalziel sent her up to Castlereagh Holding Centre for processing."

"Castlereagh? For a stabbing?"

"Stabbing a police officer."

Dalziel was no doubt cock-a-hoop over his arrest but this wouldn't do at all. If Mrs Deauville was processed at Castlereagh we wouldn't get to interview her for two or three days and as every tedious fuck will tell you, the first forty-eight hours are *the* most important in any criminal investigation.

"Sir, can you do me a favour and patch me into Kelly at the switchboard?"

"Of course, Duffy, see you later."

". . . Switchboard, this is Kelly."

"Kelly, this is Sean Duffy, listen to me, someone's off in a Land Rover taking a Mrs Deauville to Castlereagh Holding Centre. I want you to find out who it is and tell them to come back to Carrick RUC. OK?"

"Yes that's right, Sean, Constable Pollock's driving her up to Castlereagh."

"You get on the blower to Pollock and tell him to turn the Land Rover around and come back to Carrick."

"Sean, this is Inspector Dalziel's arrest," Kelly said dubiously.

"That's OK, I'll deal with Inspector Dalziel. Just get that Land Rover to turn round and return to the barracks."

"OK, Sean, I'll do it but I don't want Inspector Dalziel giving me a hard time."

"He won't. Patch me through to his office will you, Kelly?"

"OK, Sean."

A short pause . . .

"Inspector Kenneth Dalziel, admin, Carrickfergus RUC."

"Dalziel, it's Duffy."

"You finally showed up, did you? I have to tell you, Inspector Duffy, that the competence of your department leaves a lot to be desired. I found a scene of total disarray when I got there," was his opening sally. Dalziel was the son-in-law of a prominent high court judge but that didn't bother me as you knew his father-in-law probably couldn't stand him either.

"Listen to me, Kenny, if you interfere in any future CID investigations or boss around any of my men ever again I am going to come round your house and take that gnome you have with the fishing pole in your front garden and shove gnome and pole up your arse until the wee red hat comes out your bloody throat. Savvy?"

"You can't talk to me that way, Duffy, I've been promoted to—"

"I'll talk to you any way I fucking please, you useless ballbag fuck. Now I'm having Mrs Deauville brought back to Carrick to be questioned and I don't want you to interfere, OK?"

"I'm sending her to Castlereagh to be processed. In my opinion she is a Category 1 offender who needs to be centrally processed: a dead drug-dealer's wife who assaulted a police officer . . ."

"The facts aren't in but don't let that stop you giving your opinion."

"If that Land Rover shows up here, Duffy, I'm sending it back to Castlereagh."

"I dare you. I fucking dare you to do that, Dalziel!" I said and slammed the phone down.

I took a few deep breaths and went back outside.

The body had been covered with a sheet, the goat was being

held back by a kid, but the crowd was even bigger now as we found ourselves in that unhappy window between people returning from their morning dole appointments and daytime TV kicking in. The sky was overcast and drizzling but what I wouldn't give for a short thunder shower to send these gawkers indoors.

Lawson had gone out onto the street and was now locked in a battle of wills with the ice-cream-van driver who had pulled his truck right up in front of the victim's house in the exact place where the forensic team would want to park their Land Rovers. Sensing his youth and low rank, the van driver and the crowd were hassling Lawson with invective extravagant even by the somewhat elevated standards of Sunnylands Estate.

It would never do. I pushed my way through the unwashed mob and told the ice-cream-van driver to fuck off before I arrested him for obstruction.

He could see the fury behind my eyes and like a sensible chap he fucked off back to the end of the street again. Some of the crowd went with him and, satisfied with this momentum, I turned to the others.

"This is a police matter. Get back inside your houses or I'll lift the bloody lot of you!" I said, seething.

A heavy-set red-faced man with a minister's collar got in my face. "I'm the Reverend William McFaul, I'm chairman of the residents' association. How dare you speak to us like that! This is our street and our concern."

"Reverend McFaul, please tell your friends and parishioners to get back inside their homes. There's nothing to see here. These people are obstructing police officers at their work and contaminating a crime scene," I replied.

"We have a right to see what the RUC is doing on our street!" McFaul said, trembling with rage.

"You bloody don't."

"I'm a God-fearing man. I'm not used to such language," McFaul said.

"Language? You mean 'bloody'? Do you also clutch your pearls and occasionally get the vapours? Come on now, move along," I said, pushing him away from the house.

"I'll report you!"

"That's fine but just make sure you do it from the other side of the street," I said, giving him another shove.

"You are an extremely rude young man. What is your name? I am going to call your supervisor," McFaul said, taking a diary and a pencil out of his overcoat pocket.

"My name is Inspector Kenneth Dalziel of Carrickfergus RUC. My supervisor is Chief Inspector McArthur. Report me all you want," I said, giving him a last push and walking back to the crime scene with a feeling of immense satisfaction.

Lawson had found some "RUC CRIME SCENE DO NOT CROSS" tape and was stretching it in front of the house.

"Forensic are on their way," I told him. "Should be here in twenty minutes."

Before Lawson could reply, an old lady in full old lady rig popped out of the throng and began jabbing her finger in my chest. "Is this what it takes for the police to finally come? A murder? I call and call and youse take half the night to get here. It's a disgrace. The kids racing up and down the street, joyriding. Drinking at all hours. Smoking them funny cigarettes. Bad manners to the old folks. The whole country is going to the dogs."

"I quite agree, madam. What's your name?"

"Ivy McAleese," she said.

"Well Mrs McAleese, Constable Lawson here will take your statement," I said. Lawson flipped open his notebook and began writing down the woman's litany of complaints. I listened with interest: kids, drugs, loud music. The old bird didn't know how lucky she had it. She and all the good people of Belfast and the north Belfast suburbs: lucky. These were the good days. Couldn't they see the future? Entropy maximising. Neighbour against neighbour. Blood feud. The disintegration of this lost lonely province into warring camps. *The falcon cannot hear the falconer* . . . And good luck getting the cops then, love. Call 999 and it'll just ring and ring and ring.

But we're not quite down that shit hole yet, are we?

When the old lady had given Lawson a pageful I thanked her for her cooperation and ducked under the police tape with my young colleague and lifted the sheet from the body.

The crossbow bolt had hit the victim close to his left shoulder. There was very little bleeding on the denim jacket around the wound but there was a lot of dried blood on either side of his stomach . . . ergo he'd been shot in the chest first and he'd managed to make a run for it. Run almost up to his front door before they'd shot him again in the back.

"What do you know about what happened, Lawson?"

"Until forensic conclude their inquiries we don't really know anything, sir."

"Who found the body?"

"Mrs Deauville, this morning."

"Where was she last night?"

"In the house, I believe, husband never came home so she went to bed."

I touched the victim's hand. Ice cold. Rigor. Dead about nine or ten hours.

"So he's been here all night too?"

"So I gather, sir, although forensic will confirm that."

"Sergeant McCrabban said on the phone that he was a known drug dealer."

"We ran the victim's ID through the computer and half a dozen arrests came for drugs and drug possession in Bangor and before that London. He's from here originally but he's lived mostly in London, if his charge sheet is to be believed."

"That's why I'd never heard of him. When did he move to Carrick?"

"According to the local residents about four weeks ago."

"Ah so he was the new drug dealer on the block."

"Yes, sir."

"What type of drugs?"

"Sergeant McCrabban had Sergeant Mulvenny go through the house with his canine team."

"Sniffer dogs. Good thinking, that. What did they come up with?"

"Nothing, although Sergeant Mulvenny says Felix got excited."

"Who's Felix?"

"He's the heroin dog."

"Did you find any heroin?"

"No, but Sergeant Mulvenny thinks there may have been some in a couple of empty paint tins at the back of the house."

"So he's moved the drugs off site."

"Yes, sir."

"We'll have to look into that."

"Yes, sir."

"All right, now. Our victim. What do you see in front of you? We don't always have to let forensic tell us everything. We can make a few deductions on our own, can't we?"

"Yes, sir. Uhm, well, the victim's boots are clearly very expensive so he must have been making a lot of money."

I clocked the boots and yes they did look expensive. Snakeskin cowboy boots with flat soles. Slippery flat stoles that must have been a bugger to run in. If he'd been wearing sneakers the poor bastard might have lived.

"What else do you see, Lawson?" I asked, looking into his eager blue eyes. He was still a junior detective but Lawson wasn't like the usual time wasters they gave you to fill out your CID team. Lawson was smart and he had peeler wisdom beyond his years. Sooner or later some git from Belfast would spot his talent and promote him to detective sergeant and poach him away to the fraud squad or Special Branch. Five years from now

– if I was still alive – I'd probably be working for him.

"Not much bleeding from the crossbow bolt, is there?" he said.

"No. There isn't. So what does that tell you?"

"It wasn't the primary wound?"

"Exactly."

"Oh I see, sir. There's blood under the body. So he was shot in the front first, he turned, ran, and then they shot him again in the back?"

"That would certainly be my take. He must be lying on the first bolt, which is in his stomach or chest. You can't really hide a crossbow behind your back as you're walking towards someone, so I'd guess that the assailant was in a vehicle. And unless it was a drive-by (and I've never heard of a crossbow drive-by) Mr Deauville was probably approaching the vehicle, offering to sell them drugs."

Lawson nodded in agreement.

"What else do you see? Tell me about the leather jacket. Where would you get a fancy jacket like that, Lawson?" I asked, feeling the jacket's soft leather sleeve.

Lawson also felt the sleeve. "From Slater and Sons in Glasgow, sir. Three hundred and fifty quid. He liked the style so much he brought two of them. Got a fifty quid discount."

"How did you do that? Some kind of latent paranormal ability?"

"Uh, no, sir, there's a stack of receipts on a spike in his dining room. Had a look through them while we were waiting for you."

"What else did the receipts tell you?"

"Mostly receipts for furniture, white goods and dishware. Stuff you need for moving house."

"What kind of a name is Deauville?"

"Huguenot."

"Tell me everything you got on him."

"According to the rent bill from the housing executive he only moved in on January 15th – that's why we hadn't heard of him yet in Carrick CID, although he has a charge sheet as long as your arm. Robberies, burglaries and it looks like for the last year or two he's been dealing drugs."

"Heroin?"

"Sergeant Mulvenny's dog thinks so."

"How does a brand new drug dealer suddenly break into the heroin trade?"

"Don't know so, sir."

"Enemies?"

"He's not a known player, so I imagine the local paramilitaries here weren't too happy with someone muscling in on their territory. And taking the temperature of the local residents – Mrs McAleese and the minister there – apparently Mr Deauville hadn't gone out of his way to make friends."

"At least his missus was upset at his demise. What did she tell you before she was carted off?"

"Not much, sir."

"Hates the cops, eh?"

"English isn't her mother tongue."

"No need to bring her mother's tongue into the discussion, little too early in the morning for that sort of talk."

"What? Sir, I wasn't trying—"

"I know," I said wearily. "Where's she from?"

"Bulgaria. We couldn't understand anything."

"Bulgaria?"

"Bulgaria."

"How did those two love birds meet?"

"He went on a package trip to the Bulgarian Riviera, sir."

"There's a Bulgarian Riviera?"

"Yes, sir, on the Black Sea coast."

"Didn't know that. Holiday romance?"

"Apparently so, sir. She came back with him last year and they married in September. This according to Bangor RUC."

"And she doesn't speak any English?"

"Not any that she's used with us. How's your Bulgarian, sir?"

"Rusty, I've got to admit. Although it's one of the Romance languages, I think."

"No, sir. You're thinking of Romanian, which has a Latin root. It's a Slavic language."

"OK. Well, without wishing to slight the intellectual capacities of the station I have a feeling we don't have a Slavic speaker on the staff."

"We don't. Already checked, sir."

"So did she say *anything* about what happened?"

"She said plenty. I wrote some of it down."

Lawson flipped open his notebook. "When we arrived she was hugging the body and screaming *obícham te! obícham te!* over and over."

"What do you think that means? Is that his name in Bulgarian, do you think?"

Lawson gave me one of those looks that young people reserve for older people when they wish to convey their patience with the oldster's folly.

"Te is probably the tu form in Bulgarian, wouldn't you say, sir?"

"Oh . . . yes, I'm sure you're right. So she's saying *what happened to you* or *I love you*, or something like that."

"I imagine so, sir."

"Good-looking woman?"

Lawson coloured. "Uhm, I don't know. I suppose if you like that sort of thing, uhm . . ."

"No one is going to accuse you of a lack of gallantry, Lawson. Is she young?"

"Mid twenties, sir."

"Yes, good contact to have if you're dealing heroin. Young, reasonably attractive woman with a Bulgarian passport. Bulgaria is right next to Turkey, I believe, where the emerald fields of marijuana and the scarlet fields of poppy grow in the plentiful Mediterranean sunshine. And of course there's the— Oh shit, that bloody goat again."

The goat was tied to a shopping trolley that had been filled with bricks. There were about thirty bricks in the shopping trolley which probably weighed about forty pounds. If sufficiently motivated the goat could in fact have pulled the shopping trolley behind it and made an admittedly slow escape through the estate. The goat, however, being a goat, was smarter than that and had decided to eat the rope with which it had been tied to the trolley. It had been munching on this rope since we had arrived and presumably for much of the previous couple of days. Escape was now imminent.

"That goat is our only eyewitness, Lawson. Get the tow rope from my car and tie it up properly and when you've done that— Oh my God, here comes our old friend, back from the wars!" I said getting to my feet.

Detective Sergeant McCrabban was getting out of a Land Rover that he'd driven back here himself from the hospital.

I ran over and gave the big galoot a hug, which, of course, horrified him – Crabbie not being the biggest fan of outward shows of affection or human contact.

"Crabbie! It's so bloody good to see you. Jesus, can't I leave you alone for two days without someone trying to kill you?" I said, pumping his hand.

"No one tried to kill me, Sean. Mrs Deauville was just a little upset that I asked her to keep away from the body until the forensic officers came. Where are they, by the way?"

"Came and went mate, like the pack of wankers they are," I said. "Lawson, the goat, please! So how's your shoulder, mate?"

"It's completely fine. No stitches, just a plaster and a tetanus shot. No hard feelings on my part – the woman was clearly distressed. Where is Mrs Deauville, by the way?" Crabbie asked.

I filled him in on the whole sorry business, leaving out my

observations on Kenny Dalziel's competence. " . . . so she's back in Carrick now, but we'll need a Bulgarian speaker if we're going to interrogate her," I said.

"That's going to be tricky, Sean. I've checked. There is no Bulgarian consulate in Northern Ireland. I called up Queens and they don't have anyone on staff who speaks the language – they suggested that we contact the school of Slavic languages in London or the Bulgarian Embassy in Dublin."

"Then that's what we'll do. What about this first victim who you said got shot by this crossbow maniac? What's his name and where's he?"

"Morrison is his name. Unpleasant wee toerag. He's down in Larne hospital. A dozen stitches, lost a bit of blood but he's fine."

"He see anything?"

"He told me he didn't see who shot him and has no idea why anyone would target him."

"But he's definitely a drug dealer too?"

"Oh yes. Eleven convictions for possession over the last five years and he's in the files as a current dealer."

"Was he shot from a car?"

"He quote didn't see anything unquote. And quote, even if I had, I'm no bloody grass, unquote."

"I'll talk to him tomorrow. Him and Mrs Deauville, if we can get a Bulgarian speaker."

Two Land Rovers pulled up and a team of forensic officers got out, led by the grim lardy face of Chief Inspector Payne.

I shook his hand and he shook the hands of Lawson and McCrabban, who he remembered from the sad case of Lily Bigelow.

"Good to see you, Sean. You're looking well . . . for someone twice your age. Is your man going to lynch that goat, Duffy? It looks like a nasty piece of work," Payne said, lighting a ciggie and smoking it with the kind of determination you seldom saw any more in cops under fifty.

"This goat will not be harmed on my watch. He reminds me of me: determined, obstinate, omnivorous. Take him round the back of the house and tie him up, Lawson," I said.

When Lawson had gone Crabbie said in an undertone "It's not a 'he', it's a nanny goat, Sean," which brought a hideous cackle from Payne.

"Duffy thinks of himself as a she-goat. Hilarious!" Payne said.

"Don't you have work to do, mate?"

"Aye I suppose I better get cracking. You lads need to see how a professional does his job."

The crowd-control officers from the police station finally arrived and I gave them a mini seminar on how to canvas for witness statements: no leading questions, keep everything as general as possible and the old who, what, when, where, how. Incredibly and depressingly this was news to most of them.

I let them all get to work and went inside to make some phone calls.

The Bulgarian Embassy in Dublin was very cooperative and said that they would send up a translator and consular representative first thing in the morning.

Payne found me reading the first completely unhelpful statements from Mr Deauville's neighbours in the living room.

"I determined the cause of death," he announced.

"Yes, well, that one didn't exactly take Dr Gideon Fell."

"Who?"

"What did you find out?"

"You plods in CID won't have realised it but your victim was actually shot twice!" he said with unconcealed triumph. "He was shot in the back, of course, but it was a crossbow bolt in the stomach that killed him. It nicked what I believe to be the superior mesenteric vein and he bled to death. Even if he'd made it inside here he would have died."

"Tell me about these crossbow bolts."

"Well, I'm no expert on that, but they look normal to me.

Barbed crossbow bolts for target shooting or hunting. I've got the shoulder one in an evidence bag for you. The pathologist will need to remove the other one."

"Time of death?"

"About one this morning. I'm not going to be more specific than that. The last time we had a case together the medical examiner gave me an awful bollocking for being too specific about the time of death," he said, again recalling the Lily Bigelow case.

"Very good, Francis," I said, shaking his hand again.

"The boys from the morgue are here if you want to give them the nod."

I went outside and gave permission for the body to be removed as I read the last of the witness statements. None of Deauville's neighbours would admit to anything. They didn't really know the deceased, he had kept to himself, they didn't know any of his acquaintances, had never heard of any threats to his life or person.

This was also the bog-standard response to pretty much any murder in Northern Ireland, especially a murder that seemed to have a paramilitary connection. For what seemed like the millionth time in my career I had encountered Belfast's code of omerta that babes must learn at their mother's knee.

I looked at the crossbow bolt in the evidence bag. Didn't seem remarkable but I'd find out more about it.

I put Lawson in charge of a couple of constables to thoroughly search the Deauville residence before Crabbie and I returned to the station in my mercifully unfucked-with Beemer.

Mrs Deauville had been returned to Carrick CID. She was literally spitting with fury and they had put her back in the cells rather than Interview Room 1 where she couldn't wreck the two-way mirror and video-recording equipment. She wasn't bad-looking, if you didn't mind chain-smoking peroxide blondes. I'm a Debbie Harry fan, so, you know . . .

Crabbie and I tried a few questions but she appeared to have only a few stock phrases in English:

"You fucking shit . . . Six pack beer . . . Move your arse, grandma . . . Your clothes shite . . ." which were probably enough to get you through six months of life in Northern Ireland but wouldn't really do in a murder inquiry.

Her name was Elena and even after tea and biscuits she was visibly upset so I sent down a brave WPC to comfort her with a blanket and more tea and biscuits.

"How do we know she didn't do it?" I asked Crabbie. "She has a temper."

"No sign of a crossbow in the house."

"She shoots her husband and throws the murder weapon in the sea?"

"And leaves his body outside the house all night?"

"She was drunk when she did it. Wakes up this morning. Oh my God, what have I done? Calls the cops, gets the waterworks going."

"Why would she do it?"

"They had a fight? He was having an affair?"

"She seemed genuinely upset to me."

"Remorse?"

"Maybe," Crabbie conceded. "But we didn't find a receipt for a crossbow in the house."

"Who keeps receipts? Oh wait, he does. Still, let's bring a picture of Deauville and his wife to every shop selling crossbows in Ulster. If the shopkeeps recognise either of them we probably are dealing with a domestic," I said.

"You could be right. But then there's the other case."

"The other case, yes, damn it."

I made some more phone calls. Special Branch informed me that there was indeed a vigilante group called Direct Action Against Drug Dealers (DAADD) who occasionally killed drug dealers in Belfast and environs. DAADD, of course, was just one of many cover names for the IRA and its offshoots and splinter groups.

"If this was a DAADD killing they probably would have already claimed it so they could make the evening news. They're very media savvy," Trevor Finlay from Special Branch intel informed me.

"We haven't had any claims of responsibility, yet," I told him.

"Nor us."

"Meaning?"

"Might not be DAADD. Unlikely they would drive all the way up to Carrickfergus, anyway. If I was to guess, Sean, I'd say that this was something else."

"Thanks, Trevor."

I called up Roy Taylor in statistics and he told me that there had been twelve deaths by crossbow in the last thirty years, all of them manslaughters or non-prosecutable accidents.

I found out that there were two shops in Northern Ireland that sold crossbows. Both in Belfast. I called both and was told the rather disheartening information that they had sold over two hundred crossbows each in the last year. The shops were not legally obliged to keep the names and addresses of their buyers and none had. I gave them the make and serial number of the bolt in the evidence bag and unfortunately this was the most common type of crossbow bolt. Tens of thousands of them were sold in Europe every year.

Around five o'clock Lawson came back with the PCs from the house and area search. The house, rubbish bins, Mill Stream and skip search had revealed no dumped crossbow. The house search had revealed no more drugs or useful enemies list or even more useful address book but Lawson had found about a thousand quid in a paper bag under the oven and an old .455 Webley semi automatic pistol that had to be fifty years old if it was a day.

"This thing's an antique," Crabbie said, impressed.

"It looks like he never cleaned the mechanism, I doubt it would even fire," I replied.

"Should we take it to the range and find out?" Lawson suggested eagerly.

Crabbie and I shook our heads together. The dodgy-looking old thing would probably explode in our hands and Carrick CID had suffered enough today.

"Oh go on, sir," Lawson pleaded.

"We take that down the range, it misfires and gets me right in the kisser."

"You're a glass-half-empty kind of guy, sir, aren't you?"

"I don't even acknowledge the existence of the glass, son."

Crabbie nodded at the forbidding wisdom of this remark.

I yawned. "It's getting late. Case conference tomorrow morning, you lads can go home. First order of business on the morrow will be to question the wife," I said.

I typed up a brief summary of all that we knew and closed my eyes for a bit in my recliner. I must have gone straight out because I heard a voice from deep, deep in the well ask "Is he asleep, do you think? Can we nudge him?"

"Speak Lord! Thy servant heareth!" I said and opened my eyes on Constables Collins and Fletcher. "Oh it's you two. What do you want?"

"The Chief Inspector wants a progress—"

"Tell him I'll be there in two minutes. Just enough time for him to get the good whisky out of its hiding place in the bottom shelf of his filing cabinet."

I gathered my thoughts, ran a hand through my hair and went into the Chief Inspector's office to give him my formal summary of the day's events.

Chief Inspector McArthur had been our gaffer for three years now and the disappointment was beginning to show on all sides. A Scot who'd been trained at the police college in Hendon, he was a high flyer who'd probably expected to be done with his rotation in Carrickfergus RUC in about eighteen months before getting a promotion to Superintendent and a move to somewhere more interesting. It hadn't happened and I sometimes wondered if he blamed me and my bad voodoo for his career doldrums.

"Ah, Duffy, have a seat. Whisky?"

For a while the Chief Inspector and I had been on collegial first-name terms but now it was mysteriously back to "Duffy". Had I done something wrong? Already? I'd only been back from my hols a few hours.

"No thank you, sir, Beth hates it when I come home from duty with whisky on my breath," I said.

"Yes, she's right, I suppose we all should cut down on—"

"But if you insist, sir, just two fingers of that sixteen-year-old Jura would hit the spot about now."

He made me a Jura and poured a Johnny Walker and soda for himself and I sat down opposite. He read my report while I examined him. He was a boyish-looking thirty-five or thirty-six, with no grey hair that I could see in his elegantly parted locks. I dug his Top Man black suit too. Nice cut, nice lines and if I'd been fifteen years younger and liked suits or him I'd of asked him about it.

"Before we begin I should let you know, Duffy, that Inspector Dalziel is thinking of writing up a formal complaint about you."

"Is he now?"

"Yes. I tried to talk him out of it, but he's pretty adamant. Says you were rude to him over the phone. Make it go away, Duffy, eh? Apologise to him, OK?"

"Yes, sir, I'll take care of it, sir."

"Changing the subject: your team did all those blood tests we asked for last week, didn't they?"

"Yes, sir. For the annual fitness thing? Is that coming up soon, sir?"

"I shouldn't really say, Duffy, but I can tell you that we're

doing things very differently this year. We're taking officer fitness much more seriously."

"I know. I'm always telling the men that, sir. My crew is as fit
as a fiddle and I'm a model of health myself, sir. I'm just back
from Donegal; you know what it's like out there: walking on the
beach, hiking in the woods, mountain-climbing, swimming."

He lowered his voice and leaned forward conspiratori-
ally. "Hmmm, yes, well, make sure you and all your team are
here at the station tomorrow, I've heard a rumour that Chief
Superintendent Strong is coming in."

"Really? So it is tomorrow, is it? The fitness test thing?"

"You didn't hear that from me but just make sure you and all
your team are at the station in the morning and they don't go on
the piss tonight."

"Crack of dawn, we'll be here."

"Good," McArthur said finally skimming through the report.
"So you've gotten a murder case, Duffy?"

"Yes, sir."

"In Sunnylands Estate, it says here. I went there once. Its dis-
tinguishing features seemed to be religious bigotry, cockfighting
and despair."

"Cockfighting?"

"So I imagine, or perhaps dog-fighting. Unsavoury place.
Residents looked deranged and desperate to escape. Afraid to
drive my Merc through it and I certainly wouldn't park it there."

"No, sir."

He slid the report back across the desk. "All seems to be in
order here, Duffy. I take it you are not going to ask for additional resources on this one or, God forbid, over-time?"

"Too early to say, sir. The case could go in any number of
directions."

He frowned. "Well, there's no point going overboard is there?"

"Why's that, sir?"

"It's just another dead drug dealer, isn't it? No family, wife's a foreigner, he's a bloody repeat offender. You know what every-one's going to say around here: good riddance. Pardon my lan-guage, Duffy, but who's going to give a damn about him?"

I looked at the Chief Inspector for an uncomfortable five sec-onds. This kind of talk annoyed me no end.

"*I* am going to give a damn about him, sir. *My men* are going to give a damn about him. *Carrick CID* is going to give a damn about him," I said and with the rule of threes ringing in his skull I finished the whisky, set the glass down on his desk, and exited the office with enough fizzy melodrama to have made the heart of the octogenarian Bette Davis in far-off California skip a beat.

I was still grinning when I made it back to Coronation Road ten minutes later.

3: THE BIG SHEEP

"What are you so pleased about?" Beth asked as I waltzed through the door kissing girlfriend, baby girl and cat, in that order.

"Oh nothing. Just something I said to the Chief Inspector."

"Is that whisky on your breath? You know I worry about you driving with the liquor in you."

"The Chief Inspector was pouring so it barely covered the bottom of the glass."

She handed me a cold can of Bass. I popped it and took a gulp. A cigarette would have gone down well here but I was limiting myself to half a pack a day and I only had two left to get through the night.

"How was the cat in our absence?"

"He's fine, but Niamh overfed him. She gave him two tins a day."

I stroked him on the head again. He was a long, lean cat who burned off a lot of energy. "He looks OK to me."

"How's your big case?" Beth asked.

"It's a murder all right. Some lunatic going around shooting drug dealers with a crossbow."

"Will you be able to solve it?"

"I very much doubt it. No eye witnesses either because there were no eye witnesses or because they think the paramilitaries killed him and everyone is afraid to blab. Add in the fact that the murder weapon is an extremely common piece of equipment and that Mr Deauville was a drug dealer so he had many enemies and rivals . . . Nope it's not looking good for a resolution."

"And yet you seem cheerful enough?"

"Well we'll give it the old college try, won't we? You know how many murder cases I've successfully brought to trial since moving to Carrickfergus?"

"How many?"

"Zero."

"And again you're smiling, what's up with you, Sean?"

I pulled her close and got a whiff of her perfume. I brushed a line of red hair from her forehead and kissed her on the lips.

"A man's nothing without a purpose. For the last couple of months we've been treading water but now I've got something solid to work on and by God I'm going to work on it no matter what that idiot Chief Inspector has to say about it."

"You want a purpose? Change Emma and take her for a walk before the rain comes on again. Dinner will be up in half an hour."

"OK."

When I changed Emma's nappy and powdered her she fell asleep on the changing table so I transferred her to the cot.

"OK to let her nap?" I called into Beth.

"Yeah, that's fine. Hey, Niamh told me a joke. What do you get when you cross an agnostic, a dyslexic, and an insomniac?"

"Uhm—"

"An eejit who stays up all night wondering if there really is a dog," I said.

I smiled and went out to the shed to "work on rebuilding my Triumph Bonneville", a fiction Beth and I both accepted.

Shed.

Paint tins.

I had no idea sniffer dogs had gotten so sensitive so I moved my stash out of said tins and put it in a block of engine grease.

I picked up the extension phone and called Johnny Freeman, my marijuana dealer.

"Hello?"

"What's that noise in the background. Is someone murdering cats?" I asked.

"It's Kylie Minogue, as you well know."

"I suppose you heard the news."

"Of course. It was all over the *Daily Mirror*. Ian Rush is unhappy at Juventus and would love to come back to Anfield."

"Not that news. What do you know about this dead drug dealer?"

"Oh, him? Unaffiliated independent operator. Only a matter of time before he got kneecapped or topped or threatened with kneecapping and topping."

"You don't sound particularly worried, Johnny."

"I pay for protection. Twenty per cent. And still my prices cannot be beat in all of East Antrim . . . Did the drug squad seize any merchandise?"

"Nope. Nothing in the house. He must have a lock-up somewhere."

"And when you find the lock-up?"

"Everything will be under lock and key in the property room. Weighed and catalogued. Destined to remain there until the investigation is concluded. This is a murder case."

"What do they do with narcotics evidence after the case is over?"

"They destroy it."

"*Who* destroys it?"

"Forget it, Johnny. There's a whole procedure for illicit goods. A team from Belfast will come down for it and they'll take it with them and then it'll be incinerated."

"Crying shame."

"Johnny, if I could bring you back to the matter in hand. A man's been murdered here. What do you know about Deauville?"

"Nothing. Moved here from Bangor a few months ago. Worked out of Sunnylands and Castlemara. Not my turf, so I didn't care."

"Whose turf was it?"

"The UVF runs them estates, as you well know."

"Why would they kill him?"

"Because he wouldn't pay a percentage?"

"Why wouldn't he pay a percentage?"

"Because he's an idiot? I don't know."

"They shot him with a crossbow."

"Yeah I heard that."

"Why would they do that, do you think, when there are plenty of guns floating around?"

"I don't know. Aren't you the detective?"

"Helpful as usual, Johnny. Keep your head down. Bye."

"Bye, Sean and if you can somehow get your paws on any seized gear, I'd—"

I hung up before he could complete the sentence.

I went back inside the house.

"Have I got ten minutes before dinner? Want to return a video," I said.

"Yeah. It's risotto. You like my risotto, don't you?"

"Of course I do, back in ten."

I walked down the street to Bobby Cameron's house and rang his doorbell.

"What do you want, Duffy?"

"Did you hear about the killing today?"

"Aye I did. Drug dealer, no one'll miss him."

"If I wanted to ask if the late Mr Deauville had been paying for protection who would I go see?"

"I'm not telling you that."

I held up the video. "Would it help if I returned this video?" I asked.

Bobby nodded. "It might," he said and shut the door.

✿

I checked under the Beemer for mercury tilt switch bombs and drove to Video Extra on the Clipperstown Road.

I went inside with a copy of *Reds* that I hadn't watched and therefore didn't need to rewind.

"How was it?" Andy Young asked. "Not much of a Warren Beatty fan myself."

AKA: Big Andy Young. Andy Mad Dog Young. Andy King Rat Young.

Andy was the UVF deputy Chief of Staff for Carrickfergus and the person in charge of making sure businesses paid their protection money every week. If they didn't it was a brick through the window and if that didn't convince them it was the old Lagan Valley Lightning: a petrol bomb through the window . . .

"Never watched it," I said, putting the video on the counter.

"You might as well keep it. We're changing the whole shop to VHS. Everyone is."

"What will I do with my Phillips recorder?"

"Get rid of it. The format wars are over. Sony won."

"Phillips is a superior system. You can record on both sides," I said, somewhat miffed – that Phillips video recorder had cost me 500 quid.

"Doesn't matter. VHS is the industry standard now and will be until laser discs take over."

"Five years ago they said CDs were going to kill vinyl."

"They did."

"No they didn't CDs are . . . listen Andy, I'm not really here to talk about video recorders and CDs."

"I know."

"How do you know?"

"Bobby Cameron phoned me and told me you were noseying around asking questions."

"It's about this man Deauville."

"What about him?"

"Somebody shot him."

"I heard."

"It wasn't you by any chance, was it?" I asked.

Big Andy's thick white neck swivelled towards me. His eyes were narrow black slits in a menacing blue-white visage that almost looked like a human face.

"I'm no informer, Duffy."

"I know you're not. I'm not suggesting that you are."

"What are you suggesting?"

"I'm wondering why Deauville wouldn't pay protection money when he knew that he was likely to be kneecapped or worse."

"Who says he wasn't paying protection money?"

"Well he was shot, wasn't he?"

Andy shrugged and looked at the TV monitor which was playing *Jaws: The Revenge.*

"Wait a second. Are you saying he *was* paying protection money?"

"I'm not saying anything. I'm no grass," he said, never taking his eyes from the monitor.

The sound was off but a wet Michael Caine was yelling something. Probably something about a shark.

"If you keep watching, Inspector Duffy, you'll see a different ending from the cinema release. The shark blows up, just like in the first one," Andy said.

"Andy, I don't want to seem dense, but are you implying that Deauville was paying protection right enough?"

He looked at me again. "I'm not saying he was, I'm not saying he wasn't. I have no idea."

"If the Inland Revenue investigators were to inspect your business here, Andy, would everything be above board, do you think?"

"You wouldn't. We have a good relationship you and me. I

never make you pay the rewind fees."

"It's all moot anyway if you're only going to be renting VHS . . . Now tell me plain, was Deauville paying for protection or not?"

Andy checked to see that there was no one else in the shop but it was *EastEnders* time so everyone was home watching telly. He lowered his voice anyway.

"He paid protection."

"So you had no incentive to kill him?"

"No."

"This wasn't a sanctioned hit?"

"He wasn't killed by Carrick UVF or Carrick UDA."

"The local paramilitaries had nothing to do with it?"

"As far as I know, no."

"Cheers, Andy, you've been very helpful."

"No I haven't. I've told you nothing, remember that Duffy."

"You've told me nothing, check."

Back to Coronation Road in time for dinner. Risotto. Apple crumble and custard for dessert. Two of my favourites. Beth must be up to something. I did the dishes, made two mugs of tea and joined her in the living room. The TV was off, the fire was lit, the record player was on (Schubert by the sound of it). I picked up my copy of *The Times*, which I hadn't had a chance to skim through. Beth was reading a book called *Ubik*, but without much obvious enthusiasm. She was looking at me when she thought I wasn't looking. Yeah, something was going on.

"You have a good day today?" I asked.

"Yes."

"Anything new or out of the ordinary?"

"No. Played with Emma, did some reading."

"Are you at the writing stage of your thesis yet?"

"No, no, lot of reading to do yet."

"Well if you need help with the typing . . . I'm practically a touch typist now. Fifteen years in the cops will do that for you."

"Thanks, Sean," she said and looked at me again under that adorable ginger fringe.

"So nothing else happened today?" I asked.

"Well . . ."

Here it comes . . .

"Yes?"

"My father called."

"On the phone?"

"No, he came round."

"Really? I'm sorry I missed him. Your mum with him?"

"No, she had her bridge morning."

"What did he want?"

Another evasive look. "He just wanted to see the baby . . . uhm that's all."

The end of Symphony #2.

Empty grooves in the vinyl.

Silence.

The lovely opening of Symphony #3 that Schubert wrote when he was only eighteen years old, a few weeks after the Battle of Waterloo.

"Is that a clarinet?" Beth asked – an obvious ploy to distract me, that worked like a bloody charm.

"Yes. Solo clarinet. Pretty, isn't it?"

"It's good music to have in the background I'll admit that . . . oh there's Emma . . ."

"I'll take care of her."

Upstairs. Change the baby. Downstairs. Baby to Beth for a feed while I did *The Times* cryptic crossword.

Everything going great until the very first down clue "an often mature ham at the local church hall perhaps? (7)" which I fussed over ridiculously so that my completion time came in at a shocking nine minutes. The answer to the clue, of course, was "amateur". "Mature" being a pseudo anagram of "amateur" and "ham" an unkind phrase for a poor actor. I didn't get it because

I didn't realise until halfway through the crossword that more than half the clues were theatre-related.

We turned on the telly and caught the Season 3 premiere of *Miami Vice* – a show all the young cops down the station were raving about but which I'd never seen.

Liam Neeson was in it, playing a reformed IRA terrorist who wasn't as reformed as he made out.

At 9pm I called the station and asked to be put through to the duty officer.

"Carrick CID, this is DC Lawson speaking."

"Thought I sent you home."

"I came back. I'm still duty officer. Unless you want to come in, sir?"

"No, I don't. Any word on the results on our victim?"

"I have them in front of me, sir. They faxed them through an hour ago. It must have been a light day at the M.E."

"Tell me the salients."

"Time of death: between 1 and 2 this morning. Cause of death: haemorrhaging of the superior mesenteric vein."

"Anything unusual?"

"Nope. It's what we were expecting. He'd been drinking but he wasn't drunk and we're waiting for the full narcotics results."

"Was there any sign of any previous beatings, kneecappings, anything like that?"

Lawson ruffled through the report. "Nope. His body was in good shape."

"Strange that they would kill him straight away, isn't it? Usually they'll give you a good punishment beating to make you pay up. Dead men don't pay anything."

"Yes, sir. But a killing can be useful too. The old Voltaire rule."

"The old Voltaire rule indeed." (*Dans ce pays-ci, il est bon de tuer de temps en temps un admiral pour encourager les autres.*)

"How's Mrs Deauville holding up?"

"I don't know. I haven't been down to see."

"Jesus, Lawson, she's our responsibility. CID, not the station. Take her down a clean sheet and a pillow and get her some food."

"Yes, sir. Right away, sir. "

"Goodnight, Lawson. Oh wait, one more thing. I have a feeling the annual fitness test is going to be tomorrow, so if you want to call in sick this would be the day to do it."

"Nice wee run along the seafront. I'd quite enjoy doing it, sir."

"You would. Well, I'm going to have to get Crabbie and me out of it somehow. And I'm dreading getting the results of our blood work the nurse took. All right, fine, goodnight, Lawson."

"Night, sir."

"Oh, before you go, I saw that programme you've all been raving about."

"*Red Dwarf*?"

"*Miami Vice*. Liam Neeson was in it."

"Oh don't tell me anything about it! Me dad's taping it for me. Did you like the cars? Now that they've gotten rid of the kit cars the cars are pretty cool. Cool clothes, too. I wish you'd let me wear a jacket and T-shirt. It's much more practical if you think about it, sir."

"Goodnight, Lawson," I said and hung up.

I went out to the shed, lit a joint and put Robert Plant's *Now and Zen* in the tape player. On one of the songs there was a sample of Kylie Minogue's "I Should Be So Lucky". Was that co-opting or surrender?

I called up Kenny Dalziel at his house but the phone just rang and rang. I'd apologise to the useless cunt tomorrow.

I switched the music off and looked at the stars. The Great Bear rotating slowly and comfortingly across the winter sky.

Joint finished I walked back in.

Beth was upstairs getting ready for bed.

She had left her handbag on the kitchen table and neatly folded away inside it was an ordnance survey map of the

Ballypollard Road in the townland behind Magheramorne. I
knew that road and that townland.

Beth had circled a field on the Ballypollard Road for reasons
best known to herself. What could this be about? Something
to do with her father's visit? It was mysterious but there was
no percentage in asking her about it because she would know
I'd gone into her bag and looked at her stuff. If I recalled correctly the Ballypollard Road had nothing on it at all except for
the Ballypollard Wool Shop, which was something of a local
landmark because of the giant sheep statue out the front. "The
biggest sheep statue in all of Ireland", they claimed. The circle
Beth had drawn on the map was about half a mile up the road
from the Big Sheep itself, so it wasn't a wool-buying expedition.

I looked at the map until Beth called down to me to ask if I
was ever "coming up to bed?"

It had been a long day but I couldn't sleep and although it
wasn't my shift I got up to feed Emma at just after two. She
fell asleep at the half-bottle mark and I burped her over my
shoulder.

Jet the cat was sleeping in front of the paraffin heater but
when he saw that I was awake he jumped onto the baby's changing table and rubbed himself against me.

"You're awake too, eh, cat? The two men can't sleep and the
two women are out for the count. What's their secret, do you
think?"

Jet kept his own counsel while the 9th-century Irish poem
Pangur Bán floated into my consciousness; I extemporised a
translation that would, I think, have pleased Sedulius Scottus
himself, even if not my literal-minded fifth-form Irish teacher,
Dr Monroe.

How happy we are together, scholar and cat,

Each has his own work, be it study or stalking a rat.

Your shining eyes watch the ratholes, my failing eyes read
verse,

I rejoice over logic problems, you over besting your rodent adversaries.

We are pleased with our own methods and neither hinders the other,

Thus we live without tedium or envy, Pangur my brother.

And yes I *was* pleased with my method. It had been a good day professionally and otherwise, but I knew that the good days were the exception and as Noel Coward wisely reminds us, bad times are just around the corner . . .

4: A PRETTY SHITTY MORNING ON THE
BALLYPOLLARD ROAD

Voices and meows downstairs. "Sssshhh the pair of you. Daddy is still up there sleeping." *So I'm the father of the cat now too, am I?*

Yeah, I supposed I was. Rescued that cat from almost certain death in England.

I opened my eyes, embraced the light of day.

What a day. Friday the 4th of March 1988.

When I was twelve years old a gypsy boy cursed me when I stopped him from stealing my bike parked outside the pet shop in Buncrana. Nothing had happened at the time, but at the end of Friday the 4th of March 1988 when I put my head down on the pillow at two in the morning I suddenly remembered that evil-faced kid and wondered if maybe his spell had merely been delayed for twenty-five years or so.

But I didn't know that then, snuggled up in the blanket with footsteps coming along the landing.

Beth had brought me a mug of coffee and marmalade on toast.

"What's this in aid of?" I asked suspiciously.

"God, you're so cynical," she said and flounced off making me even more suspicious but also affording me a view of her fantastic bum.

Bum. Coffee. Toast. Not the worst way to start the morning. I flipped on the clock radio.

The nurses were on strike, the ferry workers were on strike and the Birmingham Six had lost another appeal against their convictions even though it was obvious to every peeler in the British Isles that they had been fitted up by the West Midlands Constabulary.

Coffee and toast done I got out of bed and looked through the window across Coronation Road to the Antrim Hills where it appeared to be flurrying.

"Was there snow in the forecast?" I shouted downstairs.

"It's only a light dusting. We'll still be able to drive," she shouted back up.

"We? Are we going somewhere?"

"What time do you have to go into work?"

"I need to be there soonish. Ten at the latest. We're supposed to be having a Bulgarian translator come up from Dublin."

"Ten? Oh we've got plenty of time then."

"Plenty of time for what?"

"Oh, just a little run in the country. I'll drive if you don't want to."

"I don't like the sound of this."

"Live a little, Sean."

"What will we do with Emma?"

"Take her with us."

"Are we going somewhere specific?"

"It's a surprise."

"Now I definitely do not like the sound of it," I muttered to myself.

I showered and dressed in jeans, DM boots, blue shirt, black sweater.

I went downstairs to find Emma and Beth in coats and sweaters all set to go.

"Wait here, let me check under the car first," I said.

I went out to the BMW and checked underneath it for bombs. No bombs but I'd always keep checking. As a student I'd listened to an aged Bertrand Russell's thoughts on the fate of turkeys being fattened for Christmas, the turkeys subscribed to the philosophy of inductivist reasoning and didn't see doomsday coming. I will.

Wife and child came out to the car. Cat staring at us anxiously through the living room window.

"I'll drive," Beth said which meant that we'd be listening to Radio 1 for the entire journey. I mentally prepared myself for an assault of Aswad, Bros, Tiffany, The Pet Shop Boys and Kylie.

"OK, you can drive, but easy on the clutch, please, this is a precision piece of machinery."

She turned the ignition and the magical mystery tour began with a trip down Victoria Road and a turn left onto the Larne Road. We kept on the Larne Road past Whitehead and on to Magheramorne

My worst musical fears were realised when they played three Phil Collins songs in a row. I made a mental note to have Collins's drum solos taped and piped into the interrogation rooms when difficult sods were cooling their heels.

"This is where we turn," Beth said, pulling the Beemer up the Ballypollard Road. Beth and even Emma started singing along to a song called "Joe Le Taxi", which chipped away at the blackness in my hard heart.

"You know you haven't had a single cigarette today?" Beth said happily as we drove deeper in the hills.

"I know, I'm bloody gasping for one," I said.

"The reason why you're gasping is because of the cigarettes, you'll see," Beth said with such uncanny prescience that a few hours later when the RUC doctor was threatening to sign me "unfit for duty" I would wonder briefly if she had the Sight.

"Wind the window down, look at the view," Beth said.

I did as I was bid. We were in a beautiful part of County

Antrim overlooking the North Channel and a big chunk of Western Scotland.

"Where are we going?"

"Have you ever been up here before?"

"I was once at that Big Sheep place where they have the jumpers."

"Yeah, we're not going as far as that. Just a wee bit further now," Beth said.

Beth and Emma sang along to the hits on BBC, I grew more nervous and more in need of a cigarette.

Finally she pulled the BMW along a lane I hadn't noticed before and stopped at a muddy field filled with half a dozen workmen. The field backed onto a little wood and beyond that lay a hamlet, a river and another wood. In the distance you could see all of Islandmagee jutting like a thumb into the water and because it was a clear day the Ayrshire coast of Scotland looked close enough to touch.

I looked at Beth. "What is this?"

"This is our new home," she said with a happy grin on her face which told me that she wasn't kidding.

"What are you talking about?"

"I've told you that I don't want to live in Victoria Estate."

"I know and I said when work eased off I'd take a few weeks and help you look for a place."

"Daddy was over yesterday and I was telling him how much I hated living in Carrick and he said that we could help him out. He's building a house and he wants it to be a model home for a dozen more that will be scattered over parcels of land he has up here. And he said that we could live in it as long as we wanted. A present for us and for the new baby. Here, let me introduce you to Vaughn, the site manager. He'll tell you all about it."

I put Emma on my shoulders to keep her out of the muck and shook hands with Vaughn, a lanky fellow with curly brown hair and likeable brown eyes. Vaughn told me all about it. A four-bedroom house on a nine-acre plot with access to woods and a riding trail. There were two bathrooms, a children's play-room, a library and a stable block.

"We could have horses, Sean!"

"It's good horse country," Vaughn said with the kind of wistful look in his eye that told me he was probably a Catholic.

I took her to one side. "What's going on, Beth?"

Her eyes narrowed. "A house for us. Away from the bloody north Belfast suburbs and those people on Coronation Road."

"Those awful people are my friends."

"You're delusional, Sean. They're not your friends. They hate you because you're a Catholic and because you're a peeler."

"I don't think that's true. Not any more."

"And they certainly hate me. I hear them gossiping about me behind my back. It's awful."

"This is some kind of class thing, isn't it? Some kind of crazy Protestant class thing."

"No! Don't you know anything about me? I'm not that sort at all. I don't care that they're working class or whatever it is they are. I just don't like them. They're rude to me behind my back and I'm lonely."

"Lonely! What do you think you'll be out here? This is the middle of fucking nowhere."

"Sean, please, not in front of the baby."

"Sorry . . . Look, I don't understand you. I wanted to marry you. You turned me down and told me never to bring it up again. Now you want us to move into Barbie's fucking – sorry – Dream House complete with bloody stables. Bit of a mixed fucking message, isn't it?"

She took Emma off my shoulders and held her. The wee lass was looking at the pair of us with bafflement in her big blue eyes. She had never seen us fight before. I had not allowed that to happen.

Beth poked me in the chest. It was unusual for her to get

physical. She must be really worked up.

"What don't you understand, Sean? Dad is giving us this house! To live in as long as we want! Who would turn that down?"

"We already have a bloody house!"

"A house I hate!"

"Aye, let's talk about hate. Your father can't fucking stand me. A Catholic peeler shacking up with his daughter! Jesus Christ I might as well as be Beelzebub himself."

"That's nonsense!"

"Is it? You want to talk about dirty looks, muttering behind backs? You don't know the half of it, love. In the old days he'd of had me horsewhipped."

"Oh my God, you are so dramatic! Listen to yourself!"

"He wants you up here because you'll only be a ten-minute drive away from them in Larne whereas I'll be all the way up in Carrick or in Belfast. No more nipping home at lunchtime to see the bairn. Leaving early in the morning, coming back late at night. Or is that what you want?"

She put her hands on her hips. "Only you, Sean Duffy, only you would react like this when someone is practically giving you a house for free! Only you. You'd cut off your nose to spite your face, you would."

"Free? Nothing's free."

"This is. No strings. It's the show house and we can live here as long as we like. I know Dad, it's his way of giving it to us forever."

"I'm happy where I'm living now. I know people. They know me. You know how hard it was to win them over?"

"You won't have to win anyone over here, Sean. It's a house in the country. Land. There's woods. Think of Emma. Think how happy she'll be. You'll be happy too, I promise."

I could see that she was trying now.

I was being the arsehole and she was trying.

"If Adam and Eve can't make it in Paradise, how are we going to make it in bloody Carrickfergus?" she said with a smile.

"You seriously think I could live here, and be beholden to your father?"

She bit her lip in that gorgeous way of hers and nodded. "That's what it boils down to, doesn't it? It's not him that hates you. It's you that hates him. Some older guy knocks up his daughter and is barely civil to him and he hasn't said one bad word to you. Not one."

"He doesn't need to say anything—"

"He drives a Jaguar and he reads the *Daily Telegraph* and so you've got this picture of him in your head that he's this fucking Colonel Blimp at the golf club who hates your 'fenian guts'. I don't know who that is, but that's not my dad! He's been nothing but civil to you, and now he's giving us a house . . . This is you, Sean. You. You . . ." she said and putting her hands over Emma's ears added "You fucking ingrate."

"I'm an ingrate? I didn't ask for this fucking house! I didn't ask your fucking father to stick his oar into my family business!"

"Is that the way you see it?"

"Aye, that's the way I fucking see it!"

She stomped over to the BMW. She put Emma in the car seat and secured her seat belt, then she got in the driver's seat in the front.

I walked over to the car and tapped the window. "So what now? You're going to fucking drive off dramatically and leave me here?"

The BMW spun its wheels in the mud and I stepped away from the splatter.

The front wheels found some grip and Beth drove out of the field and back onto the lane. I thought, for a moment, about chasing them but there's seldom anything more ridiculous to be seen than a man angrily chasing after fleeing missus.

And chasing her across a slippery muddy field would more or

less invite an encounter with the sheugh.

I looked at the blue line of exhaust smoke curling into the air like a djinn from a bottle. I heard the Beemer shift through the gears on cue until it reached the overdrive on the Ballypollard Road. She hadn't been easy with the clutch.

I walked over to Vaughn, who'd been staring fixedly at the mud during all this time.

I cleared my throat. "Horse country, eh? What type of horses? Hunters, you think?"

"Oh yes, you could stretch a hunter out here," he said.

Definitely a Catholic.

"So how long will this house take?"

Vaughn rubbed his chin. "It depends."

"On what?"

"Well, the blueprints are done and we're in today looking at the drainage. The site drains beautifully, by the way. But we'll need to get planning permission for a house from the authorities in Ballymena. This is redlined for agricultural buildings only, you know?"

"So they might say no?"

"Oh they'll say yes, Mr Macdonald is very well-connected, but it'll take a wee while."

"How long?"

"Six months, or even up to a year to get the planning permission for the house. If they give it for this one they'll have to give it for all of them along this road."

"How long to build it?"

"Four or five months if he turns the whole crew loose on it."

"So when can we think about moving in?"

"Well, if you're lucky the end of the year."

"And if we're unlucky?"

"The autumn of 1989."

"And if we're very unlucky with planning permission and building delays?"

"The spring of 1990?"

Sigh of relief.

I was a conservative animal. I didn't like to move and I liked living on Coronation Road, but 1990 seemed like a very, very long way away. The 1990s were the future. In the 90s things were bound to be very different from now. Thatcher would be gone. Kinnock would be Prime Minister. According to Gerry Anderson's *Space 1999* we would all be living in colonies on the moon at the end of the decade, although that, admittedly, seemed a little bit unlikely.

So why the big fit, Duffy? You're a lucky man. Lucky to be alive. Lucky to have Beth and Emma. So what if you end up out here in the sticks in some bullshit Proddy mansion? Small price to pay isn't it?

"Mr Macdonald's daughter, she's a feisty one, isn't she?" Vaughn said.

"Aye."

"Good-looking."

"Steady, mate. This is the mother of my child."

"You remember that line from the old John Wayne film?"

"I remember it," I said.

"Two women in the house and one of them a redhead," presumably was the quote he was referring to from *The Quiet Man*, although when I thought about my actions of this morning "Life's tough and even tougher when you're stupid," from *The Sands of Iwo Jima*, floated into my mind.

Vaughn nodded and offered me a cigarette. I was still gagging for one but I shook my head.

"Look, can someone give me a lift back to Carrickfergus, please? I've got work to do this morning."

"A lift? That shouldn't be a problem. Troy!"

Yeah, back to Carrick. Interview the victim's wife. Establish the insolubility of this case without eyewitness or forensic evidence. Log it in the yellow file. Hoof it to the flower shop and the chocolate shop and apologise big time: *I overreacted, Beth. Very generous on the part of your da. Might take us two years to move in so we'll stay here just for now . . .*

And maybe in those two years she'll learn to love this part of Carrick? Maybe, Duffy, maybe. As the Russians say, getting what you want sometimes requires moving like the knight in chess: forward and to the left.

5: INSPECTOR DALZIEL

When I arrived at Carrickfergus RUC barracks there was an air of embarrassment hovering over the place. In my experience, Ulster Protestants were capable of being embarrassed by everything and anybody so I wasn't particularly alarmed by this.

I *was* worried when Crabbie and Lawson intercepted me at the top of the stairs.

"Morning, Sean," Crabbie said darkly.

"Oh God, what's amiss? It's not about our Bulgarian, is it? She didn't escape or hang herself or anything like that?"

"No, it's not about her. She's fine. The victim support unit has been with her all morning."

"What's the victim support unit?"

"WPC Green," Lawson said.

"Oh, OK. And the translator?"

"Apparently he's at Carrick Train Station. We've sent a car for him. He should be here in about five minutes," Crabbie explained.

"So what's wrong?"

"Chief Superintendent Strong is here with a couple of people from HR and Dr Havercamp and a nurse," Lawson said.

"Dr Havercamp?"

"It's the fitness tests. The Chief Constable has given an order that this year the RUC fitness tests are to be held on the same day at every station so that people can't bunk off," Crabbie explained.

"Fitness tests? Jesus, you had me concerned there for a second. Don't worry about those, lads. That's only for beat cops. I haven't done a police fitness assessment since I moved here and that was in 1981."

"How do you keep getting out of it?" Lawson asked, amazed.

"Like I said yesterday. Do you ever listen?"

"I do, I—"

"All you do is call in sick."

"The Chief Inspector says if anyone calls in sick today they will be officially failed," Crabbie said.

"Officially failed? I've never heard such rubbish in my life!" I said. "I'm going to go see him. CID shouldn't have to do this. We don't do foot patrols or go round chasing criminals over the rooftops. We're the brains of the outfit around here."

"I don't mind doing a fitness test," Lawson said.

"Yeah, look at you. But what about McCrabban and me?"

"Don't include me, Sean. I'm fine. I've got the farm to keep me fit. Bringing the sheep in from the high bog that'll get your blood pumping and—" Crabbie began, but I put my hand on his shoulder.

"Don't worry, lads, I'll sort this one out. Fitness tests are for ordinary coppers."

The Chief Inspector was in conference with Chief Superintendent Strong, the HR goons, Inspector Dalziel and Dr Havercamp, who was one of the RUC's medical officers. I knew Kevin Havercamp well because he'd repeatedly refused to give me opiates, sick leave and methaqualone on pretty much every occasion on which I'd asked for them over the last few years. He and Strong, however, did give me pleasant enough welcoming smiles, as opposed to Dalziel, who positively grimaced when he saw it was me.

"Ah Duffy, I've been looking for you," CS Strong said in his low, pleasant Glaswegian burr.

"I've been looking for you too, sir. I just want to offer you my hearty congratulations on your promotion, sir. Thoroughly deserved. Assistant Chief Constable. It brings credit to us all, sir."

"Why thank you, Duffy, that's very good of you to say so. It's not quite official yet though, but when all the t's are crossed I'll have a wee celebration at the police club," he said, his close-cropped ginger beard bristling with pleasure.

"I'll buy the first round, sir. We're all very proud to be in your command, sir."

Strong was positively blushing now.

"Now about this fitness test, sir, I—"

"You're not getting out of it, Sean," Strong said quickly. "Out of your entire CID team only Lawson showed up to do the fitness test last year."

"CID *team*? There's only the three of us."

"Well all three of you will be doing the test this morning. Every man in the station and every man in every other station. This is coming direct from the Chief Constable."

"But sir—"

Strong leaned close and lowered his voice to convey a clandestine atmosphere: "An internal civil service report arrives on Mrs Thatcher's desk that says that the RUC is 'the fattest and least fit' police force in the entire British Isles. Not for publication of course but Mrs T sees red. She calls Jack. Jack calls all the divisional officers and he lays down the law to all of us. OK? This is coming from Number 10. You're going to bloody do your run, Duffy, and your bloody push ups and you're not getting out of it."

"OK, sir," I said meekly. "But we have quite a busy morning this morning. We have a crime victim to console and to interrogate. We've got a translator coming from—"

"You better hop to it then, Duffy. Inspector Dalziel here is leading the men out together. You're all going as a group for security reasons. I'll talk to you in a bit about your case if you want."

"Yes, sir."

"Five minutes, Duffy. Have your men meet me in the car park. Don't worry. It's only a little jog to the castle and back," Dalziel said with an incredibly smug look on his face, as if he'd already seen the future too, a future where I give up halfway wheezing . . .

"Five minutes, no problem, see you down there," I said casually.

Back into CID.

"OK, lads, we're not getting out of it, apparently. Yeah I know it's bollocks but what can you do. Is that Bulgarian here yet?"

"He is. I've sent him downstairs to the cells to be with Mrs Deauville," Crabbie said.

"Put both of them in Interview Room #1 and give them tea and biscuits while I try to find some gutties."

I changed into my old PT kit of shorts and a T-shirt and an ancient pair of Adidas gutties I found in my locker. Crabbie followed me downstairs and got changed into a similarly unused kit. I'd never seen him in shorts before.

"My God I need sunglasses to cope with the white glare coming off your legs, mate," I said.

"You can talk, look at you! Skin and bones, seen healthier corpses fished out of the Lagan," he protested, with more defensive sarcasm that he normally mustered of a morning.

But in truth I did look pretty pale and unappetising in the light of day. And in the reverse of what was supposed to happen I had in fact lost weight and muscle definition since cutting down on the smokes. What Beth saw in me I had no idea.

Lawson looked like a young Adonis in his shorts.

"Look at him, Crabbie, he's like a young Adonis in those shorts," I said.

"Adonis would have been naked, sir," Lawson replied.

"Yeah well, I wouldn't try that with Kenny Dalziel. He'll have you up on a charge. Now listen to me Lawson, I expect you to win the race, for the honour of CID," I said.

"It's not a race, sir."

"It is a race and you're going to win. It's going to be like *Chariots of Fire*. Go get your Walkman, get something good on it."

"I did bring it actually. Do you want to listen, sir?" he said playing a dozen toxic bars of Paul Hewson's singing and David Evans's tedious, predictable and barely competent chord progressions.

"What did you think of that, sir?" Lawson said, grinning like he'd just played me Sibelius's lost Eighth Symphony.

"Anodyne, conformist, radio-friendly bollocks, lacking in soul, grace, intelligence or joy," I could have said but didn't. Lawson was a fragile young man and was hurt easily.

"As long as it gets you over the line first," I said.

I led Crabbie and Lawson downstairs to the car park where it was drizzling, cold and grey. Dalziel and the other men were waiting under the overhang. No sign of the Chief Inspector or Chief Superintendent Strong. How'd they get out of it? Some pigs are more equal than others.

"There you are, Duffy!" Dalziel said. "We've been waiting for you."

I took him by the elbow and led him away from the others.

I offered him my hand and he reluctantly shook it. "Kenny, look, if I was out of order yesterday I'm sorry. And I shouldn't have raised my voice. We're all in this together. Us against the enemy you know? And I should have said congratulations on the promotion. OK?"

"Is this you apologising?"

"I'm apologising, yes."

Dalziel's face cracked a little, but then assumed its previous fixity.

"I'm sorry too, Duffy, but I'm still going to make a formal report about you. You can't say stuff like that over the switchboard and around the office. You set a bad example for the other officers. Ill discipline is infectious and without discipline what are we?"

I disengaged my hand from his, muttering "dick".

"What did you say!"

"Nothing. Are we ready to go? There's over twenty men getting soaked here."

"Twenty-six to be exact," Kenny said.

"Or over twenty, to not be exact. Come on, blow your whistle or whatever you do."

"All right! Everybody ready? Let's go!" Kenny said and started the stopwatch.

We had to run a kilometre in under eight minutes which was the distance approximately from the police station to the castle and back.

We set off at a run straight into the teeth of a stiff east wind and sea spray. Although we were going along the seafront and although we were all kitted out primarily in white shorts and T-shirts it did not look remotely like the scene from *Chariots of Fire*. Only half a dozen officers – including Lawson and Dalziel – managed to get back to the station before the eight-minute mark. Every other cop in the barracks failed. I made it in twelve minutes, just behind McCrabban. For the last two hundred metres I thought I was having a heart attack, but at least I made it in running. Some of the fatter sergeants couldn't walk the distance in under twenty minutes.

Soaked, cold and wheezing I hit the showers downstairs.

"Fitness test for CID, never heard of such a thing," I muttered to myself. I dried, changed and I was back upstairs in my office with a restorative vodka gimlet when the Chief Inspector knocked on the door.

"Come in!"

He entered with a clipboard and an air of gloom.

"Ah sir, how were the results?"

He sat down and looked glumly at the stats on the clipboard in front of him. "Everyone failed except for Lawson, Dalziel, Pollock, Hitch, O'Neill and McClusky."

"Can I have a look, sir?"

He handed it over and I was pleased to see that Lawson had indeed come in first.

"This isn't going to look good on the report," he said.

"Just do what all the other stations do," I suggested.

"And what's that, Duffy?" he asked.

"Fake the results. As long as they're on a bell curve and there are a few outliers they'll believe it."

McArthur laughed bitterly. "If only, Sean. But Chief Superintendent Strong is still here and Dalziel timed everyone, too."

McArthur looked distracted and reflective. I didn't know him well but I could tell that there was something else that was bothering him.

"This isn't about the bloody fitness test is it, sir?"

He shook his head. "Can I get a drink?"

"Sorry, sir, don't know where my manners were. Vodka gimlet?"

"What's in it?"

"The way I make it is lime juice, vodka, ice and soda to taste. It's very refreshing."

"I'll take a stiff one."

I poured him a glass. He drank it and nodded appreciatively while I topped mine up.

"Surprisingly tart," he said and put the glass on the table.

"Isn't it?" I said sitting down again.

"Look, Duffy, there's things you need to know."

"What things?"

He smiled. "I'm on my way out."

"Resigning? At your age, surely you—"

"Promotion. I'm probably moving up to divisional level in the summer. Strong's promotion to Assistant Chief Constable creates a vacancy."

"I see."

"Victor McClusky will be made the new Chief Super and I'll get his old job."

"Congratulations, sir. Superintendent. You deserve it."

"No, they're not making me Superintendent just yet but I assume that will come with the new responsibilities."

"Still, congratulations. Divisional level."

His jaw clenched. "I'm not a complete fool, Duffy, I know what you're thinking. *Here am I languishing at the rank of Inspector for the last five years . . .*"

"Promotion isn't the be all and the—" I tried but McArthur was a salesman who couldn't leave your door until he'd finished his spiel: "I know what you all think in CID. Sean Duffy collars the villains and Chief Inspector McArthur takes the credit if there is any credit."

"That's not what we think at all, sir!"

"Well, it won't be me for much longer. I'll be gone. And I'm sorry to say that I've been told that they are not going to promote you into my place even though you have effective seniority. They will never promote you, Sean. You know that, don't you? I've seen your confidential HR file. It actually says that on it. 'Not to be given additional responsibility'."

"I was told that by someone else who'd seen it."

"Red lines all over it. You have some powerful enemies and I suppose some powerful friends too for them not to have tried to boot you out before now."

McArthur wasn't to know that all my powerful friends had been killed in a helicopter crash on the Mull of Kintyre two years earlier. Now I only had powerful enemies.

"Oh they've tried to boot me out, sir, but I keep hanging on.

So who's getting your job? New broom?"

"Nope. That's why I made you apologise. Dalziel will be made Chief Inspector and he'll be running the show from August onwards. You're going to have to learn to work under him, OK?"

"Kenny Dalziel is being promoted to Chief Inspector a few months after being promoted to Inspector?"

"Yes."

"And he is going to be put in charge of the whole station?"

"Yes."

"With all due respect, sir, he's got no talent for command."

"That's the kind of talk I don't want to hear, Sean. I don't want any more comments like that from you or anyone who works for you. OK?"

"Yes, sir."

McArthur shook his head. "I share some of your reservations. I saw his wife once with a bruise on her cheek."

"The fucking bastard."

"I know . . . Look, he's going away this week for his annual leave to Eastbourne and when he comes back I expect relations between you and him to be completely different. Certainly they will need to be fixed by the summer or your life here is going to be untenable."

I said nothing. The rain was lashing the window behind the Chief Inspector's head and in the stormy lough beyond boats were struggling to make headway up the deep water channel to the port of Belfast. This was all some kind of metaphor for my own life.

"Maybe Dalziel will fail the promotion board. Surely they'll see that he's an eejit."

"I wouldn't get your hopes up. He's been practising for the promotion board for years. He's the sort of pencil pushing, risk-adverse type who'll slowly go up the ranks until he's Chief Constable."

I nodded sadly and finished my vodka gimlet.

The Chief Inspector stood up. "You'll remember what I said. No more smart-alec remarks. Make nice. OK? And remember this is just between us."

"Yes, sir," I said, feeling thoroughly beaten now.

"Oh and report to the doctor downstairs. He'll go through your blood work with you and take your pulse. You know the drill."

"Do I have to do that now? I have a witness to interrogate."

"It'll only take five minutes, Sean," he said.

I nodded and when he was gone put on a fresh shirt and tie to look respectable for the doctor.

The phone rang in my office. Switchboard said it was a reporter but I didn't have the time to talk to reporters. "Shall I say you're too busy?" Eileen asked.

"Yeah, that'll do," I said absently. Reporters, of course, hated to be told that you were too busy to speak to them.

Of course the doc's visit did not take five minutes. Not even close. I'd been avoiding Kevin Havercamp for some time, now the bugger was going to get his money's worth.

A sallow-faced, balding, heavy lidded, Uriah Heep of a man, Kevin could take the wind from the sails of even the breeziest of chaps and he caught me when I was already vulnerable.

He made me strip to my boxers and vest. He weighed me, listened to my lungs and took my blood pressure. He stuck me in a dangerous-looking X-ray machine that seem to have been trundled out of 1955 and a grim-faced nurse took a photograph of my internals.

"What's the verdict, doc?" I asked as I put my clothes back on.

"You're 10 stone nothing and your blood pressure is 150 over 95. Are you on hunger strike or something?"

"No."

"So you're just living on cigarettes and whisky now, eh Sean?"

"No. I've cut down on both, actually."

"Well, we'll talk about that in a minute. Have you had trouble breathing lately?"

"Uh, funny you should say that, sometimes in the mornings . . ."

"How were you on the 1K run?"

"CID acquitted itself well. DC Lawson won."

"I wasn't talking about your department, I was talking about you, Sean."

"If I'm honest the last bit of the run was something of a trial."

"Do you ever have any of these symptoms: Shortness of breath? Chest tightness or pain? Trouble sleeping caused by shortness of breath, coughing or wheezing? A whistling or wheezing sound when exhaling?"

"Sometimes shortness of breath."

"Do you have coughing or wheezing attacks that are worsened by a respiratory virus, such as a cold or the flu?"

"Now and again, yeah."

"Do your breathing difficulties worsen when you are exposed to airborne allergens, such as pollen, animal dander, mould, cockroaches and dust mites?"

"Maybe."

"Or when it's cold air, or like this morning when there's physical activity?"

"What have I got? Is it cancer?"

"There's no evidence of cancer on your X-ray or in your blood work."

"Well, that's a relief. Just a cold then, is it?"

"You've got asthma, Sean."

"Asthma? Are you sure? I never had that as a kid."

"Well you've got it now. We've caught it early and for that you're lucky. I'll give you a leaflet explaining how your condition manifested itself and explaining the treatment options. I won't go into detail now because I've got a lot to talk to you about and time is pressing."

"Can it be treated?"

"Yes. I'm going to prescribe two different types of inhalers for you. The first is an inhaled bronchial steroid that you will take every morning. It will help prevent asthma attacks by reducing swelling and mucus production in the airways. As a result, the airways will be less sensitive and less likely to react to asthma triggers and cause asthma symptoms. I'll also prescribe a bronchodilator which will relieve the symptoms of asthma by relaxing the muscles that can tighten around the airways. Short-acting bronchodilator inhalers are often referred to as rescue inhalers and are used to quickly relieve the shortness of breath caused by asthma."

"OK. What else did you—"

"Can we talk about the cigarettes?" he said with a black look I didn't like at all.

"There's no need for that face, Kevin. It's totally ironic, I haven't had a cigarette all day. I've been cutting down for months. I have cut down from two packs a day to half a pack. Do I get any credit for that?"

"The ironic thing about that is the fact that you expect credit for only smoking ten cigarettes a day."

I nodded. "All right, so what else am I doing wrong?"

"Can we talk about the drink, Sean?"

"What about it?"

"How many units of alcohol would you say that you drink a week?"

"I don't know. Twenty?"

"Do you know what a unit it is?"

"Yeah. A beer, a glass of whisky, a glass of wine all equal one unit.".

"How many units of beer do you drink a week?"

"Just beer? A couple of pints at lunchtime. One, maybe two, after work with the lads. I'm not a big beer drinker to be honest, not like some blokes around here. At the end of day I'll usually just have a whisky or a quiet vodka gimlet and go to bed," I said to him, not unpacking the fact that this was a vodka gimlet in a pint glass.

He looked pained.

"A pint of beer is two units. Just in beer alone you're drinking eight units of beer a day. That's fifty-six units a week, just in beer. That's twice the recommended dose for someone your age. And if you add in the vodka gimlets and the whiskies . . . You need to cut down, Sean."

"It's not just me. It's everyone in this station."

"Yes I know. And I've been telling everyone in this station. You all need to cut down on your alcohol consumption."

"How much do you drink?"

"I don't drink. I'm a Free Presbyterian."

"I bet I outlive you."

Kevin sighed and shook his head. "If I was a betting man I'd bet that you won't actually, Sean. But listen there's something else. Something more serious."

"Go on . . ."

"On your blood work you tested positive for cannabis."

I nodded.

"And in the past you've asked me for dihydrocodeine and morphine on a number of occasions."

"For me back! Jesus! I was in a Land Rover that looped the loop and I've been shot once and blown up twice."

"Opiates for pain relief and the cannabis for what?"

"We're off the record here? This is a doctor–patient thing?"

"Of course."

"Now and again just to relax."

"I'm not going to report this to any higher authority but I can't sign you as fit for duty while you're smoking dope, Sean."

"That seems a bit extreme, Kev. You know I'm the only one that does any work around here."

"I'll give you a month, Sean. You'll report to me for another blood test. If I don't see an improvement in your tox levels I'm going to put you on restricted duty. It's for your own good, you know. You have a wife and child now, I believe."

"Girlfriend and child."

"You need to change your act, Sean. Alcohol consumption down to under twenty units a week. If you can't quit try and get your cigarette smoking down to two or three a day and you will stop smoking marijuana immediately. If I see it showing up in your blood work again, I'll have you on restricted duty permanently. I can't have stoned coppers on the job, even detectives as capable as yourself. You should know better."

"It's stressful out there, doc," I said wondering what Kev would have said if he'd tested me in 1985 when at one point during the Anglo-Irish Agreement crisis I'd been taking cocaine, hash, ciggies, moonshine, Valium and diamorphine pills – usually before lunch.

"I know it is and I'm not expecting you or any of your colleagues to be Supermen, but if you want to remain on active duty you'll do what I tell you."

"Christ, this has been a miserable day so far," I muttered to myself.

"See it as a wake-up call. Here's the prescriptions for your asthma inhalers," he said, handing me a couple of scripts.

"If you put me on restricted duty, who is going to run Carrick CID?"

"Sergeant McCrabban will have to do it."

"McCrabban? He smokes a pipe. I don't see you telling him off."

"I've told him off already. Now act your age, Sean, and buck up your ideas."

I took the prescriptions and left the makeshift examination room with my tail between my legs. I clearly wasn't the only one who had gotten bad news from the doc and there was a foul atmosphere in the air. I was still punchy and pissed off when I finally went upstairs to interview Mrs Deauville with the help of the Bulgarian translator. This was where the day began to right itself and where I began to be lulled into a false sense of security. *I could fix things with Beth. My health was going to get better. Maybe Dalziel would shoot himself in the foot either metaphorically or literally before the summer . . .* And anyway there was a job to do. Interviewing a witness/suspect in a murder inquiry was a hell of a way to clear out the cobwebs. Question and answer, question and answer, building a picture, brick by smoky brick. Carving important data points and timelines out of an information blizzard, law out of chaos, order out of entropy.

Yeah, right.

6: MR DEAUVILLE'S INTERESTING PAST

The Bulgarian translator was in fact much more than a mere translator. He was actually a mid-ranking consular official called Pytor Yavarov who had been based in Dublin for nearly two years. A slight, handsome man with an old-fashioned Clark Gable moustache he had dressed himself in what he perhaps thought was the style of an old-fashioned Irish country gentlemen: tweeds, white linen shirt, brown Oxfords, with a rather attractive paisley blue tie. He was pale of face, blue of eye, with a shock of curly black hair. On perhaps any other person in Carrickfergus such a look would have drawn forth sniggers but Yavarov was sitting there with such poise and quiet assertiveness that somehow he managed to pull the whole thing off. Mrs Deauville was a different kettle of fish. Chubby, twenty-something, with dark rings round her eyes she was dressed entirely in sweats: Adidas trackie bottoms, Nike hoodie top. Her hair was a short bowl-cut dyed peroxide blonde. She was wearing a single flip flop that she flipped on and off the stubby crimson-painted toes of her left foot. Like I say, she wasn't unattractive and if she'd stayed away from the tanning shop and let her natural brown hair grow out you would have said that she was a looker. They made an odd couple sitting there in Interview Room #1 muttering together in Bulgarian, waiting for us to show up. Neither of them looked Bulgarian, whatever Bulgarians were supposed to look like.

We were watching them through the big two-way mirror that ran along one of the walls of the incident room.

"Mrs Deauville seems to have calmed down a good bit," I said.

"Well, she hasn't tried to stab WPC Warren or the man from the embassy," Crabbie said.

"Did either of you get a chance to read the reports from their neighbours?"

"I read them this morning," Lawson said.

"Fights? Screaming? Yelling? Anything like that?"

"No one heard any arguments or any disputes or anything like that. And no one saw anything on the night of the murder," Lawson said, handing me the interviews with the Deauville neighbours. These canvassing statements were practically worthless. For all we knew, Mr and Mrs Deauville might have been fighting like cats and dogs every single night since they moved in but no one in Sunnylands would ever tell us that. A drug dealer was bad, a woman who murders her husband was bad, but an informer was a more terrible creature by far than either.

"I also saw you over at the fax machine, Lawson."

"More detailed autopsy results came through."

"Anything interesting in them?" I asked Lawson.

"Death by crossbow bolt in the stomach, which we knew. But the preliminary toxicology results were quite interesting."

"How so?"

"He was clean as a whistle. He was a dealer but not a user."

"Didn't smoke the profits. Smart guy. Oh I should tell you both that Carrick's paramilitaries are not going to be claiming this one. Neither the UVF nor the UDA say they did it. My informant tells me that although Mr Deauville was an independent contractor he dutifully paid his protection money."

"But he actually didn't get any protection," Crabbie said.

"No."

"Who was this informant?" Crabbie asked.

"Andy Young."

"Well, he would know."

"Yeah he would."

"So if the UVF and UDA didn't kill him who did?" Lawson asked.

"Young could have been lying to me. There's no honour among thieves and even less among drug dealers and paramilitaries," I said.

"I just can't see anyone else driving into the heart of UVF territory to execute some random drug dealer," Crabbie said.

"There's been no statement at all so far from this Direct Action Against Drug Dealers group, which there probably would have been by now if they'd been involved," I said.

"So that leaves Mrs Deauville," Lawson said.

Crabbie shook his head. "I don't think Mrs Deauville did it either."

"Why? We haven't even talked to her yet. And she is violent, as you can testify," I said.

"Remember that other drug dealer I was telling you about who was shot on Tuesday but survived?"

"Yeah."

"Well, forensic confirms that all three crossbow bolts came from the same weapon," Crabbie said definitively.

"How did they know that?"

"The way they know things."

"You talked to someone over there?"

"Yeah. Jimmy Nichol."

"When was this?"

"When you were in with the doctor."

"What else did he tell you?"

"Apart from the victim's blood there was no DNA on the crossbow bolts."

"And all three bolts came from the same crossbow?"

"Yup."

"Where is that other victim? Morrison something, right?"

"Ivan Morrison. He's still in Larne Hospital. Lawson and I got a full statement out of him on Tuesday night."

"And he doesn't know who shot him?"

"He's not talking. Says he didn't see or hear anything. They shot him from behind and drove off in a car."

"Well, I'd like to talk to him," I said.

"Better do it soon, Sean. If some bloke shot me in the back and was going around shooting other drug dealers I'd be on the boat to England pretty sharpish."

"Good call. We'll go see him today. But I don't see how you think that the attack on Morrison rules out Mrs Deauville. How do you know she didn't shoot Mr Morrison first on Tuesday to establish a pattern and then shoot her husband on Wednesday?"

Crabbie conceded the point. "If that's true it'll be a murder charge then," he said.

Lawson seemed puzzled by this statement of the bleeding obvious. "We know it's murder," he said.

"If it was a crime of passion, we could have charged her with manslaughter, but if she really did shoot Morrison too then it establishes a mens rea and we have no choice but to take a murder rap to the DPP."

Lawson nodded. "Oh I see. So by being too clever by half to throw us off the scent she's got herself done for murder."

"I still don't think she did it," Crabbie insisted.

I looked at him squarely in the face. He had good instincts, McCrabban. He smiled at me and started his filling his pipe.

"Oi, didn't you get a lecture from Dr Havercamp about smoking?"

"He said I was as fit as a fiddle," Crabbie said.

"Did he? He said I was a mess."

"You should switch to a pipe."

"He told me to cut out tobacco completely."

"Aye. Well, he has a point, King James was against tobacco and he translated the Bible," Crabbie said.

"A hundred years from now we're going to discover that tobacco is good for us."

"No we won't," Lawson said.

"Anybody find Deauville's criminal record?" I asked.

"Yes, I looked that out for you and put it on your desk," Crabbie said.

"Run and get it, will you, Lawson?"

When Lawson was out of the room I told Crabbie about Dalziel's coming apotheosis.

McCrabban nodded dourly. "I could see it in the cards as soon as they promoted Strong to ASC. Strong to ASC, McClusky into Strong's place and McArthur into McClusky's job. That would leave a gap here and although you're the senior officer they can't promote you because you've ruffled too many feathers. They can't promote me because I have no administrative experience and I'm only a detective sergeant so it has to be Dalziel. They can't bump him from Sergeant to Chief Inspector so they make him an Inspector for now and Chief Inspector in August when McArthur leaves."

"That's a fine bit of detective work. Why didn't you tell me?"

"I didn't want to spoil your holiday. I know it's not very Christian for me to say but I don't particularly like Kenny—"

Lawson came back in with Deauville's file and we killed our mutinous conversation.

The file contained a few surprises:

Born Belfast 1945. He had gone to the relatively posh Methodist College and then to Queens University where he had briefly read English before being rusticated for being drunk and disorderly. Unemployed for a bit and, in that most turbulent of years, 1968, he had joined the police as a "special constable" but had resigned in early 1969, presumably having had his fill of beating up peaceful Catholic Civil Rights marchers. He had evidently moved to England after that, because in 1975 he was arrested for an armed robbery of a Brixton post office. The jury of his peers acquitted him of that offence but in 1978 he was convicted of insurance fraud in a case of an Irish pub that had burned to the ground. He served eighteen months in a minimum security institution and then apparently moved north. In 1980 he was arrested for assaulting a man in a bar in Bradford but the charges were dropped. In 1982 he assaulted another man in Manchester and again the charges were dropped. In 1984 he was arrested for another armed robbery on a post office and this time he got three years.

I handed the file back to Lawson. "Not a very successful criminal. But he wasn't a complete idiot. He went to Queens. All the best people go to Queens."

"Is that where you went, sir?" Lawson asked innocently.

"It is indeed."

"He had quite a varied criminal record though, didn't he? Bank robbery, insurance fraud," Crabbie said.

"Aye he's tried a few things," I agreed. "But no drug dealing. Drug dealing is a new arrow in his quiver, if you'll excuse the association."

"He's done everything except for getting a real job," Crabbie said.

"And he was a former policeman, did you see that, sir?" Lawson said.

"Well an 'Ulster Special Constable'. You can't really call him a policeman," Crabbie said, quick to defend the honour of the RUC.

"Is that like a reservist?" Lawson asked.

"No, not the same thing at all. When were you born, son?" I asked.

"1967."

"You've never heard of the B Specials?" Crabbie said.

Lawson shook his head. "I've heard of them but I don't really know what they are."

"In 1922 the Ulster Special Constabulary was set up to support the police. There were the A Specials – full timers, B Specials – part-timers and C Specials – volunteers who didn't get paid. The A Specials were absorbed into the RUC and became regular policemen. The C Specials were disbanded and that left the B Specials," I explained.

"Back in 1968 in Belfast they thought there was going to be an all-out war between the Protestants and the Catholics. The police were ridiculously undermanned so they hired hundreds of B Special constables to fill the gaps. Some of them were decent enough but there was a pretty high percentage of thugs who joined just looking for some action," Crabbie said.

"They were poorly trained, poorly equipped and the vetting wasn't all it could have been," I added.

"The B Specials performed so badly in the first two years of the Troubles that at the end of 1969 they were disbanded completely," Crabbie said.

"But maybe his police training helped him in his criminal career?" Lawson suggested.

"It doesn't look like that criminal career was too successful either, was it?"

"We don't know that. The criminal record only shows the crimes he was done for," Lawson said.

I nodded, yawned and stood up. "Good point. All right then lads, enough procrastination, let's talk to the widow Deauville."

We were about to knock on the door of Interview Room #1 when Kenny Dalziel shimmered out of nowhere and intercepted us.

"Ah, Duffy, I wanted to talk to you about a couple of things before I leave."

"Can't do it, Kenny, got to interview a witness in a murder investigation. Police work, if you know what that is."

Kenny grimaced and I could see the gears working behind those vinegary black eyes, *patience Kenny he'll pay for this, just a couple of months now and he'll pay . . .*

"You and Sergeant McCrabban both failed the run. You'll have to take it again in a month and pass it if you want to be considered fit for duty. When I get back from my holidays I'll be conducting a PT class every morning. Attendance is mandatory."

"No, I'm afraid we can't do that, Kenny. We're too busy in CID. Small department. Lot of cases. Dr Havercamp already has McCrabban and me on a fitness regime. Was that all?"

Kenny's lips pursed. "No, it's not all. I've been told that one of your witnesses is Bulgarian, is that right?"

"That's correct."

"Last year you and Constable Lawson went to Finland to supposedly follow up on a lead. That little trip cost the station a thousand pounds. And you've also been to England and Scotland on the station's shilling."

"So?"

"No trips to Bulgaria, Duffy. We can't afford to pay for all your gallivanting around. No trips to Bulgaria, no trips to the South of France, no trips anywhere, just stay within your budget. This is a case of a dead drug dealer in Carrick. If I was a detective I could close one like that in a couple of days."

"But you're not a detective, are you?"

Kenny's eyes again boring into me. I took him to the end of the corridor. "I hear you're going to Eastbourne?" I said.

"I'm paying for that. It's my holiday."

"That's not what I'm driving at. I was just thinking that's where they have Beachy Head, isn't it?"

"Yes."

"Well, don't be tempted to jump off, Kenny. I appreciate that it must be a fucking nightmare to wake up every morning and realise that you are still you, but suicide is not the answer, old cock."

It was a mild jibe, well within the bounds allowed in two officers of equal rank, but Kenny reacted as if I'd asked him to drink a pint of Margaret Thatcher's piss at the Cenotaph on Poppy Day.

"I've had enough of your insolence, Duffy. You should have been out long ago if you weren't a fucking fe . . ." he began, but his voice died in his throat before he could completely sabotage himself.

"A what?"

"A nothing."

"A 'fucking fenian', is that what you were going to say?"

"I never said that!"

"Yeah, well it's the thought that counts, isn't it? Now if you don't mind, some of us have bloody work to do around here," I said, pushing past him, marching down the corridor, knocking on the interview room door and going inside without waiting for a reply.

It was another exit Bette Davis or Rosalind Russell or even Joan Crawford would have been proud of.

7: THE BULGARIANS AND THE BEL TEL

Introductions were made and I sat opposite the Bulgarians with Lawson and McCrabban. WPC Warren excused herself and I gave her a nod of thanks for holding the fort for the entire morning.

I lit my first cigarette of the day and it tasted fantastic. Calmed me the fuck right down.

"Mrs Deauville, I am so sorry for your loss," I said and Yavarov translated for me.

A long stream of Bulgarian followed that Mr Yavarov did not translate.

"What did she say?"

"You are in charge of this investigation?" Yavarov asked in perfect and only slightly accented English.

"Yes, I am in charge," I said

"Mrs Deauville says she spent the night in police cells," Yavarov said, bristling.

"That's right."

"Was she charged with a crime?" Yavarov asked.

"No, but she could have been."

"Was she a suspect in her husband's death?"

"We can't rule anyone out at this stage."

"Her husband was murdered and you put her in the cells. I will protest this to my embassy!"

"No, you won't. You won't kick up any kind of fuss at all. Mrs

Deauville stabbed one of my officers in front of a dozen witnesses. My man has decided not to press charges, but that could change if we don't have Mrs Deauville's complete cooperation. Assaulting a police officer is a very serious offence indeed," I said.

Yavarov was clearly impressed by this (perhaps intimidating the public was how things were done back home) and a brief, furious discussion followed in Bulgarian with Mrs D.

"She will tell you everything she knows," he said at the end of it.

"Let's start with the timeline," I said to Yavarov.

"What do you want to know?" Mrs Deauville asked.

"You speak English?" Yavarov, Crabbie and I asked together.

"Of course! I am travel agent. I speak English, Turkish, German," she said.

"Why didn't you speak English before now?" I asked.

She gave us a sly knowing glance. "I not say anything without my lawyer," she muttered triumphantly.

"He's not a lawyer. You're not a lawyer, are you?"

Yavarov shook his head.

"He protect me from police tricks. Frank always talk about police tricks. Police they arrest you, put drugs in your pocket, make up lies. You will not do this now!"

"We don't do things like that in Carrick CID," I said.

"All police, all same, everywhere!" Mrs Deauville said.

I sighed. "The night your husband was murdered, where were you between the hours of midnight and two in the morning, Mrs Deauville?"

"You call me Elena. Please. No one call me Mrs Deauville," she said.

"Where were you last night between the hours of midnight and two in the morning, Elena?"

"Frank go out drinking Rangers Club. No women allowed Rangers Club so I no go. I know he come back late so I make chips and leave in pan and go to bed."

"What time did you go to bed?"

"Eleven, a little before, perhaps."

"Where is your bedroom in the house? Front or back?"

"Big back bedroom."

"And did you hear anything during the night?"

"No, I sleep until morning."

"So you have no alibi between the hours of midnight and two am?"

"I sleep."

"And what happened after you woke up?"

"I look for Frank. He not in bed or downstairs on sofa. I hear crowd outside. I open front door—" she dissolved into sobs that shook her whole body. If she was indeed a murderess she was also a pretty good actress.

I gave her a tissue and let her compose herself.

"And then what happened?"

"I hug Frank and then I call ambulance and police and then this one (she pointed at McCrabban) tells me I cannot touch my husband. I must go inside and let policemen make jokes and take photographs while Frank lies dead on ground!"

I looked at Crabbie.

"I assure you, Sean, no one was making jokes. You know I don't allow that sort of thing," Crabbie said defensively.

"So you didn't see who killed Mr Deauville?"

"I no see."

"Do you have any idea who would want Mr Deauville dead?"

"No. Frank well liked. Make many good friends."

"How did you meet Mr Deauville?"

"We meet in Villa Armira."

"You'll have to elaborate on that a bit."

She cocked her head at the word elaborate.

Yavarov explained what I was after.

"Villa Armira, Ivaylovgrad, two years ago. I am tour guide

to Roman ruins. Frank is very charming man. Very funny. We become friends. We go out. He come back for another holiday few months later. We write to one another. He come back again and this time he propose to me. We get married and we ask to move to UK. Permission granted."

"It says in our file that Francis Deauville was forty-three, you're what, twenty-five? Bit of an age gap, no?"

Crabbie shot me a *you-can-talk-Sean* look from under his eyebrows.

"Age is of no matter when people in love," Elena said dismissively.

"Very true, Mrs Deauville, very true. Now, maybe I'm wrong but I thought it was quite difficult to move from an Eastern European country to the west?"

Elena scoffed. "Nothing difficult if you have money."

"And Mr Deauville had money?"

"Frank talk to officials, get permits. No problem."

"And you got married where?"

"In London. Frank's mother come for wedding. Frank has mother in home in Frinton-on-Sea. You know Frinton-on-Sea?"

"No. I'm afraid not."

"You didn't want to live there, in England?" Crabbie asked.

"Frank have house in Bangor that he inherit from uncle. I come see, I like. It remind me of Black Sea."

"I've never heard that comparison before. House in Bangor, eh? The address?"

"4 Cold Harbour Road. Nothing there now. House burn in fire."

"A fire?"

"House burn in fire, we have insurance claim in."

I gave Lawson a look. "Go check out this fire for me, will ya?" He nodded and went off.

"So, Mrs Deauville, did Mr Deauville have any enemies?"

"Frank have no enemies. Frank makes friends everywhere he go, no enemies."

"Didn't the North Down UVF tell him to leave Bangor last year or they would kill him? Was that what the fire was all about?"

"Frank asked to leave. He leave. No hassle. We move to Carrickfergus, we make friends here. No hassle. Frank very cooperative man. Make friends everywhere. Two months in Carrick no problems. Fire happen after we leave. Whole house burn. We have insurance claim in."

"What did Mr Deauville do for a living here?"

"Like I say, he unemployed."

"Where did he get the money to pay off all these Eastern European officials?"

"He have inheritance. I tell you. Uncle who die."

"We can check that."

"Check it. Uncle die, maybe Auntie die. I give you solicitor name."

"We'll take those details from you later. How much was this inheritance?"

"I not sure."

"Look, let's not beat about the bush, Frank was a drug dealer, wasn't he?" I asked.

"He unemployed," Elena insisted.

"You never saw him with any drugs?"

"No drugs. He unemployed."

"So you had no trouble after you moved to Carrick?"

"No trouble."

"He paid the protection money in Carrick?"

"I do not know this 'protection money'. But we have no trouble before we move or after we move."

Lawson came back in with details of the fire in Bangor. Arson, but whether by the Deauvilles or the Bangor paramilitaries it was impossible to say. Insurance investigators could sort that one out.

"How many times have you been back to Bulgaria since you got married?" I asked.

Elena shrugged.

"It's very easy to check with the passport authorities."

"I go back maybe six times to see my mother and father."

"You've been back to Bulgaria six times in the last year!"

"Maybe seven. Eight? Who knows?"

"What were you doing on all these trips to Bulgaria?"

"I visit my mother and father and sisters in Sofia."

"And did you bring anything back on these trips from Bulgaria?"

She looked puzzled. "What you mean? I bring Bulgar vodka. Is good. Legal to bring three litres."

"Did you ever bring back anything gaffer-taped to your body?"

"What you mean?"

"A kilo of brown tar heroin perhaps?"

She looked affronted. "You say I drug smuggler?"

"I must object to this line of questioning, Inspector Duffy!" Yavarov said. "This lady's husband was murdered!"

"Look, I don't give a crap if you smuggled in drugs or not, I'm investigating a homicide and there's no way I can find out who killed your husband unless you give me all the details of your husband's affairs," I attempted.

She lit a cigarette and leaned back in her chair. A hardness descended over her face that I recognised from years of these interrogations. She was clearly broken up over her husband's death but come hell or high water she wasn't going to tell me anything about Frank's narcotics business lest she herself be implicated.

"I give you my word that this will just be between us," I said.

She laughed bitterly. "What value word of policeman!"

"Elena, please, you don't seem to understand how the RUC works. I'm not the drug squad, I don't care what you've done or what Frank did. I just want to catch the man who did this."

"Frank unemployed."

There followed ten more minutes of this as first I and then

McCrabban and finally Lawson attempted to get her to admit that either her husband was a drug dealer or that he had made any enemies in four decades of walking planet Earth. Elena was having none of it. There had been no bricks through windows, no threatening phone calls, no strangers accosting them on the street, no punishment beatings or threatened punishment beatings. Frank was unemployed, he didn't associate with criminals, all the trips back to Bulgaria had merely been to visit her parents and sisters.

"Mrs Deauville, Elena, look, it's in your interest to help us."

"What you do now? Say you contact immigration authority and find out if my visa in order? Threaten me? Well Frank sort everything out. My visa in order!" she said, flicking ash aggressively into the ashtray in front of her.

I tried another tack. "Was everything OK between you and Mr Deauville? Any marital difficulties?"

She smiled and said something in Bulgarian to Yavarov. Addressing Lawson she said: "Now your boss try this: blame me for Frank's death. Say I do it and unless cooperate get murder charge. Your boss good man. Yes, yes."

"Well, you don't have an alibi, do you?"

"No. I sleep."

"Ever fire a crossbow, Elena?"

"I never fire crossbow. I never see crossbow. Be good policeman, search house for crossbow."

"We already searched your house for a crossbow and didn't find one, but that doesn't mean anything. You could have walked it to the end of the Fisherman's Quay and thrown it in the sea."

"Go to crossbow shop, show crossbow shop man my photograph, ask if I buy crossbow."

I gave Crabbie a little nod and he nodded back. "And if the crossbow shop man doesn't remember you or you bought it at a second-hand shop does that mean you're off the hook?" Crabbie said.

"Why I kill Frank?"

"Why do husbands kill wives and wives kill husbands?" I said.

Her violet eyes flashed. "Frank and I very happy. He lucky to have me. I lucky to have him. Why I kill him? I love him," she said and her eyes teared up.

She didn't mean to lose it but the tears became the full water-works and all of us in the interview room were quite affected.

The policeman, like the doctor and the paramedic, treads a fine line between distance and humanity. Get too close to a victim or a suspect or a patient and you can lose yourself in the darkness of their case; but remain too distant from the suffering and the pain and you become a robot, a machine, a chilly socio-path. Like old Inspector Laidlaw across the sheugh you found yourself in the dilemma of either indulging in grief by proxy or imitating a stone.

No stone me.

I leaned across that big old oak table of Interview Room #1 and took her hand in mine and squeezed.

"We'll do our best to find your husband's killer, Elena. We want to help, we really do," I said.

She nodded and the tears flowed and the hurt on her face could not possibly be fake. You can't fake grief like that.

"You can't fake grief like that," I said to Crabbie at the coffee machine.

"Nope. I don't think you can," he said.

"You and Lawson keep at her. I have to pop home for half an hour to deal with a small family emergency, OK?"

"Is the baby all right?" Crabbie asked, aghast.

"The baby's fine, mate. Just a wee issue with moving house, you know?"

"You're moving house?"

"Maybe. I don't know."

"After we get her formal statement do we let Mrs Deauville go?" Crabbie asked.

"I don't think we can really let her go just yet, can we? She's obviously been smuggling heroin from Bulgaria every month for the last year. How else does Frank the bank robber suddenly become Frank the pusher?"

Crabbie winced. "The poor woman's devastated and as you yourself said that's not quite in our purview is it, Sean?"

"We need her cooperation and if we can use leverage to get it that's what we'll do," I said sternly.

Crabbie game me a dour look of disapproval and shook his head. I could see his point but I wanted to find that lock-up and get all we could from Mrs D.

"And get Lawson to get the local constabulary to notify the mother in Frinton-on-Sea. See if they can dig up any dirt."

"All right," Crabbie said.

"Look, no need for the long face. I'll be back in half an hour. We'll finish up with Mrs Deauville and if we're satisfied that we've gotten all we can we'll send her home. We still have this Morrison fella, the first victim, to interview before he legs it."

Outside to the Beemer in the chilly early March rain but the dark blue 1988 model 535i Sport was not waiting there like an expectant panther.

"Where's me bloody car . . . oh yeah. Shit."

Back inside the cop shop where I asked Sergeant Prentice to sign out a Land Rover for me.

A three-ton police Land Rover chugging along the Scotch Quarter, over the Horseshoe Bridge and then up the Barn Road and Coronation Road.

#113 Coronation Road where my Beemer *was* waiting for me. Park the Rover. Up the path. In through the front door.

Silence.

"Hello?"

Silence.

The fuck?

Kitchen table. A note: "Don't be alarmed, Sean. I've taken

Emma to stay with my folks for a while. You can phone me there but please don't phone me today. I know what you're like."

I crumpled up the note, grabbed the telephone and dialled the number.

"Hello?" Beth said.

"It's me."

"I knew you'd call. And I knew it would be at lunchtime. How'd your fitness thing go? Did you get out of it?"

"What's going on, Beth?"

"I think we need a little break from each other, Sean. Clearly."

"Look, I was way out of line this morning. I know that now. You want to move house? That's fine with me. You know I'm not a morning person. It was all just a bit much. I'm sorry."

A long pause.

Crying.

"I'm so glad to hear you say that, Sean. Really, I am."

"You forgive me? I know it's no excuse but I'm under a lot of stress."

Another long pause. "I forgive you, Sean. But you can't act like that in front of Emma. She's just a little girl."

"What are you doing now? I'll come down there and get you."

"No, Sean. I'm staying here for a couple of days. It's good for Emma and it's good for me."

"So when are you coming back?"

"Just give me a couple of days, OK?"

"The weekend? Sunday night?"

"Please, Sean, no pressure."

I put my hand over the receiver. "You don't know anything about fucking pressure, sister," I whispered to myself.

I took my hand off the mouthpiece. "OK, sweetie. Give me a call. Have a nice time with your folks and say hi from me . . . You didn't tell them we had a row?"

"Uhm, not as such."

"Good. OK. Give me a call. Love you. Bye."

"OK, Sean, bye."

Asymmetrical response. No "love you too". Fuck.

Back out to the Land Rover in the rain. Check underneath for mercury tilt switch bombs.

None.

Back to the station.

Crabbie meeting me in the incident room.

"Everything OK on the home front?"

"Fine. Any developments on the case?"

"Not really."

"Deauville's mother?"

"Local boys gave her the notification. She's very upset obviously."

"I imagine. Anything helpful from the local plod?"

"She says she doesn't know who killed Mr Deauville and has no knowledge of any drug dealing."

We went back to Interview Room #1 and tried another couple of lines of attack on Mrs Deauville but she wasn't giving us anything. She claimed she didn't know about any off site lock-up or garage. She denied being a drug mule. She said she didn't kill her husband and didn't know who did. The first two statements were obviously lies but all three of us believed the third.

"Did anyone threaten your husband recently?"

"No."

"Did anyone threaten you?"

"No."

"Have there been any problems with the neighbours?"

"No."

"Any anonymous letters or bricks through windows, anything like that?"

"No."

"Anyone following you, or strangers watching the house?"

A tiny hesitation before: "No."

"Are you sure no one's been following you?"

"No. Nobody follow."

"No strangers around the house?"

"No strangers."

"Are you sure?"

"Quite sure. Very sure. Everything normal and then Frank is murdered. Who did this? Who killed Frank?"

"We'll endeavour to find out, Elena."

Pause.

Reverse the shot.

Go close on her face. She's not telling you everything but she's almost certainly not the killer. Eyes – read the eyes for that kind of information.

"I no kill Frank. Someone kill him. You find!"

I pushed the chair back and stood up from the desk. "All right, Mrs Deauville I'm going to let you go, DC Lawson will take you next door to the Incident Room and give you some lunch and get you to make a formal statement. When that's done WPC Green will take you home, OK?"

She nodded sniffily.

"Mr Yavarov you are free to accompany Mrs Deauville and render her assistance, or you are free to go. If you want to stay we'll get you lunch too."

"I will help Mrs Deauville with her statement," he said.

I took Crabbie to one side. "When you let her go, have WPC Green drive her home, but get her to take her time about it. I want the house watched and I want the team to be in place by the time she arrives."

"To what end?"

"If it were me and the police hadn't found my lock-up garage full of drugs I'd want to slip out in the middle of the night and destroy the evidence. Or I might just want to fly the coop."

"It'll mean a call to Special Branch to get a covert team," he said.

"It'll be worth it if we can catch her in the act of destroying the evidence. Charge her with obstruction of justice and use that as leverage against her."

"Leverage for what? I don't think she knows anything about the murder."

"Everybody knows something."

A half dozen phone calls later Crabbie came back with a face even more sour than usual.

"What's the matter?"

"Special Branch won't do it. They say it's not a priority."

"They won't help at all?"

"They say they can't justify the expense of a team for a low-level drug dealer in Carrickfergus."

"Well that's odd. Thought they would have jumped at the chance. All right, no big deal, we'll do it ourselves, then. Find a few keen reservists to watch the place."

"It'll be over-time. Inspector Dalziel—"

"I'll pay for it out of my own pocket if I have to. Mrs Deauville will probably clock them and stay indoors, but at least our evidence won't be destroyed and she won't run for the airport."

"Aye. OK. A couple of reservists to watch the house. Then what?"

"You and I are going to go to Larne to interview this Morrison bloke."

I went to my office to get my portable tape recorder when there was a knock at the door.

The door opened and an ashen Chief Inspector McArthur came in with the early edition of the *Belfast Telegraph*.

"Page two," he said.

I opened up the paper and there over the top half of page two was a picture of yesterday's chaotic crime scene: the broken police tape, the crowd milling around the body, the goddamn goat sniffing at the victim's denim jacket.

"Fuck!" I gasped.

"Read the story, Duffy."

The story was, if anything, worse:

CROSSBOW CHAOS IN CARRICKFERGUS
By Stephen O'Toole

A murder case seemed to confound the officers of Carrickfergus CID yesterday morning. For much of the day this reporter watched as a parade of RUC men bungled an investigation into the death of a man in the Sunnylands area of the town. The victim, a Mr Francis Deauville, lay in his driveway at 15 Mountbatten Terrace for almost three hours while his neighbours milled around the body smoking cigarettes and a goat nibbled at the victim's clothing. No effort was made to "secure the crime scene" nor were forensic officers summoned to the murder.

"Is this the way murders are always handled in Carrickfergus?" I asked one uniformed RUC officer who merely a grunted a response.

The head of Carrickfergus CID, Inspector Sean Duffy, could not be reached for comment. Duffy is a controversial figure at the Carrick RUC barracks. He has been disciplined more than once by the police tribunal and on one occasion was demoted a full rank apparently because of incompetence. This murder case seems certainly to have "made a goat" of Duffy and his fellow officers in Carrickfergus RUC. Local independent Unionist Councillor Leslie Hale told this reporter that he wasn't surprised by the goat incident and that "Carrick RUC had been a joke for years." Neighbours on Mountbatten Terrace were similarly distressed by the serial blunders from the local police. Chairman of the local residents' association the Reverend William McFaul spoke of the "absolute foul language" and "rudeness" of one policeman whose identity this reporter was unable to confirm.

> Forensic officers did not arrive on the scene until nearly
> four hours after the body was . . .

I let the paper fall to the floor.

I felt light, my head was swimming. I put an arm out to steady myself.

"Fucking hell," I groaned.

"What happened yesterday, Sean?"

"What?"

"What happened yesterday, Sean?"

"It's complicated."

"Uncomplicate it."

I took a deep breath. "Well, it was a little crazy at first, sir. The victim's wife stabbed Sergeant McCrabban and Dalziel made him go to the hospital."

"Where were you when this was going on?"

"I was on my holidays, sir. I was in Donegal in the morning. It wasn't even my case!"

"Did you assume command when you arrived?"

"I had to. Because of Kenny Dalziel's blundering only young Lawson was there. He sent everybody away."

"Hmmm."

"How badly am I fucked?"

"I don't know. Chief Superintendent Strong has come down again, doubtless he'll want a word with you."

"Jesus! Strong has seen this?"

"Sean, be under no illusions, by the end of the day the Chief Constable will have seen this."

"Jesus, Mary and Joseph! What can I do?"

"Don't do anything. Have a cup of tea. No booze! Sit tight. I'll see what—"

Another knock at the door.

"Who is it?"

"Duffy, is that you in there?" Strong asked and then came

in without waiting for a reply. I've seen less purple beetroots than Strong's cheeks and forehead. Always a tall man, he looked even taller somehow when he was pissed off. His nose was a furious red and his ginger beard and salt-and-pepper hair were almost standing on end. As an ex-boilermaker who'd apprenticed in the Clydeside yards before transferring to Belfast in the early 60s he had impressively massive hands and shoulders. All this combined with his tight dark green uniform and Chief Superintendent's pips meant that he cut an imposing figure on even his good days.

Strong looked at the Chief Inspector and the spilled newspaper on the floor.

"Make yourself scarce, McArthur, I'll talk to Duffy here," Strong said in that gravelly Govan accent of his.

"Yes, sir," McArthur said.

When he'd gone, Strong went over to the drinks trolley and poured us both a healthy measure of Jura. He handed me a glass and sat down.

"Details, lad. Don't leave anything out even if it looks bad for you and your men. If you lie to me now it'll go much worse for you in the long run."

I told him everything in as cool and dispassionate voice as I could muster. The Jura helped, as Jura always does. But in truth my bap was ringing and I was having trouble keeping it together. Strong listened, drank his whisky and asked a few pointed questions along the way.

When I was done he nodded to himself and stood. "Right. It looks like you did all you could, Duffy. It was just an unlucky set of circumstances, that's all. I'll get the PR boys to formulate a response to the *Bel Tel* and any other media who pick up this story. And I'll talk to the Chief Constable when he calls."

"Is he going to call?"

"He'll have to. The minister will be on him and he'll be looking for blood. But he's not going to get it. I'm not having some jackal in the gutter press taking down one of my men."

A huge wave of relief washed over me. John Strong – son and grandson of Clydebank shop stewards – was a good man to have on your side.

"Thank you, sir."

"You are to talk to nobody, Duffy."

"No, sir."

"If anyone from the press calls you have no comment."

"No comment. Understood, sir."

"Do you have a suspect in this case?"

"No, sir. Looks like the wife didn't do it, so it's a bit of a mystery."

"That's the last thing we need. How so, a mystery?" Strong asked.

"Well, there's the unusual murder weapon and no claim of responsibility from any of the paramilitary factions or that DAADD group that sometimes kills alleged drug dealers."

"You can rule out the wife? I hear she's an immigrant? And she's clearly violent."

"Well, there's no 'definitely' in a case like this, but we were all pretty impressed by her testimony. A second man, also an alleged drug dealer, was shot a few nights ago. He lived. I was just on my way to interview him."

"Second man, eh? Also with a crossbow?"

"Yes, sir."

"Aha! So this is some kind of vigilante out to get drug dealers?"

"Could be, sir. I had young Lawson check to see if there had been any heroin overdoses or deaths in Carrick or Belfast lately."

"How would that tie in?"

"Revenge? Kid overdoses and the parents seek revenge on the dealer. Or on all the dealers. But there have been no over- dose deaths of heroin this year. And Lawson says that the deaths from last year don't link back to Deauville."

"And before that?"

"Deauville wasn't in the heroin trade. He was in England in the bank-robbing trade . . . So I suppose that brings us back to DAADD."

"If one of the paramilitary groups or DAADD was to take responsibility for the murder, would the case go away?"

"It wouldn't be solved, sir, but—"

"But what?"

"We'd probably yellow the file. Case like that almost never gets solved unless there's eyewitness testimony or forensic evidence."

"So I could then tell the Chief Constable that the case was closed?"

"It wouldn't be closed but it would be yellowed – no further action by Carrick CID, pending additional evidence."

Strong nodded to himself. "That would satisfy him. And it would probably satisfy those bastards in the press."

"Yes, sir. About that. They said some very inaccurate things about me. Maybe I should contact a lawyer or—"

"No! No lawyers. No comment. All you will do is work diligently and quietly on getting this case out of your inbox as quickly as possible."

"Yes, sir."

"And no doubt – this being bloody Belfast – there will be some kind of atrocity along in a few days to get the press slavering for someone else's hide."

"Yes, sir."

"I'll deal with the Chief Constable. Don't pick up your phone. In fact get out of the office, now. You say you have more following up to do?"

"Yes, sir, in Larne, sir. Interview the first victim."

"Good. Go!"

"Yes, sir . . . uhm, thank you, sir."

Chief Superintendent Strong stood up and offered me his big hairy boilermaker's paw. "Aye, like I say, I remember your work in the Lily Bigelow case. You did right by her and by Eddie McBain. Ed was my mentor and you did right by him. You're a good policeman, Duffy. A good copper. I don't care what the file says on you."

"Thank you, sir."

"And I am not going to have some scumbag drug dealer and some vermin journalist destroy your career, Duffy."

"I'm very grateful, sir."

"Now get out of here before your phone starts ringing and they draw you deeper into the bloody web."

8: IVAN MORRISON

The sun setting behind the Antrim Hills. Rain pounding the windscreen. Sea spray on the side windows. The Land Rover swaying in the twenty-knot crosswind as we drove along the Acreback Road.

We had no radio reception at all and Crabbie wasn't talking. He could go a thousand years and not mention the embarrassing story in the *Belfast Telegraph*. If someone was going to bring it up it would have to be me and I didn't feel like it.

"I was down here earlier this morning," I said as we drove through Magheramorne.

"Oh aye?"

"Beth had me down looking at a house."

"Where?"

"The Ballypollard road."

"Oh I know that road very well. You'd only be ten minutes from me. Well, ten minutes the way you drive. Lovely wee road, that. Have you got a view?"

"I'm not sure I want to move down here."

"It's a lovely wee quiet spot."

"I like Coronation Road."

"But Beth doesn't?"

"She says no one talks to her."

"Stop me if I'm being too personal but she's a Protestant, isn't she?"

"Oh yeah, Prod as the day is long. It's not that. It's a class thing, not a religious thing. They're working-class Prods, she's some kind of posh Prod from Larne."

"So you don't want to move?"

"Not really. But the house is going to take two years to build anyway. Lot could happen in two years."

"That it could," Crabbie said reflectively. "But it is very nice around here."

"Beth and I had a row about it. I overreacted."

"Not like you, Sean."

I laughed. "Oh you think you're funny, do you?"

He cleared his throat. "There's a wee place down this way I'm thinking of buying."

"Oh yeah? An extra field or two?"

"Considerably more than that. In fact, I'm thinking of throwing my hand in, if that's the correct expression."

"What do you mean?"

"Well, old Kerry McBride is looking to sell her acres now she's turned seventy, and she'd give them to me for a good price. That's all cattle land of course."

"Of course."

"It would put me up to 150 head and even if I got rid of the sheep, which I would, that's still a full-time job, isn't it?"

I looked at him. "What are you talking about, Crabbie?"

"I'm more of a hobby farmer at the moment. Helen does most of it, but if I take this plot, well, I'll have to come in full time, won't I?"

"You're quitting?"

"Thinking about it. Thinking seriously about it."

"You'll leave me and Lawson in the lurch?"

"Carrickfergus is more of a two-man station anyway."

"What are you talking about? We've got a murder on our hands."

"Our first murder in nearly a year."

"The Troubles could spiral up at any moment. You know they could. These things come in waves."

"Sean . . . I know. But with the farm. I have a young family," he said guiltily.

"Crabbie, mate, you can't leave because of one bad day. One bad shellacking in the press."

"Oh it's not that. I don't care about that. I've been thinking about this for some time. I've been neither one thing nor the other for a few years now. A man cannot serve two masters. A house fernenst itself cannot stand. I cannot do the farm and be a Detective Sergeant in the RUC."

Not this on top of everything else. Crabbie couldn't go. I needed him. Was that panic I was feeling?

Fear?

It was a dangerous job, a dangerous job for a man with a young daughter and you needed a steady hand by your side. Crabbie had always been that steady hand. Crabbie would always be the guy going down into the engine room to fix the warp drive and save the ship. I liked Lawson, Lawson was good, but he wasn't the Crabman.

Jesus, having trouble breathing again.

Deep breaths. Deep breaths.

"You can't go. You can't go and let Kenny Dalziel run the station. You just can't."

"The man's a fool," Crabbie agreed.

"And a scoundrel. McArthur as much as told me he beats his wife."

"The blackguard. Who hits a woman? To think we have to share a breakroom with such a fellow."

"Indeed and if he's the gaffer we can't take him outside and give him a hiding. I like that word blackguard by the way. It doesn't get enough of an airing these days. Listen, mate, if you go and Dalziel is the chief, what then? I might as well bloody quit too."

"What would you do?"

"I don't know. Beth's da's loaded. Maybe he'd give me a job."

If Beth and I are still a couple?

Crabbie nodded. "If you go and I go I suppose they'd make Lawson a detective sergeant and bring in a young DC . . . but I don't think you should resign, Sean. You are one of the best detectives I have ever worked with."

"So are you. Please don't go, mate. We need you. I need you," I said.

"I'm still thinking about it," Crabbie said.

I leaned against the steering wheel.

"Everything's just spinning out of control today," I muttered.

"Eyes on the road, Sean, come on. I'll put the radio on for you. You like Radio 3, don't you? Let me see if the reception's better."

I pulled over. "You drive." We swapped seats and as luck would have it, Arvo Pärt's *Tabula Rasa* was playing, which worked perfectly with the rain's assault on the bulletproof windscreen.

We drove to the Moyle Hospital in a contemplative silence.

A man in a raincoat who looked like a reporter but who could have just been a man in a raincoat was standing outside.

"Fifty quid if you run that journalist-looking fucker over," I said.

Crabbie ignored me and parked the Rover but it was a wasted trip, for Ivan Morrison had checked himself out three hours earlier.

While Crabbie got Morrison's home address from the matron I took the opportunity to get my asthma prescriptions filled at the on-site chemist. A pharmacist showed me how to work the inhalers. It wasn't that complicated.

Crabbie came back with the address.

"18 Old Wyncairn Road," he said.

"You know where that is?"

"No idea, but there's a map in the Rover."

Outside into the rain. Arvo Pärt. Ten minutes getting lost. Another ten finding the house. Another ten and we would have missed Ivan completely as he was nearly finished packing. The house was a cheaply built post-war prefab that smelled of damp, desperation and dope. It was built in a row behind a slaughter house at the bottom of a hill.

We parked the Rover and got out. Someone was playing Jackson C. Frank's eponymous first – and only – album which seemed apropos for the day, the estate, the weather and, you know, just life in general.

The slaughter house was quiet but it gave up the terrible stench of fear and sawdust and blood and murder.

"It reeks here," I said.

"Aye, it's bad," Crabbie agreed and he had a farm.

We knocked on the living-room window and I showed my warrant card.

"Carrick RUC," I said.

"I told youse everything," a man said from inside the house.

"You can tell us again."

He reluctantly opened the front door and we went inside.

Clothes all over the floor. A duffel bag and a suitcase open and being loaded up.

I looked at him. Looked at his twenty-two-year-old-going-on-fifty face. With his short hair and his pink skin and his beady black eyes he was like a lab rat who'd been undergoing a terrible series of experiments to see exactly when he would have a mental breakdown.

"This better be quick. I've a ferry to catch," he said.

"We want to know who shot you," Crabbie said.

"I didn't see him."

"How do you know it was a he?"

"Didn't see her either."

"One man or two?"

"I told all this to Larne RUC."

"So you won't mind telling us as well."

"I've no idea who shot me. It was dark, I was walking along, fucking huge fucking pain in my back and I went down like a ton of bricks. Car driving off pronto."

"What type of car?"

"I don't know."

"Have you had any threats lately?"

"Threats about what?"

"We know you're a drug dealer."

"Who told you that?"

"Look, Ivan, we want to help. You are not under arrest, nothing you say will incriminate you. I'm not drugs squad and I give you my word I won't pass any information on to the drugs squad."

"How can I trust you? Never heard of you. Don't know you from Adam. You're not even a Larne peeler. You could be anybody."

I showed him my warrant card again. "Read that. Carrickfergus CID. Not drugs squad, not Special Branch. I'm investigating a murder in Carrick yesterday – you might have heard of it."

"I have heard of it. Why do you think I'm packing?"

"All we want to know is who threatened you."

"I'm not talking. I'm not saying fucking anything to you, pal."

I grabbed the little lab rat by his Fred Perry Polo shirt and flung him into the aluminium walls of his house, aluminium that if it had somehow become sentient would no doubt have relished the action, having been in a previous incarnation the panels of a fighter plane or a Lancaster bomber. Ivan bounced off the briefly happy wall and gave me a hurt look.

"Hey," he said. "You can't do that!"

"You know what I'll have to do next? I'll have to arrest you and hold you as a material witness and maybe I'll throw in a charge of trafficking. I'll personally turn up for your bail hearing and I'll oppose bail and you, my son, will be inside, where anybody can get you for the next six months."

"Why would you do all that?" Ivan asked, still giving me that I-thought-we-were-friends look.

"Cos you're not cooperating."

"What is it you fucking want to know anyway?"

"I want to know who shot you."

"I didn't see who did it and by that I mean I really didn't bloody see who did it. I was walking home from the leisure centre and they just plugged me in the fucking back. That's it. End of story. Now if you don't mind I have to get back to my packing."

"Whither goest thou?"

"Getting the night ferry to Stranraer."

"Has someone told you to leave the country?"

"No. I think the message was clear enough."

"Where are you moving to?"

"Anywhere but here."

"Lucky you."

"Lucky me."

I gave him my card. "Well, if your memory suddenly clears up please don't hesitate to call. You can reverse the charges if you're over in England."

He examined the card and leaned in close to me. "I paid off every week like a choirboy. Thirty per cent of my gross. Not my net. My gross. There was no sense in killing me. Killing me was killing the goose."

"What are you saying?"

"The paramilitaries didn't shoot me. This is something else."

"Like what?"

"I don't know, but I'm not sticking around to find out."

"Come on then, we'll give you a lift to the ferry terminal."

We drove him down to the docks and saw him into the ferry terminal.

Instead of heading back to Carrick I found myself driving out along the Old Glenarm Road and then along the Coast Road.

The rain was still pouring down hard and a light mist was coming in from the sea. Crabbie thought that I'd gotten us lost again.

"Carrick's back that way, I think, Sean," Crabbie said diplomatically.

I stopped the Rover in front of a large, rectangular modern house right on the seashore. It had its own pier and mooring dock and a couple of boats were tied up there. It had big windows facing north and east and although it was all right angles its stylish minimalism worked well with the sea and sky. It was easily three times the size of my parents' cottage in Donegal. And down in the basement there was a twenty-metre three-lane swimming pool.

"Why have we stopped?" Crabbie asked and when I didn't respond he reluctantly spoke to fill the silence. "So who lives here, Sean? It's not Dalziel's house is it? I know he comes from money."

"It's Beth's father's house. She's taken Emma to stay with them for a couple of days."

"Oh."

"Do you think I should do a wee surprise visit?"

"No."

"Why not?"

"You had a row?"

"Aye."

"She's with her mother and father. She wants her space, doesn't she? Away from you."

"Is that what Helen would do?"

"Helen and her father don't get on."

"How come?"

"His new wife, May, hit Thomas for bringing mud in on the kitchen floor."

"Wee Tommy? My godson? The cheek of her. Helen and May had words, then?"

"Helen said that if May ever raised a hand to any of her children again she would put her in the hospital."

I nodded. "She would, too."

"Aye, she would," Crabbie agreed. "A remarkable woman."

I looked at the house for a couple of minutes. A light came on in an upstairs window and there was a brief glimpse of what might have been Beth's silhouette before the light went off again.

I turned the key in the ignition.

"Come on, let's get out of here, I'll drive you home."

Crabbie's house.

Quick hello to Helen and the boys.

Back along the Coast Road and the Old Glenarm Road. Back past Magheramorne and Whitehead and Eden and all the way back to the station

Night shift.

Skeleton crew.

"Have you seen this, Duffy??????????" said a post-it note pinned to a copy of the *Belfast Telegraph* that had been placed on my desk. I binned the paper and examined the note: of course it was Dalziel's handwriting.

I walked down to his office, but he wasn't in.

I took a piece of A4 paper and penned a reply.

"In answer to your note, yes I have seen it, Kenny. Nice work with the question marks by the way, most people would only do three or four, leaving me baffled as to their intent," I wrote.

I left it in the middle of his desk, checked for witnesses, fought the urge to piss in his Yucca plant, and left.

I was about to head home when I saw Yavarov, the Bulgarian translator.

"What are you still doing here? Didn't we let Mrs Deauville go home hours ago?"

"You did. There is a bomb scare on the train lines. No trains to Belfast or Dublin, tonight."

"Do you want me to drive you to a hotel?"

Yavarov smiled ruefully. "Because of the bomb scare and the train cancellations, all the hotels in Belfast are full up."

This didn't surprise me. Belfast only had three hotels in the entire city because they kept getting blown up by the IRA. The Europa Hotel had been destroyed and rebuilt four times since the Troubles had begun.

"There's actually a hotel in Carrick, the Coast Road, they owe me a favour. One of their guests was murdered and I found out who did it," I said. "I'll call them."

"Thank you."

I called up the Coast Road but it was no dice there either, even for Inspector Sean Duffy of Carrick RUC.

"Sorry, they're booked out too," I said.

"How long do these bomb alerts last?"

"They'll usually have the line checked and inspected by the morning."

"I am used to roughing it, maybe I could sleep in one your cells until then?"

"The cells? Nonsense. They're freezing. Come home with me. I've got a spare bedroom at the back."

"Really? It's no trouble?"

"No trouble at all. We'll have to walk though. I didn't take the car into work this morning. It's only a ten-minute hoof-it."

Yavarov agreed, I got my coat and we walked to Coronation Road.

The rain had driven everyone inside so it was a quiet night in the estate.

"This reminds me of parts of Sofia," Yavarov said.

"I'm not sure if that's a compliment or not."

"Sofia was not as heavily bombed as some cities in the war," Yavarov said, which didn't really clarify matters.

When we got to #113, I heated up the remains of a previous night's chilli con carne and went upstairs to turn on the paraffin heater.

"You have a daughter?" Yavarov asked, looking at the doll collection and Disney Princess colouring books and assuming that they weren't mine.

"Wife and daughter are down staying with her parents for a few days."

Yavarov raised an eyebrow but said nothing.

"You want a drink?"

"You have vodka?" he asked.

"Do I have vodka? Of course. I make a mean vodka martini and an even meaner vodka gimlet."

Yavarov grimaced. "Just vodka will be sufficient."

I handed him a half full bottle of Absolut blue label and a couple of glasses while I finished the chilli.

"Swedish? I have never had Swedish vodka before," Yavarov said.

"I'm no vodka expert, but I think it's pretty good."

Yavarov poured us a couple of healthy measures.

"*Nazdrave!*" he said and finished his shot. He reflected for a moment before nodding. "You're right, it's good. But there is something, what is the word . . . unwholesome about it."

"Unwholesome? I don't think that can be the word you're after."

"Unwholesome, no that is the word. It tastes of Sweden. It is neutral, clean, antiseptic, healthy."

I nodded.

"I think I know what you need, mate."

I went out to the shed in the rain and came back with a jar of poteen.

I poured him a shot of it.

"What is this?"

"Moonshine. You know what that is?"

He nodded. "You make it?"

"No, a bloke up the road who has a pet lion."

"You are joking with me."

"I wish."

He swallowed down a healthy measure. "This is more like it," he said.

Six more shots and a bottle of wine with the chilli and we would have praised the virtues of paint thinner.

We talked about Bulgaria and Ireland and the lack of any connection at all we could think of between the two countries. I told him that Kenny Dalziel had forbidden me to fly to Bulgaria so the murder of Mr Deauville better not have a complicated international dimension.

"You think such a thing is possible?" Yavarov asked.

"Anything's possible but I think we're probably looking at some kind of internal drug war here, or possibly a vigilante. Most likely it was some lone wolf nutjob among the Proddy paramilitaries. They're not known for attracting a high calibre of personnel."

"You don't think Mrs Deauville did it, then?"

"No. Unless she's a good actress or a KGB agent. She's not a KGB agent?"

"You think the KGB would employ someone like that to work for them?"

"Of course. Last person MI5 would suspect."

"MI5 suspect everyone," Yavarov said sadly.

"You're not KGB, are you?"

"In Bulgaria there is no KGB."

"What's the Bulgarian equivalent?"

"One does not speak of such things," he said.

"You are one, aren't you? I can tell. I've met quite a few spooks in my time. Don't worry, it doesn't bother me. KGB, CIA, MI5, you're all the same. Who gives a shit?"

"In Bulgaria it is called the Durzhavna Sigurnost. The State Security Police. But I am not Durzhavna. Believe me, if I was I would not have had to take the train up here today."

"Tell me off the record about Mrs Deauville. What's her

story? What do the files tell you?" I asked, now that he was in confidence-spilling mood.

"There is nothing to tell. She was a travel agent. She met Deauville and apparently they fell in love."

"How did she get to leave Bulgaria?"

"Her husband paid off the right people."

"Wouldn't that cost a lot of money?"

"Not much these days. Ten years ago it was almost impossible to get an exit visa. In 1988 it is a different story."

We finished the bottle of Absolut and I played Yavarov my copy of *Tabula Rasa*.

A strange look flitted across Yavarov's face. "Are you homosexual, Duffy?" he asked.

A momentary hesitation before I answered: "No."

The strange look vanished. "I like this music, but it is so sad."

"You're lucky I didn't put on the Shostakovich."

It was after one, so I showed Yavarov to his bedroom at the back of the house. The room with the weirdly unobstructed view all the way to the massive cranes of Harland and Wolff shipyard eight miles distant across the lough.

"I'll leave you to it then, Pytor. Bathroom just down the hall."

He offered me his hand and I shook it. "You're a good man, Duffy. A good man. I would help you if I could. But I cannot," he said.

"What do you mean?"

"My duty is to protect a Bulgarian citizen. Her interests must come first."

"Did she tell you something about her husband's murder?"

Yavarov shook his head.

"What did she tell you? Did she see who did it? Did she do it?"

"She did not do it and she did not see who killed him," Yavarov said emphatically.

"Then what?"

"Nothing . . . I am drunk."

"You're as drunk as me. What did she tell you?"

"She told me nothing. She does not know anything. She did not see anything. I am just talking. I am drunk. I am not a good Bulgarian. I get drunk very easily."

He yawned and swayed there for a moment until he found a convenient wall. He picked up the cat and put it down again when it gave him a dirty look.

"I will tell you Bulgarian joke," he said.

"No jokes, tell me what she told you."

"A squirrel is in a pine tree, when all of a sudden, it starts shaking. He looks down, and sees an elephant climbing the tree. 'What are you doing? Why are you climbing my tree?' the squirrel calls down to the elephant. 'I'm coming up there to eat some pears!' the elephant responds. 'You fool! This is a pine tree! There aren't any pears up here!' The elephant looks perplexed for a moment, and then says, 'Well, I brought my own pears.'"

Yavarov burst into laughter and I smiled at him. I put my hand on his shoulder. "You'd tell me if you knew anything, wouldn't you, Pytor? We're old pals now," I said.

"Old pals," he agreed. "Inspector Duffy of Belfast who has Swedish vodka and listens to Estonian classical music. And Pytor Yavarov, the son of Alexander Yavarov who was for a time in 1943 an attaché to King Boris III."

"King Boris, eh?"

"Much maligned man, Tsar Boris. History does not forgive but I say this: only two countries under Nazi occupation in all of Europe save every one of their Jewish citizens: Denmark and Bulgaria. Yes?"

"OK, mate, I believe you. King Boris – good egg. I gotta go to bed. The bathroom's down the hall, there's some spare pyjamas in the linen cupboard, don't fuck with the paraffin heater – that thing's dangerous."

I left him to it and went to my room. I was too exhausted to write the conversation down and indeed I forgot all about it until a few weeks later. It had been a bloody awful day on the whole. And my head would be a bear in the morning.

9: DAADD KNOWS BEST

Downstairs to get the milk before the starlings got to work on it. Too late: the gold top sipped from, the silver top stabbed.

Frost on the ground. Blue sky above the Antrim Hills. Mooing of cows, baaing of sheep, growling of diggers as Greater Belfast pushed deeper into the Irish countryside . . .

I took a deep breath. In a couple of years Coronation Road wouldn't be special any more. When I'd first moved here it was the last street in Carrick before the wild country of County Antrim began – country of the Ulaidh and Finn and Sweeney among the nightingales . . . But with all the construction going on now, by 1990 Coronation Road would just be part of the Greater Belfast sprawl.

Moving wouldn't be so bad. Beth was probably right.

The cat strolled up the garden path and meowed at my feet. I showed him the vandalised milk bottle.

"See this? What do you do to earn your keep around here? Keeping the starlings away from the bloody milk is your—"

A silver Jaguar was driving up Coronation Road. I put down the cat. A tall pinched man in a corduroy jacket and flat cap was driving the Jag, slowly looking for parking as if he owned the place. Who knows? Maybe he did. Maybe he'd built this street and named it back in 1953.

I clocked the number plate to confirm my worst fears: "JAG-7" it said.

"Shite," I muttered, closed the door and brought the milk in.

Yavarov was in the kitchen eating toast and drinking coffee and wearing my old red pyjamas.

"Morning," I said.

"Morning. I made coffee, have some," he said.

"Thanks."

"This was excellent drink we had last night. I can't remember it but it must have been good if you wake up without a hangover. Only bad vodka gives you a . . ." I tuned him out and lit a Marlboro. I don't care what Dr Havercamp or anybody says: a Marlboro and a good black coffee fights the demons like nothing else.

"I made toast, would you like some?" Yavarov asked.

"How did you get the toaster to work? That thing baffles me."

"It was easy."

There was a knock at the front door. I swallowed the coffee and took another pull of the ciggie.

Another knock.

"There is someone at your door."

"I know."

A third knock.

"Do you want me to answer it?"

"I'll do it."

I walked down the hall and opened the front door.

"Hello, Hector," I said.

"Hello, Sean."

"What can I do for you?"

"Elizabeth needs her books."

"What books?"

"For her studies."

"Why didn't she come and get them?"

"She asked me to do it."

Beth's father and I glared at one another. If he'd stood up straight he would have been half a foot taller than me, about six five or so, but he was in his mid sixties now and his whole body was crooked. His hair was grey and he was wearing thick George Smiley glasses. He looked, in fact, like a stretched Alec Guinness, but without Guinness's gravitas or heft. He wasn't a frail man – he kept himself fit through golfing and sailing – but there was something insubstantial about him. Some void at the heart of him that reminded me of all these upper-middle-class Prods who grew up in the mid-century good times of Northern Ireland, when working-class Prods and *every* Catholic knew their place.

"What's going on, Hector?"

"Will you let me in to get her stuff?"

"What's going on? I thought she was only staying there for a couple of days?"

His grey eyes narrowed. "What did you do to her?" he growled.

"What are you talking about?"

"If you laid a finger on her, so help me, I don't care if you are a policeman, you're a fucking dead man."

I was taken aback for two reasons: it was a good few months since I'd had a death threat, but more impressively, I'd never heard Hector swear before. And swearing in defence of one's daughter was a good thing.

"Are you going to let me in or not? I need to get some things for the baby, too."

"Help yourself," I said standing aside. "The baby's room is next to ours upstairs, Beth's office with her books is in the spare bedroom at the back."

Hector tramped upstairs.

"Is anything wrong?" Yavarov asked.

"Just a sec," I said and held up a finger while I dialled Larne. Someone picked up on the third ring.

"Hello?"

"Beth is that you?"

"Yes."

"What the hell's going on now? I thought we just had a fuck-ing tiff?" was my less than diplomatic opening.

"Sean, I just sent my dad to get some of my things, you're not rowing with him, are you?"

"I thought you said you were coming back today."

"I never said that."

"We just had a row. It was no big deal. And you were right. It's a great house. It's a lovely gesture. I said I was sorry."

"Sean, please, don't argue with my father. He's not a young man."

"I'm not arguing with him. He's upstairs getting things for Emma and your books! Why?"

She sighed. "I told you. I think we need a little time apart to think things over."

"You never said anything of the sort. What things? Things were going OK. I'd smoothed it all over with my natural charm and I already said sorry about the house."

"Sean, please, can I call you in a couple of days?"

"No. Let me drive down there with your father—"

"No! Please, Sean, I know that you're a reasonable man. Just give me a couple of days to get my bearings. I'll give you a call. I had a talk with Mum and Dad last night and it got me thinking—"

"Your bloody father, wasn't it?"

"No, well . . . look, I just want a few days. What's wrong with that?"

"I miss Emma. And I know she misses me."

"I know."

"So?"

"I'll call you."

"When?"

"What day is today?"

"Saturday."

"I'll call you tomorrow."

A long pause while Yavarov pottered about in the kitchen, the cat meowed and Hector made a hell of a racket upstairs.

"OK, Beth. Call me tomorrow. I'm not working. I'll be home."

"Fine."

"Kiss Emma for me."

"I will."

"I love you."

" . . . bye, Sean," she said and then in a whisper she added, "love you" and quickly hung up. I put the phone in the crook.

It wasn't a very original thought but I articulated it anyway: women – who could understand them?

She loved me. That was only the second or third time she'd actually said that.

I walked into the kitchen, confused, emotional.

Yavarov refilled my coffee cup.

"May I ask what's happening, or would that be rude?"

"Girlfriend's father is upstairs getting some of her stuff."

"She left you?"

"It's more complicated than that."

"Did you beat her? Is she afraid of you?"

"I never laid a finger on her and don't say 'that's where you went wrong' or anything glib and Eastern European like that."

Before Yavarov could say anything Hector came down the stairs with the cot filled with books. The cot was enormous and made of cedar, so Hector must have been stronger than he looked.

"Let me help you with that," I said, taking one end of the cot.

"I too will help!" Yavarov said.

Hector saw Yavarov and me in our matching pyjamas and gave us a withering look.

A lesser man might have felt the need to explain Yavarov's

presence and started babbling about missed trains and bomb scares but I didn't feel the need to explain anything to Hector Macdonald.

I took one end of the cot and we walked out to the Jaguar. The boot was only big enough for a set of golf clubs so we put everything in the back seat instead.

I closed the back door and looked at Hector.

"Emma needs to be burped twice after the midnight feed," I said. "Beth's not usually up for that one."

"I'll tell Jane," he said curtly.

"Oh, and you should remind her to study for her tutorial on Monday. It's Dr Byrne and he's a taskmaster."

Hector sniffed. "I don't know about that. We've been talking about having her switch to business administration. Literature's a bit useless isn't it? In life, I mean."

Beth had two older brothers but one was a site manager in Chicago and the other was running a mine in South Africa. Neither could be relied upon to take over Macdonald Construction when the old man finally called it quits. Was Beth being groomed now? Was that the plan?

"That's right, books are rubbish, aren't they?" was all I said, trying to keep the sarcasm level down to a 3 or 4.

"Some good reading in the paper though these days isn't there? I read about your latest case. Page two of the *Belfast Telegraph*."

I opened the car door. "Safe home, Hector."

He nodded, got into the Jag, closed the door and drove away.

"I do not like this man, you are lucky to escape from such a family connection," Yavarov said.

"Hmmm. Come on, get dressed and I'll drive you to the train station."

I finished the coffee, dressed, took a hit on my asthma inhaler, packed the emergency inhaler, looked under the Beemer for bombs and drove Yavarov to Carrick train station. I saw him to the ticket booth where he got a through ticket to Dublin. We shook hands and I gave him my card. I went across the road to the Railway Tavern which opened at 10 o'clock on Saturday mornings for the football crowd.

I ordered a pint of Guinness and a double whisky chaser. I thought about Dr Havercamp. How many fucking units is this, you bastard?

I gave the barman a fiver and asked if he had any crisps. Crisps and Guinness for breakfast: it was like my single days.

The Railway Tavern was a hardcore UVF bar that didn't look kindly on strangers but I was wearing my black drainpipes, my DM boots and a blood-stained Undertones T-shirt under my black leather jacket. To complete the picture of a possibly unhinged psycho I hadn't shaved and I had a *I-would-fucking-love-you-to-say-something* look in my eyes.

I finished the Guinness, looked under the Beemer for bombs and drove to the station.

The angry walk up the stairs to the Incident Room left me breathless and I took a discreet pull on the emergency inhaler. It worked like a miracle and my breathing calmed down immediately. I automatically reached for a cigarette, but realising the paradox instead crunched the packet and threw it in the bin just outside the Incident Room door.

Crabbie heard the bin rattle and opened the door. He was smiling, which made me immediately suspicious.

"It's not the End of Days, is it? Jesus is back and he's declared the Presbyterians as the only true believers?"

"What?"

"Nothing. You look pleased. What's going on?"

"A break in the case. DAADD haven't claimed responsibility for the killing but intel spotted this story in *Republican News* and faxed it to us:

Direct Action Against Drug Dealers may have executed a pedlar of heroin and other filth to our children, one Francis Deauville, on Thursday morning. Sources indicate that DAADD also attempted the execution of a drug dealer in Larne on Tuesday night. Francis Deauville of Sunnylands Estate in Carrickfergus was a smuggler and supplier of heroin. Sunnylands Estate lies in the domain of Loyalist crime lords who were doing nothing to prevent Deauville carrying out his activities. Our sources indicate that brave volunteers from DAADD stepped up to the breach and executed Deauville. He had no children or dependants but the children of Ireland will be saved from the scourge of heroin by the removal of this human scum. DAADD have frequently put all drug dealers on notice to leave Ireland now before it is too late. DAADD will not tolerate your activities and will find you anywhere! Our day will come.

I put the paper down. It's what Strong wanted. He'd be happy, and a happy Chief Superintendent was a tide that would raise all the boats. But it didn't get us off the hook, we'd still have to find out who killed him. I said as much to Crabbie. He nodded but we both knew the pressure would be somewhat alleviated. The police, the newspapers and the general public all knew that DAADD was an IRA front organisation. No one was going to come forward to testify against anyone from the IRA and no doubt, as the Chief Super predicted, there would be another IRA murder along in a few days to absorb the public's attention.

I handed the article to Lawson. "Thoughts?"

"Uhm. I've looked into the statistics and if this is true, it's the fifth alleged drug dealer the DAADD have murdered in the last twelve months; but this one is a bit unusual in its geographical location and murder weapon. They've never killed anyone with a crossbow before and only once before have they come into Protestant territory to kill an alleged drug dealer."

"But they have come into Protestant territory before?" Crabbie asked.

"Yes. They went up Sandy Row in December to kill a cocaine dealer. Alleged cocaine dealer I should say. No formal claim of responsibility because it was enemy turf."

"So if we know the group and why they did it, the only thing we have to explain is the murder weapon," Crabbie said.

"They've used it twice now. Once successfully. Once unsuccessfully. It seems a very odd choice for an organisation that is awash with firearms," I said.

"It could be a new tactic to set DAADD apart from the IRA proper, or it could just be the idiosyncrasies of one particular DAADD volunteer, I'll look into it," Lawson said.

"Good. But, Lawson, don't use the word 'volunteer' – that's their language. It's an innocuous word which they have appropriated."

"What should I say?"

"Anything else, but not that. It makes you think of the International Brigade going off to fight Franco, not some gangland hood driving about in a car shooting people out the window with his shiny new crossbow."

"Who's Franco?"

"Jesus wept. For a smart kid there are serious deficiencies in your knowledge, son."

"Sorry, sir."

"Don't apologise. Read some George Orwell. *Homage to Catalonia* would be a good start. Now, what about the Deauvilles' theoretical/hypothetical lock-up garage?" I asked.

"Nothing from the people watching the residence."

"Mrs D. didn't leave her house?"

"Not yet," Crabbie said.

"Disappointing. OK, Lawson, do me a favour and call up the shops selling crossbows and tell them we're on our way over."

"Yes, sir."

When Lawson had gone, Crabbie walked me over to his desk and handed me a couple of newspapers.

"What's this?"

"It's about our case," he said.

I shook my head. "They take us to task, do they? I don't want to read it."

"No! It's good news. Neither the *Irish News* nor the *Newsletter* have followed up on the *Belfast Telegraph* story, so we may have dodged a bullet," Crabbie said, handing me both morning papers which had only covered the story in capsule form:

CARRICKFERGUS MURDER

Francis Deauville, 43, a suspected drug dealer, was shot in the Sunnylands area of Carrickfergus on Thursday morning. Police are investigating.

MURDER IN SUNNYLANDS

A murder in Sunnylands estate, Carrickfergus, in the early hours of Thursday morning is being investigated by the RUC. The victim, Francis Deauville, originally from Bangor, was rumoured to have associations with drug dealers in the area.

Neither tabloid had run with the idea of Carrick CID's incompetence, nor had they reprinted the photo of the unattended body lying in the driveway.

"This is fantastic!" I said.

"I don't know what happened, Sean. You'd think after the *Tele* story yesterday the tabloids would have been all over us," McCrabban said.

"I know what happened. Chief Superintendent Strong, or should I say acting Assistant Chief Constable Strong, said he was going to sort this out for me," I exclaimed. "And it looks like he has. He's used his influence and killed the bloody lede."

"We owe him," Crabbie said.

"We owe him big time, mate. Does he smoke cigars?"

"Dunno."

"I'll get him a bottle of whisky. Good stuff." I looked at Crabbie for a moment and shook my head. "Not that it'll make any difference in the long run if you're quitting and I'm quitting, although I have to say that the prospect of getting a job with Beth's father seems to have vanished."

Crabbie nodded and kept his mouth firmly shut. He didn't want to ask if there was more trouble on the home front and I didn't feel like going into it just now.

"We still have to try and find the murderer. Let me get a cup of coffee and we'll get to work."

I went to the coffee machine and pressed the chocolate and coffee buttons at the same time. What came out was a surprisingly drinkable concoction that for many years I thought I'd invented until I heard tell of a "mocha".

I read through the complete witness-canvassing statements from Mountbatten Terrace, but no one had heard or seen anything. I read Mrs Deauville's full statement, but it was no help either.

I read the forensic report and called up Frank Payne to ask how exactly you could tell if all the crossbow bolts were fired from the same crossbow. He spun me some shite about score marks on the aluminium paint that I decided to believe.

Lawson's inquiries got nowhere and we took a tea break to read the paper.

"Is it better to reign in hell or serve in heaven?" Lawson asked, looking up from the *Daily Telegraph*.

"Reign in hell," I said.

"Reign in hell," he agreed.

"Serve in heaven," McCrabban dissented grimly and not completely convincingly.

At 10 o'clock Lawson and I drove to Belfast to check out the two archery shops in Northern Ireland that sold crossbows. We showed them Mr and Mrs Deauville's photographs, but no one remembered either of them buying a crossbow. We asked them questions and the more facts we got the more we were disheartened by what we heard. Combined, the two shops had sold well over two thousand crossbows in the last three years to target shooters, hobbyists and even hunters. Since crossbows were entirely legal neither shop kept a list of who had purchased them. Reselling crossbows was also legal and unregulated. The particular bolts that had killed Francis Deauville were nothing special and could be fired from any of their weapons. Again, they did not keep records of who bought these bolts.

"How close would you have to get to kill someone with a crossbow?" I asked Jake of Jake's Archery Stores on Anne Street.

"The average hunting range is fifty, maybe sixty yards. You can obviously go beyond that – even an eighty-yard shot would still be powerful enough to kill medium and even big game. The real question here is whether you can land the shot with perfect precision and penetrate the vital organ(s); most people can't do so with consistency. Which is why most crossbow hunters will prefer to take a shot from a maximum of thirty-five yards away . . ."

Thirty-five yards was much further than I'd been expecting. Deauville and Morrison could have been shot from the far side of the street.

"How long does it take to get good at firing a crossbow?"

"Most people can get reasonable accuracy with a few days' practice. Even out of the box you can be pretty accurate first time out. There's no technique. You just look down the iron sights and shoot."

"And if you had some experience with the weapon?"

"You'd be deadly. And, of course, the advantage of a crossbow over a gun is its silence. Doesn't make any appreciable noise at all. As you probably know, Inspector, even a suppressed pistol will make some noise," Jake said.

"And suppressors can affect accuracy," Lawson said.

"So a crossbow is accurate at considerable range, a barbed bolt will penetrate all manner of clothing and leather, it's completely legal and it's silent," I said. "I'm surprised more paramilitaries don't use them."

"That surprises me, too, to be honest. A hundred quid will get you a decent starter package," Jake said.

We drove back to Carrickfergus RUC and told Crabbie this unhelpful news. While I'd been out Strong had called the switchboard looking for me, so I went into my office to call him back.

He wasn't in his office and I didn't feel comfortable calling him at home so I left him a message saying that I'd been in and out of the office all day.

We spent the rest of the morning doing old-fashioned police work, combing through arrest records for crossbow offences, looking up similar crimes in the UK, Ireland and further afield and going through the evidence we'd taken from the Deauville residence.

Helpful and/or stupid criminals often kept their receipts and this was how we found the lock-up garage.

A receipt dating back to the previous December for a shed on an allotment out in Eden.

I called Harry Mulvenny from the canine unit and we went out there in the Land Rover. While Crabbie and Lawson went up front I sat in the back with Harry and his two bitches Cora and Louise. I closed the partition to the front, so we could have some privacy.

"No pun intended, Harry, but I have a bone to pick with you," I said.

"What have I done?" he said in his just-off-the-boat Scouse accent.

"You were at Deauville's house?"

"Yeah, we didn't find anything."

"You were there when Dalziel sent McCrabban to the hospital

and when forensics fucked off?"

"Yeah, so?"

"Dalziel left and when you left that meant Lawson was there by himself."

"And how is this my fault? I'm a canine officer."

"You're a sergeant in the RUC. You should have taken command. Acted on your initiative. Lawson is a detective constable with barely two years under his belt. You should have stepped up, assumed command, got forensics in, secured the crime scene until Crabbie got back."

Harry knew I was right. "Are you going to report me to McArthur?"

"No. I'm the fall guy on this debacle and there's no point getting anyone else in the shit . . . But next time remember you've got those stripes on your shoulders for a reason."

We got out of the Land Rover at a squalid little bit of waste ground near Kilroot Power Station. If this was an allotment there wasn't much evidence of anything growing.

We found Deauville's shed and the dogs were going crazy before we even opened the door.

Lawson broke the padlock with a pair of bolt cutters and inside Harry discovered a dozen bags of refined heroin. Pounds of the stuff. Not ounces, pounds.

I went back to the Land Rover and got put through to Chief Inspector McArthur.

"Sir, if you want to make someone in the drug squad happy and owe you a big future favour you should get them out here. We found a couple of pounds of heroin. It's a major score so it'll be a drugs squad case, not Carrick CID."

"I'll call Chief Inspector O'Driscoll."

"He'd be perfect, sir. And I think you should come out yourself, sir. Some good PR for the station."

"I think I will do that. Very good PR for the station after yesterday's black eye."

The rain came on, so I left Lawson at the shed and waited in the Rover until the drugs squad and McArthur arrived. Seamus O'Driscoll was another rare Catholic detective in the RUC and he'd brought with him seemingly half the narcs in the force. Twenty men and women in white evidence-gathering boiler suits.

"If it isn't Sean Duffy as I live and breathe," O'Driscoll said, offering me his hand. He was a tall, unhinged looking fellow with red hair and bad teeth, but he wasn't a bad sort. We went back aways and I could possibly have liked him if he hadn't been two years and nine months younger than me and already far ahead of me on the chain of command. We had come up together, though, so there was no question of me calling him "sir", or of him demanding it.

"O'Driscoll drove with a song, the wild duck and the drake," I said but the illiterate eejit just give me a funny look, so I dropped the Yeats.

"This is quite a big score you've given me here, Sean, I'll owe you," he said.

"You don't owe me anything. My gaffer thought you'd be the best man for the job and I agreed."

O'Driscoll grinned from ear to ear. Not a pretty sight, so I decided to put an end to it. "You could give me one big hand though. I've had a couple of men watching Mrs Deauville's house in the hope that she would lead us to her husband's lock-up. But now that we've found it by other means I'm going to take the men away. I've been paying their over-time out of the CID budget. If you want to keep up the surveillance can you pay for it out of your budget?"

"No need for surveillance. I'll just arrest her."

"Oh, OK, fair enough. Well do me a favour, Seamus, go easy on her. We don't think she killed her husband and she's pretty torn up about it."

"I'll be gentle."

"At least bring in a WPC. We did and we're not exactly cutting-edge."

"Isn't the purpose to get her to talk?"

"No, the purpose is 'to protect and serve,'" I said, giving him the motto of the LAPD.

"Oh yeah, sure, of course it is."

"I'll get Lawson to give you over the files and you can photocopy them. Standard division of duty: you handle the narco aspects, we'll do the homicide, OK?"

"Sounds good. I heard this wife of his was a foreigner?"

"Bulgarian, but don't believe any nonsense she tells you about not speaking English. She's fluent."

Chief Inspector McArthur had arrived with a reporter from the *Carrickfergus Advertiser*. I shook his hand and took my leave. Didn't need any more press attention today.

Back to the barracks on Shanks's mare.

Of course it began to rain and then hail and I was out only in my T-shirt and thin leather jacket.

Soaked when I got back to the office.

Sandra brought me tea and biscuits while I huddled in front of the single bar of the heater.

The phone rang just as I was thinking of calling Beth again.

"Hello?"

"Ah, Duffy, been trying to reach you all day."

It was Chief Superintendent Strong. A friendly voice in a cruel world.

"Sir, I've been meaning to talk to you, too. I want to thank you for whatever you did to keep yesterday's story out of the morning papers today."

He cleared his throat. "I'll admit that I did make a few phone calls into the shell-like ears of a few people who have had occasion to rely on the police for scoops and tips in the past."

"Well, I'm most grateful, sir."

"Forget it, Duffy. Tell me about the developments in the case," he said eagerly. I was a little surprised that one of the Greats of Mount Olympus would be interested in muckety-muck police work, but he had stuck his neck out for me, so no wonder he was keen.

"Well we interviewed the wife and released her."

"Released her?"

"It was our feeling that she was not a suspect or a material witness."

"What did she tell you?"

"Nothing, really. She doesn't know who killed him or why."

"She saw nothing?"

"Apparently not."

"And you definitely don't like her for it?"

" . . . uhm, like I say, I'm not completely sure, sir. But my instincts and the evidence tend to suggest that she is not to blame."

Not to blame for the murder, anyway. She'd almost certainly been smuggling in Turkish heroin – somehow – but that wasn't my concern and if CI O'Driscoll couldn't pin that on her it was no skin off my nose.

"I'd like to see the transcripts of your interview."

"I'll have Lawson fax them to you, sir."

"What else?"

"At the time of the arrest we didn't find Mr Deauville's heroin laboratory on site so it was reasonable to assume that it was at an off-site location and that she might lead us there in an attempt to destroy evidence."

"And did she?"

"No. But we found the lab by other means. An old receipt he'd kept."

"Good work! Were there drugs in it?"

"Oh yes, sir. A lot of drugs. A couple of pounds of heroin. More than we could handle, sir, so we called in the drug squad."

"Brilliant, Duffy. Who was the drug-squad liaison?"

"CI O'Driscoll, sir."

"How do I know that name?"

"Maybe from the poem, sir?"

"What poem?"

"The Yeats poem, sir. O'Driscoll drove with a song the wild duck and the drake—"

"Jesus man, I didn't tell you to start reciting it."

"Sorry, sir."

"What else, Duffy? What's this I hear about a DAADD connection?"

"Uhm, you've heard about that, sir, have you? Well, it's slightly unusual, DAADD have not claimed responsibility for the killing with a recognised codeword, but there was a story in *Republican News* strongly suggesting that they did it."

"The bastards. So it really wasn't the wife at all?"

"It's looking unlikely."

"Tell me, Duffy, do we ever catch any of those DAADD murderers?"

"If they're IRA men and there are no witnesses or forensic evidence I'd say it's going to be very tricky, sir."

"So not totally unprecedented if they get away with it, eh? If the Chief Constable starts breathing down our necks asking—"

"The Chief Constable?" I asked with alarm.

"Relax, man, I'm your shield, remember?"

"Yes, sir, thank you, sir."

"So what's going to happen next in the case?"

"CI O'Driscoll is going to arrest Mrs Deauville for the drugs smuggling."

"Maybe I'll watch it through the glass."

"The interview, sir?"

"Yeah, why not. I've taken an interest in this case and I'd like to see it through to the end now."

"That's fine by me, sir. And I'm sure Chief Inspector O'Driscoll won't mind. I believe he's based at Antrim RUC."

"Very good, Duffy, you've done well today, better than yesterday. Have a good night."

He hung up and I called O'Driscoll to warn him that acting ACC Strong might swing by to watch him work his interview magic, which alarmed him nicely. I went home, fed the cat, called Beth and got the engaged tone. I called again and I got Beth's mum, who said that Beth was out with "some old friends" and that Emma was sleeping.

I made a pint glass vodka gimlet, easy on the ice, lime and soda, heavy on the vodka.

I called up Belfast International Airport and checked to see if there were any direct charters to Bulgaria. Of course there were. Two a week from Belfast to Varna on the "Black Sea Riviera". That's how she smuggled the drugs. You bribe the officials at the Varna end and confidently walk through customs and immigration at the Belfast end. There was a chance of a random pat-down, but I knew that the immigration officers at Belfast's ports and airports were on the alert for known terrorists and the sniffer dogs at the airport were the ones who'd been trained to look for explosives not drugs. Northern Ireland's drug problem wasn't of sufficient concern yet to have narco canine teams and officers at the airports. Eventually it would be, but not yet.

I thought about telling O'Driscoll this information, but decided against it. It was his case to make and no concern of mine. I was doing the murder, he was doing the drugs. And I felt sorry for Elena Deauville.

I looked out "Fantasia on a Theme by Thomas Tallis", stoked the peat fire in the living-room grate and lay down on the floor to listen to it.

The cat crawled onto my stomach.

By the second vodka gimlet and the second iteration of the concerto much of the bad shit was going away.

Of course the real bad shit was still to come but I didn't know that then.

At midnight the phone rang.

Beth?

"Hello?"

"Sean, it's Seamus O'Driscoll, just wanted to let you know that we've arrested Mrs Deauville and taken her to Antrim RUC."

"It's midnight, Seamus."

"I thought you would want to know."

"Fine. Thanks. But there's no need to call me with further updates. You can call DS McCrabban at the station. I think he's duty detective."

"I will. Listen, Sean, Chief Super— I mean Acting Assistant Chief Constable Strong's here right enough, how do I handle him?"

"Jesus, mate, it's not Cardinal Ó Fiaich. He's just another dozy peeler."

"I'll tell him you said that."

"Goodnight, Seamus."

"Night, Sean."

The cat was looking at me expectantly and since no one else wanted to hear it I gave him the last two stanzas of "The Host of the Air":

"O'Driscoll scattered the cards/And out of his dream awoke:

Old men and young men and young girls/Were gone like a drifting smoke/But he heard high up in the air/A piper piping away,

And never was piping so sad/And never was piping so gay."

The cat yawned, not very impressed by this at all. "I learned that when I was eleven. Give me some credit," I said. "I suppose it's too old-fashioned for you, is it?"

But the wise little creature was already asleep.

10: DEATH ON THE ROCK

Sunday morning. No girlfriend, no baby girl, cold house, rain so hard it was bouncing eight inches off the pavement. Coronation Road was wet and empty and I felt isolated and alone.

With the family around and the sun shining and the kids out playing, this street seemed to lie at the centre of the earth, as Jerusalem does on medieval maps. The living room of #113 Coronation Road was the centre of the centre and the record player spinning Peetie Wheatstraw's "Police Station Blues" was the axis around which the whole universe curved.

But not today. Today #113 Coronation Road was just a cold little ex-council house with ashes in the grate and a hungry cat whining in the kitchen.

I called Beth but Hector answered the phone and claimed she was down at Larne Marina working on their boat the *Grania*.

"At this hour? In this weather?"

"Yes. You know Beth, she loves sailing."

First I knew about that, I nearly said. "Yeah, I know. She's not out on the water though, is she? It's supposed to storm later."

"Of course not."

"OK, I'll try her later. Tell her to call me and tell her I miss Emma."

I lit the fire in the living room, found a record, put it on, and thanked God for Ella Fitzgerald and a case to occupy my brain and keep away the blues.

The IRA proxy group DAADD were sort of claiming the Deauville murder and we could yellow this file soon enough but there were a few things about the case I did not like.

I took a hit on my asthma inhaler and had a cup of coffee and settled in front of the fire to think.

Think until ten anyway when I would try Beth again.

Item #1: would the IRA or its DAADD proxy really have driven deep into a Loyalist area like Sunnylands Estate to kill some random drug dealer?

Item #2: would they really have used a weapon as exotic as a crossbow when they were plenty of guns available in Ulster?

Item #3: what did Elena Deauville know about the murder that she wasn't saying?

I considered the problems one at a time:

Item #1: on the surface it didn't make a whole lot of sense for the IRA to come to a housing estate in Carrickfergus. The IRA's preference was always for soft targets. Would they really drive deep into a twisty Loyalist housing estate to kill a random pusher? The only reason they would do such a thing would be for the PR value: to prove that they could go where they pleased. Bam! We drive into Protestant Larne to shoot a drug dealer. Bam! We drive into Protestant Carrickfergus the very next night. Look at us, we can be anywhere! Yes, that worked as a reason, but then why not claim it with a recognised codeword and shout it from the rooftops? You don't want to antagonise the Loyalists and jeopardise a truce, fair enough, but then why kill Deauville and shoot Morrison in the first place? So maybe you shoot Morrison to establish a pattern, then you shoot Deauville, then you tell *Republican News* that this was the DAADD and they believe it. Everyone's happy: the press is happy, the RUC detectives are happy, parents concerned about evil doers selling drugs to their kids are happy . . . And of course the real killer is happy because he or she has gotten away with it . . .

Item #2: the crossbow is weird. Sure, the shop man could talk about its effective range and its silence, but still, why wouldn't the killer use a gun? The IRA had plenty of guns. Was it really because of the noise?

Item #3: Elena Deauville. The more I thought about it, the more I didn't like her testimony. That little look she gave. That hesitation. She was hiding something. Something important. Something beyond the fact that she was a brilliant heroin mule.

I called the station and asked for the duty detective.

"CID," Crabbie said.

"Fill me in," I said.

"On what?"

"Didn't they re-arrest Elena Deauville last night?"

"Yeah, your mate Seamus lifted her. You want the details?"

"If it's not too much trouble."

"You seem to be in a mood."

"I'm not . . . And Seamus isn't my mate. He's just a Catholic. Not all us Catholic peelers are buddy buddies, you know?"

"I thought you came up together," Crabbie protested.

"What if we did? What's the story with Mrs D., Crabbie?"

"They arrested her, took her to Antrim RUC and interviewed her. Do you want to come in and read the transcript? CI O'Driscoll faxed it over."

"No, you can summarise it for me."

"They asked her about the lock-up. She denied all knowledge of its contents. She denied all knowledge of her husband's drug dealing and she said she had nothing to do with any smuggling."

"Did Seamus believe her?"

"No. He asked how her husband could be a heroin dealer and she not know about it. He said it wasn't credible."

"And what did she say to that?"

"She said that if she knew her husband was a heroin dealer why hadn't she gotten rid of the evidence as soon as she found him dead?"

"What did Seamus say to that?"

"Seamus said that if she'd gone all the way to the lock-up in Eden and left her husband's body in her driveway after she discovered it, it would have been very suspicious and after she'd been released from custody she couldn't do it because she must have seen the policemen watching her house."

"That makes sense to me. What do you reckon?"

"She was completely hysterical after the body was found. She was in no fit state to think rationally about concealing evidence. And after she was released, as CI O'Driscoll says, she must have seen the men watching the house. They were ordinary PC's so that wouldn't surprise me."

"Anything else interesting from the interview?"

"She gave him nothing, Sean. Less than she gave us, even. Deny, deny, deny. Of course she had a Legal Aid solicitor with her this time."

"Did she ask for a lawyer?"

"Apparently she did."

"So they had to give her one."

"Aye."

"So O'Driscoll's keeping her up at Antrim for further questioning, is he?"

"No. He thinks he has enough evidence already for a prima facie case. She's already been formally charged at Antrim Magistrates Court."

"That *is* fast work. They set bail?"

"5,000 pounds."

"Steep for a guilt-by-association case."

"O'Driscoll told the court that she was a flight risk so they confiscated her passport and set a big bail. Her Legal Aid solicitor was furious, saying she was a poor widow living in a council house on benefits, but apparently the magistrate was unmoved."

"I take it no one has paid the bail."

"No."

"Unless they find her prints on the stuff I think it's going to be a tougher case to make than O'Driscoll thinks. No chain of causation, no real proof that she knew anything about the drugs. A jury might let her off. If it were me I'd offer her a deal. But then again, that's not our problem, is it?"

"No."

"Any developments on our side of the case?"

"Nothing. That story in the *Republican News* is as good as a DAADD claim of responsibility, as far as the media is concerned. Didn't make any of the Sunday papers. I don't think we'll even have to have a press conference."

"Thank God for that."

"What *will* we do next?"

"We'll appeal for witnesses. Maybe have poor Mrs Deauville go through a third police interview."

"You think she was lying to us?"

"Of course she was lying to us, she's a bloody drugs smuggler, but there was one question in particular that's been bothering me. Do you remember I asked her if she'd seen anyone following them and she sort of hesitated before she answered?"

"Aye, and she sort of stared at that Bulgarian bloke and then at us before saying no."

"Did she?"

"Yeah."

"What do you think that was about?"

"Just nerves, I thought."

"Could be," I said reflectively.

I looked at my watch. "Don't you have church soon?"

"I do indeed."

"I'll come in and take over for you."

"It's Lawson's rota."

"I'm at a loose end. Beth. You know?"

"How is everything with uh, uh . . ." Crabbie began, immediately regretting the sally. But I wasn't going to let him off the hook that easily, the poor bastard.

"So glad you asked, mate. She's staying with her parents. We had a wee row and I thought it was no big deal but apparently I freaked her out. And her da swings by yesterday and says she's switching to business administration, whatever the hell that is. And now she's away working on the family yacht like the Proddy gentry. You never had a boat as a child, did you?"

"No I—"

"Course you didn't. Son of the soil like you. Who has a boat? Nobody. I don't know what's going on, mate. Maybe this whole row about the house was a mere pretext. A *casus belli* you know?"

"Sean, I'm sympathetic, but I have to get back to—"

"Casus belli and now we're talking Latin maxims, here's one even you'll remember from your Ballymena Academy days: *contra principia negantem non est disputandum.* How can I argue with her when she's denying there's even an argument and she keeps changing the rules?"

"Sean, I have to go."

"Go then. We'll talk some more when I come in in a bit."

I dressed in a sports jacket, white shirt, red tie, black jeans, DMs. Clocked myself in the mirror, killed the fucking tie.

Under the BMW for bombs. No bombs, just the diffraction iridescence of a drop of oil floating in a puddle of rainwater.

Into the Beemer. Second gear. Third. A hard turn at Victoria Road and another onto the A2. Up to 60 mph going past the Fisherman's Quay. Going so fast the turn into Carrick police station was impossible.

As I say the Beemer, like a greyhound, needs its morning workout.

Into the harbour car park in a squeal of breaks.

Out of the car for the first cigarette of the day.

Dog walkers. Church goers. Some of them know me. Nod a hello and stand on the pier looking down into the black water of Carrick harbour. Behind me was the big Norman Castle and in that castle the well of Fergus Mor Mac Erc, King of Dalriada, the King who brought the stone of Scone from Ireland to Scotland and that sits under the Coronation Throne to this very day. The King who started all this Thucydidian bollocks if you want to go back that far. I didn't. I didn't give a shit about any of it any more. "Fuck it," I said and stamped out the ciggie and got back in the Beemer.

A kid letting his collie piss against the back wheel.

"Oi! You! That's my car."

"Sorry, mister, but when she has to go she has to go."

"What's her name?"

"I have no idea, but we call her Susie."

Everybody's such a smart ass these days. "Tell Susie to piss somewhere else."

Grumbling, I drove back to the station. When I got there Crabbie had legged it in case I laid any more of my personal stuff on him. Said morning to Lawson and went up to my office and read through the transcript of Mrs Deauville's second police interview. Crabbie was quite correct, she'd given O'Driscoll even less than she'd given us.

I wanted to know more about DAADD's murderous ways so I called Marcus Finn in Special Branch intel and although he wasn't in on a Sunday a young DC called Kenny Clarke said he was starving and would fill me in if I got him lunch.

"Lunch where?" I asked suspiciously.

"I'm not picky."

"I'm not even in Belfast. I'm in Carrick."

"Well then, I'm sorry. I'm not authorised to give out this kind of information over the tele—"

"Meet me at the Europa Grill in twenty minutes."

"What do you look like?"

"A depressed policeman."

"Aren't all policem—"

Click. Twenty minutes of hardcore Beemer driving later.

"Ah, Inspector Duffy, I believe," an amiable-looking eejit of a man in a red jumper said.

We sat in the window overlooking Great Victoria Street. He ordered the most expensive steak they had and I got one too. I'd put it on CID expenses.

"So tell me about DAADD," I said.

"He was a kindly man, but he just couldn't cope with family life so he left when I was eight to seek his fortune in Australia."

"You're hilarious."

"Wow, tough room. You don't have much of a sense of humour, eh?"

"No. DAADD?"

"Well, they're your standard IRA front organisation. Not much to them really. They've been growing in the last few years, of course, because intel-wise we've been on the back foot in so many areas."

"Back foot how?"

"Remember that chopper crash on the Mull of Kintyre?"

"I remember reading something about it."

"Very clever idea. Get all your top MI5 and Special Branch agents with expertise in the IRA and put them all in one helicopter and then fly that helicopter into a mountain in Scotland. Great thinking. Anyway we've been struggling since then and that coupled with all the new money and weapons flooding in . . ."

"What new money?" I asked as the steaks came. Both of them overcooked.

"Tons of new money. Money from Americans and Libyans and Russians . . . And then, of course, there are the general intelligence failures. So many IRA spectaculars in the last five years: the Maze Escape, the Brighton Bombing, Enniskillen."

"What does it all amount to?" I asked.

"What indeed? What indeed? A lot of our informers have turned up dead. Even some of our agent handlers."

"Smart guy like you must have some theories."

"Oh, there are lots of different theories."

"Like what?"

"Incompetence."

"That one makes sense. What else?"

He lowered his voice. "There's the theory that the IRA have a mole in the higher ups in the RUC or MI5."

I laughed. "Next?"

"There's the theory that Thatcher is deliberately letting the situation spiral out of control so she can wash her hands of Ulster, unilaterally withdraw and let the UN or the Americans take charge."

"I hadn't heard that one. She wouldn't do that."

"Wouldn't she? Only Nixon could go to China, remember. And it would be immensely popular in England. A few Tory right wingers would be furious for a while but they love her."

This was getting pointless. Bored intel guys and their speculations. I was an actual detective who had actual work to do.

"Tell me about DAADD."

He told me everything he knew. DAADD had attacked forty-two alleged drug dealers in the four years since they'd been calling themselves DAADD (before that they simply called themselves the IRA). Twenty-five of these alleged drug dealers had been successfully killed with a variety of weapons: pistols, rifles, shotguns, carbines. They'd never used crossbows before, but as an ad hoc group loosely under IRA command a crossbow attack wasn't out of the question.

"Really? I thought it was a completely bizarre choice of murder weapon considering the number of guns available in Ulster," I said.

"Guns yes. We estimate that the Libyans alone have given the IRA about eight hundred AK-47's and—"

"Eight hundred?" I said, aghast.

"Oh, maybe I shouldn't have said that. You won't repeat that, will you, Inspector Duffy? Wouldn't want to generate alarm."

"No. We wouldn't want that, would we?" I said, imagining the prospect of eight hundred armed IRA men descending en masse on Carrick police station – it would be a massacre. Thank you Colonel Gaddafi.

"But a machine gun makes a bit of a racket doesn't it? Even a hand-gun makes noise. No, a crossbow could be quite an effective little weapon for a group like DAADD. Differentiate them from their mother organisation. Especially when non-lethal force is required or you're doing a punishment attack. I was fascinated by the attack on Mr Morrison and since the second on Mr Deauville I've been eagerly awaiting a third. If there is one we can consider that a pattern and I'll write a paper on it. I'll send it to you if you want."

"Thanks. Well, look, I'm sorry but I must dash," I said, pointing at my wrist watch.

"You haven't got pudding."

"You get one," I said, getting up and leaving two twenty pound notes on the table.

"Where are you going?"

"Work. You've been very helpful, thanks, mate," I replied, found the BMW in the Europa Car Park, checked underneath it for bombs and drove back to Carrick RUC.

I spun Lawson my worries about the case and Constable Clarke's attempts to bat away at least one of them regarding the murder weapon.

We had nothing else on so we worked the evidence until two o'clock, processing tips from the Confidential Telephone and reading and rereading Mrs Deauville's statement. For want of anything better to do, I drove us to Mountbatten Terrace where we canvassed the neighbours again, but nobody had seen or heard anything and if they had "they wouldn't be telling the bloody peelers".

We went for an afternoon tea break at the Old Tech on West

Street and sat by the fire. The tea was warm and the shortbread was home-made. While we were in the restaurant the rain stopped, the wind changed and the snow began.

Carrickfergus lies far to the north on the 55th parallel, which also crosses the Alaskan peninsula and the city of Novosibirsk. I went to a lecture once where Jo McBain said that a hundred centuries ago Carrick and all of the north of Ireland lay under a mile of ice. But now the snow came only for a few days a year in February and March and the sea never froze. It was a miracle really, but as Dr McBain said, surely the ice *would* come again and all these pubs and houses and power stations and people would be wiped clean from the land.

No need for peelers then. No need for anything.

"Sir? . . . Sir?"

Lawson staring at me.

"What?"

"You were lost in thought."

"Aye, I was."

"Were you thinking about the case?"

"I was thinking about ice."

"I was just saying we should get back to the station."

"Yeah."

We went back to the station, where much to my surprise Crabbie was there to meet us.

"What are you doing here?"

"Wife has the kids down to visit her sister in Fermanagh."

"The house felt a bit lonely?"

"You said that, not me."

"You are allowed to admit to human emotion, you're Presbyterian, not Vulcan."

"Well . . . " Lawson said.

Crabbie and I both grinned. "Times have changed, eh, Crabbie? When you or I were at his tender age we wouldn't have dared raise an eyebrow to our elders and betters, would we? Next he'll be saying that the music of 1988 is better than the music of 1978 or 1968."

Crabbie shrugged, having no interest in the topic. As the saying goes, he liked both kinds of music: country and western. The day the music died for him was March 5th 1963 when Patsy Cline's plane had gone down.

"Here's a thought, gents. I know the weather's not good but don't you think it's about time we went down to the Glasgow Rangers Supporters Club and asked a few questions? Last place Mr Deauville was seen alive. Probably should have gone there yesterday," I said.

"It was a Saturday yesterday, they all would have been at the Rangers game in Scotland," Crabbie said.

"Do they go to every game then?"

"Oh yes. Over on the ferry to Glasgow every Saturday," Crabbie said.

"I suppose you're a Celtic supporter, sir?" Lawson asked. An innocent enough question everywhere else in the world except for Belfast and Glasgow, where the wrong response could get you a punch in the face.

"I don't give a shit about Scottish football, Lawson. As far as I'm concerned there's only one football team in the world."

Crabbie nodded in agreement. "Liverpool FC?" Lawson groaned.

I ruffled Lawson's blond locks. "The kid has learned something under our tutelage. All right lads, let's go, wrap up warm," I said.

I didn't trust the Beemer without snow tyres so we decided to hoof it. Exercise would do us good. Dr Havercamp would be proud of me. I'd been following his regimen fairly strictly. Asthma inhaler every morning. Cut down my smoking. Cut down my drinking. No pot. Stress was through the roof, though and that couldn't be good: Beth taking Emma to her parents and the *Belfast Telegraph* trying to crucify me . . .

We walked out in the snow to the Glasgow Rangers Supporters Club which was located near the bird sanctuary between the railway lines and Carrick Leisure Centre. Lawson was wearing a parka, Crabbie and me were both in duffle coats.

Until a few years earlier this had been marshy wasteground but the local council had formed an artificial lake and now it was a mini birders' paradise with quite the collection of ducks, kittiwakes, common gulls, crows, magpies, guillemots, fulmars, razorbills.

Not everyone was as enthused by our avian friends as I was.

"They make a bit of a racket, don't they?" Crabbie said.

"A racket to the uninitiated, but to me—" I began and as I explained how to differentiate the different bird calls I saw Lawson put on his Walkman headphones and tune me out – the cheeky wee skitter.

It was pretty back here behind the leisure centre. I should take Emma here in her stroller, she'd like that, I thought. Emma. Didn't Beth know what she was putting me through, taking her away from me?

If we separated now would I even get visitation rights? Family law, even in benighted medieval Northern Ireland, gave scant regard to the rights of the dad . . .

My conversation dried up and Crabbie wasn't exactly a chatterbox.

We walked around the lake.

It was a Japanese woodblock print.

Us. The snow. The water.

Lawson's Walkman, the sound of birds, and the soft airy snow falling onto the supine lake surface like a Basho poem.

We reached the Glasgow Rangers Club tucked behind the trees. This place was not from a woodblock print: a utilitarian breeze-block building bedecked with union jacks, Scottish saltires and painted representations of – presumably – famous Glasgow football players of the past. There were grilles on the windows to prevent petrol-bomb attacks and a heavy metal door.

I pounded on the door while Crabbie attempted to light his pipe and Lawson took his Walkman off.

"What were you listening to, Lawson?" I asked him.

"The usual."

"Zeppelin, Floyd, Sabbath?"

Lawson gave a little half-smile to convey the fact that I'd committed yet another generational crime.

"Not exactly," he said.

"Who then?"

"I just bought the Morrissey solo album, *Viva Hate*, not even out until next week, but I got an early release from KragTrax," Lawson said.

"Morrissey? The Manky lad who pulled out of Wogan at the last minute?" McCrabban said, astounded.

"I think that's Boy George," I said.

"No that's the one," Lawson clarified.

"Is the record any good?"

"It's not as good as the Smiths, but it's pretty good."

"Going back to our earlier conversation, don't you think the 80s has sort of reached a musical nadir after the heady days of the 70s?"

The young detective constable shook his boyish head. "Totally disagree," he said. "Popular music today is more interesting on nearly every front than the stuff that was being pumped out in the 70s. All that big boring corporate rock and—"

I pounded on the door again. "Open up in there!"

"Who is it?" a voice from within inquired.

"Inspector Duffy, Carrick RUC," I said.

"The poliss?" the voice from within asked.

"Just bloody open up!"

The door swung open and we went inside the Rangers Club. It was cold, stark, dimly lit and there was a sawdusty vinegary smell. The club was utilitarian on the inside, too, with a long crude bar that served only Harp and Bass on tap. The chairs were stacked on the tables, giving the place an even more desolate appearance. The voice from within belonged to a skinny but tough-looking thirty-year-old bloke with beady brown eyes and a misshapen shaved head which made him resemble one of the Talosians from the original series of *Star Trek*. He was wearing a Rangers away shirt and dungarees, which was an odd and unattractive combination.

"What can I do you for?"

I told him why we were here. He said his name was Teddy Pendergrass and he was the barman/janitor/bouncer for the establishment.

"Were you working here Wednesday night into Thursday morning?"

"I was."

"And do you remember serving Mr Deauville?" I asked, showing him Deauville's photograph.

"No . . . I don't think I've seen him, uhm, in here before," he said looking anywhere but at the three of us.

"You're a terrible liar, Teddy. Don't ever go into the confidence game. Now, Deauville was here on Thursday night and you remember him, don't you?"

"No, not really."

"Christ, Teddy, do you want us to lift you? Is that what you want? Now, do you remember him or not?"

"Aye, maybe."

"Was he a regular?"

"Aye, I think he was."

"Why would he come here of all the bars in Carrick to drink at?"

"Subsidised beer for club members. 50p a pint."

"He wasn't selling drugs out the back was he? Selling drugs out the back and giving you a cut of the action?"

"No! He wasn't!"

"So if I was to bring Sergeant Mulvenny and his K9 team down here they wouldn't find anything, would they?"

"What people do in the privacy of the stalls is their concern. I don't know if they're smoking dope back there or not."

"We'd have to close the place down, wouldn't we, Sergeant McCrabban?"

"Oh yes, Inspector Duffy, we'd have to. Under the Proceeds Of Crime (Northern Ireland Order) and under the Asset Forfeiture Act (Northern Ireland Order) we'd have no choice but to shut this place down and seize the assets of anyone who works here," Crabbie said, playing along.

"But here's the thing, Ted, we're not the drugs squad, we're investigating a murder. If you can help us solve our crime the drugs squad doesn't have to know about any of this and Sergeant Mulvenny's dogs don't have to come out into the cold."

Ted was desperate now. "What do you want to know?"

"Who did Francis Deauville associate with in here and who was he drinking with on Wednesday night?"

"Deauville only joined a couple of months back. He mostly drank by himself but occasionally people would go up to his table and he'd go to the bogs and sell them product. At least I assume he did. I never asked about it."

"What people?"

"All sorts of people, young, old, you name it."

"And how do you know he would sell them product if you never asked about it?"

"I never asked and I told him I didn't want to know. I didn't want to be involved and get myself kneecapped or worse."

"So how do you know he was selling drugs?"

"I'm not stupid, so I'm not. And at the end of a night he would give me a wee tip."

"How much?"

"It depended on how well he'd done, I suppose. Sometimes twenty quid, sometimes a hundred."

"Tell me about Wednesday night."

"What do you want to know?"

"His customers on Wednesday."

"He was only in for an hour or so on Wednesday before last orders."

"And who did he sell to?"

"The place was empty. You know what the weather was like."

"I don't know what the weather was like. I was in Donegal."

"Freezing so it was. And wet. I don't think he had a single customer."

"Have you ever listened to Lou Reed? The weather is no deterrent to the determined junkie looking for a fix."

"That may be the case but Frankie was drinking alone all night until his friend came in."

"What friend?"

"Some old fella. His age or older, wearing a flat cap."

"Describe him better."

"I didn't really look at him. Just an old guy, tall, wearing a flat cap over his face. They sat in the corner."

"He kept the cap on inside?"

"Aye."

"And how long did he and Deauville talk for?"

"About fifteen minutes. Frankie got him a whisky. Bells, I think."

"And then what?"

"Then the old guy left and Frankie sat there for a bit, finished his pint and he left too."

"Ever see the old guy in here before?"

"I don't think so, but it's hard to tell because his hat was down over his face."

"Do you have CCTV cameras in here?" Lawson asked.

"No."

"Did Deauville seem agitated or nervous, anything like that?"

"Nope. He seemed fine. Just like he was having a drink with an old friend . . . There was one thing, though."

"What was that?"

"Well, when I called last orders Frankie comes up to the bar and gives me fifty quid like he's just had a massive score. But he hadn't. He hadn't sold anything really."

"Did you ask him why the money?"

"No, like I say, no questions. Better not to know."

"You're going to have to come down the station with us and give our sketch artist a drawing of this guy," I said.

"He didn't look like anything. It's just a hat and a coat."

"What type of coat?"

"Just a heavy raincoat. He may have had a wee beard or that could have just been the shadow. No, there's no point getting me to draw anything."

"Regardless, you're going to have to come with us."

We took him back to the station with us and he did indeed produce a very unhelpful drawing with the sketch artist. A tall well-built man with a hat pulled low over his face. Possibly a beard or prominent sideburns. It was interesting, though. Direct Action Against Drug Dealers didn't usually meet with their victims before they shot them. Then again, maybe this was just an old friend of Deauville's right enough. Or maybe it bloody wasn't.

The snow continued to fall and at five o'clock everyone was keen to get home as driving on some of the country roads was bound to be treacherous.

I called Crabbie and Lawson into my office.

"OK lads, we'll all head home, but I think tomorrow we'll go up to Antrim RUC and ask Mrs Deauville if she's seen this mysterious stranger around, what do you lads think?"

"It's not much of a picture," Crabbie said.

"It's the best lead we've got," I countered.

"It's the only lead we've got," Lawson said.

I went into Chief Inspector McArthur's and filled him in on the details. He couldn't care less. This was a DAADD murder and those never got solved and the press wouldn't care if we didn't bring anyone in for it so therefore it wouldn't affect his career. And in a couple of months he'd be free of me forever.

I drove home carefully along the seafront and even more carefully up the unsalted Victoria Road. Irish people weren't used to driving in snow and the eejits were going far too fast, slipping and sliding every which way. Still, I got the Beemer in front of #113 in one piece.

As I was coming in the phone was ringing. I dropped everything and picked it up.

"Hello?"

"Hello Sean, I'm so glad I caught you. You were right, Emma misses you, she wants to hear your voice."

"I miss her. Put her on."

"Dadda!" Emma said.

"Emma honey."

"Story dadda! Story!"

"Story . . . Well, once upon a time there was this naughty little girl with blonde hair who was always breaking into people's houses. She was what we policemen call a recidivist so the local peeler, a very nice, generous, forgiving and intelligent policeman called Sean, told her she had to go and live in the woods for a while. She went out into the woods and she saw a cute little house there with the smell of porridge coming out the open window. Not just ordinary porridge but those steel-cut oats and honey that Daddy makes. Now this girl who we'll call—"

"Emma!"

"Goldilocks, immediately decided she would get up to her old tricks again by breaking into the house of a nice bear family . . ."

When the story was finished Emma yawned and Beth said she had to put her to bed.

"When are you coming back? You know I'm sorry, right?"

Beth lowered her voice. "To be honest, I'm getting a bit fed up here. Dad's always going on about business administration and how I'm wasting my time doing an English degree."

"Come back then! I'll come down tonight and get you both."

"In this weather?"

"It's no problem."

"No. My Auntie Anne and Uncle Robert are coming over on the ferry tonight. They haven't seen the baby. They'll be staying for a couple of days and by then I'll be thoroughly sick of it here. Can you come and get me on Tuesday morning? I've got a tutorial on Wednesday and I can get the train up to Belfast and you can watch Emma, yeah?"

"So you'll come back and stay here?"

"We'll have to have a serious talk about our future."

"Of course! I'm all about serious. You know me. And like I say, I'm willing to move whenever you want."

"And there will be no more shouting or stress?"

"Listen, Beth, that morning you went down to Larne I had my RUC medical and I've been told to cut down on the drinking and the smokes and the stress and I've been doing it. I'm a new man."

"Sure you are, Sean Duffy."

"What's with you and the boats?"

"I've always sailed. You didn't know that?"

"No."

"I've got all these hidden depths you don't even know about. Some cop you are. This is Dad's new boat. It's a restoration job. I was going to take it out today, but it was impossible with the weather."

"We'll go out in the summer. I've never been sailing before. I imagine it'll be fun," I said, lying like a trooper.

"OK, Sean, I'll call you."

"Bye, Beth."

I hung up feeling happy. Two good phone calls with Beth in a row. DAADD getting us off the hook by sort of claiming responsibility for the Deauville murder, a possible eyewitness

. . . things were looking up.

I made a hot whisky, heated up some soup for dinner, put on Ella Fitzgerald and sat in the living room with the TV on mute.

I quickly unmuted the telly. Something had happened in what looked like Gibraltar.

People had been killed. The killers had been, who? Men in balaclavas. Terrorists? No. No, the killers had been SAS soldiers and the people they'd shot were an IRA active service unit.

Damn it, I was going to have to pay attention to this. I put down the whisky and got my notebook. The BBC was being cagey with the details but RTE from Dublin were jumping right in. They said that the IRA unit had comprised two men and a woman and that they'd been planning to blow up some sort of British army post while the guard was being changed. RTE didn't know the men's names but the woman was a young girl from Northern Ireland called Mairéad Farrell.

The BBC said that the IRA unit had been killed in a gun battle. RTE were saying that they had been executed while attempting to surrender.

"Jesus, I don't like the sound of this," I said to the cat. "Thank God the weather's terrible." Snow and rain would deter the rioters, but for how long?

I turned the TV off and listened to comfort music while I drank hot whiskies and had only my second and third ciggies of the day.

Comfort music? Standard stuff: Schubert, Mozart, Mendelssohn.

I lit the paraffin heater and went to bed.

While the snow fell I found myself dreaming of Spain. I dreamed of palm trees and beaches and copper-haired Mairéad Farrell spread-eagled on the street in a white martyr's blouse and Red Army Faction flares.

I dreamed of the nameless, faceless SAS men celebrating in their army barracks in Hereford. Woodbines and Carling

Black Label and rugby songs. I dreamed of Tariq ibn-Ziyad, the Conqueror, and I dreamed of the great rock named forever in his honour, Tariq's mountain, Jabal Tāriq: جبل طارق

I dreamed of Molly Bloom, transported to grey Dublin, lying in her marriage bed, day-dreaming of her past erotic adventures in a sunlit Gibraltar.

A dream within a dream.

. . . and the sea, the sea crimson sometimes like fire and the glorious sunsets and the fig trees in the Alameda gardens yes and all the queer little streets and the pink and blue and yellow houses and the rosegardens and the jessamine and geraniums and cactuses . . . Yes. Oh yes. Yes.

Mairéad and Molly. Molly and Mairéad. Two lost girls. The blood coiling under Mairéad's twisted body, merging with the scarlet of her hair; Molly's hair splayed over the white of her wedding sheets.

I woke before the dawn and lay in the darkness watching the indigo flame of the paraffin heater. I was unsettled by the dream and annoyed at myself for dreaming it as I trumped down the stairs wrapped in the duvet to stoke the fire. I put on the kettle and took a puff on my inhaler. As if completing a conversation I explained things to the cat. "As you well know when your legs twitch after your phantom mice it's only a silly dream, lacking divinatory or prophetic or any other content, and a cat of your standing in the feline community and a man of my age should not be vexed by the foolishness of dreams."

The foolishness of dreams which, in this bellicose corner of this malicious little island, had the ability to change instantly into nightmares.

11: THE LADY VANISHES

Nothing under the Beemer. Careful drive along Coronation Road to the station. Everyone in the barracks full of the talk of Gibraltar. Undisguised triumph. *We got three of those IRA bastards, that'll learn them.* No appreciation that this small tactical success will have strategic consequences. As soon as the weather improves there will be riots in West Belfast and when the coffins come back for burial there will be three massive IRA funerals. So often in Ulster a tactical success led to a strategic reverse and vice versa.

I flicked through the morning papers. Mairéad Farrell did not, in fact, have red hair. It was more of a chestnutty brown. She seemed like a nice girl. They all seem like nice girls. If the SAS and MI6 were telling the truth they were plotting to blow up the changing of the ceremonial guard. Twenty young men and God knows how many civilians. *If* the SAS and MI6 were telling the truth. I'd met spooks and blades and they lied like they had invented the concept.

I'd only just taken a sip of my coffee when Chief Inspector McArthur came in with a huge grin on his face.

"Did you see the *Newsletter* this morning, Duffy?"

"No."

He handed me the paper. The headline and pages one to three were all Gibraltar, but lo and behold there was a big picture of him on page four taking the heroin out of Francis Deauville's lock-up.

"This is great for us, Duffy. For the whole station. No more scary phone calls from the Chief Constable now, eh?"

I let him speak and smiled and nodded in the right places. He was right, though – better to have the press off your back than on. When he was gone I rounded up Lawson and McCrabban for the drive to Antrim RUC. We had a picture to show Mrs Deauville now and maybe she would remember something.

Lawson made the courtesy call to Antrim RUC to let them know we were on our way but when he put the phone down he looked puzzled.

"What's the matter?" I asked.

"She made bail," he said.

"Mrs Deauville?"

"Yeah."

"Who paid it?"

"Her legal aid solicitor got an envelope full of fifty pound notes and a typed note that explained that this was for Elena Deauville's bail."

The envelope full of fifties and the note were standard paramilitary procedure, but why would the paramilitaries bail her? Perhaps she or her husband had set up this arrangement for herself in the event of her arrest?

"We better go talk to Mrs Deauville and find out who her mysterious benefactor is. At what time was she bailed this morning?"

Lawson looked pale. "It was last night. At 9pm. The solicitor wanted her out pronto so she walked the bail money over to the barracks."

"And the police just released her?"

"They had to."

"And no one told us?"

"Nope. But in their defence last night everybody was pretty

preoccupied by the news from Gibraltar."

"How is that a defence?"

"Uhm, well—"

"What if she's skipped?"

"They took her passport, didn't they?" McCrabban said.

"Why are we talking? Let's get over there."

We got in a Land Rover and drove up to Sunnylands estate but of course she wasn't there.

The police evidence tape was still across the door and I had to use my skeleton key to get in. There was no evidence of packing, her jewellery was still in the box upstairs. At the back of one we found a semi-secret drawer filled with twenty pound notes. She wouldn't have forgotten that.

"Don't think she's been home at all," Lawson said.

"She hasn't. Come on. Let's find out where she did go."

Back to the barracks. I left a reservist at her house in case she did return. No direct flight to Bulgaria today but via London or Paris no probs with a duplicate passport. I circulated her description to the ports and airports. I called up O'Driscoll to get his take but he seemed to think it was no big deal.

"So what? She made bail. She'll still have to appear in court in two weeks."

"You don't get it, mate. She's not at home. She's flown the coop."

"And lose five grand bail? No way. They're in a council house living from benefit cheque to benefit cheque."

"They're major heroin smugglers, Seamus, for all we know they have fifty grand stashed away."

"You've always been a worrier, Duffy. She'll show up in court, you'll see."

I hung up on him. Seamus was a decent bloke but he had never been a top-quality peeler and his horse sense was way off on this case. There was something seriously wrong here.

"Get me her solicitor on the phone," I said to Lawson.

The solicitor was an old pro called Carol McCauley out of McCauley and Wright in Antrim. She filled me in on the bail envelope and the note. This was not the first time she'd had such an unusual bond payment and if these Troubles went on it wouldn't be the last.

"I'm not interested in the money, Carol, in fact I'm not even that interested in your client's career as a heroin smuggler—"

"She's been charged with obstruction of justice. That's all. There's no evidence of anything else."

"Which explains why the bail was a mere five grand."

"The magistrates listened to a load of circumstantial evidence from the RUC drugs squad—"

"Carol, look, as I say, I couldn't give a shit about the drugs or the bail money. I'm investigating her husband's death. Mrs Deauville may be in danger. She may have been a witness in her husband's murder. That's all I care about."

"So what is it you want to know?"

"What did she say to you about the murder?"

"She never spoke to me about the murder."

"And what did she say about the bail money? Where did it come from?"

"She said that she had no idea. She said that maybe some of Frank's friends had helped her out."

"That seems unlikely. He was an independent operator. After you got her out last night where did she go?"

"She asked to be left at Antrim bus station."

"And is that where you left her?"

"It is."

"And she got on a bus?"

"Uhm, no, I didn't actually see her get on a bus."

"Well you've been very helpful, we'll take it from there."

"Is everything all right? Do you think she's OK?"

"I have no idea but she didn't come home last night. If we're lucky she's just skipping out on the bail."

"And if we're unlucky?"

"She's dead."

I filled in Lawson and Crabbie and got them working the phones.

Yes, there was a 9.30pm bus from Antrim to Belfast, delayed until 10pm because of the snow. But there were only two passengers on that bus and both of them were men.

There were no trains running because of the snow.

We got in the Land Rover and drove up to Antrim. We showed Mrs Deauville's mug shot around the bus station and to the taxi drivers at the taxi rank. No one recalled seeing her. The bus station had a good CCTV system and because of all the hijackings in the early 80s all the Ulsterbuses did now too. A scan of the buses leaving Antrim between 9pm and midnight revealed no Elena Deauville.

"She didn't get a bus, she didn't get a taxi, she didn't get a train. What did she get?" I asked Crabbie.

"It's time we got serious. Up the alert level at Interpol and you and I will have to go through the security footage at Larne harbour from last night until this morning."

We drove to Larne Harbour and went through their tape. It was hard to say for certain but it seemed that no one resembling Elena Deauville got on the one ferry that had left last night before weather had cancelled the sailings. Because of the rough seas the boat had only attracted thirty passengers. Ten of those were women and none of those women resembled Elena.

"She could have been wearing a wig or disguised herself," Crabbie said and we went through the tape again to double check.

No Elena.

No Elena at the airport either.

There were many ways to get over the land border between Northern and Southern Ireland so it was possible that she'd slipped across to Eire. But who had driven her and where had they crossed on that snowy night with so many country roads closed?

"I don't understand it," Lawson said.

"I think I do," I said.

"Me too," Crabbie said.

"Well you first then, Crabman," I told him.

"Her husband's killer sent the bail money. And when she was bailed he followed her to the bus station in his car. It was snowing and the buses were delayed so he offered her a lift to Carrick."

"And then what?" Lawson said.

"He killed her," Crabbie said.

"Why?" Lawson gasped.

"He didn't like the fact that she was spending so much time in police custody? He was worried that if the charges started to mount up she would tell what she knew?" he suggested.

"What did she know?" Lawson asked.

"I have no idea," I said.

"She may have just skipped," Crabbie added. "Staying with a friend on a cold night. Maybe she'll show up tomorrow large as life."

"I hope to fuck she's gone to Bulgaria. We'll follow her and I'll charge three first-class plane tickets to Carrick RUC and when Kenny Dalziel comes back from his holidays he'll have a heart attack," I muttered.

We sat in the Incident Room to await developments.

There were no developments.

I called Beth's ma and told her I was gonna be at the station.

We watched TV. *Miami Vice* repeat on BBC2:

Brenda: "How do you go from this tranquillity to that violence?"

Sonny Crockett: "I usually take the Ferrari."

I sent Lawson home after the show and I went to my office to check on the border crossings. No sign of Elena Deauville.

Crabbie came in to see me before he went home.

"Any news of Mrs Deauville?"

"No. You want a drink?"

He shook his head.

"What do you think, Crabbie?"

He sat down opposite me. "My take: she didn't run. She's in a sheugh somewhere with a bullet in her."

"My take too. She knew something. I should have gotten it out of her."

"Don't blame yourself."

"I do."

He shook his head and stood up. "I hate to ask, but, uhm . . ."

"It's better. It was all a misunderstanding. She's coming back. I think."

"Well that's good."

"It is good. Joni Mitchell, you know?"

"What?"

"Big Yellow Taxi."

"What?"

"You better go, mate. Those roads are going to be bad tonight again."

"Aye. See you."

He left. More TV. An *Open University* programme on quince:

Guy with a beard: "Most varieties of quince are too hard, astringent and sour to eat raw unless 'bletted' (softened by frost and subsequent decay)."

I found myself falling asleep in my office chair. Doing that a lot lately. Probably because of repeated head trauma. I'd been knocked out more than the average peeler. Head trauma, asthma, stress – a bomb under your car: occupational hazards for your Northern Irish cop.

Woke up at one. Checked all the crossings and hospitals for Mrs Deauville. Nothing. Checked with the constable at her house. Nope.

Out to the car.

Talk radio.

DJ spouting bullshit about the Gibraltar killings without the ballast of anything resembling facts.

Pulled in to Coronation Road, nearly killing the cat.

I parked the Beemer and picked him up. "Used one of your nine lives, there, mate," I said.

Took the cat indoors and fed it and watched the snow come on again.

Joyce again. Dubliners snow. The snow general all over Ireland. Falling on Coronation Road and Carrick Castle and all over County Antrim.

Falling on the grave the honest men of Milltown Cemetery were digging for Mairéad Farrell.

And on the grave that a bad man of unknown origin was digging for Elena Deauville.

12: THE ANGRY FATHER

The next morning Lawson came into my office with a file.
"What's this?"

"Remember you asked me to look into all the recent heroin overdoses?"

"Yeah."

"Here's one for you that I missed initially. In Bangor last November young lad called Joshua Redmond has what in the papers is called a cocaine overdose. But nobody dies from a cocaine overdose – very few anyway – so I looked into the case. He actually died from a cocaine–heroin speedball. Father had an angry outburst at the funeral 'against drug dealers and their protectors'. Said they should all be killed. Few days later our friend Francis Deauville is told to leave Bangor by the UDA and the UVF."

"Tell me about this angry father."

"Lorry driver. Criminal record for GBH. Six three and in one of the mugshot photos he had prominent sideburns."

"Tell me about the GBH."

"Bar fight in Newry four years ago. Put a bloke in the hospital with a broken collar bone and another man with a fractured neck."

"He beat up two men?"

"Yup."

"Tell me about the kid."

"The kid was only fifteen. The parents were divorced and he was living with his mother in a different part of Bangor from his dad."

"It's got the feel of a wild goose hunt. Let's go see him anyway."

Beemer to Bangor through the North Down suburbs. A gentle part of the province with the nickname: "The Surrey of Northern Ireland".

Mr Redmond's flat, however, was in the Kilcooley Estate, which judging from the terrifying murals of gunmen everywhere was firmly in the control of the UDA.

Redmond's place wasn't hard to find: it was the one with the big rig parked outside.

Doorbell.

Game faces.

Barking Alsatian dog.

"Who the fuck is it?"

"It's the police. Carrickfergus RUC."

"Is this about my road tax?"

"No, it's about Francis Deauville."

He opened the door and kicked the dog behind him into a living room where it came to the window and salivated, growled and barked at us. Redmond was a big, hairy man who looked like Giant Haystacks, the wrestler from off the telly without Haystacks's charm and charisma. Bereaved father, though, so I was prepared to cut him a lot of slack.

"We're homicide detectives looking into Francis Deauville's death," I said.

"That scumbag?"

"You knew he was dead then?"

"Oh yes, I knew. Had a few beers that night."

"After your son died you threatened to kill the drug dealers who sold him the heroin."

"I did," he said grimly. "But I didn't kill that fucker Deauville. Wish I had. Wish I'd thought of it."

"Where were you last Wednesday night?"

"France, driving me lorry."

"Can you prove that?"

"Mais oui. Let me show you the paperwork."

He showed us the paperwork and yes he was in France at a weigh station in Dijon at midnight on the night of the killing.

"How do these weigh stations work?"

"You have to be there in person. They check your licence and weigh your vehicle."

I didn't even have to look at flight schedules to see that it was impossible to get from Dijon to Belfast in the time available. Mr Redmond was not the killer.

"What do you think?" he asked snatching the documentation back.

"You have a pretty good alibi," I said. "Maybe you hired someone to do it?"

"Do you have any children, Inspector Duffy?"

"A little girl. Emma. Not yet one."

He nodded from big sad brown eyes. "Wish I *had* killed Deauville. He was filth in human form. Off the record?"

"Off the record."

"If you find the killer tell me who it is and I'll buy him a drink," he said, his voice cracking.

I looked at Lawson, but Lawson was seeing what I was seeing. This was the face of an innocent man unless he too had rehearsed this scene for the benefit of the police, which it must be said, some people do.

"I'm really sorry about your son," I said and he could see that I was.

"Off the record again?"

"Sure."

"I loved my boy. He was a good lad. Fell in with a bad crowd round here. His mother couldn't cope. If I'd had custody I would have took him driving with me all over Europe. Shown him another way. Another world. I shouldn't have said anything at the funeral. Should have kept my mouth shut and bided me time. There's talking and there's action, isn't there? Knew a driver years ago in Birmingham. His daughter was beat into a coma by her boyfriend. Lovely wee lass. Smart, funny, very pretty. Now she's in a wheelchair, brain-damaged. Can't feed herself, can't talk. This guy – my mate – says nothing at the trial. Says nothing after the verdict. Nothing to the press. Just a humble wee man content to accept the justice of the court. The boyfriend gets three years in prison. His daughter has a life sentence. Their family is destroyed. So he waits. He waits and waits and of course the boyfriend is released after two years for good behaviour. Again my mate waits so it's not obvious. He finds out where the boy lives and he watches him and he waits. A year goes by after the boyfriend is out of prison and then he and his brother visit the boy in his new flat. They knock on his door and the lad opens it and they go to town on him with tire irons . . . That's the way to do it, Inspector Duffy. No threats, no outbursts at funerals. Don't draw attention to yourself. You wait and wait and when the time is right you strike. You'd do the same if someone harmed your Emma, wouldn't you, Inspector?"

"I would," I said immediately.

"We all would. You – the police, the courts, your job is to rob fathers of our right to natural justice. If I'd kept my mouth shut I could have murdered Deauville in due course. But somebody did it for me."

"Someone you know?"

"No."

"The wife, though. Killing her's not so easy is it?" I said. "Would you kill her as well?"

He shook his head. "Have a good day, Inspector," he said and closed the door.

On the ride back to Carrick I let Lawson drive while I thought. A vengeful parent might kill Deauville but you wouldn't kill him and then wait a couple of days and kill the wife too. Not out of revenge. Not after the blood pact had been fulfilled and honour satisfied. You'd kill Elena for different reasons. Because she knew something: she'd witnessed the killer stalking them, she'd seen the killer's car parked outside her house, her husband had confided in her that he'd had threats . . . something like that.

I went back to the station and read the transcripts of her two police interviews but there was nothing new in them.

O'Driscoll's Q&A had been about the drugs so that was excusable. This was on me. I had botched this one. I had had her in my interview room and I had let her go home without telling me everything she knew. It was my fault that the killer was going unpunished. It was my fault that Elena Deauville was dead.

13: THE PAPER, THE SCISSORS AND MICHAEL STONE

You know what I'm talking about. You've seen it before. You work the case from every angle but the case still dies. Like a cardiac team in casualty with the family just outside the glass we did everything we could for the Deauvilles. But Mr Deauville's murder went unsolved and Mrs Deauville's disappearance went unsolved. At any other time perhaps we could have generated some interest in the media but for the public in Belfast it was all Gibraltar all the time. The IRA, ahem, *volunteers* were being shipped home from the Rock – the funerals were going to be the biggest thing since Bobby Sands.

Things weren't so bleak for me, though. Beth returned with Emma no questions asked. If it had been a punishment it had been an effective one. If it had been Beth just getting a little breathing room it also had been effective. She seemed happier and I was relieved.

"So we'll start looking at houses then, shall we?" Beth said.

"We will."

My Coronation Road days were numbered.

I was relieved too that for now my name was out of the papers and I was down to four ciggies a day: after breakfast, lunch, dinner and before bed. Find me the Catholic RUC man that can do better.

But nothing changed the fact that the case was dead-ending.

No forensic or eyewitness testimony on Francis Deauville. Nothing at all about Elena. We dug into her background and through Interpol the Bulgarian police gave us what they had, which turned out to be very little. Ordinary childhood and high school. Excelled in English and history, had indeed met Francis Deauville where she claimed she had met him (at the ruins of a Roman town) and apparently fallen madly in love.

Francis's CV had more scope for enemies. All those heists over the water. Crooks always fell out over who fucked up in the jobs that went wrong and who got more than his share of the loot in the jobs that went right. Francis must have made many enemies in England. Any one of them could have come over on the boat to kill him.

But that wasn't it either.

This was local. This was personal. This was something specific about Francis himself. All my instincts told me that and the little clues told me that too.

So the days went on and the nights went on and there was no change. We were a small department and there were other cases. It wasn't time to put the Deauville file away but pounding the beat and working the phones was giving us nothing. Although I was wary of journalists I did a couple of interviews for the papers including an English-language Bulgarian paper called *The Sofia Echo*.

Ordinary day in the barracks. The snow long gone. Rain now. Warm drizzle.

"Phone call for you, Inspector Duffy," Sandra said.

"Lads, I better get this. To be continued."

I went to my office and picked up the receiver.

"Duffy, Carrick CID," I said.

"Hello, Sean. It's Pytor Yavarov."

"What can I do for you, Pytor?"

"I'd like to talk to you about the Elena Deauville disappearance."

"Do you have information?"

"I would prefer it if we talk in person."

"I can be in Dublin in two hours."

"I am already in Belfast. I do not want any nosy inquiries from my colleagues in the embassy if I am seen talking to a stranger who then turns out to be a Northern Irish policeman."

"OK, we'll meet in the centre of Belfast. But it's going to have to be a quick meeting. Those IRA funerals are this afternoon and traffic will be a nightmare."

"Do you know of a discreet place?"

"Let's meet in the last snug on the right of the Crown Bar in half an hour. OK if I bring Lawson and McCrabban?"

"Do you trust them?"

"With my life."

"I will see you in half an hour."

Twenty-seven minutes later Lawson, Crabbie and I walked into the Crown Bar and ordered three Guinnesses and three Irish stews.

Yavarov was waiting for us in the snug, huddled over a lager and vodka chaser. He was nattily dressed in a wool raincoat and a tweed jacket with a red cravat underneath. He declined a Guinness and a stew, even though we explained that that's what you ate and drank in here. The Crown was a Victorian saloon that still had its original gas lights and fixtures and fortunately for our purposes was equipped with many individual booths or "snugs" that allowed one privacy.

"So what's this all about?" I asked Yavarov.

"I read about Mrs Deauville's disappearance in *The Sofia Echo*," he began. "It is fortunate that I did so. No one told us in the embassy that she had gone missing."

"I contacted Interpol and I assumed they would have contacted you," I said, quick to defend my reputation against a charge of professional misconduct.

"Interpol did not contact us."

"Well, you know now. She's been missing for a week and there's no sign of her anywhere. We've checked the ferry ports and the airports and we're certain she didn't get out of Northern Ireland that way. The border's another matter. There are hundreds of unofficial crossing points and she could have used one of those."

"She could be alive?" Yavarov asked.

"She could be. She was last seen at a bus station in Antrim but she didn't get on any of the buses. Who knows, maybe a friend drove her over the border and she hid out in the Irish countryside before getting a plane somewhere."

"Why would she run away?"

"Because she was worried she was going to be charged with heroin trafficking? That's five to ten years in prison," Crabbie said.

"You had no evidence of her direct involvement in the drug trade," Yavarov said.

"So why do you think she ran?" I asked.

"If she ran it was because she did not trust the police to protect her," he said definitively.

"Protect her from what?"

"In Bulgaria the police can be bought and sold for a few Lev."

"The RUC is incorruptible," Crabbie said.

"That is not what I hear. I hear you work with Protestants to kill the IRA. I hear you let the IRA and the UVF divide up Belfast between them for the purpose of selling drugs and running protection rackets. I hear you let Protestant and Catholic gangsters kill drug dealers who do not pay them protection," Yavarov said.

Some of that, of course, was true.

"That may happen. But not in my manor. There are no free passes for murder in Carrickfergus," I insisted.

"You I trust to do the right thing, Duffy. Perhaps I would have kept this information to myself if I did not trust you," Yavarov said and finished his vodka. He took a sip of the nasty-looking lager.

"You have tried Harp?" he asked.

"Yes," we all said together.

"It is good, no?"

"Maybe it's an acquired taste," I said to be polite. (Belfast pub Harp was an acquired taste like coprophagia or getting pissed on by hookers.) "Now, Mr Yavarov, you've come a very long way this morning to tell us something. Why don't we end the small talk and you just tell us what it is you think we should know."

"When I met Mrs Deauville before you began your tape recording she told me something she did not wish to tell you."

"What?"

"The day her husband was killed Mrs Deauville and her husband were in the pub in Carrickfergus for a drink. When they walked home Mrs Deauville thought that someone was following them in a car. Mr Deauville told her that she was talking nonsense but she grew up in Bulgaria in the bad days. She knew when she was being followed."

"What car?"

"A blue Ford Escort."

"That's not as helpful as you think it is, Mr Yavarov. There must be 5,000 blue Ford Escorts in Ireland," Crabbie said.

"Perhaps this will help," Yavarov said, sliding across a piece of paper.

When I opened it it was a licence number: AIU 9785.

"That's a Derry licence plate," Crabbie said.

Yavarov looked at us and shrugged. "It may not mean anything."

He had nothing more to add but this was bloody gold.

"We'll certainly investigate it, Mr Yavarov. Now if I were you I'd get home, the IRA funerals for the three volun– people who were killed in Gibraltar are due to start in half an hour and I imagine the trains are going to be packed and the city is going to be one huge traffic jam."

He stood up. "I hope you will be able to find Elena Draganova."

I shook his outstretched hand. "I hope so too."

We saw Yavarov across the station and headed home in the Beemer before the funeral procession began.

When we got back to Carrick RUC we went straight to the computer in the Incident Room. Finding out who drove AIU 9785 was the work of a moment. A few mouse clicks on the Macintosh and a sift through the National Vehicle Registry database.

The car belonged to one Harold Selden, forty-five, who lived in the Scissors Area of the Creggan Estate, Derry.

"What's a lad from Derry doing all the way down in Carrickfergus?" McCrabban asked.

"What's a *Catholic* lad from Derry doing all the way down in a Protestant housing estate in Carrickfergus?" I countered. For if he lived in the Creggan he was definitely a Catholic as all the Prods had been driven out of that part of the city two decades ago.

"I think we can guess why he was so far out of his territory," Crabbie said.

"What?"

"Scouting a hit for the DAADD?" Crabbie suggested. "Smart play. Bring in an assassin from the outside who won't be recognised down the chip shop later."

"Maybe some eccentric assassin who likes to shoot his victims with a crossbow?" Lawson mused.

"Look him up on the criminal database, Lawson."

That also was the work of a moment. "No criminal record," Lawson said, with obvious disappointment.

"That doesn't necessarily mean he hasn't done anything," Crabbie said. "It could just mean that he's a good criminal who doesn't get caught."

"Who fancies a trip to Derry?" I said cheerfully.

This suggestion was not met with universal enthusiasm.

"Now?" Crabbie said.

"Why not. What else are we going to do?"

"It's such a hassle to get up there and the day's nearly over," Crabbie said.

"You're afraid, aren't you?"

"No. I'm not afraid of Derry. I've been there before."

"You can admit it. There's parts of Belfast that scare me, but Derry's great. Derry people are wonderful. Love to go back to Derry. Derry's my home."

"Yeah, cos nothing bad's ever happened in Derry," Lawson muttered.

"What's the matter? Are you afeared too?"

Lawson shook his head. "No, but Crabbie's right. It's getting late. Those big funerals are on. Shouldn't we let the local peelers bring him in for questioning?"

I shook my head. "Look at the pair of you. Well, I'm going out to the car. You're free to join me if you want."

Of course they both traipsed after me but I saw Crabbie check his sidearm twice and Lawson looked as pale as William Joyce when they took him to the drop box at Wandsworth Prison.

"If you're worried about the hour let's see if we can't light up the Glenshane Pass, eh?"

"Sean, don't kill us. I have three kids and Lawson's got his whole life ahead of him."

"Sensible speed boys. You know me."

It was eighty miles from Belfast to Derry on the M2 and the A6. A one hour and twenty minute run according to the Automobile Association. I did it in 59 minutes dead. The BMW 535i lapped it up like a kitten licking cream.

We stopped outside Harry Selden's house, a nice wee three-bedroom semi-detached job in the Scissors area of the Creggan. One of the nicer parts of the sprawling estate. By the murals all around this was heavy IRA land, but there were few wee muckers or watchers on the streets today.

"Maybe there's a football game on?" Crabbie suggested.

"Nah, around here everyone's glued to the telly watching the funerals."

We knocked on Harry Selden's door.

"Go away!" he said.

"It's the police," I said.

"The police? Now?"

"Yes."

We heard Mr Selden trump down the hall and violently open the door. I couldn't help but like Harry as soon as I saw him because he was a rotund man in a cardigan with thinning black hair and a jovial shine to his cheek. He had very dark eyes and little brown caterpillar eyebrows. He was about my height and we would have made a good Laurel and Hardy standing together if we'd put on 30s garb and he'd grown a bristle moustache. I brought to the forefront of my mind the possibility that he had murdered both Elena Deauville and her husband Francis and that took the edge off my admiration.

"Mind if I ask you a few questions, Mr Selden?"

"You know the funerals are about to start?"

"Sorry, I thought they'd be over by now."

"No. I was watching it. They're just finishing the service. Have you got any identification?"

I showed him my warrant card.

"You're a Catholic?" he said accusingly after reading my name.

"Yes."

He pointed his finger at me. "You as good as killed those kids in Gibraltar. That wee girl. You work for them uns that have done it. You know what you are?"

"A policeman come to ask you some questions?"

"A traitor."

You'd think they'd be more original with their dialogue. Like

I hadn't heard this a million times since I'd joined the force.

"Where were you on Wednesday the 2nd of March, Mr Selden?"

"I was in the hospital getting me appendix out."

"What hospital?"

"Altnagelvin."

"When did you enter the hospital?"

"The previous Friday. I took ill in the *council* chamber. It was an emergency."

"And on the Wednesday you were still in the hospital?"

"I was nearly in a bloody coma. I had septicaemia."

"You seem better now."

"Yeah, they finally let me out last Saturday. I was in hospital for an entire week. Missed a week of *council* business. What's this all about?"

"Can we come in and talk? Maybe a cup of tea?"

"No, you can stand there or you can fuck off. You're not coming in and you're not getting any tea. What's this about?"

"On Wednesday March 2nd your Ford Escort was seen in Sunnylands Estate, Carrickfergus, following a man who was murdered on Thursday morning. How do you explain that, Mr Selden?"

"I explain it very easily, Mr Duffy. My car was stolen from right in front of my house while I was in the bloody hospital."

"And did you tell the police it was stolen?" Crabbie asked.

"Oh, it speaks, does it? Does the wee blond one speak as well, or is he your ventriloquist's dummy?"

"Can you answer Sergeant McCrabban's question?"

"Why didn't I report my stolen car to the police? Because I have no truck with the police. I don't recognise the RUC as a police force. It is an arm of the British state. An occupying army. No, *Sergeant McCrabban*, I will never report anything to the police or go into a police station for any reason."

"That's convenient. So you say your car was stolen but there's no proof that it was stolen," I said.

"Who said there was no proof? I never said that. I just said I never told the police. I told the insurance company, though. And I've got the claims forms to prove it. Just hold on a wee minute there and I'll get them."

He slammed the door in our faces and returned a moment later with the insurance form that certified the fact that he had reported his car stolen on March 5th, the day he had gotten out of hospital. Northern Ireland was one of the few places in the world where you didn't need a formal police report for stolen property because so many people refused, like old Harry, to have anything to do with the RUC.

"So you get out of hospital and you notice your car was gone and you immediately called the insurance company, is that right?" I asked.

"That's right. But my mother who lives with me noticed that the car had been gone for about four days. She doesn't remember when. She hasn't been too well herself. A stroke."

"I'm sorry to hear that."

I showed the form to Crabbie, who read it and nodded. He passed it to Lawson who also read it.

"Now, do you mind, I want to watch the TV and me mum will want her tea."

"I just have a few more questions," I said.

"Do you know who I am?" Selden said, snatching the form back from Lawson.

"Harold Selden of the Creggan Estate?"

"*Councillor* Harold Selden of Derry City Council. And your harassment will not go unnoticed at the next Derry City Council meeting, Inspector Sean Duffy of Carrickfergus CID."

Another door slam.

"What was that you were saying about Derry people being wonderful, sir?" Lawson said.

I turned to McCrabban. "He's developing quite the lip, young

Lawson, isn't he?"

"Aye. I don't entirely approve of that," Crabbie said.

Quick drive to check on Selden's story at the hospital. Ruptured appendix, blood poisoning, finally released from the hospital on the Saturday morning – a full 48 hours after Deauville's death.

"Pretty good alibi that, in a coma, in hospital, in Derry," McCrabban said.

"Indeed," I agreed.

Silent drive home in the car.

Snow flurries. No radio reception to speak of.

"He doesn't look a bit like the artist's sketch, anyway," Crabbie announced as we neared Carrick. "The strange, tall DAADD assassin who eccentrically has drinks with the person he later assassinates."

"Aye, none of it really fits," I agreed and dropped the lads at the station before heading up Coronation Road.

Beth met me in the hall with a can of Bass. Now that I had formally committed to leaving this street, she was much happier. This estate, these people, were only temporary constructs to be put up with for a while. My class-war comments had hurt her too and she was pretending not to be mortified by these DUP-voting, country-music-listening, self-immolating-in-chip-pan-fire Proddies.

"Did you take your inhaler?" Beth asked.

"I did."

"And no cigarettes?"

"No. Only two. Thank God I've been busy, how does anyone quit smoking when you've got nothing to occupy your mind?"

"Don't ask me, I never started. How'd the funerals go in Belfast?"

"Don't ask me. I was only there for half an hour and then we went up to Derry."

"Derry? Really?"

"Yup."

"That was a fast run there and back."

"Thank you. Glad somebody appreciates it. What have you been doing all day?"

"Watching your offspring. Reading. Which I'm going to get back to. Watch Emma, will you?"

"My pleasure."

I sat in the living room by the fire and played with Emma. Put the record player on. "This, Emma, is Luigi Boccherini, now people are going to tell you that he's courtly, old-fashioned, even boring, but you just listen to the warmth of that melody, eh?"

Emma was ignoring me and trying to choke herself to death on a Lego brick. I removed the brick from her gob and helped her make a tower. Warm house, girlfriend, baby girl and kitty – what more could a man ask for? Yeah, the missus was a bit on the high-maintenance side but I was fighting an age gap. Nah, take your pleasures where you find them and this was the good life.

At 6pm I made us some dinner, put on the BBC news and my jaw dropped.

It was on every channel.

I called Crabbie immediately. "Are you watching this?"

"I was just going to pick up the phone and call you," he said.

The IRA funerals at Milltown Cemetery in Belfast had been attacked by a rogue, presumably deranged, Loyalist gunman called Michael Stone. He had fired an automatic pistol into the crowd of mourners and thrown hand grenades at Gerry Adams and Martin McGuinness. Three were dead and dozens were wounded. It could have been many more. And what made it worse, somehow, was that the whole thing had been captured live on television. Michael Stone had thrown his grenades and run towards the motorway where the crowd had caught up with him and almost beat him to death.

It was the worst incident of the Troubles since the Enniskillen bombing back in November when the IRA had blown up a dozen civilian mourners at a Remembrance Sunday service. That had been a bad one. The father of a nurse who'd been murdered – Marie Wilson – had gone on Irish television and publicly forgiven the bombers in an act of Christian charity. This had shamed the IRA and since then the bombings had wound down and we thought things were actually going to change. But I suppose nothing ever changed in this three-hundred-and-fifty-year-long blood feud.

Beth came into the living room. "What's happened?" she asked, seeing my face.

I told her. And we watched the news footage. "I hate this whole fucking country," she said and I could do nothing but nod my head in agreement.

14: A TASTE OF HONEY

The next morning we had to report for duty as normal but nothing felt normal about that day. We knew there were going to be riots and if the Belfast police were overwhelmed they would be calling for support from the surrounding districts.

I had a little meeting with Crabbie and Lawson in my office. "I imagine they'll be looking for officers to do riot duty. It'll be over-time and danger money but I don't want either of you doing it. I'm not banning you from doing it, but I'm telling you it's fairy gold. You can get seriously hurt. And we're detectives. A cut above the ordinary peeler, you know?"

It was the same speech I gave every year during Marching Season. There was an element of hypocrisy in it because sometimes I did riot duty and crowd-control duty when I wanted to (when Muhammad Ali came) and sometimes you couldn't help it, when we were ordered into a DMSU team; still, when we had the choice I preferred not to go and not to let my men go.

"It's easy money," Lawson said. "And some of them boys on the nights get triple and even quadruple time! That's barrister's money!"

"Let them get their triple time. We've a murder and a disappearance to solve."

"No one gives a crap about this particular murder. Everybody wants it to go away," Lawson grumbled.

What age was Lawson now? Twenty-one? Twenty-two? How did he get so old so quick?

"You're dismissed, Lawson."

After he'd left the office I poured Crabbie a glass of the sixteen-year-old Bowmore. "You really want to quit and leave him in charge? Dalziel running the station and him running CID?"

"I thought you liked him."

"I do like him, but if we both go this place is doomed."

Crabbie looked out the window at the rain lashing the Belfast docks. "It's all doomed anyway."

The phone rang.

"Inspector Duffy, CID," I said.

"This is Stephen O'Toole from the *Belfast Telegraph*, we're running a wee story this afternoon about police harassment of elected Sinn Fein councillors, care to comment?"

"Not much to say about that, Mr O'Toole, we here at Carrick RUC have excellent relations with all the elected representatives in Northern Ireland."

"So you're denying that you have a policy of harassing Sinn Fein councillors?"

"There is no such policy. Sometimes we have to question councillors or judges or even journalists in the course of an investigation but that's all. I don't have the time or inclination to harass anyone."

"Thanks very much, Inspector Duffy."

"Anytime."

He hung up. Crabbie gave me the old raised left eyebrow. "Trouble?" he asked.

"I hope not."

The story, when it appeared that afternoon, did not mention my name at all, but if I'd been a bit smarter I would have realised that this was merely a shot across the bows. Harry Selden was a man with pull.

Two days after the Michael Stone incident there was another

horrific encounter on live TV. Two British army corporals from the signals regiment took a wrong turn into another IRA funeral. When they tried to reverse out of the street, the crowd seized them, pulled them from their cars, stripped them and lynched them on live TV.

That night the Protestant and Catholic districts of Belfast *both* came out in riot.

Beth was shocked. She had only hazy memories of the early 70s. She didn't know things could get this bad.

"Maybe building this house is a bad idea, Sean, maybe what's best for Emma is to get out of Ireland completely."

"What do you mean?"

"Everything's falling apart. All the smart people are getting out. Both my brothers have gone, Dad's thinking of selling the business."

"I'll admit to having had similar thoughts."

"Is it too late for you to get into the Met?"

"The Metropolitan Police? Yeah, it's too late. I'm thirty-eight now. They don't take new recruits aged thirty-eight."

"But you're not a new recruit, you could join as a detective, as a detective inspector."

"I knew one guy who managed to pull that off," I said thinking of Tony McIlroy. "But for that to work you need influence."

"Daddy's rich."

"I mean influence over the water. The Met's not going to take me ... What would you do in London?"

"Anything. As long as it was safe. Look at Kenneth Branagh's parents. They did the right thing. They got him out."

"You might be right, Beth," I said reflectively. "I've done my bit here in Northern Ireland and I've achieved nothing."

Next day I let Crabbie and Lawson volunteer for this mythical quadruple-time riot pay while I drove up to Derry again and parked the car just down the street from Councillor Selden's house.

I followed him on his rounds to the Sinn Fein Advice Centre and to the Spar Supermarket and to the butchers. Nothing interesting. Nothing untoward. But a couple of times he doubled back to see if he was being followed, which *was* interesting.

I drove over to the infamous Strand Road police station, introduced myself and asked for the intel officer. A Detective Sergeant called Linda Quinn (a woman *and* a Catholic no less) gave me some interesting stuff about Selden that wasn't in the files.

"Oh yes, we're pretty sure that Selden's a player," she said with satisfaction, in a soft County Armagh accent.

"IRA?"

"IRA indeed."

"How high up?"

"Oh, not very high. He's getting on a bit. Forty-three, I think. If you haven't made command by forty you sort of take a back seat."

"What about DAADD?"

"What's that?"

"Direct Action Against Drug Dealers."

"Oh yes, those fellows. No, they don't have much of a presence in Derry. For the moment anyway. DAADD's more of a Belfast group. Up here the IRA just kills or kneecaps the drug dealers that have upset them. They don't need a cover organisation in Derry, they've already got the public on their side."

"I know, I almost joined myself after Bloody Sunday."

"So that's something you and Selden have in common, then."

"What?"

"He was in the police. He joined the IRA after Bloody Sunday."

"He was in the police?"

"Didn't you know that?"

"No."

"Well, not the real police, the B Specials."

"The B Specials?"

"They were a reserve force in the 1960s. They were notorious for—"

"I know what they are. This is too weird to be a coincidence."

I explained that Francis Deauville, my murder victim, had also been in the B Specials.

"Maybe not that weird a coincidence. There must be thousands of people who served in that force," Linda said.

"Where would I find the records of people who served in the B Specials? They're not in the RUC service files."

"You'd have to go to the records office in Belfast. All those old paper files. Probably all falling apart. In fact, you'll probably find they have all been, quote, damaged in a flood, unquote, in case there's anything embarrassing in them."

"It's embarrassing enough that an ex B Special became an IRA player."

"There's more than you think. Bloody Sunday changed everything up here. But I'm glad I'm here, in Derry, not in Belfast with all that rioting. That's where you are, isn't it, Inspector Duffy?"

"Carrickfergus. But close enough." Hmmm, Harry Selden in the B Specials, just like poor old Francis Deauville. I thanked Sergeant Quinn and drove back to the Creggan to sit in front of Selden's house and think.

I'd only been there fifteen minutes when he came out of his house holding a paper cup and walked it over to the Beemer.

I wound down the window.

"I brought you a cup of tea, Inspector Duffy. It's a cold day to be sitting out here," he said.

"Thanks," I said taking the tea and putting it in the cup holder.

"Now, if you're interested I'll be home for about half an hour and then I'll be walking to the Sinn Fein Advice Centre for my weekly advice clinic. Then I'll be picking up some sausages for me mother at the Spar."

"How's she doing today?" I asked.

"Oh she's a little bit better today. She's improving rightly just like the doctor said she would."

"You do right by your mother, Mr Selden. It's nice to see," I said.

"You have to stick by your loved ones."

"Especially women. The way women are treated in this country. It's positively medieval."

"That's true. Look at poor Mairéad Farrell, shot by your friends in the SAS," he said.

"And look at poor Marie Wilson. Blown up by an IRA bomb while laying a wreath for those who fought against Hitler . . . oh, silly me, I forgot, the IRA was on the same side as Hitler. They conveniently forget that little fact in the Sinn Fein manifestos, don't they?"

His lips thinned and he did not reply.

"B Specials, eh?" I said.

"What's that?"

"You were in the B Specials."

"Where did you get that information?"

"Is it true?"

"For a very brief time before the Troubles began I had a part-time job as a—"

"Do your friends in the IRA know about this curious career choice of yours?"

"I don't have any friends in the IRA. I'm a Sinn Fein councillor, in case you have forgotten."

"My memory would really have to be going bad – you've reminded me of it often enough."

"A councillor cannot be harassed by a policeman, not if the policeman wants to stay out of the newspapers."

I laughed at him. "Do your research! It's a bit late for that. Tell me, did you serve with Francis Deauville in the Specials? Is that how you know him?"

"I don't know any Francis Deauville."

"Sure you do. He was on the six o'clock news. The IRA shot him because he was a heroin dealer. Interesting that you would deny knowing him, though. Interesting that your car would make its way from this safe little street all the way down to the twisty dangerous streets of Sunnylands Estate in Carrickfergus," I said.

"What are you implying, Inspector Duffy? Are you implying that I crawled out of my sick bed, somehow got all the way to Carrickfergus to murder a man I don't know for reasons that are oblique and all this without any of my doctors or nurses noticing?" Harry asked, his plump jovial face assuming a sinister aspect. He'd been getting gradually bigger and paler as the conversation had gone on and now when he leaned back on his heels he wasn't Oliver Hardy at all. Now he was Mr Potter from *It's A Wonderful Life* or maybe even Sydney Greenstreet from *The Maltese Falcon*. Like many big, heavy men he was light on his toes. Dainty, almost. I liked that. I opened the car door, got out and stood facing him.

"I'm implying that you had something to go with Francis Deauville's death. I'm implying that had something to do with Elena Deauville's disappearance. Another woman who was not treated well on this fair isle."

"Me? You're accusing me, a councillor on Derry City Council?"

"I'm accusing you, a player in the IRA."

"That's a serious charge."

"I'm a serious man."

He stared at me for a minute and then walked away in disgust. Halfway across the street he turned to face me. "I'm a serious man too," he said.

When he'd gone back indoors I threw the tea out the window. If it hadn't contained piss, spit or poison I was a Chinaman.

I looked at my watch. It was nearly three. Might as well have a quick pint and call it a day and go home for me tea. No point staking out Selden's house any more, not when he'd made me and probably already had his goons following me.

I drove to a phonebox and called Beth.

"Hello?"

"Beth, it's me, I'm up in Derry, but it's a bust up here so I'm coming home."

"Thank God you're not in Belfast. There have been terrible riots. It's on the news."

"I think Lawson's up there. I hope he's all right."

"Lawson, yes. We really should have all your colleagues round for dinner some night. We've never done that and we should. And your boss too."

"Sounds like the sort of thing married couples do."

"It does," she agreed.

"Is that a proposal? I think you missed Leap Day."

"I did, didn't I?"

"I can't keep track of you. One minute you're for leaving the country and having me join the Met and the next you want my boss round for tea so we can brown-nose him."

She bit her lip and nodded. "You're right. I have to make my mind up. We both have to do a lot of thinking about the future. Anyway, I have to go, Sean, Emma's at Jollytots and it's after three. I'm picking her up but I'm having Janette Campbell watch her while I go to the library to work. OK to get your own dinner tonight?"

"That's fine. Maybe I'll make us something."

"Ooh, I'd like that. Bye."

"Love you."

"Love you too."

Love you too, eh?

The whole province can go to hell but I got an "I love you too." Those few days at her parents' had maybe been her "Big Yellow Taxi" moment too.

I drove to the Joyce Cary pub for a quiet pint before hitting the bleak treeless joys of the A6 again.

The place was deserted but it would fill up at quitting time.

I ordered a Guinness. "You wouldn't have any food, would you?" I asked.

"*An rud a lionas an tsuil lionann se an croi,*" he said.

"Well I've an eye for grub if you've got any."

"There's only the lentil soup left. Vegetarian. Vegan, actually, if you can believe it."

"Sounds horrible. I'll take it."

I ate the soup and drank the Guinness. A pretty young woman with what appeared to be a black eye came in, ordered a gin and tonic and sat by herself in the corner.

A few minutes later, from a different part of the pub, a young man came over to the bar to order a drink, but when he noticed the young woman he left the bar and sat down at her table opposite her.

I sighed inwardly. Men. They were all fucking clueless.

The young man started pestering the young woman, who was actually shaking now. I put down my soup spoon and walked over.

"Oi mate, take it easy, she just wants to be left alone," I said.

"How is it any of your business, pal?"

"Come on, mate. Just head on. You really don't want to do this."

If it was Carrick, or even Belfast, I would have flashed my warrant card but you didn't do that kind of thing around here.

"Do you want to go outside and discuss it?" he said.

"No, I don't. Move on, son, look at her, she wants a bit of peace and quiet, OK?"

One of his fingers poked me in the chest right in the middle of my Che Guevara T-shirt. His big greasy paw on my T-shirt? I grabbed his wrist with my left hand and bent the finger back with my right. He gasped in pain.

"Just go home, son," I whispered.

"OK, OK, let go!"

He scurried out of there and I said "excuse me" to the girl and returned to the dregs of my pint.

Five minutes later she was standing next to me at the bar. In the Jameson mirror I could see that she'd been very attractive before the punch in the face. Very attractive after the punch in the face. Dark curly hair, blue eyes, pale. A very Derry look. She had a handbag and a shopping bag and nothing else.

"That was kind of you," she said. "I didn't need that aggravation after the day I've had."

"Do you have a place to go tonight?"

"Yes, I'm going to stay with my friend Siobhan. If he comes looking for me he'll never look for me there. He'll think I'm with my mum and dad but I won't be. I'll be at Siobhan's. She's a friend from work. He doesn't know her."

"That's a good plan," I said.

"Siobhan's ma is a social worker and she's got connections with the police. She can get me one of them what do you call them things? Restriction order?"

"Restraining order."

"Aye, one of them."

"Yeah, that's the way to go about it. Stay with someone he doesn't know and let the courts and the police handle the whole thing. Smart thinking."

"I'm Mary, by the way."

"I'm Sean."

She gave me a frail, ashamed smile. "I couldn't ask you for one more big favour though, Sean, could I?"

"How much do you need?"

"Oh, it's not that. I just want to go home and get some clothes for work. He probably won't be there. He doesn't knock off *his* work until five. But if he is home he'll fucking give me a hammering, so he will."

"Where is this place?"

"Dungiven Street. Round the corner. Do you know it?"

"Aye, I know it."

I looked at my watch. It was nearly 4 now.

"If we're going to do this we need to do it right now. Can you be in and out in fifteen minutes? I really don't want a confrontation."

"I can be in and out in five."

"That's good. Where does your friend Siobhan live?"

"Siobhan . . . Oh, she's out near Altnagelvin."

"I know where that is, too. I can run you over."

"I don't want to put you to any trouble."

"It's no trouble, it's on my way back to Belfast. Let me call home first."

I put fifty pence in the bar phone and called home.

Janette Campbell was over babysitting. "Hello?" Janette said.

"Janette, it's Sean, there shouldn't be any hassles but I may be a wee bit delayed in Derry. Can you tell Beth?"

"You're in Derry and might be delayed. Is that the message?"

"Yeah. I should be home on time, but you never know."

"OK, Sean."

I hung up and walked back over to Mary. "Come on, love, let's get this show on the road before your husband gets back."

"He's not my husband. I wouldn't marry the likes of him. Just my boyfriend. Ex-boyfriend."

We walked out to the Beemer. I pretended to drop my lighter and looked underneath it for bombs. No bombs. We drove out to Dungiven Street. Quiet little residential block of redbrick back to backs. We walked to the front door and she gingerly took out her key and put it in the lock. She turned the key and leaned in the doorway with a whispered "Nate? Nate?"

She turned to me "No Nate," she said.

I looked at my watch again. "Fifteen minutes, mind. It'll be better for all of us if he never knew you were here."

I followed her into the hall.

They did it very professionally indeed.

A man was waiting behind the door with a sawn-off shotgun. Another man came out of the side room with a pistol. Both men were wearing balaclavas. Both guns were pointing only at me. Mary walked along the hall, into the kitchen and straight out the back door of the house without turning her head once to look at me.

"Don't move," the man with the pistol said. "When we tell you to, we want you to lie down on the floor."

There was no play that wouldn't result in my immediate death. I put my hands up and when ordered to I lay down on the floor with my hands behind my back.

They stripped me of my weapon.

They handcuffed me and took my wallet and the knife in my sock.

Classic honey trap. Oh Duffy. Eejits fell for honey traps, not you. Not an experienced peeler like you.

15: THAT PETROL EMOTION

Things are different in the movies. When the IRA take a policeman or a soldier hostage in the pictures what follows is an often philosophical and historical argument about the British presence in Ireland and the crimes the Brits have committed against Irish rebels. In real life what happened was what had happened to the two corporals in West Belfast: the hostage is stripped and beaten and then summarily executed. There's no philosophy, no history, just a savage beating and then a bullet in the brain.

If the IRA want specific intelligence from the hostage then there will, of course, be graphic physical torture until the victim tells them everything he or she knows. Hundreds of tortured victims had been found over the years lying by the side of the road or buried in shallow graves.

I had seen bodies where the paramilitaries had drilled into victims' kneecaps, wrists and ankles. I'd seen bodies where the eyeballs had been gouged out, where the victim's feet had been blowtorched, or where the victim had been castrated and forced to eat their own genitalia until they'd choked to death. None of this was necessary. That initial blow torch to the feet would make anyone talk. The rest was just for the sadistic pleasure of the torturers.

I knew all this and I knew there was absolutely no point trying to lie.

Truth right from the start, that was the way to go.

It wouldn't stop them hurting me. It wouldn't stop me from being terrified but it was a *tactic* and in a situation like that you need to cling to something. I decided to cling to truth.

A hood was thrown over my head and I was bundled outside to a waiting car. I was chucked in the boot and driven a short distance.

Taken out, dragged to a house and sat on a chair in the middle of a room with several people already in it. I could hear a petrol can being sloshed around in the background. Dousing someone in petrol and threatening to burn them alive was another old torturers' trick. I didn't want that, either.

"There's no need for the petrol or anything else. I'll tell you everything you want to know," I said.

"OK. What's your name?" a voice asked.

"Sean Duffy of Carrickfergus RUC."

"So you're admitting that you're a policeman then?"

"I am."

Grumbling and muttering from those assembled in the room. He's admitted he's a peeler: what else needs to be said?

"Why were you in Derry?" a different voice asked.

"I was investigating the murder of Francis Deauville and the disappearance of Elena Deauville in Carrickfergus."

"Who are they?"

"Francis Deauville was a heroin dealer probably executed by DAADD. Elena Deauville was his wife, who went missing."

"What's the Derry connection?"

"A car belonging to Harry Selden was spotted in the vicinity of Deauville's house shortly before his murder. The car was following Deauville."

"Harry Selden?"

"Aye."

More muttering from the men in the room. Four distinct voices, possibly five.

"Don't lie," a voice said.

"I'm not lying."

"We won't hesitate to torture you if we have to to get you to tell the truth."

"I believe you," I said.

"We've got a can of petrol here and we're in a derelict house. We could just pour this over you, light a match and leave."

"I smell the petrol. I know you could do that. Please don't! I'm telling you the truth!"

Silence and this was more terrifying than the questions. There could be a gun at my temple right now and I wouldn't even know it.

I was afraid of the darkness.

Afraid of the pain.

My whole body began to tremble. I was having trouble breathing.

"I'm having trouble breathing," I said.

"You'll be having more trouble breathing in an hour or so," a voice said.

A few guffaws.

"You know Harry Selden's a councillor, don't you?" a voice said, a different voice, higher-pitched but vibrating with authority. It was a voice I recognised from the TV. This was almost certainly ****** **********, the IRA commander in the city and a prominent leader in Sinn Fein.

"He may have mentioned that to me," I said.

"What exactly is his connection to this murder case?"

"All we know is that his car showed up in Carrick and he may have been following the victim. But Selden says his car was stolen."

"Was his car stolen?"

"Apparently it was. He put in an insurance claim, although he didn't report the car stolen to the police."

"He wouldn't go to the police."

"That's what he said."

"It sounds to me, Inspector Duffy, that this wee trip up here was a wild goose chase," ****** ********** said.

"That may be the case."

"You're a very brave man driving around the Bogside in an unmarked police car. Very brave or very stupid."

"Very stupid it turns out."

"You're from Derry though, are you? That's a Derry accent is it?"

"I went to school here."

"And you're Catholic."

"Yes."

"A Catholic policeman."

"Yes."

"You know there's a bounty on Catholic RUC men."

"I know."

"You don't seem particularly scared."

"I'm fucking terrified. I have a wife and a kid. A little girl. She's just begun talking and walking."

"We all have wives and kids . . . All right, time's a factor here. I don't think we need to send a message with this one. He won't give us any trouble . . . You won't give us any trouble, will you, Sean Duffy?"

"I won't be any trouble."

"So you'd appreciate it if we didn't set on you on fire or didn't beat the shit out of you?"

"I'd very much appreciate that."

"Are your parents alive?"

"Yes."

"I'm sure your mother would be happy to know that you didn't suffer."

"Yes."

"There's plenty here who would love to use you to get revenge for what happened in Gibraltar and what happened at Milltown Cemetery."

"I know."

"But if you're a good lad and just do everything everyone tells you and don't play silly buggers I can promise you a quick and painless death and a body that won't upset your wife or mother if it ever gets found. That's the best offer you're going to get today. Fair enough?"

I swallowed hard. I had one play and it wasn't much of a play. I'd been to school with Ken Kirkpatrick who was now the IRA quartermaster in Derry. And I'd been Deputy Head Boy to Dermot McCann when he was Head Boy. Dermot was an IRA martyr who'd nearly killed Mrs Thatcher in Brighton (fortunately no one knew my part in that affair).

"Look, I don't know if it'll help but Ken Kirkpatrick knows me. He knows I'm not a bad guy."

"You know Ken Kirkpatrick?"

"I went to school with him. I went to school with Ken Kirkpatrick and Dermot McCann."

"Dermot's no longer with us."

"I know, but if you talk to Ken—"

"We're not talking to anybody! I'm in charge here. Now, I've offered you a nice little arrangement. You be quiet and do as you're told and you go gentle into the good night. If you start to get on my nerves it's the petrol can. Fair enough?"

"Fair enough," I said.

"Right, well I'll say goodbye then, Sean. Another team will be along in a few hours to take you out of here. The big lad here will be watching you until they come. His instructions are very clear: if you cry out or move from that chair he'll shoot you on the spot. If you try to bribe him or try to talk your way out of it or ask for a glass of water or open your mouth at all he'll shoot on the spot. That's clear, isn't it?"

"Very clear."

"Good. Come on, lads."

Everyone left the room except for the Big Lad. I could hear

him breathing and turning the pages of a newspaper. I waited for a count of two hundred after they'd gone before I tried speaking to him.

"What are you reading?" I attempted.

"Sport."

"Oh yeah? I'm a big Hugh McIlvanney fan myself."

"Not that. *Roy of the Rovers*."

I wanted to connect with the Big Lad but I wasn't exactly a regular reader of *Roy of the Rovers*.

"Haven't read it for a while. Is Ben Galloway still Roy's manager?"

"Ben Galloway?"

"Yeah, sort of a Bill Shankly figure?"

"Bill Shankly?"

"The Liverpool manager?"

"Are you a Liverpool fan?" he asked.

"Yeah, are you?"

The Big Lad got up from his chair and leaned real close to my head. "I'm Man United. Fucking hate Liverpool. And I fucking hate you, Duffy."

He banged the jerry can off the side off my head. "You want this petrol all over your fucking face?"

"No."

"One more word out of you and it's human torch time. Get me?"

"Aye. I get you."

Several hours later a different five-man team took me from the Big Lad and threw me in the boot of a big Volvo Estate.

There was much discussion and some argument and finally they got going and drove me way out into the middle of nowhere into the yellow dark, the red dark, and the deep blue dark . . .

16: OUT HERE IN THE WOODS

I had fallen and I couldn't breathe and they were going to shoot me. All I had to do was close my eyes and await the nothingness. How easy that would be.

And I was so tired after all these years of this.

Being a peeler.

Being a peeler in the police force with the highest mortality rate in the world. Hated by all sides. Your life on the line every day. It was no surprise that it was ending this way. In a shallow grave in the woods. Killed by half-baked, unprofessional PIRA volunteers: a geography teacher, a stupid young man and a silly girl.

Close my eyes, check out, leave them all behind . . .

But Emma.

Emma's face.

And Beth.

Open my eyes. Hoist myself up onto my knees. In front of me black soil and under it a line of chalk and under that . . .

"You have to give me a moment to make my contrition!" I demanded.

"What did you say?" the woman asked.

"You have to give me a moment to make my contrition. And then you can shoot me in a State of Grace," I said, breathing deep, clearing my lungs and clasping my hands together in prayer.

"He's a Catholic?" the woman asked, shocked.

"Didn't you know?" Tommy said.

"No. I thought he was a Prod."

"He's the lowest form of life there is that walks this earth. A Catholic RUC man," Tommy snarled.

"Allow me to make my peace, for God's sake," I said.

Hard-to-read expressions behind balaclavas, but she seemed upset and the other kid wasn't too happy either.

"Please! I'm from Derry, like you. Please. You have to give me a chance to make my peace," I said, breathing in hard again, clearing my lungs and shuffling closer to the chalky ground.

"No, pal. There's going to be no last-minute confession, no contrition, no State of Grace for you," Tommy said and raised the revolver.

"What would Dr Martin say about that?" I attempted, naming the headmaster of St Malachy's where Tommy could have been a teacher.

The revolver twitched. Tommy's eyes widened under the mask.

A lucky guess.

The woman looked at Tommy and then back at me.

"What did you say?" she asked.

"We know all about you Tommy, who you work for, we've been watching all of you," I said.

"You've been watching us?" the woman said, aghast.

"What else does he know?" the young man asked.

"He doesn't know fucking anything!" Tommy said. "He's just playing for time."

I put my hands together in prayer. They were still sore from the handcuffs but I'd been uncuffed for almost ten minutes now and the blood had returned to my fingertips. "It's too late for me, I can see that," I began. "But you'se are all going to go down for killing me. For certain. Now if you don't mind I'm just going to compose myself: *actiones nostras, quaesumus Domine, aspirando*

praeveni et adiuvando prosequere: ut cuncta nosta oratio et oper-
atio a te semper incipiat et per ta coepta finiatur . . ."

The woman was looking at me, appalled, she would have been even more appalled if she knew that this was the prayer before action, not the prayer before death.

I leaned forward towards the big piece of flint lying there in the chalk.

Strange stuff, flint. No one really knows how it's made or where it comes from. Without it the Neolithic revolution in the British Isles wouldn't have happened. No hand axes, no spears. No Newgrange, no Stonehenge.

Flint.

The young man took the .45 from her and walked towards me. He pointed it at my head.

"Shut the fuck up with them words! Now talk. How do you know all this shit about Tommy and him being at St Malachy's and Dr Martin?"

I looked at him. "You know what the penalty is for killing a peeler? You get an automatic life sentence and they'll give you a thirty-five-year tariff before they can even consider parole. You won't be out of prison until 2023. How old will you be then? Sixty?"

Tommy looked at the others and shook his head. "He's bluffing. He has no idea who we are and no one else has any idea either."

"Your whole plan has been fucking compromised, if there even was a plan. I only arrived in Derry yesterday. Isn't a honey trap usually planned well in advance? This was a last-minute operation. And since when did the IRA kill coppers and bury them in the woods? You disappear traitors. You bury informers in the woods but policemen you *display*, don't you?"

"Yeah, what the fuck are we doing up here? Why didn't we just shoot him and leave him in a sheugh outside of town?" the young man asked.

"They want me vanished forever. No murder inquiry, no body, they want me wiped from history. Why is that? Who are you really doing this bit of dirty work for?"

The young man let the .45 drop to his side and turned to face Tommy. "Aye. This whole thing's a big bollocks, so it is. Answer us, Tommy. What are we doing up here in the mid—"

The edge of the flint thumped into his calf and he went down like a poleaxed gazelle. He fell sideways and I threw the big piece of flint at Tommy and hurled the spade after it. The kid was screaming so hard I must have severed a tendon. I jumped on top of him, rolled him, easily grabbed the .45 from his hand and kept rolling, expecting the .38 slugs to come roaring towards my head.

But Tommy was too slow. Glacial. Standing there flinching, trying to compute his comrade's cry of pain, trying to understand the flint's trajectory, trying desperately to grasp what had just happened.

The big piece of flint and the spade missed him by a mile and when he finally understood what was happening and his eyes cleared, he saw me on one knee pointing the black army-issue .45 at him. He raised the .38 and was surprised again when a hole appeared in his sport jacket under the pocket. A small hole in the front and a massive exit wound in the back through which came bits of ribs and lungs and heart.

A heart shot from a .45 at this range was almost instant death but I shot him again anyway in the head and his skull shattered like a coconut ventilated by a claw hammer.

The young man was clearly paralysed by the flint but to be on the safe side I shot off his right knee cap.

Only her left, but foolishly she started to run and I had no choice. The first shot missed but then I nailed her in the back and she went down like poor dead Mairéad Farrell falling for-ever in that car park back in Gib.

I got to my feet and walked towards her. The round had taken her in the left-hand side near the small of the back. I turned her over and I saw that she was bleeding out to the right of her belly button. There was no place to put a tourniquet. She looked at me desperately but I shook my head. Keeping an eye on her writhing, screaming friend, I knelt beside her and took her hand.

"You fucking fuck, Duffy," she said.

"Yeah."

"You fucking bastard," she said, sobbing.

"I'm sorry."

"Like fuck you are," she said squeezing the hand, hard.

"Do you want a benediction?"

"No . . . Yes."

I took off the balaclava. She was a blonde with green eyes. About twenty-eight years old. She looked nice and intelligent too. Such a fucking waste.

"What's your name?"

"Karen."

I made the sign of the cross and said quickly: "Here lies Karen. *Ave Maria, gratia plena, Dominus tecum. Benedicta tu in mulieribus, et benedictus fructus ventris tui, Iesus. Sancta Maria, Mater Dei, ora pro nobis peccatoribus, nunc, et in hora mortis nostrae.*"

I thought she would be dead by "mother of God" but amazingly she was hanging in there. I looked at the exit wound again.

What the hell? The blood was oozing out rather than haemorrhaging. The big .45 round had somehow missed all the major blood vessels. It had winged her, catching only fat and stomach. She must be under the fucking protection of St Jude. I ran back to Tommy, picked up the .38 and ripped the jacket off his back. I ran back to Karen. "I think you're going to live," I said and pushed the jacket down hard on the exit wound.

"I don't believe you," she groaned, her eyes wide, wanting to believe it.

I took her hand again and squeezed. "I think you're going to make it. By all rights a big calibre round like that should have torn you up inside but somehow it missed all the major blood vessels."

"I'm bleeding like fuck!"

"Of course you are but it's not arterial bleeding. Hold that jacket over the wound and don't try to move."

I let go of her hand.

"Don't leave me!"

"I have to go. Your mates will have been expecting one gun shot, perhaps two, but not four. The .45 made a racket that you could hear for miles."

"Don't leave me!"

"You'll be OK. Keep the pressure on the wound, OK?"

"OK."

"Now listen to me: when they come they're probably going to want to move you. If they move you you'll start to haemorrhage and you'll bleed to death before they can get you to a hospital. Do you understand?"

"I understand."

"What's your blood type?"

"B positive."

"OK, I'll go and get help."

"Duffy . . . Sean, what if . . . what if, they want to just finish me, so I don't talk, so they can get out of here?"

"Are they the sort that would do that?"

"I don't know."

I thought about it for a second.

"All right. I'll leave you the .38. If they try any funny business just fucking shoot them. And don't fucking shoot me as I'm running off."

"I won't shoot you," she said.

I put the .38 in her right hand and for a split second the barrel was pointing right at me but she didn't pull the trigger.

"Hang tight. And tell your young friend there to hang tight.

He'll live too," I said and ran off into the forest, circling round through the trees to the right, well off the trail.

Going downhill without a gun in your back made this little trek an entirely different experience.

My asthma didn't play up in the slightest.

A lovely old wood – in spring it would be full of bluebells.

When I reached the fire-break at the bottom of the hill, I could see two men arguing with one another.

Both of them were carrying shotguns. Nope, correction, one of them was carrying an AK-47.

I decided not to try to intercept them or attack them or arrest them. If anything went wrong and that guy opened up with the AK I was toast. Burnt-soda-bread-full-of-holes toast lying in the bottom of a sheugh.

Arrest would be nice in theory. But they would never talk. No one ever talks. And I wasn't going to push my luck.

I drifted deeper into the forest and kept going south until I reached the car park.

No one was here now, but there was the big stolen Volvo estate they'd brought me in. I looked through the window and didn't find a key but the door was open and those big Volvos from the late 70s had an easy-to-smash plastic dash and steering column.

In a manner that would have impressed the best teenage car thief, I had smashed the plastic, sparked the car and got the steering lock off in under two minutes.

I took a sniff of the dangling Pine Barrens air freshener to get the smell of blood and death out of my nostrils.

I drove out of the car park and headed north until I saw a road sign for Derry. It was so early that traffic was non-existent and in fourth gear I managed to get the big old diesel Volvo up to 75 mph. I tried Radio 1 but it was all Whitesnake and Billy Ocean and George Michael and Cheap Trick.

I drove to Strand Road RUC like a banshee on her broom

and was about to go into the station when I thought better of it, accelerated past the cop shop, drove up Asylum Street and towards the Bogside.

Squeal of breaks and a three-gear down shift and I stopped at a house in Heaney Street. I ran down the drive and rang the bell. I kept ringing it until Ken Kirkpatrick opened the door holding an ancient-looking pistol.

He recognised me immediately, even though it had been nearly fifteen years.

"Sean Duffy," he began. "I never thought I'd see the likes of you again. Not after you'd taken the King's shilling."

Arses like Ken Kirkpatrick were always coming out with old-timey phrases like "taken the King's shilling", but I had no time for his bullshit today. Ken Kirkpatrick was the Provisional IRA quartermaster general for Derry and as such was the number 3 or number 4 IRA man in the whole city.

"Kitchen, now," I said and marched into the house.

"What do you want, Duffy?" Ken said following me into the back kitchen.

"Listen, Ken, I got lifted last night by an IRA active service unit, taken to a derelict house, interrogated and then they took me out to Glenblane Forest to shoot me this morning. They fucked it up. I killed one of your men and shot one of them in the knees and a wee lassie in the back. There's two more of them up there. The woman is bleeding to death. She needs a couple of pints of B positive blood and she needs to go to a hospital. If you go now you can get a team there and save her."

"What?"

I slapped my hand on the kitchen table. "Fucking wake up, Ken! Glenblane Forest. One of your ASUs tried to kill me. I turned the tables and there's a girl called Karen bleeding to fucking death. B positive blood. Did you get all that in your skull?"

"Yes, I got it!"

"Make some fucking phone calls! I'll leave the room. If you need more details I'll be in the bloody lounge."

I went into the living room and sat on a musty leather sofa.

Quiet in here. Ticking grandfather clock, old bookcase full of nineteenth-century hardbacks, family portraits . . .

Exhausted.

So very tired . . .

Don't go to . . .

Don't . . .

A hand on my shoulder.

Ken shaking me awake.

"Sean, here's a mug of tea. Way you like it. Milk, two sugars, am I right?"

"That's right. Thanks. Was I asleep?"

"You've been asleep for an hour."

I sipped the tea and looked at Ken. Pale as a ghost, chubby, his ginger hair now almost entirely gone. He had run to fat and baldness like his da.

"Can I ask you something, Sean?"

"Sure."

"Why didn't you go to the police?"

"Is everything sorted? Did you get the girl?"

"We got her. We brought the team in. The lad's going to be fine too. They're both in Altnagelvin Hospital."

"What did you tell the hospital?"

"We'll say it was a punishment shooting gone wrong, we found both of them by the side of the road."

"What'll you say about the dead man?"

"We'll think of a cover story. Accidental discharge of a fire-arm, something like that. Why didn't you go to the RUC, Sean?"

"The police would have taken all day to comb the forest for the ASU. They probably would have waited until they could get army back-up. The girl would have bled to death."

"What's that to you? They were trying to kill you, weren't they?"

I shook my head. "I don't know, Ken, I've seen enough death. Been responsible for enough death."

"But you'd be a big hero in the RUC. Not many peelers survive hits like that."

"Who wants to be a hero? And hero at the expense of some wee lassie's life?"

"This is yours," he said, handing me my wallet, police ID, watch and even my gun.

"Jesus! I wasn't expecting . . . thanks," I said. "Where did this come from?"

"It was dropped off. By the uh . . . at the highest levels."

"I appreciate it."

"So what will you tell the police about what happened today?"

"Not much I can tell them after coming here."

"You're not going to mention any of this to anyone?"

"I won't if you won't."

"We won't."

"Then I won't. I'm compromised now. Coming to your house. Not going to the station. Nah, I'd rather this whole little operation went away. Better for the cops not to be even more suspicious of me. And better that I don't become a fat revenge target for the Derry brigade of the IRA," I said, emphasising these last words.

Ken nodded slowly. "Even though you killed one of our operatives I think the consensus in Derry will be that the local brigade of the IRA is in your debt."

"Thanks, Ken. I don't want to become a *special project* of the dead man's family."

"I'll see that you don't. No one from the Derry Brigade or from Tommy Flaherty's family will be looking for revenge. Sound OK?"

"Sounds OK."

I could tell there was something else he wanted to say but Ken's mouth closed and he didn't finish the thought.

I drank the mug of tea and put it on the coffee table. I yawned and stretched.

"Can I call you a taxi or do anything else for you, Sean?"

"A taxi would be great, Ken. I've got my car parked on Dungiven Street."

He made the call and he walked me down the hall when the taxi arrived.

"I know we're on opposite sides, Sean, and the circumstances aren't the best but it was good to see you. You seem to be good at what you do. You're what the old men would call a *worthy opponent*."

I grimaced. "Getting caught in a rookie-mistake honey trap? I'm a worthy nothing. I'm a fucking eejit, Ken."

Again Ken's mouth opened and closed again. I looked him in the eyes but I couldn't figure him out.

The taxi honked.

I opened the front door.

Ken waved to the taxi driver and held up two fingers, meaning two minutes. He took my sleeve and led me onto the porch. He lowered his voice so that whoever was sleeping upstairs couldn't possibly hear:

"Funny thing that honey trap, Sean. I looked into it. Whole thing was organised in minutes. Do you know how long these things normally take? Weeks of preparation. Weeks."

"That is strange."

"And can I tell you something else. The order to lift you came from Dublin."

"Dublin?"

"From the top brass. From the Army Council."

"What are you talking about?"

"You've strayed into some deep waters, Sean. Operations in

Derry are always handled by the Derry Brigade but the order to lift you came from the IRA Army Council in Dublin. The top boys here weren't too happy about that, which is why it wasn't difficult to get you your wallet and gun back."

"Deep waters? What deep waters? I'm investigating a murder of a drug dealer."

"Could you have antagonised somebody in the course of your investigation?"

"I certainly annoyed the hell out of Harry Selden."

Ken shook his head. "Harry's not a major player. He doesn't have the authority to order what happened to you."

"That's what I thought. So am I in any immediate danger? I have a kid now."

"Oh?"

"A wee girl, Emma. Walking and nearly talking. I wouldn't want anything to happen to her."

Ken rubbed his chin. "There will be an internal inquiry about what happened to you. A post-mortem. It'll take a few weeks to sort everything out. I imagine you'll be safe until after that's concluded but if someone in the Army Council wants you dead I wouldn't want to be in your shoes."

I grinned at him. "Like many other people before now, Ken, this person will learn that killing me isn't so fucking easy."

We both smiled sadly at this bit of bravado.

Ken opened the front door and stepped back inside. "You didn't hear any of this from me. OK?"

"OK."

"Write down your telephone number and if I hear anything I'll give you a call."

I gave him my card and walked out to the taxi.

"Where to mate?"

"Dungiven Street."

Dungiven Street.

A really thorough look under the Beemer for bombs. A big

hit on the asthma inhaler from the glove compartment.

"I'm alive," I said.

The Beemer didn't understand but growled in sympathy when I put the key in the ignition.

I drove to Waterside Railway Station car park and pulled the Beemer into an empty spot. Early yet. Only a few people around.

I took out the picture I had in my wallet of *Michael Tramples Satan* by Guido Reni and gave a prayer of thanks to Saint Michael the Archangel, the Patron Saint of Policemen, and then another to Mary the Mother of God, who had had her hands full watching over me for the last few years.

I took out my emergency hip flask filled with a 1967 Balvenie Vintage Cask – a gift from my father on Emma's birth (we all should have such fathers). Twenty-one-year-old whisky and the removal of the imminence of death: no man on that morning anywhere in Ireland felt as glad to be drawing air as I did then.

I got out of the car and walked to the Waterside Train Station wall, and then, like Elizabeth Smart in her memoir, I sat down and wept. Ten minutes of tears. Ten solid minutes of them. The refrain of "Big Yellow Taxi" playing deep in my hippocampus.

They would have killed me. They really would have done it. And that poor man . . . that poor stupid geography-teaching man.

"Are you OK, son?" a passing nun asked me when I had just about recovered.

"Thank you, I'm fine, sister," I said, getting to my feet. "I was just having a wee moment."

She looked at the hip flask and my crumpled Che T-shirt.

"Are you a married man?" she asked, a little impertinently.

"In a way," I replied.

"Get away home to your wife then, and stay away from the

strong liquor. It is the curse of Ireland, is the strong liquor."

"Yes, sister."

Back to the Beemer.

I looked underneath it for bombs, didn't find any and put the key in the ignition. The big throaty, comforting engine roared into life. I drove cautiously out of Derry and then gunned it on the A6. By the Glenshane Pass I was doing my usual ton and change and I reached 115 mph by Maghera.

When I made it back to Coronation Road it was 8.00 but Beth was still in bed.

I stripped and climbed in beside her.

"Sean?" she said sleepily.

"It's me."

"I'm furious with you."

"Why?"

"Jeanette said you'd be late, but I didn't think you'd be out all night."

"Sorry."

"Where have you been? I was worried sick. I called John McCrabban and he thought you might be on a stake-out."

"Aye. It was something like that."

"You have to call me and let me know. Anything could have happened. I was worried, Sean!"

"I know."

"I'm serious!" she said.

"Next time I will."

"You better. I was so worried. I called John."

"You said."

"Did you have car trouble?"

"No."

"You stink of petrol."

"Oh. Yeah. Had a bit of trouble with a jerry can. Might have got some petrol on me. It was a long night."

"You'll have to shower."

"I will. Listen, Beth, I'm just going to shut my eyes for a minute. Let me lie in if I manage to drift off, will you?"

"Do you think you *can* drift off? It's a very sunny morning."

And if she said anything more I didn't hear it for sleep has always been a friend to lucky men and drowned men and those very lucky men indeed who are pulled living from the sea.

17: THE OLD FILES

I woke at noon plus forty and schlepped myself downstairs for the 1 o'clock news. Can a Mick schlepp? *I* can, so fuck off.

Beth was in Belfast, Emma at Jollytots. Don't care what Dr Havercamp said, this was a day for herb. I'll give him Lawson's piss if he does a random.

Shed. Moonshine. Resin. Joan Armatrading.

Back inside.

Cold shower. Shave. Shirt. Blue sweater. Sports jacket. Black jeans. DMs. Lucky Che T-shirt lying on the bedroom floor. Still lucky. Pet the cat. Under the Beemer for bombs. Really good look today.

Somebody in the IRA Army Council wants you dead. Why? I'm nobody. On a dead-end investigation. Had to be a reason, dig deep, dig all the way to boiling iron at the centre of the earth.

Along the sea front to Carrick RUC.

Crabbie in the Incident Room, Lawson making coffee, down-hearted because there wasn't any riot duty scheduled for the day.

"Case conference."

Crabbie and Lawson sat down and I closed the door.

"What I'm about to tell you doesn't leave this room, OK?"

"Why?" Crabbie asked suspiciously.

"I made some questionable calls in the course of an

investigation yesterday. I did it with the best of intentions to
save a young woman's life."

Crabbie sighed. "I'll get us some tea and biscuits and when
I've got them why don't you tell us everything, Sean?"

When I was done with the explanation Lawson's eyes were
wide. Crabbie's only display of emotion had been to fill, empty
and re-fill his pipe.

"So what do you think?" I said.

"I'm happy that you're still with us, Sean," Crabbie said. "That
was a close one."

"It certainly was."

"But you should have gone to Strand Road police station," he
said firmly.

"I concur, sir," Lawson said. "They could have at least
attempted to round up the cell that kidnapped you."

"You know they would have demanded army back-up to go
off on a manhunt in the forest and by the time the army had
arrived the girl would have been dead and the rest of the cell
probably would have escaped anyway," I said.

"But it would have been the right thing to do," Crabbie said.

I nodded. Crabbie was a policeman who would never manu-
facture evidence or take fruit from the jurisprudential poison
tree or knowingly break the law. Crabbie had doomed-Edward-
ian-expeditions-to-the-Pole concepts of rectitude and discipline.

But he was also an old friend now and I could see the emotion
behind his eyes. If he'd known Ken Kirkpatrick he would have
done exactly the same thing. He would have saved the girl too.

"How much danger are you in now, do you think, Sean?" he
asked, blowing pipe smoke towards the ceiling.

Lawson said nothing, his head still spinning from all of this.

"I don't know. I really don't know. Ken Kirkpatrick says there
will be an internal inquiry following yesterday's events. He says
I'll probably have a week or two until this person in the Army
Council is able to act again. She's only just come back, but I'm

going to ask Beth to take Emma away and stay with her parents."

"A sensible precaution for starters," Crabbie said. "But maybe for your own good you should report what happened to Special Branch."

"You know what they'd do to me. Disciplinary proceedings and then the sack. And then possibly criminal charges for aiding and abetting a terrorist suspect."

"That's probably true," Crabbie said. "But if the IRA are gunning for you?"

"The IRA are gunning for all of us, all the time, and as a Catholic peeler I've had that bounty on my head for fifteen years."

"Do you want to come and stay with me? Way out on the farm no one can get close without us hearing their car."

"That's the one advantage I have of living on Coronation Road. It would be the bold IRA team that comes down there trying to kill me deep in Loyalist turf."

"Aye, although don't forget Francis Deauville. Somebody got him. Somebody got him with medieval technology," Crabbie said.

"First things first, I'll get Beth and Emma to safety and then I'll weigh up my options."

"We need to figure out what this all means," Lawson said.

"We bloody do," I agreed. "And quick."

"As I see it the honey trap was not a random crime of opportunity. It wasn't designed to lift a policeman, it was designed to lift a specific policeman: you. And there's only one reason why, really, because you were getting too close to Harry Selden."

"Which means that Harry, despite being in a coma, was somehow involved in the murder of Francis Deauville," Crabbie said.

"We're sure he was definitely in the hospital?" Lawson asked.

"Yup, we are. Interviewed his doctors and his nurses. It was him and before you ask, no, he doesn't have a twin brother, or any other brother for that matter," I said.

"And on Harry Selden's say-so the IRA Army Council ordered a hit on you? Is Selden really that important?" Crabbie asked.

I shook my head. "I don't understand it. Ken Kirkpatrick says he's only a minor player. He says he's not even a particularly big cheese in Derry. And he's certainly not on the IRA Army Council like ****** *********** ."

"So what could this be about?" Crabbie asked.

"It's *something* to do with Selden. And it's something to do with this case we're working on. And it's something to do with Selden and Deauville working together in the B Specials all those years ago."

"We better get moving then, Sean. This is urgent, I'll get my coat," Crabbie said.

I smiled at him. "Where do you think we're going?

"I think we're going to Belvoir Park Records Office where they keep the files on the B Specials and after that I think we're all driving up to Derry to talk to Mr Selden."

"What say you, Lawson?" I asked.

"You know my motto, sir: all for one and one for all."

"My motto is: don't trust whitey and whitey is everywhere in this fucking town. Let's keep all this quiet for now."

BMW. Radio 3. A2. M5. South Belfast.

The nice part of Belfast.

Parks, the Lagan, trees, attractive houses spilling down to the water's edge. You'd hardly think there was a war going on.

"You'd hardly think there was a war going on," I said.

"This is what it's like on my farm," Crabbie said. "If we didn't have TV we could be living in the good old days."

Belvoir Park Records Office was in the same complex as the Belvoir Park Forensic Science Laboratory. A top-notch, modern, state of the art facility for processing evidence from all the criminal cases in Northern Ireland and even some cases from Scotland and the Republic of Ireland too.

A few years after our visit a 3,000-pound IRA truck bomb,

that you could hear up to twenty miles away, reduced the entire structure to rubble, but that was in the future and on this particular March morning everything was shiny, sparkling and new.

The B Special records were in a sub-basement in old cardboard files that were covered with dust and mildew. If someone in RUC Clerical had really cared about preserving these records they would have been transferred to microfiche, but no one gave a shit about the B Specials, who'd been in them and what they had done.

The librarian, an ancient WPC called Fogerty, took us to the shelf stacks and explained that the records were alphabetised by last name.

"That should be easy enough to sort out," I said.

But, of course, it wasn't.

Harry Selden's cardboard file was there all right, under S, but the paper documentation inside the file was missing. Francis Deauville's cardboard file was there all right, but the paper documentation inside the file was also missing.

WPC Fogerty was perplexed. "I don't understand it," she said. "Even if they never made a single arrest or ever even turned up for duty, at the very least there should be date of birth, height, weight, home address, total pay, date of swearing-in and date of discharge."

I showed her the empty files. "There's not even a blank piece of paper. There's nothing at all. Is that usual?"

"I don't know. I've never really looked through these files."

"Let's do some random sampling."

We looked through thirty or forty random B Special personnel and not a single one of them was completely empty and most had several pages of documentation detailing the reserve policeman's arrests, etc.

"This is most unusual," WPC Fogerty said.

"Who has access to these files?" I asked.

"Anyone who has access to the records building. As soon as

you're inside all you have to do is walk down the stairs to the basement."

"And who has access to this building?"

"Anyone with a police, army or grade 4 civil service ID would have access," she said.

"So that would be how many people in Northern Ireland?" I asked.

"Thousands," she said.

"Tens of thousands," Lawson corrected.

"If you wanted to take a file with you, how would you do that?"

"Oh, you can't take these files out of the building. You can photocopy them if you want but they can't leave the building. I make sure everyone's aware of that and you have to come past the librarian's desk when you leave."

"But what's to stop you just walking out with the contents of the files rolled up in a newspaper or shoved in your pocket?"

"No one's ever stolen a file," she protested.

"Au contraire, WPC Fogerty. Someone indeed has stolen the files of Francis Deauville and Harry Selden. What about CCTV cameras on the front gate?"

"Well yes, but we have 200 personnel in here and we get thousands of visitors to the RUC, RIC and army records rooms upstairs."

"Would you have any idea when these files could have been removed?" I asked.

"No. They could even have been taken from the old RUC HQ building before we moved here a year ago. And the records department there was open access. No cameras. Just flashed your ID to the security guard."

"So even if I got young Lawson here to go through the CCTV footage from the front gate checking every single visitor you've ever had in this facility—"

"Why me?" Lawson protested.

". . . ever had in his facility to see if any of them are suspicious, and I don't even know how he would possibly determine that, it wouldn't actually make any difference because the files could have been removed from the old RUC HQ building, where there were no CCTV cameras in the records department?"

"That's right."

I sighed. "And there are no copies anywhere else?"

"No," WPC Fogerty said.

"Thank you very much WPC Fogerty, you've been very helpful," I said.

Outside to the Beemer. Even in the police forensic lab car park I got down on my knees to check for mercury tilt switch bombs.

We had an early lunch in Belfast and then decided to drive up to Derry for what felt like the millionth time in this investigation.

Brave face on it for the lads, but the fear.

The fucking fear.

Deep waters.

Hits ordered in from Dublin.

Hit pieces in the newspapers.

What kind of a case was this? Who wanted it to end? And why?

Need time. If I have time.

Get Beth and Emma out of the house and think.

Think, think, think.

Drive and think.

Crabbie was sitting next to me in the front seat going through his notes. He didn't like what he was reading there.

"What's the matter, mate?"

"I just don't see a way through this. We're in an information void. Whatever Harry Selden and Francis Deauville were up to in the B Specials will forever be a secret because Selden won't tell us and Deauville's dead."

"Do you think Deauville told his wife and that's why she's disappeared?" Lawson asked.

"That's what the killer thought, anyway. Even if she didn't know. The poor wee lass was silenced because she might have known," Crabbie said.

I was fed up with the same old roads, so at Claudy I cut over onto the Longland Road to go into the city via Strabane and the A5. It was on that lonely stretch of nothingness through the bleak treeless foothills of the Sperrins that I noticed a car on our tail.

"We're being followed," I said.

Crabbie looked in the mirror. The car was a black Ford Escort XR3i. We both knew what that meant. "Aye I see it," he said.

"Oh my God! Is it the IRA? Are they going to get us?" Lawson said, alarmed.

I patted the Beemer's steering wheel. "I'd like to see them try to get us. But no, it isn't the IRA, son, it's the bloody Special Branch."

"It's policemen? Maybe it's just the traffic police."

"No, it isn't traffic. They're in plain clothes. Now why are they following me do you think, Crabbie?"

"I wouldn't like to speculate," Crabbie said.

"Me neither. Look at them. They think they're being terribly discreet. Is there a seat belt back there, Lawson?"

"Yeah."

"Put it on. I'm going to lose the bastards in Strabane."

"Sean, is that wise?" Crabbie asked.

"If any of us were wise we would have chosen a different profession. Now be a good 'un and click my seat belt for me, will ya?"

Crabbie clicked in my seat belt and did his own belt too.

"What are you going to do, Sean?" he asked.

"I'm just going to lose them. We don't need meddling from those boys."

"If you say so. How will you do it?"

"Just before Strabane proper there's a wee road through a

housing development, I think it's called the Wood-something Road – there's a hill that obscures the view and at the end of that there's a sharp turn onto the A5 going into Derry. If you know what you're doing you can lose them on the Wood-something Road, scream onto the A5 and be halfway into Derry before they know what's hit them."

"If you're going to do that slow down now. Get them accustomed to a lower speed in top gear," he suggested.

"Good idea, mate, I'll cruise along in third."

"What are youse doing? You're running from Special Branch? That can't be a good idea," Lawson said.

I downshifted to third gear and reduced my speed to 40 mph. The Ford Escort reduced its speed and dropped way back to avoid being seen.

We came to a small hill just after the village of Artigarvan. We were a mile and a half from the A5 turn. This was the moment. On the reverse slope of the hill I'd gun it.

I crested the hill and as soon as the Ford disappeared in the rear-view mirror I pushed down hard on the accelerator pedal. The BMW screamed up towards 60 mph. I hit fourth gear and now we were doing 70. The outskirts of Strabane went past in a blur and the A5 turn came faster than I was expecting.

A Tayto Crisps lorry was coming towards the junction. I could either hard-brake, stop and let it pass or try to beat it. If we stopped the goons would catch us.

"A lorry!" Lawson screamed.

"Damn it," I yelled and gunned the engine and drove through into the junction in a horrible fishtail of screaming tyres and honking horns. I accelerated hard away from the crisps lorry, waved a friendly apology to the driver, switched to fifth gear and in thirty seconds we were going north east at 100 mph.

The Ford Escort was nowhere to be seen.

"All right back there?" I asked Lawson.

He tried to reply but couldn't quite manage it. McCrabban

showed no visible change of emotion.

I parked the BMW outside Harry Selden's house but when I rang the doorbell his mother, who appeared to be in rude good health, said that he was at a council meeting. We found him at his office in the Guildhall and a pleasant young secretary told us we could wait and that he would be along presently.

Harry Selden was not pleased to see us when he eventually showed up.

"Inspector Duffy and I see you've brought a couple of body-guards with you," he said mirthlessly. He was wearing a blue checked seersucker jacket and checked trousers over a shirt that seemed too tight on him. His tie was black like his fucking heart. Definitely no Oliver Hardy vibe today but perhaps there was a hint of northern working-man's-club comic. I asked if we could talk in his office.

"You can have five minutes," he said. "I'm a busy man."

We went inside his office, which was a tastefully decorated job overlooking the River Foyle. Big comfy leather chairs, nice big desk, nice watercolours. You could do good work sucking money out of the Brits in this office.

"So what is it now?" Selden asked.

"I suppose you already know that after we had our little chat I was abducted by the IRA."

"I don't know what you're talking about," he said, looking me, rather impressively, straight in the eye. He held my gaze but only for a three count and then his gaze shifted to his feet.

Christ, the guy was no poker player. Give me two days with him in an interrogation suite and I'd have him singing "When The Saints Go Marching In" and the name of every girl he necked in the back row of the Regal Cinema. Lifting a Sinn Fein councillor wouldn't be easy though, without any evidence. Not impossible, of course, but not easy.

"Well, as you can see, your chums weren't able to give me a hole in the back of the head."

"No? How'd you escape? Magic powers?"

"Just a bit of luck, actually."

"You should write fiction, inspector."

"Fiction is redundant around here, don't you think? Reality is so much worse. I was kidnapped, probably at your orders."

"You've a great imagination, pal."

"I've got a terrible imagination. That's why I'm living in Northern Ireland in the 1980s. Anybody with any imagination would have hightailed it out of here long ago."

"Yeah, well, you can piss off now."

"What's the next trick? Another smear attack in the press, or you going to try and get to me in Carrick?"

"I despair, really, I do," Harry said and gave Lawson and McCrabban a sigh. "Can youse talk sense into him? I've looked into this case of yours. I don't for the life of me see why you are trying to drag me into it. I was in hospital in Derry with blood poisoning when they shot this drug dealer fella in Carrickfergus. Teleportation is not one of my gifts."

"Your car was in Carrick tailing the dead man."

"My stolen car."

"There can't have been many Catholics in the B Specials back in 1968," I said.

"Oh it's back to this again, is it?"

"It's back to this again."

"You're one to talk about Catholics in the police."

"Touché, Harry. What did you and Frank Deauville get up to together in the B Specials in 1968?"

"I never heard of this Frank Deauville before you started bleating on about him."

"That's not what your file says," I attempted.

A smile flitted across his lips.

He knew. He fucking knew the files were gone. His file. Deauville's file. Harry knew.

"What file's that?" he asked.

I said nothing and as I guessed he would, he filled the dead air with more nonsense: "Are you talking about my old police records? What do they say?"

I got up from the comfy leather sofa. Lawson and McCrabban got up too.

"We'll see ourselves out," I said.

"Is that it?" he asked.

"You'll be hearing from us again," I said.

"No I won't. That's harassment. Next time you want to talk to me, you can talk to my solicitor first."

I nodded, said goodbye to the secretary and walked down the stairs with Lawson and Crabbie.

When we were safely back in the Beemer, Crabbie shook his head and lit his pipe.

"Aye," he said.

"Yeah," I agreed.

"What?" Lawson said. "What did I miss?"

"He knew about the missing file. The question is how?" McCrabban said.

"How indeed?"

18: INFERNAL AFFAIRS

Home to Coronation Road. Emma excited to see her Da-da-da, Beth in good form reading *Ubik* while I made the tea: spagbol for everyone, Chilean red and garlic bread for me and B.

After dinner we took Emma up the road for a walk.

"The man in that house builds ships. The man in that house was a prisoner of the Japanese. The man in that house has a pet lion," I said.

"The woman in that house makes gin in her bathtub. The woman in that house is divorced and has a huge crush on Daddy," Beth said.

I put Emma to bed and when I came downstairs Beth was thumbing through my albums.

Time for The Talk.

Don't mention the kidnapping or the promise of being burned alive or the dead man or shooting a girl in the back.

Don't mention the fear.

The fear in the chair.

The fear in the walk up the hill.

The fear that the men will, in due course, try it all again.

Secrets.

Secrets were poison. Especially in the six counties: a fake world built on fantasies, secrets and dissimulation.

But sometimes you needed to dissimulate.

"Is this Robert Reich any good?" she asked, holding up a record.

"Do you like xylophones?"

"God no!"

I took the record from her. "Listen, Beth, there's this threat thing that has come down from intel. It's against my life. Nothing to get panicky about but it's against me personally not just against the police in general. We don't know if it's real or not, but I'd prefer it if you and Em moved back in with your folks for a few days. "

"We only just moved back here!"

"I know."

"This isn't your way of kicking us out, is it? I didn't like being away from you, Sean. I tried it and I didn't like it."

"That's good to hear. I'm not kicking you out. I hate being away from you and Emma, but this is some scary stuff."

She nodded and bit her lip. She understood.

"One question. If it's too dangerous for us to stay here, why are you staying here?"

"It's not too dangerous. Nothing's going to happen. This is just a precaution. If someone is lunatic enough to drive by the house and maybe try and have a go I want you and Emma well out of it. Nothing is likely to happen, but I'd be able to handle everything better knowing that both of you are safe."

She was tearing up now. She put her arms round me. I hugged her and carried her to the sofa. "How long for?"

"I don't know. A few weeks maybe. Until I put this investigation to bed. I've stirred up something strange, something deep."

"When do we have to move?"

"You'll have to go by the weekend. The threat becomes a bit more imminent after the weekend."

"What does that mean?"

"I can't really explain, but you should go sooner rather than later."

"I have my last tutorial tomorrow and then we're off for the term. I could have my dad come with one of his vans the day after."

"You don't have to take all your stuff. But, yeah, the day after tomorrow is a good idea."

"OK, Sean, if that's what you want," she said sadly.

"Don't worry. It's probably nothing. We get this sort of thing all the time. It's always bollocks."

"And after that I want to look at permanently moving away from here."

"I've already agreed to that. I'm a man of my word."

She kissed me on the lips. "That you are," she said.

The next day I got up early and made everyone pancakes for breakfast. I dropped Emma off at Jollytots and Beth down at the train station.

I drove to the barracks feeling gloomy.

Lawson was waiting for me with a cup of coffee in the car park. Whenever Crabbie sent Lawson down to the car park to wait for me with a cup of coffee it was invariably because there was bad news waiting for me upstairs that he wanted to warn me about.

"Oh shit, what now? I haven't failed another physical, have I?"

"No. It's not that, sir. There are two men in your office."

"What two men?"

"They wouldn't say."

"How'd they get in? What if it's an IRA hit squad or one of those stripograms?"

"They're policemen."

"All stripograms are policemen."

"I think they might be Special Branch."

"So ugly stripograms."

I was trying to get a smile out of Lawson but it wasn't working.

"Gimme that coffee."

Coffee. Asthma inhaler. Stairs.

Four men in my office: two goons from the internal investigation unit of Special Branch (one called McWhirter and a
Jock called Nelson whom I'd encountered before); our ineffec-
tual union rep, Sergeant Price, and Chief Inspector McArthur.
McWhirter had a flasher vibe about him – skinny and pale and
I'll bet his hands sweated something chronic. Nelson had a face
like Brian Clough getting sodomised with a pineapple.

"Were you boys having a séance?" I asked.

"Maybe for your days as a free man," Nelson said.

"That doesn't make any sense," I said, shooing him out of my
good swivel chair.

"This is serious, Sean," McArthur said.

Nelson handed me a manila envelope.

"Is this an invitation to your birthday party?"

"Open the envelope and then we'll see who's laughing,"
Nelson said.

I opened the envelope. It was a series of photographs of me
going into Ken Kirkpatrick's house.

"A known IRA man. An old friend of yours from Derry. You
show up at his house at five in the morning. Stay for 90 minutes
then head out again. Lots of handshakes at the door," Nelson
said.

I handed the photographs back to Nelson.

"You want to explain yourself, Duffy?" McWhirter asked.

"Nope."

"I think photographs of you consorting with the IRA quartermaster for Derry is pretty fucking serious," Nelson said.

"Yeah well you shouldn't think so much, Nelson, you might
break your head."

"A plain clothes undercover team took photographs of you
going into Ken Kirkpatrick's house," McWhirter said.

"Where are the plain clothes undercover teams when you
really need them, eh?" I muttered.

"Duffy, I think you have to explain this. It looks very bad with all this talk of IRA infiltrators and—" Sergeant Price said.

"You think I'm an IRA mole? Me? I don't know whether to laugh or cry. This is what you geniuses in internal affairs have come up with?" I said, addressing the two Special Branch goons.

"A Catholic boy from Derry, who we know attempted to join the Provisional IRA after Bloody Sunday," Nelson began. "Know that for a fact from a number of sources. Who we know has had numerous disciplinary and other offences, yet mysteriously manages not to get the sack even when I personally get him to give me his resignation. Whose case files have never involved the prosecution of a single IRA man. Not one. For anything. Not so much as a parking ticket. Maybe instead of attempting to join the IRA in 1972 you did in fact—"

"March zipped by, didn't it? I didn't realise it was April the first already," I said.

"Did in fact join the IRA and have been working for the Provisionals ever since," Nelson said.

"If I were a mole wouldn't it be smarter to have me prosecute a few low-ranking IRA guys and have me rise up the ranks in the RUC? Wouldn't it be more efficacious for me to join the intel branch or, here's a thought, Special Branch?"

"You might not be the only one. There might be dozens of you," Nelson said.

I looked at Sergeant Price and McArthur.

"You don't have to say anything without a solicitor present, Sean," Sergeant Price reminded me.

I pulled out a bottle of whisky from my desk drawer. "Can all of you gentlemen please leave my office? I have work to do."

"Sean, these men have come all the way from Castlereagh to put these allegations to you," McArthur said.

"And they can go all the way back to Castlereagh."

"You're not even going to attempt an explanation?" Nelson said.

"An explanation? I was doing police work. You should fucking try it some time."

"Why did you evade us yesterday?" McWhirter asked.

"What do you mean?"

"We were following your car on the Strabane Road," McWhirter said.

"Were you? I never noticed. You must have been doing an amazing job. Normally I'm pretty observant about these things. Now listen, I'm a busy man, so unless you've got an arrest warrant in another brown envelope, which I don't think you have . . . well then, you know, fuck off."

Nelson stood and put the manila envelope under his arm. "This time it won't be you getting the sack, pal, it'll be you getting the sack and then going to the old grey bar hotel. You could be looking at twenty years, Duffy. But don't worry, I hear they treat policemen really well inside. We'll be talking again," he said.

"I don't think we will."

Nelson and McWhirter left and I waved Sergeant Price away with them.

That only left the Chief Inspector. He took the seat opposite me and refused a drink when offered.

"What's all this about, Sean?"

"This guy in Derry, Harry Selden, he's up to his neck in the Deauville murder case. I went to an old friend of mine, Ken Kirkpatrick, to get the lowdown on Selden."

"Is this Kirkpatrick chap in the IRA?"

"He is, but he's a friend of mine who has helped me out with info in the past. He gave me some good stuff about Selden."

"Well?"

"Selden is a low-level IRA commander and a medium-level Sinn Fein politician. Ken filled me in on all that."

"What does he have to do with the Deauville case?"

"Quite a lot, I think. Deauville and Selden served together

in the B Specials. And Selden's car was seen following the Deauvilles shortly before Mr Deauville's murder. He claimed it had been stolen. He wasn't driving it because he was in the hospital, but I don't like the coincidence."

"Who *was* driving the car?"

"We don't have eyewitness testimony because our eyewitness, Elena Deauville, has vanished."

"What about that artist's sketch you have?"

"Looks nothing like Selden."

McArthur leaned back in the chair, put his head in his hands and sighed. "Special Branch thinking one of my men is an IRA infiltrator? The timing is awful," he muttered.

"Yeah I know, I'm sorry, sir, what with your promotion board coming up."

He hadn't meant to say that out loud and he was embarrassed now. He stood up, straightened his tie.

He leaned on the desk and looked at me. "Man to man, you're not an IRA mole are you, Duffy?" he asked.

I almost laughed in his face. Laughter of despair this time. If senior policemen thought moles could be found by simply asking them outright it was pretty worrying. And if even McArthur thought I might be a mole, what the fuck had I achieved here at Carrickfergus RUC? What had I achieved in my entire police career? Nicking a few villains here and there while all around me King Chaos ran his Carnivale.

"No, sir, I'm not the mole."

"Good show, Duffy. I believe you."

"Thank you, sir."

"Maybe you should lie low for a bit, take the rest of the day off, couple of days maybe?"

"Won't that look rather suspicious?"

"Everything you do will look suspicious from now on but why stir the pot?"

When he'd gone I called the only influential friend I had left.

"Hello?"

"Sir, it's me, Sean Duffy, I'm sorry to bother you."

"What is it, Duffy?" the brand new Assistant Chief Constable Strong replied.

"I've just had a rather unpleasant encounter with an internal affairs team from Special Branch. Did you know about this?"

"Of course not. What's going on, Duffy?"

"They've got photos of me coming out of Ken Kirkpatrick's house in Derry. They think I'm some sort of IRA agent. It's absolute rubbish, sir. There's this Jock sergeant who's got it in for me . . . Anyway, sir, you're the only important friend I've got, I don't want to be railroaded here. They're talking about sending me to prison."

"What is this about, Duffy? What were you doing in Derry?"

"I was investigating the Deauville case."

"Have you made any progress?"

"Some. I've learned that Harry Selden and Deauville were in the B Specials together. Selden's car was seen near to Deauville's house just before the murder. The two of them are linked somehow."

"How?"

"I don't know."

"Why would this Selden character drive all the way to Carrickfergus to murder this Deauville fellow?"

"I don't know, sir."

"Do you have any eyewitnesses to the killing?"

"None, sir."

"So what exactly have you got?"

"Uhm, only the fact that Selden's car was seen following Francis Deauville before the murder."

"Who saw this?"

"Mrs Deauville."

"Hasn't she gone missing?"

"Yes, sir."

"This wasn't in her statement."

"No, sir. She told the Bulgarian translator that she saw a car following them and wrote down the number plate."

"So this is all hearsay evidence. Completely inadmissible in court."

"Yes, sir."

"Let me see if I understand you, Duffy. DAADD has claimed responsibility for this killing but instead of pursuing that angle you're following some insane lead from hearsay evidence? Is that what you're telling me?"

"Sir, they haven't actually claimed responsibility. Not formally. There's also the B Special angle. We know both men served in the B Specials because it's in their criminal record file, but when I went to look at the B Special files for Deauville and Selden to see if they had served together or done a joint arrest or anything like that, well, the files were gone, sir! Total dead end, sir."

A long silence.

"Hearsay evidence and missing files, is that what you're telling me, Duffy? And now you've been seen going into a known IRA man's house at five in the morning? And you wonder why Special Branch is interested in you, with your extremely patchy service record?"

"Sir, I—"

"Son, I'm going to have to tell you how it is. Clearly no one has told you how it is for years so I'm going to have to be the man to do it. I'm an Assistant Chief Constable now. I'm very high up the food chain. I can't afford to be dragged down by a man like you, Duffy. You've had some successes in your career but also some notable failures. If you're going to fuck this case up like you've fucked up in the past I'm going to have to cut you loose. Do you understand me, son?"

"I think so, sir."

"Can I give you a piece of advice, Duffy?"

"Of course, sir."

"File the Francis Deauville murder as an unsolved DAADD killing. Case closed pending further developments. File the Elena Deauville disappearance as a bloody missing persons case. Case closed pending further developments. Move on to other business. Don't go back to Derry. Keep your head down. Do you hear me, Duffy?"

"Yes, sir."

"Now I will see what I can do about these Special Branch detectives. But I won't be able to get the ants off your back while you're sticking your arm into the ant hill."

"Thank you, sir. I appreciate anything you can do, sir. Got a lot on my plate at the moment."

"Have less on your plate, Duffy. Close those cases, move on, don't make pointless fucking waves."

"Yes, sir, I understand sir."

"Goodbye, Duffy. Don't call me again. It's always a long-distance call up here at ACC rank. I don't think you can afford the charges."

Dialtone.

Another friendship burned. Well done, Sean. Well done.

19: LIFTED

Living room, mulling it all over. Gears turning. Patterns forming. Something told me that I'd been given everything I needed to solve the equation. It was all there. It was a complicated equation but somehow I knew that it was all there. A better detective would have put it together now. Where was Miss Marple when you needed her?

Knock at the front door. Early morning. Post-milkman but pre-starlings.

Looked through the peephole. Two goons. Didn't recognise them. One was wearing a raincoat and a dark grey suit. He had a moustache, copper hair and beady brown eyes. He was about forty. The other one was a woman about five years younger than him, with her hair in a blonde ponytail. She was wearing the uniform of an RUC Superintendent. She had odd yellowish goblin eyes.

I unhooked the lock and opened the door with my foot, coffee cup in one hand, Glock in the other.

"Yes?"

"We'd like you to come with us, Inspector Duffy," the woman said. "I'm Detective Superintendent Baker, this is Detective Sergeant O'Neill. Would you mind not pointing that gun at me?"

"I'll keep the gun pointing at you until I see some identification," I said.

They showed me two warrant cards that seemed convincing enough.

"What's this about?"

"We'd like to ask you some questions."

"What about?"

"Personnel stuff. Your record."

"Am I about to win police officer of the year?"

"Not exactly."

"Specifically what questions about my record?"

"Allegations of corruption and about your connections with the IRA," Baker said.

"I'll need to get dressed," I said.

"Can we come in?" Baker asked.

"No, you can wait in your car. I'll be five minutes," I said and closed the door.

I pulled on a pair of jeans and a sweater and left a note for Beth. "Police business. Should be back in a couple of hours."

I went to the car. Of course the anti-corruption unit was driving a brand new Mercedes Benz. No irony or integrity worries there.

"I'll sit in the front seat if you don't mind, I need to stretch my legs out," I said.

"That's fine," Baker said and got in the back.

I sat in the plush Merc seat. O'Neill checked for mercury tilt switch bombs and got in beside me. There was a tape of Willie Nelson's "Pancho and Lefty" in the player and it kicked in when he turned the engine on.

"What's the last thing you want to hear after you've given Willie Nelson a blow job?" I asked O'Neill.

"I dunno," he said.

"'I'm not Willie Nelson'," I said.

O'Neill grinned until he caught Superintendent Baker's face in the rear-view mirror.

Divide and conquer, Duffy. That's how you'll beat them. That and keeping a cool fucking head.

We drove up to Castlereagh Holding Centre and they led me down to a sub-basement interrogation suite.

Tape recorder spooling.

Water flowing in pipes.

Baleful dungeon noises.

Creepy distant heathen laughter.

The corruption stuff was bullshit and they knew it. Chicken shit rule-breaking, fiddling the over-time claims . . . it wouldn't wash, but that was only the starter.

"So, Inspector Duffy, how long have you been friends with the top brass of the Derry Brigade of the IRA?" Baker asked.

"I know a lot of people in Derry. Some of them are in the police, some of them are in the IRA, some of them actually work for a living. It's a small city. Everybody knows everybody else. Contacts are useful for a policeman, especially for a detective. Good to keep all the channels open."

Baker nodded, put a box file on the table, opened it and began looking through its contents with a bit of theatrical tut-tutting.

"What we can't figure out, Duffy, is whether you're incompetent, unlucky or whether you're working for the other side," Baker said.

"Duh, duh, duh . . . " I said, making a fake organ noise.

"The Tommy Little case no arrests, no convictions. The Lizzie Fitzpatrick case no arrests, no convictions. The Lily Bigelow case, one arrest but you allowed the suspect to escape the jurisdiction . . . do we need to continue? I think you see the pattern here," Sergeant O'Neill said.

"In 1972 you joined the IRA, didn't you? You've been working for them ever since, haven't you?" Baker said.

I held out my wrists. "That's brilliant. Absolutely brilliant. It's a fair cop, gov. Take out your notebook. I'll tell you everything."

Sergeant O'Neill did in fact take out his notebook. Baker frowned and her little goblin eyes twitched.

No one said anything and the silence worked me. I was actually getting a bit concerned now.

I attempted an ingratiating smile, which I'm sure looked ghastly.

"Come on, guys, you can't be serious. I've worked with MI5. Why don't you ask them about my loyalty!"

"Yes, MI5, that's another interesting one," Baker said, taking a photocopy of the story about the crash in the *Irish News* and pretending to read it. "Apparently you were supposed to get on that helicopter with all the top MI5 agents in Northern Ireland, that helicopter that flew into the mountain on the Mull of Kintyre. Got off at the last minute, didn't you, while all your friends in MI5 died?"

"That's not what happened. I broke my leg and the pilot wouldn't let me fly."

"Hmmmm," Baker said.

This was getting annoying. "We all know the real collusion problem in Northern Ireland," I said.

"Oh yes and what's that?" Baker asked.

"That's between Special Branch and its informers in the Loyalist paramilitaries. One day there's going to be a reckoning for all the civilians, all the Catholic civilians, you've let die in Loyalist attacks, to protect your agents."

I stood up and headed for the door.

"Where do you think you're going?" Baker asked.

"I don't have time for this. This may be how you get your kicks but I've an actual job to do. Next time you want to question me you better have an arrest warrant. And my solicitor and my union representative will need to be present. If you come to my home again I'm going straight to the newspapers. I can just see the *Guardian* headline now. 'Catholic RUC Man Harassed by Protestant Police Establishment'."

"I'm a Catholic!" O'Neill protested.

"You're an Uncle Tom, that's what you are," I said.

"You haven't heard the last of this, Duffy," Baker said.

"I don't know how things work here, but in CID before we even think about bringing a case to the Director of Public Prosecutions we have to have witnesses, chains of causation, motivation, forensic evidence. You've got none of that. You've got nothing."

"If you're a mole we'll get you."

"I'm not the bloody mole."

Door slam. Stomp along the corridor. Upstairs. Another dramatic exit.

Asthma inhaler. Played it badly. As always. Hothead.

Downstairs.

Desk Sergeant. "Can you call me a taxi, mate?"

Outside into the cold air.

Hands shaking.

Cigarette. Fucking stress.

Taxi back to Carrickfergus.

Thinking.

Thinking . . .

Newspapers . . .

Upstairs to my office. A fifth of whisky.

I called Carrick Library to confirm a fact about their collection.

I summoned Crabbie and Lawson into my office, gave them a summary of the internal-affairs accusations and what Assistant Chief Constable Strong had suggested we do with the case.

"So what are we going to do with the case?" Crabbie asked.

"I've been mulling that over. There were three prominent local newspapers printed in Belfast in the 1960s: the *Belfast Telegraph*, the *Irish News* and the *Newsletter*. There's three of us. We'll look up the names Deauville and Selden in the indexes and if nothing comes up we'll look up every incident involving the B Specials from say 1966–1969."

"That was when the Troubles were kicking off. The B Specials will be mentioned all the time. We'll practically have to read every single issue of every single paper," Lawson said.

"We better read every single issue of every single paper just to be on the safe side," Crabbie said.

"I've just checked with the librarian. Carrickfergus Library has all three papers in either hardbound or microfiche edition," I said.

"Take us weeks," Lawson said.

"We better get cracking then," Crabbie said. "I'll take the *Newsletter* if you don't mind. Good farming stories."

"I'll take the *Irish News* cos it'll be shorter than the *Telegraph*," I said.

"I'll take the *Telegraph* then," Lawson said gloomily because, as we all knew, the *Belfast Telegraph* had more pages.

"When do we start?" Lawson asked.

"No time like the present."

Seven hours library time later, exhausted and bug-eyed and without finding anything helpful I drove back home to Victoria Estate.

It was raining.

Coronation Road was quiet.

It wasn't destined to stay that way.

20: OUT OF THE SILENT PLANET

Beth had already changed into her PJs and was reading a CS Lewis science-fiction novel from the 50s. Lewis was from Belfast but you wouldn't know that if you'd ever heard him talk in the poshest voice in the world on the BBC, explaining the existence of evil or how God is able to listen to a million people praying at the same time. (God exists outside time and thus has an infinite amount of time and patience to listen to our prayers, poor sod.)

Emma was asleep upstairs. I was reading *Tristes Tropiques*. The music on the record player was Chopin.

Drizzle outside.

I looked at Beth. I wanted to tell her about my troubles but the Derry stuff would only upset her and the Special Branch investigation was nonsense. Her legs were curled up underneath her and she sat there: elfin, boyish, coiled, quiet.

Jet the cat came in and rubbed against me. With a great deal of hassle I had installed a cat flap in the back door so he could go out at night but he seldom ever went out after dark. He'd been Lily Bigelow's cat and had lived most of his life in her flat in London and wasn't that confident about patrolling these streets at night. Streets of Carrickfergus that abutted the Irish countryside and were therefore full of the smell of other cats, stray dogs, foxes and God knows what else. I petted the cat and looked at Beth.

She caught me looking.

"What?" she said. "You look worried."

"I'm not worried."

"Sean, please, come with me to my parents tomorrow. I know you're not a fan of Larne, but we don't really live in Larne, it's more Ballygally."

"I'm not worried. I've got a two-week window before I should be worried and even then I can't see anyone coming onto Bobby Cameron's turf to knock off a peeler without his permission."

"What *are* you thinking about then?"

The lie of the previous sentence? Special Branch railroading me into a jail cell? The fact that ACC Strong and CI McArthur could no longer be counted on to back me up against the bureaucrats and bullshit artists . . . Take your pick.

"CS Lewis was a good friend of Louis MacNeice, who grew up just round the corner from here. MacNeice would come back to Carrickfergus often to visit his parents and sometimes he'd bring WH Auden or CS Lewis with him. They would walk around Carrick together, maybe they even walked down this very street."

"Really?"

"Cool, huh?"

"It is, actually."

And thus distracted, Beth returned to her book.

We went to bed at midnight, checked on the girl, left food for the cat. Slept.

Three am is when they come. The Devil's Hour. When most terminal patients slip away in hospices and hospitals. When the human body is at its weakest. When even the bakers and milkmen are still asleep.

Drizzle on the quiet street and the hills beyond.

No watchers. No dog walkers. Nothing.

Cloudless night. Sickle moon. Constellations rotating about Polaris. Orion. The Great Bear. The Little Bear. Everyone asleep. But not me.

Living room. Staring at the embers. Worries. I looked for something gentle to put on the record player.

Peggy Lee. Peggy Lee singing about *Enttäuschung* – nothing more comforting than that.

Then an odd thought came to me. Something ACC Strong had said: *Hearsay evidence and missing files, is that what you're telling me, Duffy? And now you've been seen going into a known IRA man's house at five in the morning?*

If he didn't know about the Special Branch investigation until I mentioned it, how did he know that I'd arrived at Ken Kirkpatrick's house at five in the morning? Had I said that to him? I didn't think so.

Was it possible that Strong was my secret persecutor? Had he set Special Branch on me? Is that how it worked in the upper levels of the RUC? You prove your ability to command by being prepared to sacrifice your own men?

What motivation could he have for doing that? Would my scalp and a few other scalps and a vigorous internal anti-corruption campaign help prove to Mrs Thatcher that he was the one she should appoint as the Chief Constable's successor?

It was strange, too, that Internal Affairs were coming after me at the same time as the IRA's Army Council and the bloody papers.

Strange, but not, perhaps, a coincidence?

My head hurt.

Phone ringing in the hall.

At this hour!

Probably the Carrick switchboard and I was *not* duty detective tonight.

I picked up the receiver. "What is it? You've probably woken the baby!"

"Get out of the house, Sean! They're coming for you. Get out now!"

I believed it instantly. It was Ken Kirkpatrick from the Derry IRA.

"Beth and Emma are with me!"

"That won't stop them. Get them out, Duffy. Now!"

I slammed down the phone and looked through the hall window. A Ford Transit van was parking itself right outside the gate.

I ran upstairs, three steps at a time.

I shook Beth awake and put my hand over her mouth.

"Mmmffff?"

"IRA hit team. They're going to kill us all. We have to get out!"

I ran into Emma's room, scooped her up, took Beth's hand and stopped at the top of the stairs.

Too late.

A sledgehammer smashed through the front door and it came off its hinges.

If we went down the stairs we were all dead.

Once before my home had been invaded but I'd had more time then. Time to think. Time to move the paraffin heater. I had no time now.

No time. No gun. And a wife and child to protect.

I opened the bathroom door and pushed Beth inside.

Emma began to cry.

"Up there!" a voice said from the bottom of the steps.

I closed the bathroom door as I heard men charging up the stairs. "We'll go out the bathroom window onto the wash-house roof and into the back garden," I whispered.

The window had recently been painted. Would it open?

I tugged and it wouldn't budge.

Men nearly at the top of the stairs.

I gave Emma to Beth, took off my T-shirt, wrapped it around my fist and smashed the window through. I lifted Beth and Emma up and shoved them through.

"He's in there!"

A bullet came through the bathroom door. And then two more bullets. I jumped head first through the bathroom window, scraping my back on the broken glass as a machine gun tore through the bathroom door's handle and lock.

I got half a hand up to stop myself landing face first on the wash-house roof but I still bashed my nose.

Blood in my mouth. Ringing in my ears. I turned to see a man in a balaclava standing in the bathroom with an AK-47. Another man behind him.

Beth had already jumped down into the garden with Emma. I rolled off the roof, fell, landed on the wet grass with a thump, got up and dragged them towards the hedge separating us from the Bridewells' garden.

Machine gun bursts and tracer set the night on fire.

I shoved Beth and Emma over the hedge and dived through the bush after them.

Bullets buried themselves in the garden path where I had just been standing.

The gunman and his companion jumped down onto the wash-house roof. Another gunman came through the back door. The man on the roof jumped down. At least three of them in the back garden now. All of them with machine guns.

And I had nothing.

I ran Beth and Emma through the Bridewells' garden and we smashed through the wooden picket fence between us and the McMurtrys' house.

More tracer and machine gun fire in terrifying parabolas of red death behind us.

"This way!" I said and we ran across the McMurtrys' back yard and vaulted the low wall between the McMurtrys' and the Ferrins'.

"There he goes!" a voice said and all three men emptied their clips after us.

A pause while they reloaded.

The air filled now with car alarms and burglar alarms, dogs barking, birds squawking, Emma screaming.

We ran through the Ferrins' vegetable garden, demolishing their tomato plants on bamboo runners and I helped Beth climb the metal fence between the Ferrins' and Bobby Cameron's house.

"When you get over to the other side bang on Bobby Cameron's back door until he opens up!" I said to Beth. The fence was seven foot tall but Beth was limber. When she dropped down on the other side I passed Emma over the top to her. Beth took her and looked at me through the wire mesh. Bobby's was the last house on the terrace and there was no way out of his back garden but the way we'd come.

"What if Bobby doesn't open the door?"

"He has to. If we try to go to the street they'll kill us."

I started climbing the fence.

The men had all reloaded now and I was an easy target. The machine guns danced and I threw myself over the lip of the fence and landed in Bobby Cameron's garden. Beth was nowhere to be seen.

"Beth!"

"She's inside," Bobby said, running out the back door naked and holding an M249 light machine gun.

"Violet will look after her and the baby. Here," he said handing me a revolver.

I took the gun and as the hit squad ran from my garden into the Bridewells' garden we opened up on them.

The M249 is a belt-fed weapon that fires from an open bolt. When the trigger is pulled, the bolt and bolt carrier move forward under the power of the recoil spring. A cartridge is stripped from the belt, chambered, and then discharged. A simple weapon. Simple but very, very effective. The M249 can fire 200 rounds a minute. Before it was taken out of service in the US

Army to be safety-featured it was known as the SAW because it could saw through just about fucking anything. Bricks, armour plate, humans . . .

An AK-47, even three AK-47s, were no match for this wall of death.

The SAW demolished the Ferrins' greenhouse, the McMurtrys' wall, my hedge. I fired the revolver at the three gunmen but it was redundant and unnecessary in the face of the M249's devastating blanket of fire.

Brass cartridges spewed all over the garden, the SAW sang and Bobby yelled with delight: "Come on! Come and get it! Come on!"

He hadn't hit any of the IRA hit team, but he didn't need to. They weren't fools. The SAW was the gateway to hell and the man wielding the M249 looked like a fucking maniac.

They ran back into my house and when the cartridges finally ran out of the belt on the machine gun I heard the Ford Transit van accelerate away down Coronation Road.

Bobby stood there, holding the smoking gun, naked, happy, the SAW's echoes bouncing off the houses as far away as Fairview Park.

I went into Bobby's house to check that Beth and Emma were unhurt.

I hugged them and told them it was over and then I dialled the station and told Mary to tell RUC command to set up a roadblock. It probably wouldn't be quick enough but you never knew.

Back to the girls.

Emma and Beth were terrified but unharmed.

I hugged and kissed them both again and held them *tight*.

"It's OK, it's OK, it's OK, baby girl. We're safe. The bad men have gone," I said to Emma as I held her.

Beth said nothing. She was in shock. Violet waved me away and put a blanket round her. She gave Beth a cup of sweet tea while Bobby led me out to the back garden where the smell of gunpowder and war was prehistoric and rusty and terrible and beautiful.

"Friends of yours?" Bobby asked.

"IRA hit team."

He nodded. "No Loyalist would dare come onto my street."

"I thought no IRA team would either."

"They'll know better next time. Now, listen Duffy, we have a bit of a problem. The police will be here in five minutes. This machine gun—"

"I'll say the IRA team dropped it when they followed me out of the bathroom. I picked it up and ran with it and then turned it on them. Wipe your prints off it. And I'll get my prints on it."

Bobby wiped down the machine gun and I picked it up. It was so hot it seared my wrists and I immediately dropped it again. Prints imprinted. Job done.

Everyone in Coronation Road and Coronation Crescent and Victoria Estate was out now in their nightshirts and pyjamas, amazed, scared, excited, incredulous at this turn of events.

For the kids this was better than a chip pan fire or when Paisley came electioneering in his open-top car and camel-hair coat.

This would be a night they would tell their children about. When the demons came to Coronation Road and fled.

Now the excitement was over the shakes were starting. And the chills. Need a blanket and a cup of tea to ward off shock.

"Good woman, your Beth," Bobby said.

"She feels like nobody likes her on the street. You couldn't encourage them to be a wee bit friendlier, could you?"

"Aye."

"Not that she'll be staying here for a while."

"This kind of thing is enough to put you right off the neighbourhood."

"Yes."

"I suppose I better go inside and get some clothes on," Bobby said.

"Aye," I agreed and stinking of cordite, sweat, gun oil and adrenalin I waded through the fire, shell casings and massacred tomato plants, back over the walls and hedges into my own garden, where Peggy Lee was still singing about disappointment, where the cat was yawning and where, faintly in the distance, I could hear the sirens from cop cars, Land Rovers and ambulances Dopplering their way onto the stave of the night's music in a manner that was not displeasing to me at all.

21: AFTERMATH

Street full of people. Safe now. Army helicopters flying in big curves above Carrickfergus. Above them the Great Bear drooping his protective paw over all of us.

Cops, soldiers, press. Press – *like to see you fuck with me now Special Branch, yeah, maybe in due course, but not now*. And you too, Dr Havercamp. I dare you to put me on restricted duty. I double dare you.

Kids looking at me in wonder. Bobby Cameron smoking a cigarette and drinking a can of Bass, *no officers I didn't see anything, I slept through the whole kit and caboodle*.

A solitary crow on the telegraph wire.

A solitary crow with a knowing, sleekit black eye.

Cut to:

Larne. Next morning. Saying goodbye to Beth and Emma. Safe now in her father's house. "How long will we have to be here, Sean?"

"Not long. I feel it. Things are coming to a head."

Cut to:

Carrick RUC. My office. A report that the getaway Ford Transit had been found burned out in Eden Village next to the skid marks of an Audio Quattro.

Cut to:

Carrick RUC. Chief Inspector McArthur's office. Chief Inspector McArthur reading the story about me surviving a gun attack on my home in the *Belfast Telegraph* and "it's also in three of the London papers! Three of them, Sean. Maybe they'll give you the Queen's Police Medal."

"I already got one of those."

"Maybe they'll give you the George Cross!"

"Maybe they'll give me the Victoria Cross."

"Oh no, they can't do that, you have to be in the army or the—"

Cut to:

Coronation Road. The workmen installing the iron front door and bullet-proof windows at #113. "They'll need a rocket launcher to take you out now, mate."

"Don't give them any ideas."

Cut to:

Beth looking at houses for sale in Scotland. "I've had it with this bloody country."

"I don't blame you."

Cut to:

Ownies Pub. Crabbie, Lawson and me at the table upstairs overlooking the lough and the Marine Gardens and the Castle. Three Guinnesses in front of us. Three whisky chasers already gone.

We'd done good work in this pub. Case conferences, strategy, working out our plans.

"The papers think this was a random attack on a Catholic peeler and that's good. I don't want the Army Council to know that I know that this was personal."

"But why, personal?" Crabbie asked.

"It's because of this case. Something about Selden and Deauville and the B Specials. Ken Kirkpatrick hinted I was close to something."

"But you say Selden is only a mid-level player. Intel says he's only a mid-level player," Lawson said.

"Exactly. That's what makes it so bloody weird. The Army

Council isn't going to risk an operation in Carrickfergus because I got on the nerves of Harry fucking Selden."

"So what do we do?" Crabbie asked.

"Only two things we can do: 1) Drop the case and let it be known that we are dropping the case, or 2) Keep digging through the newspapers and following up on the other leads until we find out what the connection is. I'm not going to make you guys go with me here. If I'm in jeopardy, you're in jeopardy. I'll take a majority vote."

Lawson was the first with his hand in the air. "There is a third possibility, sir. We tell everyone who asks that we've yellow-filed the case but we keep digging. That's what I think we should do."

"Yeah, that's smart." I agreed. "Crabbie, are you in?"

Crabbie looked at me. "Do you even need to ask?" he said indignantly.

Cut to:

Carrick Library. Reading through old newspapers.

Cut to:

My office. Following up on the other leads.

Cut to:

Beth's parents' house in Larne. Any other girl would have gone to pieces. Hospital time. Shock. PTSD. But as I said: hidden depths, bottom, holding it together – for now – for the sake of Emma and me.

"How are you doing, sweetie?"

"I feel like we're in the bottle city of Kandor."

"The what?"

"Your knowledge of Superman is as bad as your knowledge of Philip K. Dick."

Her turf-blown features, looking at me, right through me. Elizabeth of the waves. Elizabeth of the holding it together.

I kissed her.

She tasted of red wine and tears. No wonder for either.

"Where are your folks in this great pile?"

"They're in the front room with Emma."

"Who's upstairs?"

"Nobody."

"Come on."

"Sean, no, we can't, your car's running, I—"

We ran up to the bedroom.

Ten minutes was enough.

You want the best sex in the world? Ever? Have three men in balaclavas fire Kalashnikovs at you and your girlfriend and miss. And fucking miss.

Cut to: Carrick Library.

Long days, long nights and then:

Lawson staggering towards me from the microfiche machine. He had a box of film and a photocopy in his hands. He looked terrified.

"I found it," he said in an awed whisper. "It was here all along."

Here all along, like an unexploded bomb from 1968. You can kill a man and disappear his wife and disappear the files but you can't unmake what happened.

History knows.

And Morrigan knows.

And Death knows.

"What is it?" I asked.

"We can't discuss it here. I've photocopied the story and put the microfilm back in the box."

"You certainly win the tinfoil-hat award. OK, then, if we can't talk here we'll go to my office."

"We can't go to your office, sir. We'll have to go to Ownies or somewhere neutral like that."

"What are you talking about?"

"We can't go anywhere near a *police* station."

"Oh shit," I said.

"Oh shit indeed," Lawson replied.

22: WHATEVER HAPPENED TO THE
LIKELY LADS

It was 1968. That Wunderjahr *when bliss was it in that dawn to be alive and to be young was very heaven*. The kids had had enough of their parents' wars and their parents' rules and, most of all, their parents' music. Paris was erupting, London was erupting, San Francisco was erupting and even dear old Stone Age Belfast was erupting.

After fifty years of discrimination over jobs and housing, Catholics had taken a leaf out of Martin Luther King's playbook and begun demonstrating for equal treatment in the state of Northern Ireland. Demonstrations had led to riots and counter-demonstrations from the likes of Ian Paisley and his rabble. Violence descended like a black cloak over Ulster and twenty years later it was still here. In 1968 one of those little acts of violence was the shooting of a couple who had rammed a police checkpoint. A police checkpoint manned by auxiliaries, by the B Specials, who had shot at them with their .303 Lee Enfield rifles left over from the war.

The story itself barely got a mention, and the coroner's inquest a hasty month later only gleaned a couple of paragraphs and two sad little black-and-white snaps of a boy and a girl.

The young couple were Maria McKeen (seventeen) and Patrick Devlin (nineteen), driving Patrick's father's Morris Minor. It was the same week a dozen other people died. The overburdened coroner was brief and to the point. *The young couple were going to the Grand Opera House for a show. They were late, but that was no reason to charge through a police checkpoint, especially in these troubled times. The police had no choice but to assume they were terrorists fleeing justice. A tragic case indeed, but no criminal charges were necessary.*

The three B Specials manning the checkpoint were Francis Deauville, Harry Selden and, wait for it, one John Strong who later transferred to the RUC and began rising up the ranks.

Rising up the ranks to Assistant Chief Constable.

John Strong. Read the name, but don't even say it out loud.

"What does this mean?" Crabbie asked in a whisper.

"Let's go find out. Don't mention this to anyone. No one. If anyone asks what we're working on tell them that post office robbery from 1986."

"What's that thing you're always saying about paranoia, Sean?"

"Not me. William Burroughs. A paranoid man is a man who knows a little about what's going on."

"That was it," Crabbie said.

Don't trust whitey and whitey is fucking everywhere.

We walked out of Ownies and went to the station to research the case.

There was no case.

No criminal charges. Nothing in the files.

"We need to talk to the parents," I said.

The electoral records told us that although the Devlin family had moved to England the McKeens were still here, living way up the coast in Cushendun.

BMW.

A2.

The causeway road.

James McKeen had had a stroke and had good days and bad days but Judith McKeen was clear-eyed and angry and sharp as a tack.

"Maria was a mezzo soprano. Very cultured wee girl. Very beautiful. Such a voice. They were going to the Grand Opera House to see *Tristan and Isolde*. Patrick had got his father's car especially. Such a good boy. The idea that he could ever have a run a checkpoint . . ."

"Even if they were late?"

"Even if they were late."

"What do you think happened at that checkpoint?" I asked across the tea cups in that little house in Cushendun village.

"Old Jackie Finnerty the undertaker told James that she'd been interfered with. Now James never told me that at the time. I suppose he thought that it was better I didn't know, but it came out years later on one of his bad mornings. Jackie Finnerty was ninety by then but when I put it to him he said it was true."

"I'm sorry to be so indelicate but what do you mean interfered with?"

"She was raped. Raped by those three B specials is my belief."

I looked at Crabbie and Lawson. Both of them would normally be scribbling in their notebooks, but notebooks can be seized by Special Branch and by your station chief.

"I'm sorry to press the point but how do you know it wasn't Patrick who did it?"

"Patrick wasn't that sort of boy. Patrick was a very shy, very good boy. And it wouldn't make sense, would it? He rapes her and then she goes on with him to the opera house?"

"Definitely rape, not just ordinary sex?"

"Jackie Finnerty is dead now but he saw a lot of bodies in his time and he said rape. He said you always know."

"Why didn't you go to the coroner with this story?"

"My husband James did go to the coroner but the coroner said that she'd probably had sex with Patrick and did he really want his daughter's reputation dragged through the mud? And that was that. James wasn't a fighter and I didn't know at the time."

Judith McKeen looked at us and we looked at her. Her strong dark eyes and her thick grey hair and her strong bony hands.

"Are youseuns looking into this?" she asked.

"We are," I said.

"The police investigating the police?" she said sceptically.

"The police investigating the police," I insisted.

"Can I tell you what I think happened?" she said quietly.

"Please do."

"They were drunk. The three of them. Drunk on duty. The coroner said there had been some 'light drinking on duty', whatever that meant. And they stop this car on the coast road and Maria's all dressed up to the nines, looking gorgeous and one of them touches her and Patrick yells blue murder and they shoot him and rape her."

"Would you give us permission to have Maria's body exhumed? Recently there have been a number of successful prosecutions following the recovery of what is known as DNA evidence. That seems very unlikely in a case like this but you never know what—"

"When they had to move the cemetery to Ballycastle because of the new road James said he didn't want poor Maria to be all dug up and jiggered about and reburied miles away from all of us. So we had her remains cremated and scattered in the sea just out there. When my time comes that's what I want too."

"I see," I said.

"We have no one here now. Maria's brother, Kevin, is in Canada. He has a hotel in Calgary. We never see him. He's very busy."

"Grandchildren?"

"Not yet. Not ever, I think. It'll be a lonely few years when James goes."

I looked at Lawson and McCrabban to see if they had any questions but neither of them had anything.

"Where are these men now? The men who done this?" Judith asked.

"One of them's dead and we're investigating the other two," I said.

She nodded.

"You'll do your best. I can see that. All three of you," she said. "Now I better go see to James. This has been one of his bad afternoons."

"Will you do me one more favour?" I asked at the door.

"What's that?"

"If anyone asks you about this conversation I'd prefer if you didn't say anything about it," I said.

"They've got you afeared these men? Have they?"

She could see it in my eyes, so there was no point in denying it. "There is an element of risk in this investigation so it's probably best if we keep it quiet until we're sure of the facts," I said.

We drove back to Carrickfergus RUC along the coast road, to give us plenty of time to talk.

"Thoughts, gentlemen?" I said.

Lawson leapt right in. "They were drunk, like Mrs McKeen said. They were probably patting her down or grabbing her arse or something, the boy goes for them and they shoot him. In for a penny in for a pound, rape the girl, and then kill her."

"And then what?" I said.

"They concoct their story, everyone believes it, they get off," Lawson said.

"That's not what he means. He means how has this led to Deauville's death?" Crabbie said.

"Any thoughts?"

"Do you have a hypothesis, sir?" Lawson asked.

I looked at both of them. "I believe I do have a working hypothesis that fits with the information we have available."

I didn't say anything and continued to drive along the road.

"Well go on then, sir," Lawson said.

"Unfortunately I have zero evidence for any part of my hypothesis. Nothing I can present to the DPP, nothing that I could take to any of our superiors."

"Go on, Sean, you have to tell us what you're thinking."

I pulled over to the side of the road and we walked to a pub in the picturesque village of Waterfoot in the Glens of Antrim. Quite the dissonance between the story percolating in my brain and the beauty of the surroundings.

A pint. A cigarette. A think. I made sure we got a table outside in the empty beer garden where our only listeners were the cows staring at us over the stone wall.

"They didn't plan on rape. Not at first. The rape comes near the end. They've been drinking but they don't consider themselves to be bad men. Three concerned citizens working as reserve policemen. Salt-of-the-earth types. Two Prods and a Catholic. Just like the three of us."

"Very different from the three of us," McCrabban said, with as grave a voice as I've ever heard him use.

"Young couple stop at the checkpoint, impatient to get going. Cops are being overbearing and a little lascivious. Just light banter. Maybe the girl gives the policeman lip. Maybe the boy. They take the boy out, rough him up, one thing leads to another. The girl goes for them. They point the rifles at the boy and one of them has the bright idea to teach the wee lassie a lesson. She won't talk, and if she does no one will believe her. Teach her a lesson and let them go. This is Ulster: whatever you say, say nothing. They take turns and she's screaming and the shy boy finally cracks. Tries to take down one of them. But it's no go and they shoot him. And then they feel they have no choice and they have to shoot her. And then it's a pact in blood between the three of them: Deauville, Selden and our good friend and lord protector Assistant Chief Constable Strong."

I took a sip of my Guinness and continued.

"The years go by. The B Specials are disbanded. Strong joins the RUC proper but Selden and Deauville take very different paths. Deauville goes to England and drifts into a life of petty and not so petty crime. Selden moves back to Derry and when Bloody Sunday happens, like every other Catholic man in the city he attempts to join the IRA. They take him in. He slowly moves up the ranks. He's a plodder. Not a gunman or a planner or a thinker. Just a plodder. He'll never go anywhere, but then he has an idea. What about his old friend John Strong who he's heard has joined the RUC. What's he up to these days? And he finds out that John Strong has made quite a career for himself. He's going places. And he arranges a not-so-accidental meeting with John Strong. And he tells Strong that all this beautiful life you've made will end if I tell people what really happened to Maria McKeen and Patrick Devlin back in 1968."

Crabbie filled his pipe. "I don't like where you're taking this, Sean," he said.

"And at first Selden just asks for a few bits of information here and there, maybe a tip-off or two about an upcoming raid. And maybe it even goes two ways, maybe Strong gets information from the IRA as he moves up the ranks and the IRA high command realise that they have a very important operational asset indeed. Both men help each other. Both careers blossom. Selden does in fact become something of a player and as a reward gets to be a councillor."

"But no one in Derry knows this, only the Army Council itself," Lawson said. "That's why your mate Ken thought Selden was a nonentity."

I looked at Crabbie and he knew it was possible, maybe even probable. There *was* an IRA mole and that mole was John Strong.

"An Assistant Chief Constable who belongs to the IRA," Lawson said, gasping over his drink.

"An Assistant Chief Constable, maybe Chief Constable in waiting who is their creature to his very boots. What a coup that would be."

"And everything's just peachy for a few years but then

Deauville returns from England with a new wife and a new game," Lawson said.

"And he spots his old friend John Strong in Carrick. Maybe at the Rangers Club," Crabbie suggested.

"And Deauville's not like the IRA. He's not subtle. He's not interested in the long game. He sees that Strong is a wealthy man, an important man and he asks for money. A lot of money. If Strong pays him a handsome cheque every month poor Elena won't have to risk life and limb smuggling heroin from Bulgaria every six weeks," I said.

"And after this chance meeting with Deauville, Strong tries to contact his handler immediately. But where is Harry Selden? Harry's in the hospital. So Strong decides to act on his initiative. I'll shoot the blackmailing bastard myself. Can't use my service revolver but it's dead easy to buy a crossbow somewhere. And then I'll get Harry to get the IRA to claim the hit. End of problem."

"But the IRA didn't want to claim the hit, they're pretty protective of their and other groups' kills, aren't they? And it was only with reluctance that Harry got that DAADD claim out into the press," Lawson said.

We finished our drinks and stared at the sea.

"We have no proof and we're not going to get any proof," McCrabban said. "Strong is far too clever to admit anything."

"What if we wore a wire and confronted him? I mean you, sir, you confront him?" Lawson asked.

I shook my head. "Crabbie's right. Those Jedi tricks aren't going to work with him. Overtly or covertly he won't admit anything to me. And we'll have played our hand. He's a very dangerous opponent. The most dangerous opponent we've ever had and he'll destroy us all if we bring him in and only wound him."

"And what if we're wrong? What if we bring him in and accuse him and we're just dead wrong?" Lawson said. "The high jump for all of us."

"I don't think we're wrong. Strong told me to drop the case. He needs it gone. He's come at me on two fronts, through Special Branch and through the IRA."

"He can't know that we suspect him. You have to tell Strong that we're yellowing the file. DAADD claimed the kill and we're letting it drop for lack of evidence. Similarly with Mrs Deauville, we're letting the case lapse," Crabbie said.

"Then what?" I asked.

"Then you write a letter to Harry Selden on official stationery telling him too that the case is closed and that the RUC regrets any inconvenience it may have caused," Crabbie said.

"Agent and handler both get the good news and both think they're in the clear. I officially move on to other work, meanwhile we try harder than ever to nail the fucker," I said.

23: THE ACC

First things first. Letter off to Selden. Full-throated apology. Regret any inconvenience. Blah, blah, bloody blah. Then wait for the other shoe to drop.

Two days later the phone rang in my office.

"Hello?"

"Duffy, it's John Strong."

"Sir, I wasn't expecting to hear—"

"It's a pleasure to talk to you, son. I don't want to embarrass you but you're quite the hero now, after what happened to you at your home," ACC Strong said.

"From zero to hero, isn't that the expression, sir?"

"Now, now, Duffy. Don't be facetious, I always knew you were a good policeman. And I hear you're in the running for a medal?"

"Another medal, sir. That'll be my second."

"You are in a cocky mood this morning. So, uhm, what are you up to these days?"

"Nothing much, sir, a post office robbery from a few years ago that we can't seem to crack."

"Whatever happened to that case you were working on with the French name?"

"Oh, the Deauville case? You were right, sir. There was no juice to it. DAADD murdered the poor chap and we've no eye-witnesses or forensic evidence of any kind so we're dropping it.

Moving it to the yellow file. Moving onto other business."

"I think that's probably for the best, don't you?"

"Yes, sir. I'm sorry to have let you down, sir. It's yet another homicide case that goes unsolved, sir, and it won't do my reputation any good for bringing DAADD or IRA men to justice but—"

"No need to finish that sentence, Duffy. You're doing the right thing. And there's some of us up here that know you're a good policeman. Special Branch still causing you problems?"

"They're still investigating me, I think, sir."

"I'll see what I can do to get them off your back."

"Thank you, sir, I'll get you a drink next time you're down the police club."

"I won't get there as often as I'd like now, not with all my new responsibilities."

"Of course, sir."

"Bye, Duffy. Good to see you've decided to become a company man again."

"Yes, sir. Straight and narrow for me from now on . . . Sir, I'd like to get you a wee something for all your help, though. You're a Rangers man rather than Celtic, am I right?"

"Of course!" he said, laughing. "But you don't have to get me anything."

"I'll find something nice, sir. Tickets to an Old Firm game or something like that."

"You don't have to do anything, Duffy. Just keep your nose clean. Bye, Inspector."

"Bye, sir."

He hung up.

A Rangers fan who goes to the Rangers club and is seen there by Francis Deauville? Yeah, that would work.

The IRA Council would get the message from two different sources now. Their mole was safe. *Yeah don't worry, lads, Duffy's not as smart as he thinks he is and he's safely neutered.*

A third Army-Council-sanctioned attack on Sean Duffy seemed an unlikely possibility.

Time for Duffy and crew to get working.

We told the Chief Inspector we were running down leads on the PO robbery and started doing leg work. We took Selden and Strong's photographs to the crossbow shops, but no one remembered either man. At the Rangers Club the barman liked the look of Strong as the tall man in the flat cap but wasn't completely convinced it was him and "wasn't completely convinced" was not something you could take to court.

We tried to look up the coroner on the McKeen–Devlin deaths but that old complacent lying bastard had died ten years previously.

We ran the missing persons reports on Mrs Deauville but there was no give there either.

We discreetly accessed John Strong's personnel file but all that was in there was a hagiographical ascent to glory.

We looked into the possibility of exhuming Patrick Devlin and examining the wounds on his body but the family wasn't in the country any more and an exhumation was not something you could keep quiet about. And even if we did pull up poor old Patrick Devlin from his final resting place, only a pistol shot in the back of the head could possibly be strong enough probative value to indict a high-ranking policeman – every other gunshot wound could be turned by a good lawyer into the kind of wound you get in a melee from running a roadblock. Attempt to take down Strong with evidence like that and we'd be blowing up all our careers and putting our lives in jeopardy. The exhumation of Patrick Devlin would have to be a last desperate roll of the dice.

We did finally find Harry Selden's "stolen" car burnt out and forensically dead in a wrecker's yard in East Belfast. No help at all on that score.

Days like this.

Nights like this.

The Troubles simmered in the background, an entire generation scarred by the brutal murders of the two corporals and the
three IRA funeral mourners on live TV.

Throw in the "punishment" shootings and the firebombings
and the attacks on cops and soldiers.

Old news now. Most of that stuff wouldn't make page one of the
Irish papers and wouldn't get mentioned at all in the British ones.

My old gaffer and one of John Strong's mentors, Superintendent
Bertie Hare died of coronary heart disease. Dress uniform for
his funeral in the rain at Victoria Cemetery. ACC Strong didn't
show up. Busy man. A Church of Ireland priest telling the men
gathered round the grave that he was "confident in the resurrection of the flesh".

I was glad someone was confident.

Fortunately we had a few real minor cases that allowed us to
hide the big case: a shoplifting gang, joyriders, coal thieves.

March advanced into April.

Beth grew more and more agitated at her parents' house.
More and more depressed about living in Ulster at all. "That
house Dad's building for us feels like it's a prison."

"Then we won't move in there."

"But Northern Ireland feels like a prison."

"Ulster as existential prison. I've had those thoughts. Many
times."

"They do my exact masters course at Glasgow University.
It's better, actually. They have teachers there who'll let you do
comic books as well as contemporary fiction."

"Glasgow University? Sounds good."

"I'd transfer my work done. I could finish the whole thing in
under a year."

I'd lost one girlfriend to a Scottish uni. Could I lose two?
That's the way history goes, says Nietzsche. Wash and repeat.
Until all feeling is gone and everything fades into nothing. Wash
and repeat.

Walking insomniac around Carrickfergus.

Down Coronation Road, Barn Road, Taylor's Avenue. The dream engine spilling vowels on Victoria Estate. An audiobook on my Walkman. Poems. Berryman. Huffy Henry and Amy Vladeck. Huffy Henry and Louis MacNeice.

Others lines from other poems:

The blots on the page are so black they cannot be covered with shamrock . . .

The falcon cannot hear the falconer . . .

And this from the opera the dead couple in 1968 did not get to see:

Frisch weht der Wind/Der Heimat zu
Mein Irisch Kind/Wo weilest du?

Where indeed?

He was out there, like a spider at the centre of a web. A dangerous opponent. One mistake, one false move, and me and Lawson and Crabbie were all going to go down. How can you mess with a man who has the IRA *and* the police on his team?

Even a clown like Dalziel assumes a new light. You're an eejit, Kenny, a complete fucking eejit, but at least you're not a traitor.

24: DRIVING MUSIC

B elfast does weather well. Especially rain.
   One night I grabbed the lock-pick kit, the Glock and the
raincoat and walked down the path of 113 Coronation Road in a
downpour from Ezekiel 38.

Lightning danced around the occult chimney at Kilroot and
the yellow cranes above the dry dock at the shipyard. Thunder
boomed across the lough. I looked under the BMW for mercury
tilt switch bombs but the brave boys who plant such things were
all abed tonight.

It was late.

Stupid o'clock.

I drove up Coronation Road and turned right on Victoria
Road. The estate was deserted. The Beemer purred down
Victoria Road past the graveyard and the butchers, past Lawson's
house and the supermarket.

We came to a rest at the newly installed traffic lights, which, of
course, were red, even though there wasn't another car around
for miles.

I put one of Lawson's CDs in the player. It wasn't the LA rap
one that he and all the kids at the station and even John Peel
were calling a classic. It was a band called The Butthole Surfers
from Texas. I looked at the CD case while the light stayed red.
The album was called *Hairway to Steven*.

The light went green and I turned right.

The BMW wanted to stretch itself.

Up the Marine Highway, heading for the city.

Belfast: beautiful in its brokenness.

All cities will look like this in the far future: ruined and fractured, walled and utilitarian. This is Earth's only city. A Belfast that vibrates in the present and the past and in the days to come.

Burned-out cars. Bomb sites. Wet horses tied to girders. Dead televisions in the rubble.

Like the man said. The dead man in the forest outside Derry with his strange map and his interesting opinions. We were once creatures of the savannah, whose lives were mapped by the journeys of the great migrating herds across the rift valley. We can't live like this. Stationary, on top of one another. It's bad for our mental health.

It was so windy the cranes were swaying at the shipyard and the army helicopters had been grounded. Good night for a smash-and-grab raid somewhere with the choppers down and the police huddled in their barracks. Remember that if Special Branch forces me to resign and I'm looking for a career change.

I drove up the Antrim Road, past Our Lady of Lourdes, past the zoo, and then I curved down again through the empty city streets to the Shore Road.

I knew where I was going.

The address from the personnel file.

I parked the car outside the Assistant Chief Constable's house on the Belfast Road. A big granite three-floor job on the water's edge of Belfast Lough. I put on gloves and a balaclava. I took the Glock from the passenger's seat and put it in my raincoat pocket. I examined the lock-pick kit to make sure everything was in order.

I got out and walked to that big iron gate.

Rain was pouring down my neck between my raincoat and my Che T-shirt.

Sea spray was splashing against the gable wall.

Lightning again hit the power-station chimney.

I looked at the Beware of the Dog sign.

"Dog better beware of me."

I climbed over the gate and dropped down the other side.

Way to deal with an attack dog is to offer it your left arm. He'll bite it and hold on and then you punch him in the eye with your right fist. No need for a gun. Amateurs and farmers shoot dogs.

I stood there, waiting.

No dog.

I walked down the long driveway past the rose bushes.

Onto the porch with its empty milk bottles and a garden gnome in an English bobby's uniform. Strictly against regulations, that. Standing order 222, "Display nothing in your car or your house that might indicate that you are a member of the RUC."

Have to have a word with him about it.

Yale 1970s front door lock. Easy peasy. Leaky tumblers. Pick it with a screwdriver if I needed to. Lock-pick kit it anyway. Tension wrench in bottom of lock, pick in top. Feel for the tumbler, turn, hey presto the door is open.

Safety chain behind the door.

Pliers from lock-pick kit could snip through it in a second but there was no need. It had been placed too close to the catch, with too much slack, and it wasn't that tricky to lift it off with my gloved fingers.

I stepped into the house.

I walked into the hall and then into the living room with its big windows and the view over Belfast and North Down.

I caught my balaclavaed reflection in the glass.

Why are you doing this, Duffy? Why do you always have to be so fucking theatrical? You weren't always this way. Don't you remember that row you had with your philosophy tutor at Queens when he was recommending the stance Camus takes in *The Myth of Sisyphus*? Melodramatic and narcissistic and false you called it. You were right then, you're wrong now.

I mean just look at you: raincoat, gloves, gun, balaclava. It's pathetic. Age hasn't matured you. It's made those traits that were ticks in the twenty-five-year-old into full-blown affectations in the thirty-eight-year-old. And affectations is putting it politely. Haven't you grown up at all? You have a child, for Christ's sake, isn't that supposed to wise a man up?

I stood there looking in the window glass, saying nothing. Frozen there half in and half out of the rain, an image flickering in the lightning like a ghost.

I sighed, gently closed the front door and sat down on the sofa.

I was disgusted with myself, sitting here in Assistant Chief Constable Strong's living room at midnight, getting his carpet all wet.

The bold move would be to put something on his stereo. Something loud, Beethoven if he had any. He comes down in his dressing gown, bleary-eyed, holding his service revolver in front of him and I'm sitting there on the sofa waiting for him, like a stone cold motherfucker.

I take off the balaclava and he sees it's me.

"It's all right, Margaret," he says to the wife and then comes over to the stereo and turns it off.

"What's the meaning of this, Duffy?" he says.

And I stand up and I tell him that I know what he's done. I let it all out. "You had me lifted in Derry! You gave me up to the IRA! Your own man. To protect your arse!"

Yeah something like that.

I put my head in my hands and sighed.

I looked at the Glock in my right hand.

I got up and, still dripping, walked over to the stereo, rifled through the CDs. There wasn't any Beethoven anyway. No classical music at all, in fact.

A black Alsatian walked into the living room from the kitchen.

It wasn't expecting to see me and after a moment's shock came over and sniffed my hand. I took the glove off to let him better get the measure of me. An intruder who deserved to get bitten or a friend of the family?

He must have smelt *cop* because he licked my wrist and lay down on the living-room rug. I rubbed his belly and he liked that.

It was time to go now, time to flee, but Dozy Duffy didn't go. Dozy Duffy found himself walking upstairs.

He opened the door at the top of the stairs which was a bathroom. Another door which was a child's bedroom, with a fifteen-year-old boy sleeping in a race-car bed that was nearly too small for him. Another bedroom was a spare room and another bedroom was the master bedroom.

Moonlight was illuminating the face of Assistant Chief Constable Strong and the long red hair of Mrs Assistant Chief Constable Strong, whom I'd met once at the police club in Kilroot.

Look at you two lying there. You don't know how close you are to death, how close that boy is to losing a father. I'm boiling with fury. I'm an avenging angel for my own daughter who, but for a stroke of luck, would be fatherless.

And Maria McKeen and Patrick Devlin and all the others you have betrayed.

Look at you. A killer by proxy. A coward.

I have come for you, Strong.

I shook my head again.

No.

Theatrical. Ridiculous.

I closed the door, walked back onto the landing and down the stairs. I patted the dog and went out into the rain. I carefully closed the front door behind me. There was no way to put the safety chain back on the hook but chances were they wouldn't notice that, or they'd think they'd forgotten to do it. Or they'd think it was elves.

The dog was watching me through the frosted glass part of the door. It began to bark.

Of course.

I ran down the path, climbed the gate, quickest ever look under the Beemer, got in and drove; I was a good bit away when I saw the bedroom light come on in the rear-view mirror.

"That was a close one."

I accelerated up the A2 and kept accelerating as the dual carriageway became the M5. I drove into Belfast but the city was deserted. I don't know what I was expecting or hoping for. An ambush? A riot? None of those things.

Back out of the city along the Shore Road. To Carrickfergus. The North Road and finally up to Knockagh Mountain. It always comes back to here.

I got out of the Beemer and walked around the monument and watched the lightning stab great red electric forks over the glacial valley. Some strikes as far away as the Galloway hills in Scotland.

The rain poured down onto me.

And I was not baptised and I was not cleansed and my anger did not abate.

But a thought was growing.

A plan.

A way of getting the bastard. A way of getting all of them.

What was the thing that they feared the most?

Blackmail. Blackmail had started this ball rolling.

Yeah, it would be theatrical and I'd just renounced theatrics in that big speech to myself. But fuck it. Foolish consistency/ hobgoblin, all that jazz.

I grinned and took a hit on my asthma inhaler. I got back in the BMW, stuck in NWA's "Fuck Tha Police" and for the final time in this case I drove to Derry.

25: THE OFFER

I parked the Beemer two roads over and checked the street for Special Branch observation teams. Last thing I needed was internal affairs dicking with me now. No vans, no Volkswagen campers, no eejits sleeping in cars.

Harry Selden couldn't believe it when he came downstairs to wonder why his stereo had suddenly come on and he saw me standing there listening to *Willie Nelson Live* in his living room. He was wearing a navy blue dressing gown and slippers and holding an ancient-looking shotgun that would probably take us both out if he squeezed the trigger.

"What the hell?"

"Put the gun down, Harry, I'm unarmed and I've important things to discuss with you. Do it now, before I'm forced to tell you my Willie Nelson joke."

He turned off the stereo and lowered the shotgun.

"Get out of my house. My mother's sleeping upstairs."

I sat on the sofa. "I'll take a cup of tea."

His really rather adorable visage contorted into the sort of rage Oliver Hardy contorted into when James Finlayson started smashing up his car in *Big Business* (1929).

"No tea, Duffy, get the fuck out of my house before I call the police."

"I thought you had no truck with the police."

"Get out, Duffy!"

"Lower your voice, Harry. Mother's sleeping upstairs."

"What the fuck is the meaning of this? You're going to be in all the papers tomorrow."

"No, I don't think I will. To quote Bugs Bunny, it's mongoose season, and you're the fucking mongoose."

"Have you lost your—"

"I know everything, Harry. I know about you and Strong and Deauville and that couple you murdered back in 1968. Maria McKeen and Patrick Devlin."

He was momentarily taken aback but he recovered himself quickly enough. "We didn't murder anyone. We were exonerated by—"

"It doesn't matter. I don't care. 1968? Might as well be 1868 or 1690 or May 29th 1453, I don't give a flying fuck."

He seemed confused now. I supposed he'd been expecting moral indignation and he wasn't getting any.

"Go and make the tea and be quick about it."

He made the tea and came back with a mug and a couple of digestive biscuits. I dipped the biscuit and sipped the tea.

"Have you seen my personnel record, Harry?" I asked.

"No."

"Well, your friend John Strong has, and sorry reading it is, too. The shit I have had to put up with over the years. You wouldn't believe it, mate. Promotion holds, demotions, suspensions without pay . . . And now they're going to put some fucking connected Proddy bastard called Dalziel over me. Best years of my life I've given to the RUC. For what? So I can look under my car every day for bombs, so I can walk about with a big fat target on my back?"

"I don't understand, what is it—"

"I want what John Strong has. I want a pay cheque every month from the IRA into a Swiss bank account. Nothing extravagant. Nothing you can't handle. Let's say 10 grand a month. Gaddafi gave you five million dollars so I know you're good for it. Or pay me direct from Noraid in America if you want."

"I don't know what you think you're—"

"I'm not done! And I want Strong to forward my career in the police. Immediate promotion to Chief Inspector and eventual promotion to Chief Super. Strong will become my mentor and he'll make sure I rise up through the ranks with him."

"Duffy, what—"

I took out my Glock and pointed it at his face. "I'm not fucking done," I snarled. "And I want an end to attacks on my family. A permanent end. I want it to be known on the Army Council that I am one of the good guys now. I am not to be touched."

"You're wearing a tape recorder," Selden said.

I shook my head.

"Search me, top to bottom, I don't care."

I held the gun in the air and he searched me for a wire and found nothing.

"Now we can talk, right?" I said.

But still he was suspicious. "I don't know what you think you know—"

I yawned. "So tired of this shit. You blackmailed Strong into becoming an IRA agent because of what happened in 1968 and since, oh I don't know, maybe the last decade or so you've been running John Strong as your agent. The most important agent the IRA has in the police."

"That's fantastic. Ridiculous, I—"

I pointed the gun at him again. "I'm in no mood, Harry. I'm just tired. Tired of all the nonsense. I'm as good as married. I have a wee girl who you tried to kill. You'll pay me until I hit my twenty years in the police in 1994 and then I'll retire with the rank of Detective Chief Superintendent and maybe an MBE and I'll move to Spain and live on my pension and on the considerably higher sum you've put in the Swiss bank account."

I finished the tea. Hopefully there wasn't rat poison in it.

"You've got 48 hours to think it over. If you choose to decline my generous offer I'll have to go public with my allegations. And my proof."

"Proof?"

"Proof."

"What proof? Proof of what?"

"You'll see. Maybe no one'll believe it, but fuck it, I don't care. Look at my eyes. Look at them. I'm done. Done with all this bullshit. So what if I pull the temple down about our heads? I'm fucking exhausted by all of you."

I stood up.

"It's too risky for me to come up here, what with intel watching you and IA watching me. I never want to have to drive onto this bloody street again. From now on you'll be servicing me . . ."

"Wait a minute, Duffy, we haven't discussed anything. I haven't committed to anything. I don't know if any of this is possible. I—"

"Here's the first step. You and me and Strong are going to meet. None of us can ever be seen together so it's got to be somewhere safe at night. On my turf. Somewhere I control. At that first meeting I'll bring my Swiss bank account number. You two will bring nothing. No IRA hit team, no bodyguards, no guns, nothing. Understood?"

"I haven't agreed to any—"

"Furthermore, you will not discuss our little conversation today with anyone except John Strong. I want the deal to be in place before the Army Council is approached. I don't want them thinking I'm some rogue fucking lunatic like Deauville who is going to ruin everything for them. I want them to see me as a friend of John's and yours and a potentially valuable asset in my own right. Is that clear?"

"Duffy, look, what you're saying is all very well but—"

I got close to his face. "Rule number 1: only discuss this with John Strong for now. Rule number 2: only the two of you at the first meeting. Rule number 3 is the same as rule number 2: no bodyguards, no minders, no drivers, nothing like that. I will be alone. And if anything happens to me before the meet, you're all up the spout."

He nodded. He was beginning to process it all now, beginning to figure out the angles.

"About this proof," he said.

Ah, so that was the line that was really worrying him.

"Proof that the pair of you murdered Deauville and disappeared his wife."

"What is it?"

"You'll see it. And after the first meeting, when we've established some trust, you and I will never have to meet again. The money will go into my bank account and Strong and I can meet socially or at work."

"How will we ever be able to trust each other?" Selden asked.

"Mutual blackmail. I've got a hold over you and as soon as that first cheque goes into my bank account from the IRA you've got a hold over me. It'll be in both our interests to keep quiet. Everybody wins."

"And the Deauville case?"

"Yellowed. No one gives a shit about a fucking drug dealer and his fucking heroin-smuggling wife."

"And the McKeen–Devlin case?"

"Old news. No one gives a shit about that either."

Selden looked me up and down. "I don't know, Duffy," he said slowly. "This doesn't seem like you."

"Doesn't it? From the boy who tried to join the provisionals in 1972 but was turned down by Dermot McCann? From the young man who has realised that dirty cops and Loyalist thugs are the real enemies of the people of Ireland? But ultimately from the old man who's just sick and tired of all of it and the only thing he wants is a quiet life? Let me finish my career in safety and get my pension and move abroad. Ten grand a month? Small price to pay for keeping one of your prize assets in place and keeping a lippy peeler off your back."

He nodded.

"Well?" I asked.

"Perhaps something can be arranged," he said.

"Good. It's the smart play for all of us. Now this is where we meet. There's an abandoned factory in Carrickfergus called Courtaulds. I know it well and it's close to my house. It's my turf and it's safe. Tomorrow night at midnight in the turbine room. That'll give you nearly two days to think it over. If you're not there by 12.05 there's no deal and fuck it, I'll go to the press. Yes, I know Strong will try to bring me down and probably he will bring me down but no one will ever really trust that fucker again and they'll be watching him like a hawk."

"Tomorrow night. Midnight. Courtaulds factory, Carrickfergus," Selden said, still not completely convinced.

"No guns, no surprises. Just you and Strong. I'll bring my bank account number and my proof of your complicity and we'll take it from there," I said.

"I'll talk to him."

I laughed. "He's not going to be happy."

"We've had many such difficult conversations," Selden said.

"I'll bet you have. This is the beginning of a beautiful friendship," I said and offered him my hand.

He shook it tentatively. I walked to the front door and turned. "No tricks! I am not a problem. A problem is something that can't be solved with money. I can be solved with money. OK?"

"OK."

I drove out of Derry just as the sun was coming out of the bit of the Atlantic Ocean that embraces the coast of Western

Scotland. On a whim I drove east to Tor Head and followed the trail to the top of the promontory.

From here it looked like I could see the whole world.

With no one around for miles and miles I allowed myself a clenched-fist cheer. Just one. They were only half in the bag.

I followed the A2 back to Carrickfergus, driving right past Judith McKeen's house in Cushendun.

Back to Coronation Road.

Fed the cat and went to sleep on the living-room sofa.

No one came to kill me in the night and if they were going to come it would have been last night.

Probably.

Hit the bricks. Look under Beemer. Crabbie and Lawson in my office. I told them what I'd done and then I told them the plan.

"Strong and Selden have to come to see what this proof is. They'll be expecting me to come alone but I won't be alone. They'll check that I'm not wearing a wire before we talk and I won't be wearing a wire, either. But Lawson, you'll be there in the corner with the boom mike and the high-gain antenna hooked up to the tape recorder. Almost as good as a wire."

"And you'll get them to incriminate themselves?" Crabbie said.

"I'll try to."

"And what if it's a double cross and they bring a couple of gunmen with them?" Crabbie asked.

"You know that factory. We can see for miles round there. If we don't like what's coming we can get out of there. But anyway, you'll be there with a Heckler and Koch MP5, as will Lawson and me . . ." I suddenly realised I'd been getting ahead of myself. "Uhm, that's if you lads are in. I should have—"

"Of course we're in, sir," Lawson said matter of factly.

Crabbie nodded vigorously. "Oh aye. We're in. Do you think there's anyone else we can trust though? For back-up."

"I doubt it," I said. "What do you think?"

"We'd have to lie to them. As soon as we mention that we're trying to trap ACC Strong . . . well, alarm bells will be ringing. And if we lie to them and Strong shows up . . . Confusion, to say the least."

"In house," Lawson said. "The three of us. We'll take him down."

26: THE FACTORY

The abandoned factory was a movie trailer from an entropic future when all the world would look like this. From a time without the means to repair corrugation or combustion engines or vacuum tubes. From a planet of rust and candle power. Guano coated the walls. Mildewed garbage lay in heaps. Strange machinery littered a floor which, with its layer of leaves, oil and broken glass was reminiscent of the dark understorey of a rainforest . . .

Yeah, I know.

Circles.

That's why I'm getting out. I wasn't joking about retirement, but I have a slightly different plan, one that won't involve me selling my soul to the paramilitaries.

Crabbie signalling me with his torch.

The torch on and off and on and off to tell us that a car was coming.

A momentary ellipse. A fragment of a second. But enough to move us from prologue into body . . . This was it. I was confident. I had prepared the ground. Walked the terrain. I had sent home the aged night watchman, telling him that there was a police operation underway. I had gotten the best bullet-proof vests and Heckler and Koch MP5s from the armoury. I had taken Crabbie and Lawson to the UDR base in Woodburn and gotten two hours' range time shooting the MP5s. Shooting, reloading, shooting until they were utterly familiar with the gun. Lawson was the more—

Crabbie was running towards me.

"What is it?" I said.

"Two vehicles. One of them is a van, one of them is a car. I don't like it."

"We can abort. We can get out of here before they pull up," I said.

"I don't know," he muttered.

"Let's see who gets out of them," I said, running to the broken window.

I checked my watch. It was five to twelve.

Sure enough it was a van, but there was only one man in it: Selden, wearing an anorak and carrying a torch. The other car was a white Bentley Mulsanne Turbo – Strong's car. How did we not twig that he was on the take? Jesus.

"False alarm," I said to Lawson. "Everything's going according to plan."

Lawson was hiding in the deep shadow in the corner of the factory with his sound-recording equipment.

It was all deep shadow in here, perfect for vanishing men. There was only one working light from an arc light the night watchman had set up. The only ambient sources were the street lights on the dual carriageway below us and the stars and moon. Lawson was next to the arc light switch and at the first sign of trouble was to kill the light. Would he know what trouble meant? He'd have to.

Selden and Strong walked up the path to the factory entrance together. Thick as bloody thieves.

"OK, Crabbie, get in the corner over there and cover me," I whispered.

I zipped up my leather jacket.

Leather jacket, bullet-proof vest, jeans, Adidas gutties, lucky Che T-shirt again.

When they came in the door it was Selden, the handler, who said: "Hello?"

I let them walk in a little further before I answered: "Gentlemen, it's good to see you."

"About this—" Strong began, but Selden cut him off.

"Come over here, Duffy, I need to know that you're not recording this."

"Why would I do that? It's going to incriminate me as much as it'll incriminate you."

"Nevertheless."

I walked over, carrying the machine gun.

"I thought you said no guns," Selden said.

"No guns for you, but I'm not meeting the two of you without protection. Get on with your search. I'm wearing a vest but it's loose enough for you to look underneath it."

Selden patted me down and found no wire.

"He's clean," Selden said.

Strong looked around the factory. "Are you alone?"

"I'm alone."

"What about the redoubtable Sergeant McCrabban?" Strong said suspiciously.

"You'd think he'd believe one bad word about you? He worships you. All the men do. They'd throw me down a well if I lifted a finger to you . . . What about you, though, did you keep your side of the bargain? You kept the Army Council out of it?"

"Of course!" Selden snapped. "I wouldn't dare present them with a problem like you for a third time. I'd be the one making that trip out to the forest."

"Good. Then everyone kept their word."

"Now, what about this proof of yours?" Strong said.

"An eyewitness saw you and Deauville talking in the Rangers club. He drew an uncannily accurate picture of you and when I showed him your photograph he confirmed it. He'll never think of it again until I go public with revelations but then he'll be able to back me up 100 per cent."

"What's his name?" Selden demanded.

"No, no, no. Now it's your turn. What happened March 22nd 1968? Quid pro quo."

"Quid pro quo is you giving us your informant's name."

"Quid pro quo is us both trusting one another and being able to fuck one another, now what happened March 22nd 1968?"

A long pause before Strong shrugged.

"If there's no wire what difference does it make?" Strong said.

"Tell me."

"Not much to tell. It wasn't even our fault. It was Frank Deauville. It was all him," Strong said.

"What did he do?"

"We stop the car. They're not suspects, they're not anything, Harry says to wave them on but Frank says no, the wee lassie might have something concealed under her dress."

"And then what?"

"Well, we'd all been drinking a bit. It was a cold night."

"What happened?"

"Frank looked under her dress, or tried to, and she slapped him and then he lost it. He dragged her out of the car and then the boy comes running round and he's on top of Frank . . ."

"What happened?" I asked.

"Frank threw the boy off and swung his rifle round and shot him. The bullet went through his heart, killed him on the spot."

"The whole thing was an accident," Selden said.

I shook my head. "No, it wasn't an accident. The girl was raped."

"Frank's blood was up. He was furious. We couldn't stop him," Selden said.

"Couldn't or didn't want to?" I asked.

Strong shone his torch in my face. "How do you know all this?"

"I'm a detective. I find shit out."

"OK, now you know what happened. What's the name of this eyewitness?"

"Who shot the girl?"

"What's got into you, Duffy?" Strong said, his radar pricking up by my insistence on the details.

"Who shot the girl?" I asked again.

"Frank insisted that we all shoot her. He would have shot us if we didn't," Selden said.

"My rifle jammed," Strong said.

Aye, maybe so, but you pulled the trigger, didn't you?

I turned to Selden. "And when did you recruit John into the IRA?" I asked.

Selden shook his head. "We all drifted apart after that. I didn't know what any of them were doing until I saw Frank's name in the paper in '83, I think. He'd solved some kind of big bank fraud case."

"And that's when the blackmail started?"

"Blackmail's an ugly word . . . We scratch his back and vicey versey, like you said," Selden said.

"Who is this eyewitness?" Strong demanded.

"I've written down their name and address on a piece of paper. I've also written down my bank details and I've put them both in this envelope," I said, reaching into the inside pocket of my leather jacket.

Strong took the envelope and shoved it into his sports coat pocket.

"And you haven't told anyone else what you know?" Strong said.

"Nope."

Strong looked at Selden and nodded. Selden took a step back away from me. "There's been a change of plan, Duffy," Selden said.

"What change of plan?"

"Well, you were right," Selden said. "I couldn't go to the Army

Council with a third request to kill you in as many weeks. I'd be a joke. In fact, worse than a joke, I'd be fucking dead. So I had to keep my mouth shut about our little talk. No help coming from the high command."

"And obviously I couldn't bring in any of *my* colleagues," Strong said.

"But for heaven's sake, this is Ulster. It was easy enough to round up four men in Derry who would kill somebody no questions asked."

"What four men?"

"Us four men," they said, coming in the door.

They'd obviously been in the back of van, waiting for their cue. Double cross. He was going to take the envelope and kill me.

The leader was a pale, beady-eyed man who was an odd amalgam of a Staffordshire bull terrier and Charles Hawtrey. The other three were archetypes: an old one, a tall one, a skinny young one. You can think of them as *Carry On* actors too: Syd James, Bernard Breslaw, Jim Dale. No Kenneth Williams, I'm sorry to say. But it's OK. You don't really need to think about them at all. In forty-five seconds all four of them would be dead.

The men were carrying assorted weapons: an AK47, double-barrelled shotguns, a revolver.

Strong and Selden pulled pistols from inside their jackets.

"Six against one. Seems a bit unfair, no?" I said.

"Fuck me, Duffy, what a headache you were. It's your own fucking fault, you know, you just wouldn't let it lie, would you?" Strong said.

The seven 'p's.

Proper preparation and planning prevents piss poor performance.

Hands into fists. Drip of endorphins soothing the lizard brain.

Again that old, old thought: *fear is power*, son, *fear is the precursor to action*.

A look of alarm in Strong's eyes. "Why are you smiling, Duffy?"

"Kill the light!"

The light went out.

It was pitch black.

I hit the deck and immediately all six men fired into the space where I had been.

I crawled through the rubble.

Fire above me.

A terrifying noise bouncing off the walls.

I crawled in a diagonal, away from the gunfire. The shotgun men shot both their barrels immediately, the AK man went through his clip in a few seconds, the men with pistols fired intermittently into the darkness.

Ping! Ping! Ping! all around me. "Jesus!"

I kept crawling through glass and muck and oil.

Something hot screamed past my face.

"Return fire for fucksake!"

Were they dead?

Oh fuck, had I killed them too?

Two muted flames shooting towards the gunmen.

Crabbie was behind a turbine in one corner. Lawson was behind a cast iron door in another. Both of them had suppressors on their MP5's, not just for the noise but to screen the muzzle flash.

"Return fire!" I screamed unnecessarily.

They knew what they were doing and they had targets to shoot at: the dusty yellow flames from the barrels of the men shooting at me.

Crabbie fired.

Lawson fired.

Turning round and lying on the ground in sniper mode I fired.

The range time paid off.

Range time always pays off.

Three men went down.

We all shot again and two more men went down and one made a bolt for the back door.

"Lights!"

The lights came on and I got to my feet and pointed the MP5 at the vacuum where the baddies had been standing. Jim Dale, Haughtrey, Breslaw and James were all dead. Selden was bleeding out from a hole in his chest the size of an orange.

"Is everyone OK?" I screamed.

"Not a scratch," Lawson said.

"Crabbie?"

Silence.

"Crabbie!"

"I think I was hit."

I sprinted over to him. "Where were you hit?"

"I'm fine. Go after. Strong, Sean! He's getting away," Crabbie said.

"Are you OK?"

"I'm all right. It was just a scratch. Go after Strong."

Lawson came over to the pair of us.

"Run with me to the car!" I said and we ran through the factory. "Did you get everything on tape, son?" I asked.

"Yes, sir."

"All right. I want you to call Special Branch, not the regular police. Tell them what happened. If they can find Superintendent Baker get them to send her. Play her the tape if necessary."

"What are you going to do?"

"I'm going to try to catch Strong before he does anything stupid."

27: RUNNING FOR THE BORDER

I dashed out to the BMW. Strong was getting away in his Bentley Turbo making for Belfast.

"Your family's back that way!" I yelled after him, but he was gone. He wasn't going back to be with his wife and kids while the cops closed in. He was trying to get away.

The 1988-89 Bentley Mulsanne was a mean piece of equipment. 400 brake horse power, twin-turbo 6.75 litre V8, top speed of 140 mph.

I got in the Beemer without looking underneath it for bombs.

"Here we go," I said and drove out of the factory and onto the onramp for the dual carriageway. At this time of night there was almost no traffic.

Perfect. Just me and him.

The Bentley was a mile ahead now. He was making for the M5, heading for the city and a million ways to escape after that. Yeah, that Bentley turbo was some car all right. Look at it go.

I laughed.

I was driving the BMW 535i sport with a 5-speed Getrag manual transmission. I knew the specs off by heart: 0–60 mph in 6.5s. Top speed (computer-limited): 128 mph. Top speed (without computer limit): 146 mph. Needless to say, I had showed my warrant card and had the dealership remove the computer limit.

The Bentley was about to get fucking crucified.

We reached the hill coming into Newtownabbey. The mercury tilt bomb under my car did not go off because there was no mercury tilt bomb.

Don't make a habit of this, Sean.

I grinned at myself in the rear-view. I was alive. And the killers were dead.

I was alive and the killers were dead but the man who had sent the killers was getting away in a souped-up Bentley. Smile gone. Shit, I couldn't even see him any more.

Surely he couldn't outrun me in that big boat?

I turned on the police scanner.

Reports of a white car doing over 100 mph at Mullusk.

He was already at Mullusk?

I'd have to shovel some more coal on to catch him.

I ate the tarmac on four wheels.

I ate the M5 and the M2 coming into Belfast.

I ate the motorway out past Dunmurry.

I ate Ballyskeagh and Moira.

The BMW's speedometer nudged upwards.

110 mph. 120 mph. 125 mph. 130 mph.

Christ, this thing could fly. I pushed the accelerator all the way to the floor.

150 miles per hour.

Portable siren on. Roof light flashing. Lane ahead cleared. On the big diagonal across Ulster.

The motorway was a relatively recent development and this BMW was brand new, so it was possible that this was the fastest anyone had ever driven in Northern Ireland outside of the Ulster Grand Prix circuit and even there . . .

Screaming down the M1 and then the A3 towards Armagh.

What traffic there was moved aside.

Cars blurred.

I couldn't risk fiddling with the tape deck at this speed so I turned on Radio 1 and prayed for something good.

John Peel was on repeat but Peelie was playing something way out of his comfort zone.

"This isn't really my cup of tea, but I think this might be the beginning of a new form in metal music. Or not. Send the kiddies to bed, get headphones for granny. Here for your delectation is Slayer and their song 'Raining Blood'."

I cranked the volume, which turned out to be a good move.

Ulster dematerialised.

I was flying over it.

I was seeing it from the air.

I was peering through the Mir space station window.

I was unfolding one of poor dead Tommy's secret maps.

I knew exactly where he was going. He was on the A3 now, the Monaghan Road, he was heading for the border just ten miles from Armagh.

Traffic cops didn't have the juice to catch us in their Ford Sierras and Ford Escorts.

After Slayer came Motorhead's "Ace of Spades".

Perfect.

Armagh. Milford. Madden. Middletown. He was heading for the Irish Republic all right. There was a checkpoint at the formal border where the A3 became the N12. But the checkpoint didn't matter because he was going to ditch the Bentley somewhere along here where the road ran parallel to the border and where there were no boundary walls or fences or anything of the—

I hit the brakes.

The Beemer screeched to a halt, fishtailed, thought about rolling, decided against it, fishtailed the other way and stopped.

There was the car. Ditched in a sheugh. Or sheughed in a ditch if you preferred.

Door open, Strong gone, out into the night.

Where was this place?

I got bearings. Typical border landscape. Boggy sheep fields rolling down the hills to a river.

The river. Yes. That's where he'd go.

And then I saw a trail through the grass. No blood. Just a big heavy running man.

I got out of the Beemer and followed him across the grass to a stream that I learned later was called the River Cor. The other side of the river was the Irish Republic. A place beyond my jurisdiction.

The moon came out from behind the clouds. And I saw him at the top of the rise beyond the river.

"You can't touch me, Duffy! This is the border! I'm over the border!"

"What are you going to do? Run and hide for the rest of your life?"

"Fuck off back to Belfast!"

"We'll extradite you from whatever rat hole you bolt to!"

"Oh you will, will you?"

Hadn't he learned anything about me from my file? Maybe not the greatest copper in these islands, but everybody, even my worst enemy, would agree that I was a stubborn son of a bitch. I'd fucking nail him if he went behind the Iron Curtain or a beach in Brazil or the Amundsen-Scott base at the South fucking Pole.

I looked at the tiny river separating him from me.

Was I going to be stopped by this . . . puddle?

Fuck that.

"What are you doing, Duffy? This is the Irish Republic!"

I waded into the river. It only went up to my knees. If he'd had more bottle he could have driven his car over. No need to abandon a decent car.

Strong pulled out his gun.

He shot once.

Missed.

Shot again.

Missed.

Click.

Click.

Click.

"I think you'll find it's empty," I said, crossing the stream into Southern Ireland.

Reverse the shot.

Him looking at me wading the river. Nemesis.

Back to me, looking at him.

He still could have run. Run to the top of that hill, jumped the little barbed-wire fence, gone on through the sheep shit and the bog.

But he knew he was beat.

He put his hands up.

"You can't touch me, Duffy. It's illegal."

I got to within six feet of him, took out the Glock and pointed it at him.

"You know why Death lets me live, John?"

"No, Duffy, I don't."

"Because I give him so much business."

Hammer back.

"Please! No!"

"As I see it, there are four possibilities. Number one, I let you run. You run. You probably get caught but you might escape and assume an identity and live out your life on an IRA pension. That might be a good punishment for you. Always worried, living in fear. Number two, I shoot you. I shoot you and pick up the shell casings and carry your body back across the river. Fireman's lift. Easy. What happened? Oh, he was making a run for it. Didn't quite make it. I shot him in Northern Ireland, no diplomatic incident, no need to involve the Guards."

"Please, Duffy—"

"Possibility three. I slug you across the face, drag you back across the river, deny you ever made it over and bring you in for trial. And then there's possibility number four. We'll get to that one in a minute, but first you talk."

"What do you mea—"

"Tell me about the crossbow. We couldn't figure that one out."

"The crossbow?"

"The crossbow."

"I was fucked, Duffy. Deauville saw me at the Rangers Club and my only contact was in the hospital. Deauville was going to start blackmailing me. I had to end it. I had to kill him before anything got going. My son had a—"

I put my hand up to stop him.

"I get it. Francis Deauville pops up out of nowhere with his big mouth just when you were on the verge of promotion to ACC. You couldn't shoot him with your gun because it would be traced back to you. You couldn't get the IRA to get you a stolen gun because your IRA contact was in the hospital gravely ill, but your son had a crossbow. You take the crossbow, practise with it in that big back garden of yours. Get good at it. Shoot that guy in Larne to establish a pattern and then you shoot Deauville, toss the weapon in the sea, and when Harry is out of intensive care he tells his mates in DAADD to call it in as one of theirs."

"You see, Duffy—"

"I'm not done, Strong. Never interrupt Columbo when he's doing his final fucking speech. But DAADD refused to admit to the killing lest it start a turf war, so Harry got that story printed in *Republican News*, which was good enough for us. The car. I should have paid more attention to the car. You couldn't follow Deauville and shoot some tosser in Larne in your big fucking Bentley so you took the train to Derry and borrowed your mate Harry's car. And squared it with him when he got out of the hospital. Am I right?"

He nodded. "You've solved it. You've figured it out as you always do, Sean."

"Who bought the crossbow? We showed your photograph at

the archery shops."

"My wife bought it for Teddy."

"Your wife. Should have thought of that."

Still keeping the gun on him I sat down on the grass and took my leather jacket off and opened the Velcro on the bullet-proof vest.

"That's better. Sweating like a bastard in that thing."

"Who were those men with you?" Strong asked.

"Lawson and McCrabban."

"I knew it! I told Harry that you'd tell them, that the whole thing was a set-up."

"But Harry was sceptical about your psychic ability?"

He took the envelope out of his jacket pocket. "It's a blank piece of paper in here, isn't it?"

I nodded.

"Tell me about Mrs Deauville," I said.

"Oh, I had nothing to do with that. Harry was out of the hospital then. He took care of all that."

"Took care of it how?"

"I didn't ask."

"Took care of it how?" I asked and waggled the gun in his direction for emphasis.

"Killed her. Abducted her from the bus station in Antrim," he said.

"Why'd you do it, John?"

"She knew too much."

"I don't mean that. Why did you do all of it? Work for the IRA, betray your friends, the police, everything?"

"I had to do it! Harry was blackmailing me. It would have been the end of everything. And it wasn't so much. They never wanted so much. It's like the red telephone, isn't it? The red telephone between the Kremlin and the White House. A line of communication. That's what I told myself. We have a mole in their upper echelons and they have moles in ours. We keep each other honest."

"So you were doing the police a favour?"

"In a way, yes. Besides, all this . . . what's the point? You know. You're a Catholic. You know. It's all a sham. What's that line, 'On the dunes and headland sinks the fire' . . . You know the rest. Smart boy like you."

What eejit can refuse quoting memorised poetry:

"'On dune and headland sinks the fire/all our pomp of yesterday/is one with Nineveh and Tyre.' Is that what you mean?"

"That's the one, Duffy," Strong said, sitting down on the grass.

"That's the reason you sold us out? Apart from the money and the fear? And you as the red telephone?"

"You've had those thoughts too, Duffy. We've all had the same conversations. What's the point to any of this?"

I took off my vest and let it drop next to Strong. "Aye, I've had those thoughts. You ever watch that Carl Sagan bloke on TV?"

"I've seen him."

"Civilisations rise and fall and rise and fall, and eventually the sun goes out and the earth dies and then all the suns go out, and all the civilisations die and eventually entropy maximises, the second law of thermodynamics wins, and there's nothing in the universe, no light, no atoms, nothing . . . But just because the world's ending, doesn't mean you give up. It was the great heretic Martin Luther who said 'If the Apocalypse was coming tomorrow, today I would plant a tree.' Wise words. And that's how we win: by sticking up a middle finger to the darkness closing in. I'd love to shoot you, John. For all your crimes and lies. I'd love to do that. But I'm not going to. And I'm not going to arrest you, either. On your feet. Back over the border. Any funny business and it's a bullet in the brain. Pick up my vest and leather jacket. Hold them out in front of you."

He picked up my gear and started walking towards the river.

"What *are* you going to do?" he asked.

"We're going to spin this as a mad vendetta by a clearly unstable Harry Selden against the Carrickfergus RUC who had been hassling him about a dead drug dealer and a missing persons case. Your name won't come up. I made sure Harry didn't tell the IRA Army Council that you'd been compromised. They all still think you're pure."

"What *are* you going to do?"

"We're going to run you as a double agent, John. The IRA will get you a new handler and you'll tell them you had no idea what Harry was up to. You'll tell them everything we want them to know from now on, but this time you'll be working for the good guys. If you're worried about Special Branch not believing me, don't be. I've got your whole confession on tape. Lawson recorded it with the high-gain antenna. You don't need wires when you have one of those."

"Shit," he said. "Where are you taking me now?"

"Special Branch. There's a Superintendent Baker that I may have offended with a joke about Willie Nelson. You might help me get on her good side."

Strong looked down. "I'm sorry about all this," he said.

I had no compassion for him at all. "You will be, mate. You will be."

We walked back across the River Cor and I handcuffed him at the car and put him in the back of the Beemer.

"We'll get your car out of the sheugh and fixed and back to your house. Appearances will be everything here. You didn't know what Harry was up to and you were home the entire evening. Savvy?"

"Savvy."

I patted the BMW's roof and drove north.

The radio crackled back into life when I got within range.

"Inspector Duffy! . . . Inspector Duffy! . . . Inspector Duffy!"

"This is Duffy, what's up, Lawson?"

"Oh sir, it's Sergeant McCrabban, sir, he's dying!"

28: DETECTIVE SERGEANT JOHN 'CRABBIE' MCCRABBAN

The Royal Victoria Hospital.

Casualty.

John McCrabban in emergency surgery for an AK 47 slug in his stomach.

Lost a lot of blood in the ambulance.

Should have been with him.

Should have been there with him instead of chasing down a traitor.

Screech of brakes as the BMW pulled into the ambulance bay.

"You can't park that here!" a policeman said.

I showed my warrant card. "Inspector Sean Duffy, RUC. If that man in the back of the car gets out I've told him you'll shoot him, so you'll have to shoot him. He's very dangerous."

"Yes, sir."

Inside the hospital.

Doctors and nurses in the trauma wards. A busy night for the RVH.

Lawson saw me at the Reception Desk.

"Sir!" he said.

He'd been crying.

"How is he?"

Lawson shook his head. "I'm so sorry, sir. I didn't realise

how badly he was hurt. I was checking the bodies and waiting for Special Branch like you said. I didn't realise Sergeant McCrabban was unconscious until Superintendent Baker showed up and I went looking for him."

"How was he in the ambulance?"

Lawson sniffed. "Haemorrhaging. He's lost so much blood. I don't think . . . The men in the ambulance said he wasn't . . ."

"Oh God."

I turned to the nurse at the desk. "Where's John McCrabban?"

"He's in the OR."

"Where is that?" I demanded.

"Sir, you can't go in there. It's a sterile environment. You'll have to wait here."

I waited.

And waited.

Helen and the boys arrived.

I hugged Helen. I hugged the boys.

Beth and Emma arrived. Beth was in tears. "Oh my God, Sean."

We paced the corridor.

Waited.

Lawson talking to me at the Coke machine.

"I didn't realise he was hit, sir. I didn't know he was down. He told you to go. I thought it was just a scratch, I—"

"Ssshhh. It's going to be OK. How can a bullet kill John McCrabban? It would be like a bullet trying to kill a fucking oak tree."

Beth, Emma and I played with Crabbie's boys.

We got Helen a cup of tea.

Seizing a moment when the kids were quiet, I went to the Catholic chapel and had a heart-to-heart with the Virgin.

"Yeah, I know. I know. I fucking know, OK? But this will be the last time. Just this last time and I won't ask any more," I said.

29: THE CHIEF CONSTABLE

If you really have to get shot, Belfast is one of the best places to do it. After twenty years of the Troubles and after thousands of assassination attempts and punishment shootings Belfast has trained many of the best gunshot-trauma surgeons in the world.

After four hours Crabbie was discharged from the OR and given into the hands of some of the best nurses in the world.

The head surgeon talked to Helen.

She hugged him and turned to us. "They think he's going to pull through."

Tears.

The complete waterworks from all of us.

From the OR to the recovery ward.

There was Crabbie. Bandaged. Sedated. Plugged in.

Only Helen allowed in to see him at first. But then the rest of us permitted to stand by his bed "as long as we were quiet".

"How is he?" I whispered to Helen.

"He hasn't spoken a word, but the doctor says he should be—"

"Sean, is that you?" he asked, opening first one eye and then the other.

"It's me."

"Did we get him?"

"We got him . . . But don't worry about that now. Helen's here and the boys—"

"Is Helen here?"

"Of course I am!"

He looked at Helen. "You're here, Helen?"

"Yes!"

"And the boys are here?"

"Yes, Dad, of course we are."

He shook his head and frowned. "If you're all here, who's looking after the farm?" he said dourly.

Back to Carrickfergus RUC.

The farm remark already legendary.

Upstairs to my office.

Me falling asleep at my desk while typing up the report.

A knock on my door.

"Sean?"

The door opened. Chief Inspector McArthur was standing there with another man, the Chief Constable of the RUC, Jack Hermon.

I snapped to my feet.

"Sir, I had no idea—"

Hermon waved me down.

"How's your man, Duffy?"

"Sergeant McCrabban, sir? He's on the mend."

"Good to hear it. You probably need to get some sleep, don't you?"

"I haven't finished the report, yet, sir, I was just typing it now. We, uhm, need to get the story . . ."

Hermon turned to Chief Inspector McArthur. "I'd like to talk to Inspector Duffy, alone, if that's all right."

"Oh . . . Yes, of course," he said and left the room. Hermon sat down in the chair opposite.

"Help yourself to a whisky," I said, gesturing towards the drinks trolley.

"Little early for me," he replied.

"Yeah. What time is it?"

"Not quite noon . . . This has been a terrible business," he said.

"Yes. It has."

"Glad McCrabban is on the mend."

"Yes, sir."

"But, Strong. Dear, oh dear. I trusted that man. I thought he was an up-and-comer."

"If my, our, plan is going to work, sir, you'll have to continue to trust him, sir. At least in public."

"Perhaps I will take a wee dram," Hermon said and poured himself a fifth of the sixteen-year-old Jura – the best whisky on the drinks trolley.

"Look, Duffy, I'll need a good man to be one of Strong's handlers. Someone intimate with the details of the case, someone who can bully him when he needs to be bullied and someone who can—"

"Let me stop you right there, sir. I'm very flattered but I don't know if I'm that man. I'm thinking of quitting, actually. Moving to Scotland in a year or so. My girlfriend, Beth, wants to go. She doesn't feel safe here, obviously. And we have a child together, so I need to go with her."

Hermon smiled. "I read about your girlfriend Beth on that attack on your house. A remarkable young lady, it seems."

"Oh, you wouldn't think it to look at her, but she's a toughie," I said.

Hermon stood up. "Scotland's not so very far away," he said. "In fact, if I'm not mistaken that's it, there, that blue line on the horizon."

"Yes, sir, I believe it is," I said and couldn't stop a massive yawn.

"We might be able to arrange something for you even if you lived over there. The part-time reserve perhaps. How many years until your twenty-year-pension, Duffy?"

"I've actually quite a bit to go, sir, 1994 will be my twenty years and you can't accumulate pension years in the part-time reserve."

Hermon frowned and looked into his whisky glass. "Exceptions can be made. Exceptions are made all the time in special circumstances."

"And for McCrabban too? He's thinking of retiring as well."

"For John McCrabban, a good man, yes, for him too."

I thought about what other concessions I could ask for. "And if I do stay here even part-time I don't want Kenny Dalziel to be my gaffer. I like Chief Inspector McArthur and I get on well with him. He's due a promotion but perhaps he could get the bump in salary and still, somehow, keep his job."

Hermon nodded. "All of that can be sorted out in due course. The first thing we have to do is, as you say, get our story straight."

Two hours later. Outside to the BMW. Exhausted. Need my bed. But not home. Not yet. Into Carrick to visit a jeweller's shop.

Down the A2 to Larne.

Knock on Beth's door. Her parents and her in the kitchen. Giving them the public version of the previous night's events.

Her father shaking my hand.

Later. In the playroom with Emma.

"Glasgow University, eh?"

"Yeah, it's super modern. The English department, anyway."

"In about a year from now?"

"I think that's how long it would take to get everything sorted."

"Have you heard of a thing called the part-time police reserve?"

"I've heard of it."

"You're a reservist in the RUC but not the full-time reserve, I wouldn't be on call. I'd only have to come in seven days in a calendar month. I could get it all over in a week or I could do two shorter stints."

"What do you mean?"

"I can retire with a full pension in 1994. If we live in Scotland I can get the ferry over and do my seven days a month easily.

The rest of the time I'll be a stay-home dad and look after Emma."

"Will you still be a detective?"

I shook my head. "No, that's not going to be possible. You can't be a part-time detective. But it won't matter. Crabbie's probably going to do the same thing. He wants to concentrate on his farming, so he'll be moving to the part-time reserve too."

"Who will run Carrick CID?"

"Lawson will do it. They'll promote him to Detective Sergeant and maybe get him a DC. It'll take me a while to train him up. Me and Crabbie. It'll take us that year and then we can both jack it in for the reserves."

Beth bit her lip and pushed a gorgeous line of golden hair from her face. "And we'll be out of all of this in our house over the water."

"We'll be out of it in our house over the water."

"And in the meantime?"

"Bobby Cameron is having the council install speed bumps and a one-way system on Coronation Road. No more drive-bys. And the man who had the vendetta against me in the IRA is dead. Oh, and I think you'll find the neighbours are a bit friendlier now too."

"Is that everything?"

"One more thing."

I started to get down on one knee.

"Let me put a stop to that straight away, mister," she said, pulling me back up again.

"Don't you wanna—"

"No!"

"But your dad . . ."

"Yeah, he'll be annoyed, won't he?" she said happily. "Can you cope with us just living in sin, you big Catholic weirdo?"

"I can cope with it," I said.

She grabbed the ring box. "At least let me take a look at it to see if you're a cheapo as well as a weirdo . . . Nope, not a cheapo. Very impressive."

"You want to try it on?"

"No, I don't."

"Shall I return it?"

"Keep it in a safe place."

30: O MASTERFUL BLEAK COP

A café just outside of Newry in the shadow of the Mourne Mountains. Thunder rumbling in from the Irish Sea. Rain lashing the windows. It's early. The café is deserted but for a couple of long-distance lorry drivers wolfing down Ulster fries and mugs of tea.

I've got my back to the door, a cup of coffee and *The Times* cryptic crossword.

Fourteen down: "The rich and powerful fear you, o masterful bleak cop."

Hmm. What can they mean by that?

The café door opens and a big heavyset man in a raincoat and a flat cap barges in. For a second he looks like trouble and I reach for the revolver in the pocket of my leather jacket.

"Some weather!" the man says, takes a table on the opposite side of the café and orders bacon and eggs.

I watch him for a minute but he's soon lost in the football pages of the *Sun*. I leave the revolver alone and go back to the cryptic crossword.

I still can't get the clue. My brain isn't working this early in the morning.

The door opens again and Assistant Chief Constable Strong comes in looking harassed and afraid. His tie is askew and he hasn't brushed his hair. He's buttoned his anorak with the wrong buttons. This will never do.

I wave at him and he comes over to the table and sits down opposite me.

"Fix your coat and run a hand through your hair," I tell him.

"I can't do this, Duffy!" he wails.

I grab his knee under the table and squeeze it, hard.

"Lower your voice and calm down," I tell him.

"I can't do this," he whispers.

The bored, sarky, pretty waitress comes over. "What can I get youse?"

"He'll have the same as me. Toast and a coffee," I tell her.

"Marmalade or jam?"

I look at Strong.

"Uhm, uhm . . ."

"He'll take the marmalade, love," I tell her.

"I can't do this, Duffy, if they find the wire I'm a dead man," Strong says when the waitress is gone.

Today is his first meeting with two members of the IRA Army Council in a pub in Newry. He's wearing a mike and a tape recorder, both of which are in his no doubt very sweaty underpants. MI5 are watching his every move but I'm the last person he wanted to see before driving the last part of the journey in his Bentley. I'm his handler. He thinks if he can convince me that he's not ready I'll call the operation off.

But I won't do that. I would never do that. One slip, one really thorough pat-down search and Elena Deauville and Maria McKeen will get the justice they deserve.

"They're not going to search you. They trust you. And if they do search you they'll never grab your bollocks – they're far too shy for that," I tell him.

"I can't do this, Sean."

"You can do it. It's what you've been doing for years. Except now you're going to be telling them what *we* want them to know."

When the coffee comes I slip him an aspirin.

"This is a Valium, it will calm you down and give you confidence and make you more alert," I lie.

He believes me and swallows the pill.

I spend the next ten minutes talking him down from the ledge. He doesn't touch his toast.

I look at my watch.

"It's time to go. Follow me to the loo in a minute and I'll check your gear."

He follows me into the bathroom and I fix his tie and check the mike and the tape recorder. It's all fine.

Back to the table. I make him take another sip of the coffee.

"Just do exactly what we told you and everything will be OK," I tell him.

He gets to his feet and nods.

He walks out of the café as if he's on his way to an execution, which, in truth, he might be . . .

I return to the cryptic crossword.

"The rich and powerful fear you, o masterful bleak cop," I say to myself.

O masterful bleak cop is a weird thing to say, it must be an anagram of something, maybe a—

"Peter Falk as Columbo," I say and fill in the clue. The final remaining clues tumble in pretty easily.

When I've paid the bill and gone back outside the rain has ceased but a cold wind is blowing in from the sea and the mountains are caught in its bitter grip. The southern rim of the sky is thinning from grey to black. The rush hour is over and the road is quiet and in the dense empty silence you can hear the alarms of wood pigeon and the cries of hawks.

I walk to the Beemer, look underneath it and get inside.

A spook called Wilson taps on the passenger's side window. I unlock the car and let him in.

"Did you gentle his condition, Duffy?"

"He's as good as he's going to get," I tell him.

"If he doesn't have a heart attack he might be quite a useful little asset," Wilson says with satisfaction.

"We'll see. You'll take it from here then, will you?"

"Aye. We'll take it from here."

"I'll be off then."

"Safe home."

Up along the motorway and into Carrickfergus. I drive to #113 Coronation Road where there is a giant For Sale sign on a board in the front yard.

I go inside, where Beth and Emma and Jet the cat are waiting.

Beth is poring over the forms for Glasgow University, where her potential supervisor has said that it would be fine for her to study Frank Miller's *Batman* as a response to Henry Miller's *Air Conditioned Nightmare*.

"Oh, I got sent some estate listings today. What do you think of this place?" Beth asks, handing me an estate agent's brochure. It's for a house overlooking the sea in Portpatrick, Scotland," she says.

I look at the house with its falling gables and ivy-covered windows and overgrown garden and path down to the water. It's practically a ruin but the location is terribly romantic.

"It'll be perfect. Let's go take a look at it."

31: SILENCIO

Blue. Big sideways swathes of blue. A universe of blue. A great blue engine. A machinery of blue.

Beth was manning the tiller, showing Emma how it worked.

I was up front in all that blue.

We had left Carrickfergus early, at five am, just as the sun was coming up as it is wont to do in August, at this hour, in these latitudes.

It was a straight run across the North Channel with only one tack. McCrabban and Lawson were sitting gingerly in the back, wondering if it was really a good idea to let an infant steer the boat. Wives and children had been invited but Helen was no sailor and didn't trust the little boys on board and Alex didn't have a steady girlfriend yet. It was warm already but Crabbie was dressed for an expedition to Ice Station Zebra with a massive windbreaker and multiple layers under that.

"Are we in any danger?" Crabbie asked nervously.

I shook my head. "It's a gorgeous day, not a cloud in the sky. We should be fine."

Gorgeous indeed.

When we cleared Belfast Lough Beth decided to hoist the big green spinnaker sail.

"You boys need to help," Beth said to Crabbie and Lawson. "Alex, you pull on that sheet over there and Crabbie, you pull on that sheet here."

"What sheets?"

"The ropes. The blue rope and the red rope."

We raised the spinnaker and the main and a curly-haired, freckled-faced, deeply concentrating Emma steered the *Deirdre* out of the lough and into the Irish Sea.

We were heading for the Scottish coast. Carrickfergus was behind us now, even the castle looking small and grey on the shoreline. Jet the cat came up on deck after falling asleep on a rope coil. He decided that the moving watery realm was not for him and went back down below.

"How's the farm going?" I asked Crabbie as I handed him a cup of tea.

Crabbie, unlike every farmer on the face of the earth, did not spend the next ten minutes complaining about how difficult it was to be a farmer.

"It's all right," he said.

"And your health?"

"Mustn't grumble," he said.

"Does he ever grumble?" Beth asked and Lawson and myself both shook our heads.

"He doesn't grumble but his frown could fell a gazelle at fifty paces," Lawson said.

Yeah, that frown. Last week McCrabban and I had driven to Judith McKeen's house in Cushendun and told her that the two men who had shot her daughter were both dead. Both themselves shot. She nodded and when she asked if the third B Special had had anything to do with it I had said no, that he was innocent, and that was when Crabbie had frowned. It was a lie, a necessary lie, but a lie nonetheless.

"What type of boat is this?" Alex asked.

It was a small Bermuda-rigged two-masted ketch with a cabin and bunks for four. It was a carvel-built design from Harry Brace's private yard on the Clyde. The planking was teak, which was extremely rare for a Scottish yard. 1947 or possibly

1948, although the man who'd sold it to Beth claimed it was from the 60s because he thought – wrongly – that its venerable age would decrease its value. It was only thirty-two foot long but the design was such that it looked much roomier when you were down below. It was a beautiful-looking craft with its sleek hull, weathered teak decks and brass fittings. By far the stand-out craft in any marina filled with 1980s white fibreglass mono-hulled cruisers and ugly speedboats.

"It's a ketch," Beth and I said together.

Two and a half hours later we dropped the sails and motored into Portpatrick harbour. I threw a stern line to a helpful kid on the shore and he tied us up onto a cleat while I jumped onto the pontoon and ran a line forward. Portpatrick couldn't compare with Oban or Port Ellen or Tobermory but it was a lovely little place nonetheless and I could see that the lads were delighted by the whole experience of getting up early and sailing over to Scotland for lunch.

We ate at a fish restaurant and found the house for sale on a cliff just outside of town. It had once been a lovely three-bed-room, but that once was probably about 1910. The roof looked none too stable and it had a garden full of weeds and nettles. However, the view across the water to Ireland was to die for.

"It'll certainly take some fixing up," Beth said and I could tell that she loved it. The lads agreed that it was just the place for us.

I put in an offer there and then and the estate agent told us that the current owners would almost certainly take it.

After thoroughly exploring "our" house we took Emma to a park back in town.

"There's Kilroot Power Station there across the sea. It's hard to believe that we live so close. I should get a little boat, myself," Lawson said, like me, now thoroughly convinced by a nautical existence.

"There's an old joke: the two best days of a boat owner's life are the day he buys his boat and the day he sells his boat," Beth told him, but I could see he didn't believe her. The hooks were in. It had been that big green spinnaker sail.

We stayed for dinner in Portpatrick and it was late when we headed out of the harbour again.

On the journey back Crabbie joined me on the foredeck and we talked tactics.

"They'll take my recommendation that Lawson pass for sergeant and be promoted to head of Carrick CID," I said. "I think he'll be ready to take over in about a year or so."

"Yes, that sounds about right," he agreed.

"And we'll both resign as detectives and move to the part-time reserve," I said.

"That will suit me down to the ground," he said. "I can concentrate more on the farm."

"We'll teach him everything we know and let the new generation handle things for a while."

"Aye."

The sun began sinking behind the Irish coast.

The yellow dark, the red dark, the deep blue dark . . .

Stars in swirls. A sickle moon. Silence.

Between Ireland and Scotland not a ship or a plane or another vessel.

Just the night itself and the flat black sea that makes a noise like singing.

The cat asleep. Emma asleep. Beth reading Frank Miller and allowing Lawson to hold the tiller.

Yes, the plan would work out fine.

We'd train Lawson and we'd move to Scotland and I'd finish out my time as a reservist. One more year of murder cases that don't get solved and missing girls who never come back and, as a sideline, handling the flighty, paranoid, highly strung Assistant Chief Constable Strong – an absolute menace of a man whom I would have to keep on a very tight leash.

And after that just a few more years of commuting to Belfast by plane and ferry, doing humdrum police work so I didn't blow my agent-handling cover: foot patrols, traffic work, paperwork.

It was nothing I couldn't handle.

I had Beth and Emma.

A boat called *Deirdre*.

Two excellent friends.

It would be a good life.

Good enough.

Adrian McKinty's Sean Duffy Thrillers

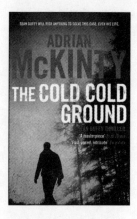

The Cold Cold Ground

Book one in the Sean Duffy series
Adrian McKinty

'If Raymond Chandler had grown up in Northern Ireland, *The Cold Cold Ground* is what he would have written' *The Times*

Two dead.

One left in a car by the side of a road. He was meant to be found quickly. His killer is making a statement.

The other is discovered hanging in a tree, deep in a forest. Surely a suicide: she'd just given birth, but there's no sign of the baby.

Nothing seems to link the two, but Detective Sergeant Sean Duffy knows the links that seem to be invisible are just waiting to be uncovered. And as a policeman who has solved six murders so far in his career, but not yet brought a single case to court, Duffy is determined that this time, someone will pay.

'Told with style, courage and dark as night wit' Stuart Neville

'An exciting new voice' Ian Rankin

ISBN 978 1 84668 823 2
eISBN 978 1 84765 795 4